BLACK INK HEART

LAURINDA LAWRENCE

Blue Velvet Press

Thank you to *Faiz Foundation Trust* for permission to use the poem by Faiz Ahmed Faiz

Laurinda Lawrence

laurindalawrence.com

For Mum—you always said I would.

PROLOGUE

*N*akita had to have the shoes. The fluorescent yellow Crocs on the feet of the homeless man symbolised two men who had once been so important to her. One man she had tried to forget, but she knew now he had to be remembered. The other she needed to forget, wanted to forget, was trying to forget... couldn't forget. Once those same shoes had brought her to tears of laughter. Not now. Now she wanted to give vent to the feelings that consumed her.

To run and seek comfort in tears.

Yet she stood, rooted to the spot on the cobbled pavers, totally transfixed by those stupid shoes.

No one at the bustling shopping centre could have been aware of her distress. They wouldn't know her heart had come to a standstill and that a pair of shoes were her undoing.

And now, the cruel joke continued.

The homeless man, who appeared weathered more by years of hard living than age, sat on a bench seat puffing away on a rollie outside the Plaza. His Corgi, stretched out by his side, looked better fed than he did; tongue lolling, without a care in the world. The two were not an unusual sight, turning up in various places around town from time to time.

A rattle of a long line of trolleys assaulted her eardrums, breaking the spell. Nakita stepped out of the way to avoid being run down by a bored-looking trolley boy. While everyone else was making a beeline to the sanctuary of the air-conditioning inside, she took a deep breath, stepping closer to the man. *This is it, Nakita.* In the past she might have been too cautious to go near him, but now an inexplicable anger mounted within her at the injustice of those shoes turning up now.

She narrowed her eyes at them. *How dare they?*

She stepped towards him without further thought. "Excuse me?"

"Why hullo there, pretty young lady," he drawled.

She held her breath to avoid inhaling the stream of rank smoke that enveloped her.

"Would you like a rollie, love?" He held out his pouch of tobacco with grubby, nicotine-stained fingers.

"No. I want to buy your shoes."

CHAPTER 1

"To new adventures." Will raised his beer in his customary salute.

"To new adventures," Nakita agreed, clinking her glass against his schooner.

They sat across from one another at a rustic wooden table in front of The Gull. Dorley Point hadn't long woken from its winter slumber to greet a steady procession of summer holidaymakers, some caravanning, many braving the oppressive heat of their tents to enjoy the usual beach and lagoon activities. Campers and day-trippers from the city wandered and cycled by, more interested in checking out the waves than watching where they were going. Dorley Point was a tiny, sleepy village on the east coast of Australia. A short drive from town, it had a pristine beach that filtered into an estuary. The only road in was the same road out—a steep and spectacular drive through coastal bush land.

Nakita didn't mind the invasion of the beach town she called home, since it brought back her brother, and she was especially delighted not to be sharing her fun-loving twin with anyone else for a change. Even though they were twins, they didn't look a scrap alike.

Will had baby blue-eyes and olive skin with scruffy, light blonde hair, while Nakita was fair with brown eyes, her thick red hair noncommittal to being either curly or straight, but happy to settle for being wavy at best, and fuzzy in humid weather.

"Happy birthday, Kit."

"Happy birthday, Will. I don't know how you get me to do this."

"Do what?"

"This." She nodded to the drink he'd just put in her hands. "I only meant to have one." She was sure that her brother being the youngest, gave him some kind of magnetic power of persuasion. He had always had this indefinable quality that made her want to give in, just to please him.

"It's a celebration, Kit." Will leaned back, resting on the stone wall behind him, his wide blue eyes looking at her warmly.

"Will, you seriously need a haircut, your hair is so long now and you're so tanned. You look like a hobo."

"It takes a huge effort to achieve the hobo look." He laughed, shaking his long blonde fringe from his eyes and looking around. "Geez, this place is seriously understaffed. How long does it take to whack together a chicken snitty? You'd think they'd prioritise us, considering you work here and we're locals."

"That's precisely why we are waiting," Nakita said, using her 'I'm-six-minutes-older-and-more-responsible-than-you', big sister tone, although her own stomach rumbled at the tantalising scent of salt and pepper squid drizzled with lemon. "Hmm...they do seem flat out. Perhaps I should help?"

"No way, Kit, you already are." Will nodded towards the pile of cutlery in front of her that she was wrapping meticulously in crisp white paper napkins. "Would you quit with the origami for two minutes? You're not even meant to be working. Miriam would kill you if she saw you doing this on your birthday."

"Relax. If I don't do it, no one else will. Besides, it's kind of therapeutic. I get satisfaction bringing order from disorder." She straightened as she polished a dull spot on a tablespoon.

"Do you realise when you get really anal you pull this weird face like you're trying not to smile?"

"I do not."

"Yeah, you do. You did that exact same face whenever you polished our shoes every Sunday night before school. I spent all of Monday trying to scuff them up. It was so not cool to have polished shoes."

"I've always been such a dedicated sister." She smiled. "Hey, so you haven't told me about your last adventure. It's been six months, Will. It nearly killed me."

"You know you're the only reason I come back? Next time, you are coming. It'll be a blast. Can you imagine us two backpacking? We'd have to lay a few ground rules, of course. If you could just remember that you're not my mother, we'd be sweet."

She continued, focused on folding the napkins, ignoring his barb. He hated it when she mothered him. But someone had to, and in the end there was no one else around putting up their hand.

He reached across the table, taking her by surprise. "Nakita, Nakita, as endearing as you are, and believe me, I really do love you, I can't help but think that you're letting your life slip by. You never go out, you're already saddled with a mortgage and doing the most boring possible degree that you could think of. You've just turned twenty-two. C'mon, who does that?"

"Smart people, Will," she huffed. "People who want to get ahead in life. Besides, I couldn't just let the house go. We grew up there. It's the only link we have to who we are—well, who we were."

"Kit, I get that you've got brains, and it's good to be financially independent, set goals, and all that crap, but you're taking this whole 'life plan' way too seriously. All you do is work and uni. Shit, that's all you've done since we left school. This is supposed to be the best time of our lives—when we get to go out into the big wide world, throw caution to the wind and make mistakes before we settle down to all that adult stuff. I mean, when are you getting out of this backwater town?"

"Look around," she motioned to the people overflowing the popular beachfront pub, "Dorley Point is the place to be."

"The place to be, or the place to retire?"

She rolled her eyes. "What's the big deal? It's less than ten minutes into town, forty to the city. It's not like I'm a recluse. I do stuff. My fun is just different to yours."

"Yeah right, I'm talking about you getting out and actually living, not hanging around libraries and that old folks' home in your spare time."

"At least I've got goals," she muttered, pretending to scan the menu she knew off-by-heart.

Now I can't bring up his totally reckless attitude towards his future. Normally she was the one doing the lecturing. She would eventually get to the fun stuff, but first she needed to secure her career; once she had career stability, she could focus on the things she wanted to do. It seemed everyone was on her case about the same thing these days.

"How 'bout we make a birthday deal?"

She raised an eyebrow. "A birthday deal?"

"Yeah. A bet." He said, leaning forward.

"Okay, give it." Clasping her hands together, she gave her 'patient sister look', but the truth was, her curiosity was piqued. She loved nothing more than making bets with Will. The stakes were always high, and once they agreed on the conditions, it was a rock solid contract between them. It was their love economy, for as much as they were opposites; if there was one thing they had in common, it was their stubbornness. Making wagers was a language they'd spoken since they were little. It had started with simple competitive things like running races and had evolved over the years into stakes that were at times costly, or downright hard to follow through with. But as a matter of pride, neither of them would back down. Once they'd sworn with their hands over their heart, there was no way out.

"Right, here's the deal. You've got two years. By your twenty-fourth birthday, if you haven't become a bit less of a virgin, you must do something."

"What? You think I need to lose my virginity, like it's something to be discarded?" She waved a napkin in his face. "I'll have you know that, in the nineteenth century, one's virginity was not only held sacred, but was highly sought after."

"Yeah, okay, okay." He put his hand up. "Poor choice of words— you've read way too many olden day books... What I meant was, just become a little less 'life-experience virginal.' Let loose a little. Stop trying to control everything and just let life happen. Instead of this whole 'I'm in control of my destiny' thing you've got going on."

"And if I don't become less 'virginal'?"

"Then there'll be a list of things you have to do," he paused to add effect, motioning with his hands. "Much like a bucket list."

"A bucket list? I'm already doing my bucket list. I'm at uni, paying off the house. I'm writing a novel..." she trailed off, unable to think of anything else to add. The truth was, she'd majorly stalled on that novel she'd been writing, well over a year ago.

"Yeah, I know, I know—just hear me out. This will be no ordinary bucket list, it's a bucket list with a twist. More like an 'anti-bucket list.'"

"Okay... I'm listening."

"This will be a bucket list of stuff you'd never want to do."

"So why would I do it?" Trying to follow their conversation was proving increasingly difficult after three drinks.

"If you lose the bet, you've got to do the bucket list."

"What's the bet again?"

"Okay. Well, you've never been out of the country, so how about you have to go overseas before the time you reach twenty-four, and if you don't, you must complete the anti-bucket list?"

"Overseas? Easy done. I would love to go overseas. And what about you? What's at stake for you? Will you become more virginal?" She quipped, delighted by her own joke.

"You really shouldn't snicker at your own jokes."

"I did not."

"Yes, that was a snicker. Anyway, by then, I should probably settle down a bit and become a bit more responsible since almost-twenty-five is ancient. So, if I'm not enrolled at uni within two years, I'll have broken my end of the bargain and I'll have to do my 'anti-bucket' list."

"You go to uni? I'll believe that when I see it." She wriggled in her chair, excited at the prospect. If there was one thing she knew it was that her brother had to start thinking about his future. "Where do I sign up?"

"Got any paper in that bad-boy?" he asked, eyeing her oversized handbag. She rummaged through and fished out a pen. "Just write it on the back of the beer coasters."

She handed him a pen as he turned over the beer coaster bearing the image of a seagull in flight. "Alright, so give me something you'd never do?"

"That's easy. Skydiving." *No way I am ever going skydiving.* Her legs trembled at the mere thought of it.

I wonder where I should go? Europe? Definitely Europe, I must talk Annie into going with me.

She could just see herself and Annie exploring historical ruins, wandering through art galleries, sipping lattes on French sidewalks. A trip with Will was out of the question; he preferred high thrill action, partying and eating at questionable places.

"Actually, how about we start with your list?" she suggested, nervous at the prospect of an anti-bucket list.

"Too easy," he handed back the pen and coaster. "Well, I'd never for the life of me read one of those Jane Austen books you love to read."

"Haha, I have a spare copy I'll lend you. If there is one thing I am certain of, William, it's that you won't have enrolled at uni in two years time."

"That's where you're wrong. I've got goals too. Put me down for crosswords and one of those boring puzzles you like to do."

"What about visiting a Jane Austen book club with me?"

"Yeah, why not? You may as well add on one of those fancy poetry reading nights and those cooking classes you like to do... Other suggestions?"

"What about a Disney movie marathon?"

"Ugh, okay. I could fall asleep just thinking about doing any of those."

"This is going to be so great." The thought of her brother doing any of the things on the list that grew before her eyes had her biting back a smile.

"Hmm... let's see... you can also put me down for wearing those god-awful rubber shoes people wear..."

"You mean Crocs?"

"They're the ones—Crocs—for a day."

She clapped. "Hilarious."

"I don't plan on losing this bet, Kit. I'll pick up a woman from the library, learn the tango, and sleep the night with a woman without having sex." He leaned forward on his elbows, his eyebrows raised in challenge.

"Like that's an achievement," she grimaced. But try as she might, she couldn't stay angry at him.

"Oh, and put me down to visit the old fogies' home for a game of bingo or to read them a story, or whatever it is you do there."

"Oh, this is seriously fun. I want you to do all this right now. Okay, my turn..."

She chewed the lid of the pen. *The hard part will be narrowing my list down.* "I am so confident that I will never have to do this list that I'm going to go all out. You can be scribe this time." She passed him the pen and a second beer coaster.

He printed her name at the top. "Shock me, Nakita."

"Well, I already have skydiving. Hmm, put me down for a fake tan, a skinny dip, a motorbike ride, I'll sleep the night fully clothed, shoes and all."

"Come on, up the ante."

"Okay... let's see... a pole dancing class." *Ew, that's so tacky. No way am I doing that.*

"Now we're talking."

"I'll get a guy's number at a nightclub, drink you under the table, smoke a cigar. Get a nude portrait by a male artist." *Never going to happen, may as well go extra all out.* "Plus, I'll get a tattoo." She leant forward and gave her best 'how-do-you-like-me-now,' expression.

Will looked at her, his eyes widening. *Good, I shocked him.*

"Kit, with us, a deal is a deal, right? There's no breaking this. No matter how high the stakes are. It's an unbreakable covenant, we're forever sworn."

"Yeah, I know." She tapped the beer coaster on the table, giving him a cocky smile, "My stakes are higher than yours, I might add, an indicator of how adamant I am that I'll never have to do anything on this list."

"These beer coasters, henceforth, shall be a contract that bindeth us in everlasting agreement," he said, in his most solemn tone.

"As it is written, so shall it be done," she added.

"Hand over heart, Nakita." They rested their hands over their hearts in oath, smiling at each other.

She raised her half filled glass. He raised his empty one.

"To Europe," *Under no circumstances am I getting a tattoo. Ever.*

~

Two years later

Nakita pushed open the heavy door of Ink Guild. She wanted to turn and run, but Will was right behind her, ensuring she kept her side of their deal. Part of her hoped that he'd let her off the hook, but she knew he'd never give in, and neither would she. She'd never broken a promise in her life and she wasn't about to start now; even if this was her absolute worst nightmare.

A tattoo. Great. Today you're joining the ranks of inked up girls. Classy. A shudder crept down her spine.

The cheerful ding of the doorbell was at odds with the scene before her. Stepping inside, she paused, seeing a bronzed centaur warrior that dominated the corner rearing up with bow and arrow. It was almost as tall as she was. She studied it for a few moments; it was stunning. Glancing around, surprised this time by the parlour itself. She'd expected it to be covered wall-to-wall with questionable photographs of inked body parts. The crisp smell of tea tree oil pervaded the space, but the counters were clean and the shop was tidy. Sophisticated framed inks lined the walls. Nakita stepped across the room to examine a matador and bull—a dramatic depiction; the matador's chaquetilla was as precise as the fury in the bull's eyes. *It's more like an art gallery.* Nakita let out the breath she was holding.

"Look at the use of colour in this artwork. Whoever did this has some serious talent."

A woman about her age appeared behind the counter. Nakita swallowed hard, trying to keep calm. With arms covered in a mish-mash of birds, feathers and curly script, the woman was just what she'd expect in a tattoo parlour; she was a colourful human canvas with her hair shaved almost to the skin on one side and long on the other. Her jet black hair had garish stripes of bright blue, and prolific rings and studs obscured her face. She was a walking, talking pincushion.

"How can I help?"

"Hey there. My sister was hoping to get a tatt today," Will piped up. He was loving every second of her discomfiture.

Pincushion's eyes, framed with startling drawn on eyebrows, looked her up and down. Nakita glanced down at her olive-green top and favourite autumn print skirt that fell slightly above the knee. Fiddling with the single gold hoop in her ear, she tried to regulate her breathing, sure that her pulse was about to beat out of her neck.

"Well, this is your lucky day," Pincushion said, her manner as blunt as her haircut. "Last client chickened out from the pain mid-tatt. Want his spot?"

No, I don't want his spot. I never want a tattoo. Nakita couldn't help her gaze flitting to the front door, but it returned with new resolve to the shrapnel-pocked face of the girl. She nodded, forcing a smile, thrusting a clipboard into her hand.

"Okay, you'll have to wait ten minutes. Fill this out. I'll tell Nox you're here."

Nox? Now that sounds like a tattoo artist's name.

Nakita started conjuring up an image of how menacing this Nox was going to be as she sat down next to Will, who was flicking through a folder on the coffee table before them. She leaned towards him and whispered, "I think we should go. I don't think this place is very professional."

"What do you mean, not professional?"

"Shh," she pinched him in the ribs.

"Argh! We sealed the deal. Stop trying to buy time." He moved to another couch. "Don't forget, I've got a list of stuff I don't exactly want to do either."

"Are you kidding me? Your list is nowhere near as bad as mine."

"Well, if I recall correctly, you were half-tanked when we wrote that list. I was a little more prudent," he teased, tapping the side of his head with a smug expression.

When she was sure Pincushion wasn't looking, she launched the closest cushion at his head, but to her annoyance, he caught it and eased back with a smile.

"Thanks. Love you too."

Huffing in frustration, she picked up a folder from the table, hoping to find a design that grabbed her. Although the pictures were excellent artworks, she couldn't say she'd choose to have one on her body, forever.

"What are you going to get?" Will asked, bringing a folder closer to his face, his eyebrow raised.

"I have no idea. Nothing stands out, they're too cliché. I don't want anything common or dark," she said, eyeing a tattoo of the angel of death.

Where am I even going to get this tattoo? Lower back was out—they were called 'tramp stamps' for a reason. Boobs and butt were definitely a no-go zone—it all just seemed so tacky.

She put her head in her hands. If only she'd followed through with the bet with Will and gone backpacking around Europe like she pledged to, then she wouldn't be here making the most irresponsible decision of her life.

Will stood and stretched, yawning loudly, bringing her back to reality. "I'm going to get a kebab and a coke, want one?" She shook her head. Even though her stomach rumbled, the last thing she wanted was to be belching mid-tattoo. Will struggled to sit still for more than five minutes and even though he would never admit it, he had a fear of needles.

No sooner had he left than the doorbell chimed again and a little girl resembling a dark-haired cherub bounced inside. Her brown curls bobbed up and down as she chatted to a woman in her mid-fifties who came huffing and puffing behind.

"Hawo, Kara," the girl said to Pincushion.

"You're going to have to let Lennox know he'll have to find someone else to mind Emmylou for the time being," the older woman said. "Mum's broken her hip and I'm going to have to be by her side until she recovers."

"That's no good. I'll let him know, Lorraine."

"Emmylou, remember to keep practicing your 'R's like I taught you."

Emmylou screwed up her cute button nose and made an 'rrrhg' sound as she shook her head. She was so adorable, Nakita laughed, capturing the little girl's attention.

"What's yawa name?" she asked, pushing her fringe from her eyes with her forearm.

"My name's Nakita."

"Are you getting a tattoo?"

"Yes, I am," Nakita answered, pressing her knees together so she didn't squirm in her seat.

A smile lit up the little girl's face, exposing a row of white baby teeth. "My daddy's the best tattoo man in the whole wild world." She exclaimed, spreading out her arms.

Nakita chuckled. "Wild? Just as well I'm getting him to tattoo me then."

"I'll help you choose." Emmylou plopped down next to her. "So what's it going to be today?" she asked, jumping straight into a tattooist-client role-play that she'd obviously witnessed before. Taking a purple folder from the coffee table, she flipped straight to the back. "I like this one." She pointed a stubby finger at Smurfette holding a daisy with a dreamy expression on her face.

"Hmm, I do like Smurfette, but I think she's too bright blue for my complex—my white skin."

The little girl squinted at Nakita's arms and nodded.

Smiling to herself, Nakita picked up another folder that looked a little more promising. It wasn't so hard-core, yet tribal markings and Celtic symbols just weren't her thing, nor did she want a phrase or a word.

Wow, this is seriously difficult.

She continued flicking through the pages, her breath catching as she came to a photo of a bare-chested guy wearing a pair of low-slung, black jeans. Her eyes strayed over his body. Broad, lean and muscular, his sun-streaked, dark hair was pulled back in a loose knot with a few wisps hanging untamed around his face. A simple inscription in another language ran down the left side of his ribs; while his torso wasn't completely covered with tattoos, two full sleeves were accompanied by a sine tattoo that snaked up one side of his neck. He had a sculptured jawline and brooding eyebrows. She could tell those slightly full lips would have done some damage in their time.

But it was his mysterious, leaf-green eyes that brought her heart to a standstill. He looked like a musician from the cover of a rock magazine. She wasn't normally a fan of long hair and tattoos, yet he was undeniably gorgeous. She drank in his image, her gaze travelling over his hair and face, working down his inked shoulders, hard chest and cut abdomen and kept coming back to those eyes. Something entirely unfamiliar squeezed tight in her belly.

"That's my Daddy."

"Oh, ah..." Nakita tried to close the folder.

"Hey Chipmunk, you telling stories about me again?"

Turning toward the amused voice, her stomach lurched as she noted it was the guy from the folder. He was leaning against the door-frame, those eyes on her, arms folded and a lazy half-grin. She glanced down at his photo, the pages still pinned open in her lap by two pudgy hands.

This is Emmylou's dad? My tattooist?

She couldn't breathe, couldn't swallow, couldn't return the easy smile on his face. She stared back, mutely. *Oh dear God, how long has he been standing there?*

"Daddy! Daddy!" Emmylou squealed and leapt into his arms.

"I missed you, Chipmunk." He tossed Emmylou in the air and was rewarded with more squeals.

He looked just as he did in the photo, save for his grey shirt and a longish, scruffy looking beard that obscured the angles of his handsome face. She had the urge to reach out and trace those lips.

What? Nakita, get a hold of yourself. He's a tattooist. He has a beard. Not to mention a child... and clearly a partner.

Fidgeting with the hem of her skirt, she focused on controlling her breathing; pursing her lips discreetly, she imagined she was sucking each breath through a straw.

Emmylou placed her hands on either side of her father's face, rubbing his beard. "Daddy, Nakita's getting a tattoo and I'm helping her choose."

"Nakita, is it?" His eyes flicked over her once again as she stood to accept his hand.

"Yeah, hi." Managing a small smile that felt more like a grimace, her entire focus turned to the feel of her hand in his and the effect of his eyes on her. She'd always had a thing for green eyes and his were even more disarming in real life; they had that way of knowing how to look at a woman.

"Nox." He introduced himself, one brow raised a little in a questioning look. He was probably wondering what a girl like her was doing there. She figured she didn't exactly look like the poster child for a tattoo parlour.

"Emmylou, your afternoon tea's ready now," Kara called. Emmylou gave Nakita a small wave and skipped over to Kara.

"So, you ready?" he asked, his eyes marking hers.

She could only manage a small nod as she swept past him, concentrating on not inhaling a deep breath of his musky, wooded cologne.

Ugh. Where is Will when I need him? The studio had a similar feel to the waiting room. A kitchenette ran along the back wall, a small two-seat couch filled the corner, and an eclectic selection of chairs sat around a low coffee table. By the window was an imposing black leather tattoo chair, which she couldn't help eyeing as an instrument of torture, wondering who else had suffered there already. There were more framed artworks and an illustration of a steampunk view of a city with recreated scenes of the Victorian past fused with futuristic elements that took up a large part of the wall.

"Did you do this?" she asked, forgetting her shyness as she leant in to appreciate the complex illustration.

He nodded, running his fingers through his hair, pushing back the stray bits that fell forward again. "It's kind of an outlet for me. You like art?"

She nodded eagerly. "I seriously love it. But I don't have an artistic bone in my body. That sculpture in the foyer, did you do that too?"

"Yep." He closed the door.

"It's *really* good."

"Thanks," he said, watching her, then seeming to come back to himself. "So... let's take a seat." He motioned her to the couch while he straddled a stool. Something about the way he moved made her more aware of his physical presence.

"So, did anything in the folders grab you?"

"Ah no, not really," she lied, rubbing her sweaty palms along her thighs, hoping she was imagining the amusement in his eyes.

Will tapped on the door and walked in.

Thank God. As annoying as Will was, he was quite useful in social situations. He greeted Nox with a handshake as if they were good buddies from way back and then sat next to Nakita.

Nox eased back a little further on the stool. "Okay," he continued, "usually when customers come for a tattoo they have a few ideas about what they want." He rubbed his beard, regarding her. "Are you sure you've put enough thought into whether you want one? They are kind of permanent."

"Allow me," Will said, throwing his arm around her. "The fact of the matter is, a bet was lost. The consequence being, she gets a tattoo."

"I've tattooed plenty of people who've lost bets, but deep down they usually want one. Are you sure you want this?" He turned to her.

"No." She returned his intent gaze, aware of the irony of her answer.

He turned to Will. "She obviously doesn't want to get one, so let her off the hook."

"That's not an option," they said in unison.

Nox motioned between them. "Wait, are you twins or something?"

Will smiled and nodded.

"Ahh." Recognition dawned. "Look, I'm not going to argue. I've tattooed people for dumber reasons. Where do you want it?"

"I was thinking... on my hip?"

"So, I'm guessing you don't have any others?" Nox rubbed his chin, his eyes skimming her body.

"Gosh, no!" her skin seared at his perusal.

Her answer brought a twinkle to his eyes and a barely perceptible smile to his lips.

"Yeah, she's a tattoo virgin." Will paused and then shrugged. "Not to mention a virgin in general."

Nakita sucked in her breath. "Will!"

"Maybe you could tattoo a chastity belt around her hips?"

"William James Faulkner!"

Nox choked on his laughter. He'd been in many situations as a tattooist, but this was different. *Do chicks still blush these days?* The ones he knew didn't. Nakita's lips were in the shape of a perfect 'O'. She'd blushed when he'd first caught her checking out his photo in the folder, but now she was bright red. Surely her brother wasn't serious? She looked to be in her early twenties. It just didn't seem possible. Even though she had 'good girl' written all over her, she was all woman.

"How about you tell me things you like?"

"Things I like?" She bit the side of her lower lip as he watched.

"Yeah... things that turn you on." *Hmm... poor choice of words.* "I mean, like your hobbies, stuff you like to do." One thing he never did was sleaze on his clients; even if she was a brown-eyed, gorgeous redhead with a body like a man's idea of a playground.

"Well, I guess I enjoy reading, baking, and, um... cats?"

"Cats?" He winced

"Yeah, I like cats. I have a cat." She sat poker-straight in her chair, her hands poised on either side of the couch, as if she was about to spring out.

"You know, as good as those things are, I'd stay away from books, cupcakes or cats in that general area." He nodded towards her pelvis, hoping she'd get the gist.

There she goes, blushing again. She was as geeky as hell, but damn she was hot.

"I'm telling you, stick with the chastity belt." Her brother clearly enjoyed stirring her, but the affection between them was obvious.

"Chastity belt," she murmured, looking up. "A key. That's what I want. A key," she said with a faraway look in her almond-shaped eyes.

"A key?" he repeated, somewhat mystified. Nox decided right then that he'd draw those eyes—though he doubted that he'd be able to capture the expression in them. She had a captivating, sexy quality, like the leading ladies in the old movies his mum used to watch.

"Yeah, a key, a secret garden key. Right here." She stood, pointing low to the front of her hip.

"You sure?" She rewarded him with a slow smile that sent jolts through his stomach. "Okay, a secret garden key it will be then." That smile was having a peculiar effect on him.

"Oh geez, Kit, can't you come up with anything more exciting than that?" Will groaned.

"It's not like I asked for a 'My Little Pony', Will."

Nox laughed out loud this time. For someone extremely uptight, she was kind of sassy. "Do you want me to run a search so you can choose a design?"

"No, I want something original." She stood up and walked over to the wall. His eyes followed the sway of her hips, taking in the curve of her arse.

"I like the feel of your artwork. Can you design it?" She turned to him suddenly, unfolding her arms. "I don't want to see it beforehand. Just do it. I trust you."

She trusted him? There was something about this girl that made him forget himself. She wasn't the kind of girl he'd ever go for: geeky, virginal, and seriously neurotic—but then, surprising. He groaned inwardly. *Who am I kidding?* "Are you sure? Because, if you don't like it, a coverup is even bigger."

"I'm sure." She tucked her chin in.

"Alright, one secret garden key coming right up," he said, as though he were her very own personal genie. He raked his fingers through the front of his hair. "I better make it good, it's not every day I get to tattoo a virgin." Her eyes connected with his from underneath her eyelids for a fleeting moment; she gave him a timid smile. And somehow, giving this girl her very first ink was becoming even more enticing.

~

Nakita forced herself to watch from a distance as Nox sketched a design. She knew if she started deliberating, the perfectionist in her would never settle on anything. Will had skipped out on her and left to go play pool with Byron. As soon as he left the room, her body, already overly conscious of Nox's presence, went into overdrive again. She was acutely aware of her tattoo artist's proximity in relation to hers.

He was leaning over a table, his brow furrowed deeply as he worked on her key. Nakita found her eyes drawn to him, admiring his height, the way his shirt moulded to his chest and shoulders, the loose bits of hair that fell free of his man-bun that he kept pushing back. His left hand moved swiftly and fluidly as he drew. Now and then he would pause briefly, rub his beard and glance up at her. Each time she was caught out staring at him, but her eyes seemed to have a will of their own and kept going back for more.

"Okay. You're up," he said, putting his pencil down and looking at his picture as though it satisfied him. "I'll just put this through the machine so I can transfer the stencil on you. You sure you don't want to see it first?"

Maybe I should take a tiny peek? What if I hate it?

"No." She shook her head, not wanting to elaborate further. "So long as there are no skulls or grim reapers. I think it'll be fine."

"Your call." He stood looking at her as though she were an enigma. "Jump up on the couch then and lay down."

Thick dread jammed somewhere between her throat and her gut. She walked over to the black chair with leaden feet. *What the heck am I doing?* She lay down, hoping he didn't notice her movements were stiff and awkward or that she was quivering uncontrollably.

"Okay. So you're going to have to pull the front of your skirt down to just above the bikini line," he said, turning away. She knew most days he saw more flesh than she was revealing right now, but to her it was a big deal; exposing that part of her body to a man that she'd just met seemed so intimate.

Get a hold of yourself. He's a tattooist, for goodness sake. You're making this into something it's not.

"Ready?" He came over with the stencil. She trained her eyes to the ceiling. "Okay, so you want it about here?" he brushed his fingers in a flicking motion over her sensitive skin.

His touch sent a thrill of heat coursing through her body. "Yes. There's good." *Just breathe, Nakita.* She closed her eyes and visualised breathing through a straw.

"You okay?" She felt his touch on her arm and opened her eyes, to see his expression, somewhere between amused and concerned.

"I'm fine. Just breathing," she said, realising she probably looked ridiculous.

"Breathing's good, keep doing that." She might have been embarrassed except for the warmth in his green eyes as he smiled at her. Her stomach did a flip-flop. She visualised the straw.

At first she tried to ignore his touch as he cleaned her skin, but then she thought to allow herself the guilty pleasure as his hands worked deftly, the lightest brush on her hip sending electrical tingles through her pelvis. An awkward silence hung between them.

"So, you from around here?"

"I grew up in Dorley Point." *Oh thank God, he's making conversation.* She was too nervous. Though she wasn't exactly shy, she took a little while to warm up with people she didn't know. But then he was on a whole other level. And she'd never been in a situation like *this* before.

"Dorley Point, eh? Where do you live now? On campus at the uni?"

"It's that obvious I go to uni, huh?"

"Ah yeah, pretty much."

There he goes, smiling at me like that again. Just stop it.

"Actually, I still live in the same house I grew up in. I work at The Gull—the pub just on the beach."

"I go to Dorley Point for a surf now and again. I always see this old guy power walking around in nothing but speedos and joggers."

"Oh, that's Martin, he's a great guy. We do yoga together on the beach some Sunday mornings. You should see him; he's super flexible and a total health guru."

Stop blurting, Nakita.

"I'm a visual kind of guy and you're drawing some pretty vivid images for me right now."

"I really admire him. No, no, no, not like that." She sat up, her eyes widening at his expression, which was becoming more amused the more she talked.

"Relax, sit back. I get you."

"Okay, sorry." She reclined back on the seat, shivering, knowing by the contraption he was holding near her skin that he was about to begin.

"Okay, no going back?" His green eyes held hers in question. She held her breath, suspended in time. But she wasn't sure it had anything to do with the fact he was about to inject her with ink. It was his eyes. They were injecting her with a warmth that reached to her toes.

"No going back." She repeated, realising their eyes still held.

"Slight sting."

"Ouch." *Just block it out.* "He inspires me. I love old folk, especially when they break out of the stereotype and remind us that life is still worth living when we get older." *You're rambling, Nakita.*

"Are we talking about Martin again?"

"Yeah, I'm sorry. I talk way too much when I'm nervous, and I'm really nervous. He's added hand weights to his repertoire now."

Nox paused his work and looked at her in a way she couldn't

decipher. "Really? Well, I'll have to get back there for a surf some-time soon and get some inspiration."

Pressing her lips together, she was determined to be quiet. Her belly tremors disappeared as the white-hot pain of the needle took over, and yet there was still something incredibly intimate about him tattooing her that even the pain couldn't dull. She tried to appear unaffected, but when he looked up and caught her watching him, she immediately averted her gaze, but not before she caught that gleam of recognition in his eye. He was obviously very experienced with women, and she wasn't sure how that made her feel.

"So, what was the bet with your brother, if you don't mind me asking?" His focus on what he was doing was intense as she tried to find the words to answer him.

"Well, we've had this thing ever since we were kids, that when we make a bet, we follow through on it, no matter what. For us, a bet is more like a contract. It's binding. A few years ago, Will and I made a bet on our twenty-second birthday. Whoever lost the bet would have to do a list of things we'd never want to do."

"You mean, kind of like the opposite of a bucket list?"

"Exactly. Well, recently, we turned twenty-four. I haven't made good on my deal and neither has Will."

"So a tattoo was on your list?"

Her eyes focused on a flash of straight, white teeth as he smiled. She resisted the sudden urge to reach out and run her fingers along his jawline. She shook her head.

I don't even like beards. What's with me today?

She cleared her throat, "It was at the top—well, at the bottom really. I threw it in because I was adamant that I would follow through on the bet—I never expected to have to do it."

"How'd you lose the bet?"

"Well, I had to travel overseas before I turned twenty-four and Will had to enrol at uni." She shook her head, studying the cracks in the ceiling. "I just got too busy. I'm at uni part-time. I work. I have a mortgage. I have responsibilities. I just don't have time or money to go gallivanting around the world."

He nodded as though he understood, which was oddly satisfying. This encouraged her to go on. "An old friend of mine says some people have roots and others have wings. I guess I'm a roots kind of girl. Will sprouted wings a long time ago." She gasped, wincing at the sharp sting.

"Sorry, it's a sensitive area. So what are you studying?"

"Accountancy." She wished she could say something more cutting edge, like journalism, or a travel writer. Anything more exotic than an accountant. "And before you start with any jokes about boring accountants, trust me, I've heard every single one of them more times than I can count."

He smiled easily. "No, I admire a person who follows their dreams."

She looked at him from under her eyelashes to check whether he was having a go at her, but he gave nothing away. She changed the topic; unsure she wanted to continue discussing her dreams. "So, you live around here?"

"Yeah, I've only been open for about six months. I rent a small unit in town. It's not much, but it's just me and Emmylou... the way I like it."

Her body tensed at his words.

"You need a breather?"

She held both her hands to her forehead. "No, I want to get it over with. I knew tattoos hurt, but I had no idea it would be this bad."

He paused and squeezed her shoulder reassuringly. "You're doing great. I've seen plenty of tough blokes go to custard in this chair." He refocused on the tattoo. "So why'd you get the tattoo done first if it was at the bottom of the list?"

"Well, I figured if I did the worst thing first, the rest would be easy. Just about everything on the list either terrifies me, goes against my common sense, my sense of propriety, or my personal convictions."

"So which one does this come under?"

She thought for a moment. "I'd say all four."

His teeth flashed again, "Well, I'm honoured to be part of this experience with you then."

Oh lordy. Why was just looking at him more painful than the tattoo?

"Here I am, Daddy." Emmylou came running in as though she'd been summoned and plonked herself on the floor by the tattoo chair with paper and crayons.

Nox looked to Nakita for approval.

"It's fine with me." Nakita said, relieved to have a distraction in the room.

"Emmylou, you'll have to sit quietly."

"Okay, Daddy," she said, in what sounded like her 'don't-you-remember-I'm-a-perfect-angel' voice. Nox made a 'sure-you-will' face. For a few minutes Emmylou chatted quietly to her crayons, while Nakita and Nox slipped into easy silence. Emmylou stood suddenly, her head tipped towards Nakita. "What's your favourite animal?"

"Hm... let's see. I guess I'd have to say giraffes; they have such graceful long necks."

She looked into Nakita's face as though their conversation was of the utmost importance. Nakita tried to ignore the feel of Nox's eyes on her as she talked to his daughter. "Oh, and I also love cats. I have a cat called Moopsy. She's a Persian and very lovely."

Nox shifted and grunted. Clearly not a feline fan.

"Can I call you Kitty?" Emmylou asked.

"Sure, you can call me Kitty," Nakita answered, not sure she really liked this new nickname, especially as she noted the amused gleam in Nox's eye.

"Can I come to your house?"

"Emmylou, you can't invite yourself to people's homes."

"But Kitty's my fwend, Daddy."

"Maybe we can arrange something," Nakita offered feebly, hoping Emmylou would drop it.

"Yay! I'm going to tell Kawa." With that, she up and left the room.

"Now you've done it," Nox muttered, his focus never leaving the tattoo.

"Done what?"

"My daughter can be a little vixen, you know you're going to have to follow through on that. She won't let up till you do." He remained focused, his strong brows knitted together.

"Then I guess I'll have to," she answered, embarrassed that she'd put the idea in Emmylou's mind.

"Okay, honey. You're done." He wiped the excess ink off her skin. "Take your time getting up and have a look in the mirror."

"I'm so nervous," she said, finding an odd pleasure in him calling her honey. He looked down at her, every bit as magnificent as he was in the photo she'd seen of him—even with a beard.

"How do you think I feel? If you hate it, you'll always remember me as the guy who gave you that awful tattoo you never wanted."

On liquid legs she walked towards the mirror. Looking at her hip, she gasped.

CHAPTER 2

*N*ox took the opportunity to answer a few texts while he stood near the pharmacy counter waiting for his prescription. He kept one eye on Emmylou, who was busy eyeing off the giftware that probably looked like treasure to her four-year-old eyes. He stalled mid-text, instantly recognising the very female voice asking the pharmacy assistant questions about vitamins.

Nakita. Something about her presence had stuck with him, as if she was taking up real estate in his thoughts. He couldn't put his finger on exactly what it was about her, but he'd found himself noticing how his other female clients moved and spoke in comparison. She didn't have the rough edge in her speech and manner like some women—she was all silkiness and curves. He couldn't remember a time when he'd found a woman so intriguing. Letting out a shallow breath, he tried to get his body to follow his mind. He'd been hoping to see her again. *Who are you kidding? You think she'd be remotely interested in someone like you?* But then, he could swear there'd been something that passed between them. He'd replayed that scene over more than a few times.

He wished he wasn't running into her now when he felt like crap.

All week he'd been dead tired, the smallest exertion had him out of breath. During one of his sessions with a client, his vision started to blur and he was cold, but sweating profusely; he'd cancelled his other appointments. That afternoon he'd been so lightheaded that he put cartoons on for Emmylou and slept until she came into his room after dark, putting her pudgy sticky hands on either side of his face and pleading, "Daddy, I'm soooo hungwy." As she chatted animatedly about Peppa Pig and ate eggs on toast for the third night in a row, he tried to enjoy the moment and ignore the hot rock of guilt and despair that sat heavy in his gut.

Taking a deep breath, he took Emmylou's hand and went to the next aisle where Nakita stood. She wore a denim skirt and a stripy blouse that hung loosely off one creamy shoulder as she leaned forward taking a pack of panty-liners off the shelf. He almost turned back, but she looked up straight at him.

"Kitty!" Emmylou ran over and clutched her around the legs. The panty-liners fell to the floor. A smile lit Nakita's face as she looked down at Emmylou. He wasn't sure quite what to do, so he stooped to pick up the packet and held them out to her.

"Ah, thanks." She flushed a pretty shade of pink that was only enhanced by the two thick braids that hung over her shoulders.

"Hey, how's the ink?" he asked, trying not to sound breathless; his heart skipping a beat at the warmth of expression in her gorgeous dark eyes. *Stupid heart.* It was doing all sorts of funky things these days.

"I love it." She smiled. "It's more beautiful than I could have imagined; I love the lace and how you made the key look antique; it's kind of elegant for a tattoo. I still can't believe I've got one. It's my little secret nobody knows. Well except for you, Emmylou and Will." There was something gratifying knowing she liked his design. He stood there watching her tugging on the end of one of her long plaits. He'd never been much of a fan of braids, but damn they looked sexy on her. He'd observed from his short time with her that she fidgeted when she was nervous and knowing he made her nervous filled him with an odd satisfaction. Or maybe it was just wishful thinking on his part?

"What are them?" Emmylou asked, pointing at the pack of panty-liners in her hand.

"Oh, they're ah..." She looked to Nox for help.

"Ladies' business. You'll find out when you're a lady." That was as much as he was telling her today. He didn't want to think about Emmylou becoming a teenager someday—chances were he might not get his someday.

"Lennox Conrad?" The pharmacist called his name, holding up a basket overflowing with medication. Nakita looked towards the counter.

"So, what you up to?" he asked, rubbing the side of his neck, pretending not to notice.

"Well, actually, I've been putting notices on the community boards around town. I'm looking for a housemate to generate a bit of extra income. The house needs some TLC. Nothing's been done to it since long before our dad passed away and Will's always travelling."

"If you like, I could put a notice up in Ink Guild."

"Ah thanks, but it's okay. I appreciate the offer, it's just that..." She glanced away.

"Yeah, I hear you. I suppose I wouldn't want to live with any of my clients either." He raised his eyebrows. "Although, come to think of it, you're now one of my clients."

Oh shit, I'm flirting.

She stood there smiling, delicious and shy.

"Hey, I think they're calling your name again, Lennox Conrad." Was he imagining that her eyes were sparkling and that she was flirting back?

He wanted to ask for her number, or for a date, or to visit the bloody cat, whatever the hell its name was. "Ah, yeah. I better go." He ran his fingers through the front of his hair. Torn.

"Me too. See you later." She said, suddenly looking flustered. He watched as she walked away. *Damn.* With a shy smile she glanced over her shoulder to him. She was interested. He let her go. He was no catch for her; he was no catch for anyone now.

~

Stilettos, seriously, what was I thinking?

Although she enjoyed wearing all things feminine, stilettos were the exception. And the dress she was wearing tonight had looked rubbish with flat shoes. Once she got to the beach club where the engagement party was already well underway, she'd be on firm ground. She just had to get there first. Walking on her tiptoes to prevent her heels from sinking into the grass, she made her way past the long line of parked cars pausing to text Will.

Here. Be there in a sec.

Continuing in the dark towards the lit up beach club in the distance, music drifted down from the open windows muffled by the roar of the ocean.

"Okay, shoes, you're coming off." Lifting her heel, she pulled at one, then straightening she was knocked hard off balance. A hand clamped over her mouth, an arm compressing her chest. Liquid fear shot through her veins. For a fleeting moment she thought it was Will fooling around, but as her head was reefed back mercilessly by the hair, she knew she was in trouble. Her scalp burned, causing tears to spring to her eyes. She cast wildly to and fro, hoping for someone— anyone. She could see the glow of the club; hear the faint murmur of voices mingled with the latest pop songs. Her hair was suddenly released. Seizing the moment, she bucked wildly. Something sharp pierced her side. Ice-cold dread flooded her veins. She froze. What she knew by instinct was a knife, pressed into her even further.

"Now, Princess, you can do it my way, or the hard way." A voice came low and menacing in her ear. The words were surreal, as if from a movie script. She tried to nod, her whole body arching backwards. He was dragging her to a grassy section that led down into the sand dunes; her insides screamed the words she couldn't form on her lips. *No, not this. This can't be happening. Oh please God, help me!*

Forcing her down onto the grass, her assailant pinned her arms above her head with one powerful forearm. Releasing his other hand from her mouth, he reached under her dress and yanked at her underwear, viciously tugging them down. Her mouth was free. She found her voice and screamed with everything inside her. Leaning back, he slapped her hard across the face and ear with full force. Momentarily stunned, the world tipped, and for the briefest moment, all she could process was how brilliant the stars were in the night sky. Everything went from hazy, slow motion to startling clarity as she felt him pressing up against her, trying to gain access.

Fight. The words came to her.

"Help! Help me! Will!" She shrieked. She heard a loud crack as a punch landed on the underside of her jaw and her teeth clashed together, the pain and shock dizzying.

"Nakita!"

Will? Was she imagining it? She grappled feebly, losing hope to free herself, her limbs were weak and useless. As the attacker's arm lifted to make a fist, she watched, paralysed by fear. He smashed her hard across the cheekbone.

There was an explosion of pain, then nothing.

A thick fog enveloped her senses. It was as if her eyes, her ears, her mouth, all her senses were stuffed with cotton wool. Her cheek throbbed painfully, radiating to her eye. Moaning, she reached up to touch her face, confused. Where am I? Pushing up she met resistance as she was firmly pushed back down. She lay there a moment blinking, willing her eyes to see. Dark shadows slowly turned into a pair of legs. It dawned upon her that she was in someone's arms. The hems of party dresses, long pants and high heels came into view.

High heels!

Everything that had just happened came back with startling clarity; she was at the beach, the engagement party. She was being attacked. *Will!* She pushed up desperately, only to be pulled back down again. Turning to the side she found her head was cradled in someone's lap; she brought a hand to her face and found it was swollen and numb. Her friend Carmen was on her knees beside her, smoothing hair off her face. She looked to be crying.

Nakita tried to push up. *I'm okay.* The words formed in her mind but she couldn't say them as she sank back down. It was like being trapped in one of those dreams she couldn't escape from; no parts of her body were working as they were supposed to. She couldn't hear a sound. In the distance a red light flashed. *An ambulance? I don't need an ambulance. Do I?* All at once her ears cleared and were assaulted by sound. The blaring ambulance. Panicked voices. Sobbing. Chaos. Ice was pushed gently against her cheek, as the lights grew closer. What was going on? Why wasn't anyone telling her? She pushed up again and fought this time against all the hands that pushed and pulled her back down. That's when she saw the top of Will's head, white blonde hair sticking out in its way. Everyone stepped back as paramedics moved towards him.

He lay unmoving in the sand.

Something was terribly wrong.

Nakita let out a wail and sank into darkness as the stars tipped once again.

CHAPTER 3

*W*ill was dead. Her beautiful brother was dead.

She sat in a daze on the front porch of Miriam and Antony's house. Most of the mourners had gone, only those closest to him were left. She just wanted everyone to leave. It wasn't that she didn't appreciate their kind words and gestures, but nothing could be said, nothing could be done to take away the searing pain that burned her insides but somehow left her stone-cold.

She was grateful that Miriam had taken care of the funeral preparations and hosted the wake since she was barely functioning. Mim and Antony were the grandparents she and Will had never had. They were the owners of The Gull and had lived around the corner in a cosy, tree-lined street for as long as Nakita could remember, they'd been there for Will and Nakita as their world had crumbled little by little—now her world was completely unravelled.

The afternoon sunlight filtered its rays through the autumn trees, casting dappled fingers on everything it touched. Once she'd have thought it pretty, but the encroaching shadows reminded her of the approach of yet another endless night. Morning brought its own dread.

Many times as kids, she and Will had played in this yard, climbed the trees and made burrows in the autumn leaves. They'd laughed and rolled around, gleefully stomping on them and enjoying the sound of them crackling underfoot. Together they would examine the explosion of colours, the intricate veins and designs on each leaf, judging who had the finest collection. Will would roll them and pretend he was smoking. One time he even lit one. She could still recall the shock in his face when it flamed suddenly, singeing his eyebrows. Now she saw them differently. They weren't beautiful anymore. The leaves lying on the ground, once green and vital, offering shade from the summer heat, were now in various stages of reds, oranges, yellows and browns—in the throes of death and decay.

The voice of Toby, Will's best mate since kindergarten, and his mother Sharon, brought her out of her reverie. They were about to leave. She should have known this was a stupid place to hide. There was no escape.

Did they really think she wanted to hear more stories about Will? About how fun he *had been* and what a larrikin he *was*. It was all this talk in the past tense, punctuating every sentence that ripped at her heart. While they filled the empty spaces with hushed chitchat, or story after endless story of the mischief that Will had gotten into, she just wanted to forget. Forget that he ever existed, or to at least pretend he was off on some new exploit. The Himalayas were going to be his next big adventure.

"Love, we've got to get going," Sharon's face seemed to sag with the emotional turmoil of the past weeks. Standing slowly, Nakita straightened her plain, black dress. She didn't know what to say. 'Thanks for coming' didn't seem appropriate somehow. Once again she was pulled into an embrace, possibly her thousandth for the day. "Sweetheart, Will was a hero. He did what any brother would have done. He'll always be remembered for his bravery. He was such a beautiful boy." Her voice broke.

Remembered. Was. He now resides in the sphere of the past.

"Bye, Kit, when you're up to it, we'll have a schooner at The Gull, eh?"

Toby. He was the hardest person for her to look at. So many of his mannerisms reminded her of him.

"Yeah, that'd be nice." She knew she sounded as lifeless as she felt. Toby had never been as in your face as Will, but he always seemed to be in a perpetual good mood; now his head was down, his shoulders slumped. A surge of grief rolled over her again. It wasn't just her grief anymore—she felt theirs too. Life had changed forever for all of them: Toby had lost his best mate. Mim and Antony had lost a grandson. She had lost her twin. It was as though half of herself was dead and the world didn't look the same anymore. How could she face the rest of her life without him? It was too much to bear. As they left, she stumbled back down onto the stairs, her face in her hands; the endless reel of that night playing over and over in her mind, tormenting her till she was half-crazed. *If only I hadn't gone to the engagement party, none of this would have happened; Will would be at The Gull having a schooner and laughing with his mates. It's all my fault.*

She'd woke in hospital to Miriam and her best friend, Annie, trying to console her, faces puffy and blotched from crying. Will had never regained consciousness, passing away not long after arriving at the hospital. She couldn't bear to hear the details. The monster who'd taken her brother's life died a couple of days later from a brain haemorrhage sustained from a rock to the head. Knowing Will's killer was dead, was no comfort. There was no comfort.

Nakita watched, mesmerised, as a bright orange leaf detached from a branch and floated aimlessly to the ground. She undid the pin that Miriam had stuck into her lapel before the service. It was a rose pin from the organ donor society. She pressed its coolness against her lips, reliving the distress she felt when it was explained to her that Will was a candidate for organ donation and that he had registered to be an organ donor. They had asked her, as next of kin, to sign for the release of his organs. Something about those words had made the horror of it all so much more real. So final.

"Hey, Kit." Annie nudged down onto the step, wrapping an arm around her. "What you got there?" Her usual singsong voice attempted to be cheery, but fell flat. Annie sounded as drained as Nakita felt. She and Will had been good friends.

"Just a pin... from the organ donation society." She twirled the rose-pin in her fingers. "You know, Annie, I just can't reconcile the fact that people out there have parts of Will inside of them. I mean, I get that it gives others a chance at life, but for the family doing the giving, it's, it's..."

"Totally screwed," Annie finished.

She pursed her lips and nodded. "I mean, just think about it: right now his heart is beating in someone else's chest. I just can't—" Annie rubbed a gentle hand up and down her arm as she failed to continue. Under normal circumstances she'd have found her touch comforting, but right now it was irritating.

"Somehow, Kit, we need to find comfort that Will lives on in those people, that something good has come from something so dreadful."

"I know Annie. I know it's a good thing. But it's meant to happen to someone else—this is Will—my Will. Haven't I lost enough in my life?" She pulled from Annie's embrace and looked at her. "I feel like I'm being punished. I know I shouldn't be saying this, but I'm so angry that whoever has his organs has a chance at life when his was taken from him. He was so healthy." She put her face in her hands. Part of her still had the faint hope that she'd wake up from the living nightmare she was in. "It hurts so much, my whole body hurts so bad. I don't know if I can go on."

Annie pressed her cheek against Nakita's, her hot tears mingling with her own.

He's gone. He's gone. He's gone. The words, like an echo wailed into an endless gorge, reverberated through her being, sending ripples through her soul, taunting her.

Inhaling a shaky breath of cool autumn air, the reality closed around her again. The finality. After losing her mum and dad, Will had become her reason. The other half of her was gone. Forever. Now she had three reasons to never want to breathe again.

CHAPTER 4

*K*eeping her back to the brick wall, Nakita squatted to unlace her worn-out jogger. It made a squeaking sound as she eased it off her sweaty foot with a wince; blood from the blisters on her ankle had soaked through the sock. She'd been walking so long she'd lost track of time, and though her foot stung and the joints in her body were screaming for her to stop, she had gritted her teeth and kept going. Pain was a welcome distraction. Walking had become her survival. Not that she was going anywhere in particular; she just needed to keep moving; normally she would prefer being out somewhere in the beauty of nature, but now she felt more at ease with the bustle and fumes of traffic whizzing past and people going about their daily lives.

She couldn't process the fact that Will was gone. Like a silent movie, images of him would play—endless reels on repeat. Over and over and over again, memories streamed. His cheeky grin; idiosyncrasies like how he bit his nails when he was having a rare quiet moment; how grumpy and dishevelled he was in the morning; how he'd eat enormous bowls of sugary Weetbix any time, day or night.

How she knew he adored her, even though he teased her relentlessly. Never again would he throw his arm around her. Never pull her hair playfully, or take those little liberties only he could, like stealing a huge bite out of whatever she was eating, laughing the whole time she scolded him. Even in sleep she couldn't escape him. Nightmares left her gasping for air on her knees, bringing up nothing but bile. It didn't matter if she was awake or asleep; the nightmares were all-consuming.

Damn, how am I going to get home? She calculated the distance as she slid her shoe back on, clenching her teeth against the smarting flesh. Limping a little further along the main road, she looked across the street where Ink Guild stood on the corner, next to a barber and a pawnshop. It held even more intrigue for her than before. The last time she'd spent an entire day with Will was the day she got her tattoo. Now he was dead.

A sign was on the door: Closed Till Further Notice. *Strange, why would it be closed?* Despite the sign, she twisted the doorknob. There was a flash of movement in a frosted windowpane by the door. She backed up against the wall, unsure if she even wanted to see him, yet unable to curb her curiosity. As discreetly as she could, she peered through the window. It was Pincushion. Not knowing what compelled her, she rapped on the window. Pincushion came to the glass and pulled a face before unlocking the door. Her streaks had changed from vivid blue to hot pink—a lot could change in a matter of weeks.

"What is it?"

"I was just passing by and noticed the sign. Are Nox and Emmylou on holidays or something?"

"You're not family and you're not a friend, so I'm not at liberty to say." The door shut in Nakita's face.

Bitch! Nakita fumed. What wasn't she at liberty to say? Surely, if they'd just gone on a holiday, there'd be nothing to tell? She wandered aimlessly with the steady flow of people, turning it over in her mind. As she walked past the Post Office, a woman in the window caught her eye. *It's the lady who'd dropped Emmylou off. What was her name again? Laura? Lauren? Lorraine?*

Without a moment's thought, she turned and went inside. Waiting until the lady finished writing on her envelope, Nakita approached. "Hi there, Lorraine?"

"Ah, yes?"

Nakita could tell by the older woman's expression, she was trying to place her. "Sorry, I don't mean to interrupt you, but I was just wondering if you could help me? I was at Ink Guild a few weeks back... I'm a friend of Nox and Emmylou." *Nothing wrong with stretching the truth a little.* "Anyway, I've been away, and it surprised me to see the sign in the shop window. Do you know where they are?"

"Oh yes, love. Haven't you heard the news? It's so wonderful." Her face, folded with wrinkles, lit up, "Nox got the transplant. He's in hospital now, and he's doing really well. Everything went better than expected. They think it's because he's young and fit. I saw him yesterday. He's looking superb, and he's in great spirits."

"Transplant?" Nakita breathed.

"You knew about his heart?" The woman looked at her quizzically.

"His heart?" She barely managed. She felt as though the blood had drained from her vital organs and was pooling in her hands and feet, causing them to tingle, hot then cold.

"Are you okay, dear?" Lorraine inclined her head towards her, but it was as if everything was in slow motion.

"You say he's had a heart transplant? Just recently?" She clutched her tote bag tighter.

"Yes, dear, just a few weeks ago. He was waiting for such a long time, but now he's recovering in the city at Central View Hospital."

Central View... where Will...

No, it's not. It couldn't be possible...

Lorraine's voice faded back in as Nakita's vision greyed. "... awful to have to worry about such things at his age, isn't it? They said he was lucky to live as long as he did. He's such a fine fellow, too. Would do anything for anyone. It was a tremendous relief as you can imagine. The last few weeks he was going downhill fast. We were all so worried. Modern day medicine is such a miracle, isn't it? He's still got a long, hard road to recovery ahead, and I can't do a thing to help these days, with mum having broken her hip and all, but he's got good friends that will look out for him. Anyway, all's well that ends well. Such a shame for the other family. Though they say: Someone's loss is another's gain..." Lorraine continued talking, but Nakita never heard another word. Her body numbed. It was all Nakita could do to not collapse in a heap right there on the floor.

Maybe going back to Uni so soon was a bad idea? Sitting in the cafeteria, textbook open in front of her, along with a barely touched salad sandwich. No matter how many times Nakita read the same paragraph, it wouldn't sink in. But she'd needed a distraction, another focus. Before, she would have found a patch of grass outside to eat her lunch, since the noise of the cafeteria reached torturous levels, but now the clamour of people buying trays laden with food, talking, laughing, scraping their chairs on the floor, helped her to zone out. Just so long as she didn't look at the guys that hung together in packs, she was fine. Except, right now, they were goofing around, flicking rubber bands at each other. They reminded her of *him*.

Two hands slid around her shoulders. She stiffened. When she saw the hands belonged to Annie, she let out a breath of relief. She was still so jumpy since that night... *Don't go there. You don't go there, Nakita.*

Annie pressed her full cheek into hers and squeezed her shoulders. "Oh sorry, hon, I didn't mean to frighten you."

"No, you didn't," she lied, "it was just unexpected. It's so noisy in here, and I guess I'm a little jumpy."

Annie's forehead had two deep creases down the centre, her

usually soft hazel eyes, narrowed. "Yeah, well, I'm not surprised. The acoustics in this place are ghastly. Here, share these with me," she pulled a foam container of hot chips swimming in gravy out of her satchel, "You need to eat. Your boobs and booty are gone."

"I know, I can't seem to keep anything down, and I've been walking a lot." Nakita took a chip to appease her; the last thing she needed was Annie on her case. Nothing seemed to taste like anything anymore. Besides, her stomach was always tied in knots and she had no appetite. Whereas before she used to be a real foodie, baking and trying new recipes, now she baked to keep herself occupied, giving it to her elderly neighbours.

She looked into the face of her best friend. "Annie, I've got to tell you something."

Annie winced from the screech of a chair. "Say again?"

"There's something I need to tell you." Nakita raised her voice. If she didn't tell her, she was going to lose her mind. Annie's small, pouty lips pursed together, reminding Nakita of a pretty porcelain doll.

"Let's go for a stroll," she said, leaving her chips on the table with a reluctant look. Nakita packed her things away and headed for the glass doors. Pulling their jackets tighter to keep out the chill that stung their cheeks, they wandered the mostly deserted winding paths of the campus, the scent of pine needles fresh in the frigid air.

"What's going on, Kit?"

"I got a tattoo." She stated as though it were the simplest fact and not something completely outlandish and out of character.

"Wait, what?" Annie yelped, her hands flapping, "When? Where? Why?"

"Shh! Don't be so obvious. It was a bet... with Will."

"Will?" her forehead wrinkled.

"Yeah, it was before..." She'd never talked about that night to anyone apart from the police. Even then, it was as if someone had pressed play on a recording of someone else's voice. Annie and

Miriam tried giving her the opportunity to talk about it afterwards, encouraging her to see a therapist, but she just wanted to forget.

"Where is it?"

"On my hip." Nakita bit her lip, feeling like a disobedient child.

"I can't believe it. You always swore you'd never get one."

"No. I never swore on it," Nakita defended. "It was never an option. But then I lost that bet with Will, and I had to." Although somewhat incredulous, Annie had been friends with Nakita long enough to know that this was a big feature in their brother-sister relationship. Annie had wanted a rockabilly style tattoo, but every time she'd settled on one, Nakita had talked her out of it.

"Do you like it? Show me, show me." Annie clapped, her ringlets dancing around her face.

Making sure the coast was clear, Nakita lifted her jacket while pulling her leggings down to reveal the key on her hip.

"Oh, I love it, it's so vintage. I can't believe you. Did it hurt?"

"So bad."

"Why didn't you tell me?"

"I don't know. I guess I felt like a hypocrite," she said, hoping Annie would see the sincerity in her face. "You have to understand. I had no choice."

Annie rolled her eyes. "You and Will always took this betting thing way too seriously." Her comment hung in the air between them. "Anyway, it's no big deal." She said, linking her arm through Nakita's, pulling her along.

Nakita resisted. "That's not all, there's something else." Squeezing her fists tight, her nails dug into her palms, her throat constricted. She hadn't cried in days and the only way she managed was by allowing her heart to turn to cold, hard stone, to pretend *he* never existed.

"C'mon, let's walk and talk." Annie wrapped an arm around her. They walked for a while in silence; aimless in the paling afternoon sun.

"The guy that tattooed me, Nox—" She felt so stupid as she

uttered the next words. "I don't know, it's kind of weird, but I guess I was kind of... attracted to him?"

Annie watched her closely and grabbed her arm, "Did he try something on you?"

"What? Annie, no. He was very professional. I didn't know at the time—he was sick. Very sick. Annie, he was on the organ donor waiting list." She whispered the last words.

Annie went stock-still.

"Annie, he has Will's heart." She barely choked the words out.

"His heart?" Annie's eyebrows drew together in a deep furrow. "But how did you find out? It's confidential. How do you know it's Will's?"

"Nox had a heart condition. Which makes sense now, because I ran into him and Emmylou at the chemist. He was getting all this medicine. Someone who knows him told me he's recovering from a heart transplant at Central View Hospital where Will... the timing... it has to be Will's—" She couldn't finish, still couldn't believe the words she uttered.

"Oh, my gosh... I don't know what to say. Are you going to visit him? And who's Emmylou?"

"His daughter. And no, I will not see him." She tried to shrug, but her shoulders remained rigid. "There's no point. There's nothing to say. I mean, what would I say? 'Hi, nice to see you again. By the way —you have my brother's heart.'" She shoved her icy fists into her pockets. "No, he'll only remind me of everything that's been taken from me. I don't want to see him, ever again."

Annie was silent for a moment. Then she squeezed Nakita's shoulder gently. "Kit, listen; I can understand why you'd feel like that, but maybe you'll regret not taking the opportunity. I mean, seriously, what are the chances of you finding that out? It's uncanny. It's almost like divine intervention; as if you were supposed to find out. Maybe it will bring you to a point of closure? If you don't see him, maybe you'll always wonder?"

She pressed her hands to her stomach as another wave of helpless grief wrenched her insides, as did the sudden urge to be near him, to be close to Will's heart. It was a compulsion so strong that it swayed her to the core of her being. Trembling, she looked Annie square in the eyes.

"You're right. I know I have to see him, Annie."

CHAPTER 5

*H*ospitals. The smell alone was enough to remind Nakita of the losses in her life, losses that had left gaping holes: her Mum, her Dad, and now Will.

What is that hospital smell, anyway? Hand sanitiser? Antiseptic? If clinical had a smell, that would be it. It was an unpleasant reminder of the pungent stench of pain, disease and death that lingered close by. If she never had to smell that putrid, sickening odour again, she'd be grateful.

She walked through the foyer, sure she was utterly conspicuous having been a patient there only weeks before. Keeping her head down, she hoped that none of the hospital staff would recognise her. Her sudden compulsion to see him was coupled with crippling anxiety. She knew she had to face him alone. Could it be that Will's heart was drawing her to him?

Standing at the admissions desk, a wave of nausea and dizziness hit her. *This is crazy! What am I doing?* She turned to leave.

"Can I help you?" A harassed-looking receptionist voice cut through, causing her to stop in her tracks.

"Ah... yes. I'm here to visit... Lennox Conrad."

"Let's see here. Lennox. Yes, he's in the Coronary Care Unit. Go up to Level Four, turn right, room 321."

"Okay, thank you." She murmured, then walked towards the elevator, planning to head for the exit as the receptionist stopped looking her way.

Compulsion be damned, I'm out of my mind coming here. She snuck a look over her shoulder to check if the receptionist was occupied.

The elevator doors opened with a ding and Nakita found herself looking down into the cherubic face of Emmylou. Recognising Nakita straight away, the little girl took a giant leap off the elevator, landing square in front of her.

"Kitty!" She grabbed Nakita, burying her face into her legs.

An odd mixture of emotion gripped her, knowing this little girl's father now had her brother's heart. She looked up from Emmylou into the blue-grey eyes of a burly man with clipped, light brown hair and a thick, reddish beard. He looked to be about forty. With his black jeans and Harley Davidson hoodie, he reminded Nakita of a bikie. The woman standing beside him, probably in her late thirties, had long, glossy black hair, olive skin and a beautiful face. Smiling at Nakita, she revealed a lovely set of straight white teeth.

"You're a friend of Nox's?" she asked, her warm smile and expression giving away the barest hint of surprise.

"Ah yeah."

"Hi, I'm Raina. This is Pete."

"Nakita."

"Are you come to see Daddy? Can we take Kitty to Daddy, pleeease?" Emmylou bust out in her over-exuberant manner. Raina looked at Nakita as if to gauge if it were okay with her. Nakita wondered if she looked anywhere near as nauseous as she was feeling.

"Sure. But we can't stay too long because I've got to take Ronan to soccer training."

"Yay!" Emmylou took her hand, dragging her into the elevator.

Nakita vaguely registered her chattering away, but her mind was in overdrive. *What am I going to say? What is he going to think of me just turning up? He has no idea that I know he's got my brother's heart.*

Her scalp tingled. Hot, then cold.

"So how do you know Nox?" Raina asked, making polite conversation.

Nakita's mind scrambled to answer the simple question. "He, ah, gave me a tattoo."

"Have you known him long?" she continued to probe.

"No, not long." She knew she should keep the small talk going, but was too anxious to care for polite civilities. If not for Emmylou dragging her headlong down the corridor, oblivious to Nakita falling apart beside her, she would have come to a standstill.

Room 321.

She paused at the entrance. Emmylou ran in ahead. Electricity shot down Nakita's spine at the sound of Nox's husky voice. "You're back, Chipmunk? Did you leave something behind?"

"Na-ah, we found something." Emmylou danced around as she spoke, unable to contain her excitement.

"You found something?"

"Yep."

Oh. My. God. What do I say?

Nakita stood outside where he couldn't see her. Raina and Pete were in the doorway looking at her, unable to contain the strain on their own faces. Obviously, they could tell something was seriously wrong.

"I'm getting mixed signals here. Am I going to like this surprise?" Nox's voice wavered slightly.

Throwing caution to the wind, she took a deep breath, and stepped into the room with a sway; the axis of the earth shifted all over again.

∼

Nox pressed the button on the side of his bed, readjusting himself yet again. No matter how he lay, he just couldn't get comfortable; the idea of comfort was long forgotten. He thought in terms of more or less pain. The heavy-duty pain relief only took the edge off. Pain had become his normal. Tonight he struggled with as simple a task of eating his dinner. Every movement caused a stabbing pain in his sternum, which had been split open to make way for his new heart.

He looked down at his dinner with disgust. *Tasteless pea and ham soup—check. Dried out cold chicken schnitzel with congealed gravy—check. Sodden vegetables—check. Thimble-sized tub of plain ice cream—check.* The worst thing was, he'd tried to add flavour to his meal with a little packet of salt and it had all poured out in one pile, so now his meal really was inedible.

How can anyone get well eating this crap?

He pushed the tray table aside in disgust and was rewarded with a gripping pain that tore down his middle. But he wouldn't allow a complaint to pass his lips. He knew at what price he had this new heart—at the expense of someone else's life. He still wasn't sure how he felt about losing his own heart. Yes, it had been totally fucked, but it was still his heart. Surely a person's heart, apart from its usual function, was important on some metaphysical level. Deep down, he worried that somehow he'd feel different, that somehow the echoes of the last owner's heart would become his own, or that he'd start to feel differently about the people and things he loved. But so far, he still felt exactly the same, just a lot healthier—except for the pain.

He still couldn't believe he was recovering from a heart transplant. He'd given up hoping, especially in the last weeks when he'd declined so rapidly. The pager to notify him there was a potential match had gone off in the middle of the night, scaring the hell out of him. He was wide awake at the time, wondering if Emmylou would still remember him when he died. He'd never dreamed the buzzer would ever sound. It was the equivalent of winning the lottery, but in this case, the lottery was his life.

His doctors had warned him of the possibility that the organ wouldn't be a suitable match. He knew that chances were he'd be sent back home, so he didn't let himself get his hopes up. Pete and Raina had looked after Emmylou while he'd hightailed it to the hospital. As it turned out, the heart was a match. Before he knew it, he was all suited up for a transplant. The whole thing was surreal. He was well aware of the risks, the possibility he might not survive the transplant, or even if he did, that his body could reject the foreign heart soon afterwards. It was still a possibility. One thing was for sure, he didn't take this heart for granted. He had no idea who had given him this gift, but he knew that it came from someone else's loss. The whole thing was humbling in ways he could never have imagined.

There was this whole new reverence for life that wasn't there before. He was like a wide-eyed kid all over again—what was once insignificant had become somehow extraordinary. It was as if he was suspended in a sense of wonder. The only thing he could liken it to was holding Emmylou in his arms for the first time; she'd grounded him at a time when life felt meaningless. But now, it was as if every little thing was an epiphany. Just today, as a nurse changed his bedding, millions of particles of dust were hit by the sunlight filtering through the window. The particles looked like miniature galaxies floating through the air. It brought tears to his eyes. The fact he was spontaneously tearing up like a chick was disturbing. He put it down to the heavy medication he was on, and to gratitude. Basically, he'd been granted with a whole new chance at life.

Manoeuvring himself inch by inch, he finally reached the TV control and flicked through the channels. There was nothing on. He'd never been one to sit around and watch television.

Man, a beer would be good right now. He stared through the screen. *Nakita.* She came unbidden to his mind again. In the initial moments of seeing her, he'd been surprised to say the least. He was sure his smile had near split his face in two, just like his sternum had been. Since that time in the pharmacy, he hadn't stopped thinking of her. It was obvious they were from different worlds. So why had she turned up at the hospital? How did she even find out he was there?

It had only taken him all of two seconds to see that something was seriously wrong. She stood, vacant and distant, a shadow of who'd she'd been only weeks earlier. Now, she was emaciated. Her face, with its honeyed glow, was a sallow complexion. Her eyes were ringed with blue-black smudges. Even the fiery red hair that he'd instinctively wanted to reach out and touch, hung limp. Worst of all, she just stood there staring straight through him with a vague smile.

Maybe the whole heart transplant thing freaked her out? He'd tried to make conversation, but only got one-word responses for his efforts. Pete and Raina could tell he was struggling. They tried to fill the awkward silence with chitchat and frivolous interactions with Emmylou. For the first time in his life, he was thankful when she wet her pants, which she did way too often for a four-year-old. Pete and Raina had made a lucky escape, saying they'd better get her home and in the bath. Emmylou put on a fine display, crying and carrying on about when she'd see Moopsy. *Bloody Moopsy.* He'd kick that cat if he ever laid eyes on it; it was all he'd heard about for weeks, since Emmylou had a mind like a steel trap.

A nurse had come in to do the routine check-up and must have sensed the unease in the room. She gave Nakita a once-over, before turning on her heel and walking out.

Once the others left, he thought it would give Nakita a chance to open up, but she didn't. She just stood there, shuffling around, looking out the window like she wanted to be somewhere else— anywhere else—so why did she visit in the first place?

"How's Will?" He couldn't think of anything else to say.

This time her eyes turned to him. They held an expression. What was it? Alarm? Panic?

"He's away."

"Travelling again?"

"Something like that... I have to go. I just came to see how you are."

"Oh, okay then. Well, as you can see, I'm doing fine. Fighting fit. I have this new ticker." He'd tapped his chest lightly with a smile,

"She's a beauty." He knew he'd sounded like a tool, but she had totally thrown him. After he said i, she'd looked at him like he'd sprouted another head, made an excuse and left. The encounter left him reeling for hours, just like the first time he'd seen her; but this time for all the wrong reasons.

Chicks, they're all as crazy as hell in the end. He reached for his tray table, ignoring the stab in his chest, and pulled it back so he could grab the tiny tub of melted ice-cream. Hunger bore a hole in his gut. He needed to eat something. The phone by his bedside started ringing. It was probably Emmylou wanting to say goodnight.

Maybe he'd ask Raina to drop in a few sandwiches tomorrow? He manoeuvred so he could reach for it. It hurt like hell.

"Hello?"

"Hey, Nox," came Raina's soothing voice. "How you doing?"

"Well, apart from feeling like a watermelon split in two—which I guess I have, I feel really good. Fantastic, actually."

"That's great," she said in a tone that didn't sound like she thought it was great news at all. Something was up. He could tell by her tone. He knew Raina well. Over the years, she'd become like a sister to him. There was a pause and a deep breath. "Look. I need to tell you something."

Another pause came, this one longer.

His heart skipped a beat. At least he knew it could still do the ordinary stuff the old one used to.

"Is it Emmylou?"

"No, no, nothing like that. Umm, it's really hard to know how to tell you this, so I'll get straight to the point. This afternoon, after we took Emmylou to the bathroom to clean her up. We overheard a few nurses talking. One of them was asking if Nakita was the same girl who'd been in two weeks ago. Someone attacked her at the beach. Apparently, one of the nurses was in the Emergency Department that night; we heard her say that Nakita's brother was murdered... saving her life."

Electricity jolted through Nox's body at her words.

"Shit," he finally managed, closing his eyes, the room suddenly way too bright. "That explains why she looked so different and acted so weird. She probably wanted to tell me. Oh god... I asked her about Will. She said he was travelling or something..."

Shit! Shit! Shit! His heart pound hard in his chest.

"How well do you know her? I've never heard you mention her?"

"I don't really know her. She came in for a tattoo. Her and her brother had this bet... Will seemed like a really great guy. They were twins." The shock of it kept rolling over him in waves. He wished she'd said something, but if she had, what would he have said? "It must have hit her hard. She looks so different. I wonder why she came to see me?"

Raina was quiet for a moment before she spoke again. "I think I know why. There's something else I overheard. Will was a donor." There was a pause. "Nox, I'm sure you have her brother's heart. I think that's why she came."

Unable to process what she was saying, the phone fell from his grasp while blood roared in his ears.

The heart, slamming against the wall in his chest, was her brother's.

CHAPTER 6

hat was I thinking, going to see him?
Sitting at her small dining table, Nakita held her hands to her face, physically tormented by her dumb decision. Going to the hospital had been a huge mistake. She didn't know how she felt about him before, but now it was so much worse. He was so healthy and looked out-of-place sitting in a hospital bed. Clean-shaven, she'd been struck again by how handsome he was. She could see his strong jawline and the flash of a faint dimple in one cheek as he grinned in surprise when he first saw her. All she'd done was bring more anguish to herself and make everyone feel totally awkward. She'd been completely powerless to speak or do anything remotely normal, with Will's heart beating right there in his chest.

There was a gentle knock on the front door. Nakita sat for a moment and contemplated whether to answer. The knock came again, this time more insistent. She stood slowly. After a few moments of tense waiting, she went over to the window and peeked out. A slim woman with long, straight hair walked back down the dimly lit path. *Raina. Why is she here? How does she know where I live? I wonder if Nox is okay?* Her mind flooded with questions. Part of her wanted to race down the path and ask what she wanted, but something held her back. As the car door shut, she watched from her hiding place, relieved as the taillights slipped away. In the dark, she could see the outline of an enormous arrangement of flowers left on the doorstep. Strangely cautious, she went outside and scooped them up, surprised at how heavy they were. Nested inside the elaborate native bouquet was a small watercolour card of a hummingbird sipping nectar from a flower. With slow, trembling fingers, she opened it.

Dear Nakita,

By a twist of fate, I found out the truth. I have no words to bring you comfort. I have thought long and hard, but keep coming up with nothing. The whole thing is totally messed up. I wish things had ended differently. Sorry.

Nox.

P.S. I'm out of hospital in a few days. I'll be staying at Pete and Raina's until I find a rental. I know it's a long shot, and I'm probably the last person you ever want to set your eyes on, but if you want to visit Emmylou... 77 Timbrel Road, Nalangal.

She read the message, again and again, then closed it and sat for a long time staring at the flowers. The peppery, wooded scent of the proteas tickled her nostrils. *How could he possibly have found out?* She stood and tried to suck back down the tears threatening to escape, but they spilled over with a will of their own. Taking the flowers, she walked to her bedroom in a daze. Setting them on the bed, she pulled her quilt over her and lay next to them, fresh tears trickling into her hair; wishing she were the one laid to rest, and they were her funeral flowers. His words, '*I wish things had ended differently...*' resonated in her mind, a vibration that became increasingly stronger.

I wish. I wish. I wish.

But they hadn't.

Keep focused. Focus on the routine.

Make the bed. Shower. Get dressed. Make toast and a cup of tea. Take small methodical bites. Chew deliberately. Sip your tea. Focus on something... nothing... anything but him.

Breathe. Just breathe. In through the nose, out through the mouth. Slow. Make sure you feel it in your gut. Now let it out as if you are a slowly deflating balloon. Okay, now wash up: dishwashing liquid, hot water. Wash the plate, the teacup, the knife and spoon. Place them on the dish rack. Breathe in. Breathe out slowly.

No. I can't do this.

Nakita leant with her hands against the kitchen sink, taking deep, gulping breaths, but she couldn't stop the tears that chugged helplessly down her cheeks. "Oh God, please help me." She held the kitchen counter as a gut-wrenching sob wracked her body once again, her breakfast ending up in the sink just as it did every day.

Rinsing her mouth and washing her face, she still felt numb as she made her way to the door. At this rate, she was going to be late for lectures. Taking her jacket from the cloak hook, she eased into it, hearing the chink of loose change in the pocket. Scooping it out, she threw it into the money jar on the sideboard next to the front door. As she turned to leave, something caught her eye, causing her to falter. It was a beer coaster poking out from underneath a pile of bills she hadn't paid yet. With sudden urgency, she rummaged through the paperwork, pushing the bills aside until she found the two beer coasters and the letter that accompanied them. She turned over the one that said '*Nakita*', tracing her fingers over the hastily written list, her heart pounding hard. She turned the other beer coaster over that had Will's name at the top, running her eyes over the list that had his signature at the bottom. Leaning against the door for support, she thought back to the pact they'd made with each other that day. Will had not long sent her the note with her beer coaster. The tattoo she acquired weeks before was the beginning of them making good on their vow. They'd sworn with their hands over their hearts. It was their last promise to each other. She could still hear his voice, *"Kit, you know with us, a deal is a deal, right? There's no breaking this—no matter how high the stakes are. It's a covenant, we're forever sworn."*

Forever sworn...

You can't break a promise, Nakita.

Closing her eyes, she held the two beer coasters to her chest. An idea formed in her mind; an idea that gave her a glimmer of hope. With startling clarity, she knew what she had to do. Grabbing her keys, she slammed the front door. She wasn't going to uni today; she knew who she had to go see.

CHAPTER 7

"*D*iesel. Here, boy."

Nox stretched out on an old recliner that had made its way into Pete and Raina's backyard, amongst a whole mishmash of gear scattered around. Collecting odds and ends suited them, somehow nothing looked out of place. Diesel, Nox's red heeler, bumped up against him with a fat stick in his mouth.

"Sorry, buddy." Nox scratched behind the dog's ear, since he wasn't really up for playing fetch or for much of anything lately. Recovery was slow. It went against his grain, lying around being useless. He tried as best he could not to be a burden, but the recovery from a heart transplant was what it was. As far back as he could remember, he'd fended for himself and hated relying on others. The follow-up appointments were endless, but the good thing was, his progress had blown the doctors away, and it looked like his new heart was 'taking well'. Apart from the initial risk of a transplant; rejection of the organ was the biggest factor. He was going to be on anti-rejection medication for the rest of his life, which he wasn't fussed about. But apart from the pain, which was improving, he felt pretty good— bloody good, actually.

For late autumn, the afternoon sun was warm so long as you sat in the right spot and it was so good to be out of hospital, even if he was sleeping on the lounge. They'd insisted he take one of their kid's beds, but he wouldn't have a bar of it. He was indebted to Pete and Raina who had made room for Emmylou, Diesel and himself, despite their relatively modest lodgings for a family of six with two dogs of their own and a cockatoo that shrieked all day long. If it weren't for them, he would have been up shit creek without a paddle since he hadn't been able to work for a while. He'd started falling behind on his rent a few weeks prior to his operation and his landlord, who'd always been a decent guy, told him very reluctantly that he had to clear out because the 'missus was on his case'. Pete and Raina invited him and Emmylou to live with them for as long as they needed, but he wanted to find a place of their own. He had his pride too.

Pete and Raina were run off their feet with their business. Pete restored and repaired vintage cars, servicing a vast area up and down the coast while Raina did her own fair share of revamping and restoring antiques and collectables that she sold online. She also looked after the business side of things for Pete. Sometimes, Nox felt a pang of envy when he saw them having a moment together, talking or laughing. They were one of the few couples he knew who were still together and actually liked each other, and they'd been together since high school.

Their kids were respectful and knew how to have a conversation with anyone; like any kids, they carried on with the usual sibling rivalry, but knew not to mess with their dad. One hard look from Pete when the limits of his patience was reached and the kids would be as crestfallen as their cockatoo. Rodge would strut around his perch, all pissed-off, as if he owned the joint; but whenever the cocky got too rowdy, Pete would spray him with a water gun. It had to be kept out of reach of Emmylou ever since she decided to have a go. Unhappily for the cantankerous bird, by the time Emmylou's peals of laughter drew anyone's attention, he was waterlogged and indignant.

Yep, he had to get back to work and out of Pete and Raina's hair.

He knew he was welcome there; they were solid friends, but it was time to make plans. Maybe if he and Emmylou did a stint living out the back of the shop for a while... It wasn't ideal, but he just needed some time to get back on his feet financially and physically. He rubbed his temples as the stress mounted. Lately there'd been way too much time to think.

Suddenly, the dogs started barking all at once, as they did whenever someone came by the house. A few moments later, a shadow stretched over him, blocking the warmth of the sun on his body. He opened his eyes, squinting. It was Raina.

"Nox," she said in her quiet way, "Nakita's here to see you." She nodded over her shoulder to where Nakita was standing a little way behind. Nox sat up and was reminded with a sharp stab in his sternum that he couldn't move like he used to. He clutched his chest.

"Are you alright?" Raina stepped towards him, her arms outstretched.

He pulled his hand away. "Yeah, yeah. I'm fine. I just got up too quick."

"Well, I'll leave you to it. I'm in the middle of peeling potatoes. Emmylou's with me, so I'll keep her inside. Come on, Bronson." She dragged their giant Doberman away from sniffing at Nakita, who was standing by the shed, looking uncomfortable. Nox stood with effort; trying not to wince. He could tell she'd been crying.

"Sorry to turn up unannounced. I can come back at a better time —" Her voice was soft.

"No, please." He put up his hand to stop her leaving as he straightened, slightly breathless. "Now is a good time, I was just lazing around." There was an awkward beat of silence.

"You look well," she said, looking at his feet.

Thank God. She's actually going to initiate conversation this time. What was he to say now? 'Yeah, thanks for the new heart?' He didn't want to ramble on either about how grateful he was. Even though it was true, it wasn't going to bring her any level of comfort. So he said nothing.

"I got your flowers and note," she said, lifting her eyes to his briefly. He nodded, noticing the flush climb up her cheeks as she looked around at her surroundings. Anywhere but him.

"Can we go for a walk? Oh actually, that's probably a bad idea. You're probably not up for it."

"Actually, a walk would be good. I'm more than a little over sitting around." He led the way to the fence that backed onto the next-door neighbour's impressive acreage that had a couple of horses and a foal, a handful of goats, alpacas, chooks and ducks. The stretch of property set into the Australian bush blended seamlessly with the natural beauty of the landscape. Soaring, spotted gums dotted the paddocks while willow trees bowed low, by the bend of a narrow river.

They walked towards the river, the silence between them made somewhat easier by the trickle of water, noises of farm animals and a tree full of squawking, pink galahs making a nuisance of themselves which they did every afternoon as the sun sank low.

"This place is breathtaking," she commented, her eye on the foal close by its mother.

"Yeah, it's paradise. I'd love to own a place like this one day," as he spoke, the clumsiness of his words hit him full force. Here he was passing comments about his dream future while her brother was dead. Her own dreams dashed to pieces. "The neighbours are pretty good friends of Pete and Raina's and they're happy for any of us to wander in, so long as the younger kids go with someone older. The horses can be a bit temperamental," he knew he was prattling on like an old woman, but he was way out of his depth.

"So you live with Pete and Raina now?"

"For the time being. I'm on the lounge. Pete and Rai wanted me to take one of the kid's rooms, but I wouldn't have it. I closed up shop and I can't get back to it until I'm all healed up—doctor's orders. It's kind of weird to be back on a mate's couch again. Feels like I'm fifteen all over, except this time with a kid. I really need to find a place. I already owe Pete and Rai so much."

"How's Emmylou finding it?" she asked, suddenly very interested in the ground again.

"Emmylou's pretty adaptable. She shares Lily's bedroom. She loves Emmylou, even though she's eleven. The boys are good with her too. She's enjoying having big brothers."

"How many kids do they have?"

"Four. Aside from Lily, Wyatt's fifteen, Ronan's thirteen and Sy is nine. Emmylou kind of rotates between the four of them. When one of them tires of her endless tea parties, she moves on to her next victim."

Nakita had a glimmer of a smile. "She is rather tenacious."

"You could say that." The conversation halted, and he was at a loss to know what to say. They continued walking in a silence that grew heavier with each step.

She stopped. "How did you find out?"

"Some nurses remembered you. Raina overheard them talking."

"I thought it was a possibility." She shook her head. "How did Raina find out where I lived?"

"I remembered you worked at The Gull. I asked Raina to go there and see if she could track you down. An older woman told her where you lived."

"That would be Miriam."

"Yeah, that was her."

"What about you? How did you find out?" He watched her as she looked to the hills in the distance, her face full of emotions he could tell she was having trouble containing.

"I ran into Lorraine at the Post Office. I asked after... Emmylou, and she told me you'd just had a heart transplant."

"Sorry you found out like that. Though I suppose there's no easy way."

"True." She rubbed her forearms.

Was she cold or nervous? She seemed agitated, but at least she was talking. "So you're probably wondering why I'm here?"

"I am surprised. I thought I'd be the last person you'd want to see."

"You were until this morning."

"Why? What happened this morning?"

She pulled a yellow envelope out of her pocket, handing it to him. "I found these. Open it."

There was a strange unspoken tension mounting as he opened the envelope. Whatever was inside was very important to her. Of all things. He pulled out a beer coaster.

"The Gull," he read, looking from her to it.

"Turn it over."

He flipped it; on the back was Will's name and a list. He scanned it briefly. Will's signature was at the bottom.

"Is this to do with that bucket list?"

"Yeah, there's a note too. Read it."

The letter was rumpled; the writing smudged and smattered with what appeared to be tears.

Kit,

Found this the other day and had a good laugh to myself. Remember? We're both twenty-four now, and nothing has changed for either of us. You're still as boring as hell and I haven't settled down. Looks like we need to make good on our bet. I look forward to completing our 'Anti-Bucket' lists together. It's going to be a riot. I won't even ask if you've still got mine. You probably have it on file somewhere. I've forgotten what was on mine, but I don't care because I'm going to have the greatest pleasure watching you do yours. Still can't believe we're twins. There must have been a mixup at the hospital, but hey, I'm pretty glad of that stuff up.

From your 'little' bro, Will.

A strange melancholy settled on him. Will was the kind of guy he could've become mates with. Again, he didn't know what to say. He folded it up slowly.

She looked at the mountains in the distance as though she was trying to draw strength from them. "I've been sitting in my car for a long time trying to get the courage to come and see you... to ask you something." She moistened her lips. "I know I don't have the right, but I want to ask a favour, a huge favour."

As far as he was concerned, she could ask for anything. *Maybe she wants money to do the things on the list, a kind of payment for her brother's heart? How am I going to tell her I'm flat strap broke?*

"How can I help, Nakita?"

"Well, I know it sounds really lame, and you probably won't want to, but I'm just having trouble coping with his... um... passing." She wrapped her arms around herself and looked at the ground again, fresh tears in her eyes. "I feel like...." Her hand went to her neck. "It's like I can't breathe."

His heart stumbled. He had to help her, no matter what it took. "Just say what it is you'd like me to do. I want to help you."

"I know this may be weird, but I thought that since you have his heart, that since there is still a part of him living inside you, it's kind of like he's a part of you now. I mean, just think about it, a part of him is alive in you, the most important part of him."

The heaviness of what she was saying almost made him take a step back, but he kept his feet firmly planted. It wasn't like he hadn't thought of it himself, but to hear her say it and to know how much this meant to her was paralysing. She crossed her arms and kicked the toe of her shoe, focusing her attention on a dry clod of dirt.

"Anyway, I know you're going to think I'm crazy but..." A flush of pink crept up her neck, her eyes locked somewhere just below his right ear. "I thought that perhaps we could do the bucket list together... you'd be a kind of stand in for Will. And this may sound even crazier, but after hearing what you said before, it sounds like you and Emmylou need a place to live and I still need to find a house-mate. Perhaps you could both come and live with me while we do the list together?"

He couldn't have been more shocked by her request, but he tried not to show it. "Look, I'd be honoured to stand in for Will; but the thing is, I don't have any money to pay rent at the moment. I'm just scraping enough together each week to keep the shop."

"Well, that won't be a problem. I really just wanted the money to give the house a bit of a facelift, but it can wait. I won't charge you any rent, and I'll cook all your meals." Desperation laced her voice. "When I'm not rostered on at the Gull or at uni, I can take care of Emmylou while you work. It'll give you the opportunity to get ahead and keep me occupied." She halted, her shoulders slumped, as though she realised she was asking for too much. "I just thought it might give me some closure. We had this twin thing. A connection." Her voice was tight, and then finally broke. He could see everything in her was fighting not to cry.

"I'll do it." He couldn't believe his own ears as he said those three words. But something inside him compelled him to do exactly as she asked. He owed her so much more, and this was one thing he could do because he'd never be able to pay her back. She looked up, as surprised as he was at his own words.

She let out a pent-up breath, as though surprised. "You will?"

"Yeah, I'll do it."

"But don't you want to see the house first?" she asked, looking as shocked as he felt.

"No, I trust you," he said, reminiscent of her telling him she trusted him that day in his tattoo parlour, "I'm sure it's fine, or I don't think you'd invite us to stay or live there. Plus, you live at Dorley Point, and from what I've seen, it's a beautiful spot. There are two conditions, however," his voice was firm to make his point, "once I get my finances sorted, I pay you back every cent from living with you." She started to protest, but he put his hand up to stop her. "I won't take no for an answer. It's helping me out too. I was only thinking just now, how I need to find a place. The other condition is: if you feel uncomfortable with us in your house or you've just had enough, we leave. No questions asked."

She was quiet for a moment, but he could tell it was more

because she was overcome with emotion. Her brown eyes shone. It was as if he'd given her hope, a reason to continue.

"Okay, it's a deal. But I get to cook, right?"

"I'm not going to argue with that." He smiled and her eyes met his for a fleeting moment, something in her manner reminding him of the day they first met. Even though she was a shadow of her previous self, she still stirred him. His heart still kept missing beats, which he felt weird about since it was her brothers.

"Shake on it?" She put out her hand with a tentative smile through a film of tears. He took her hand, wondering what he'd gotten himself into. With her hand in his and those brown eyes looking up at him, he felt as skittish as the young foal they were watching in the nearby paddock.

Later that night, as Pete dealt another round of cards, Nox told them about his arrangement with Nakita. He knew it sounded totally crazy, but the more he thought about it, the more he could see how it could bring closure from her perspective. He explained the whole anti-bucket list thing and how she wanted him to be Will's stand in. Pete looked a little shell-shocked by his decision, while Raina sat tapping her fingers on the table, looking like she was battling herself whether to say something. She gave it all of about ten seconds before she let loose. "Nox, this is madness. You could end up doing a lot of damage to that girl."

"How so? She asked for help. It's the least I can do. I owe her."

"That girl needs time to grieve, not you hanging around the house with a kid."

"She's not exactly a girl, Raina."

"And that's the other thing, I've seen that look in your eye when she's around." She put up her hand as he started to protest. "I wasn't born yesterday. Your attracted to her. It can only end badly. She needs time to heal, not a constant reminder of her brother living with her."

"I do not get a look in my eye," he denied, but decided against pressing the matter.

"Nox, she was attacked only weeks ago. I haven't told you this, but I think you need to hear it."

"Rai," Pete warned in that quiet, stern way of his.

"Pete, he needs to know."

What more could there possibly be? Mostly Raina stayed out of stuff, but when she got something in her bonnet, she wouldn't back down without a fight. As fine-boned as she was, she was also fierce.

"After I heard those nurses talking, I did a bit of research."

"Here we go," he groaned, putting his face in his hands, "what now?" he asked, not really wanting to know.

"Look, Nox, your head's been so caught up in the fact that you have her brother's heart, that you haven't really considered why."

"Yeah, I know. Her brother was attacked. He's dead and because of that I'm alive." He felt guilty about it every second of the day.

"You didn't listen to me the other night. Maybe it's the medication. Nakita was attacked and badly hurt; she was admitted to hospital herself. That bastard had a knife. He was a known offender and had already done time for rape. If Will hadn't got to Nakita that night, he would have raped and possibly killed her. So not only does she have to deal with the fact that her twin died trying to save her life and that you have his heart beating in your body; she also has to deal with the fact that she was beaten, almost raped and killed. Nox, just one of those things is enough to cope with. She's been traumatised."

He rubbed his hand over his face, weary from it all. All he wanted was to live a simple life. Originally he'd been so focused on moving on, he never thought about all the mixed emotions he'd have at receiving someone's heart. The joy and relief he had expected, but the guilt and sense of responsibility wasn't something that crossed his mind, and it was made worse knowing he was hurting her. Now, his life was completely tied up in the death of her brother, and from what he could gather from their conversations, she didn't have any other family. The whole thing was too heavy. He couldn't imagine how she was getting through it when he was struggling; but somehow he knew in his gut that it was the path he had to take.

"Okay, look, I know you're right. I'll be careful, but I won't go back on my word. She thinks it'll bring her closure. Whether it does, I don't know, but I owe it to her to try. I've told her I'd only agree to it if I can pay her back for living there, and if she ever feels uncomfortable, she can ask us to leave. Besides, I really can't stay here. Your overrun—"

"That's not an issue, you're as good as family," Raina interjected.

"I know and you guys are family to me too, but if I can make this work, it'll be good. I need to find a rental; she needs a housemate. It'll give me a chance to get back on my feet and help her at the same time."

"I don't know..." Raina started, but Pete piped in.

"Bottom line is, Rai, he's a grown man and can make his own mistakes." Nox looked at Pete. "Decisions," Pete corrected himself.

"You're right. I just don't want either of you to get hurt. She already looks so broken. I just feel for her."

"Yeah, well, I'm not going to hurt her. If it's because you're worried something will happen between us, I can guarantee it won't. You know what I think about relationships. Plus, I really don't think she's going to go for the guy who's got her twin's heart. You have to admit, it would be kind of weird."

Pete levelled a look at him. "Since you've got her brother's heart now, you need to think of her like a brother would." Pete didn't give advice too often, so when he did, Nox listened.

"Agreed." Nox raised his soda and lime in the air. "To my new little sister."

Pete grunted, slowly and deliberately touching his schooner to Nox's glass, but he didn't smile and the expression in his eyes was sobering. With a long chug of his beer, he fixed his eyes on Nox as if to say, 'You're in over your head in your own bullshit.'

Later that night, Nox wondered if there was some truth behind that look. But in his heart he knew Nakita was completely off limits. The fact that he wasn't a relationships kind of guy was definitely going to be an arrow in his quiver.

CHAPTER 8

*I*t was late in the evening when Pete pulled up in Nox's white Kombi Van with Raina following in her car. Nakita was sweeping the front path. The lights of the cars signalling their arrival reminded her of the reality she'd brought on herself. Did she really want this man, who was practically a stranger, living with her, even if he had Will's heart?

"Hey there, darlin'." Raina came over and gave her a gentle squeeze. "It's really good of you to let Nox and Emmylou stay here."

Nakita wondered if he'd told them about the details of their arrangement. *Oh God. They must think I'm crazy.*

"Yeah, we'd just about had enough of him hogging the lounge, so we jumped at the opportunity to offload him." Pete winked at her. Emmylou was fast asleep on his shoulder, her cheek and lips all squashed up cute like a fish.

Nakita instantly warmed to the twinkle in Pete's eyes. "Come inside. I have a room ready for her." She turned to Nox, avoiding eye contact. "I've given Emmylou the spare bedroom. Yours is a little different, it's a mezzanine; I hope you don't mind." They walked up the porch steps and into the beach cottage she'd grown up in. She'd been fighting her nerves all day, worried they might not like it. Even though she'd tried to make it look and feel cosy, apart from being outdated it was worn and rundown in places, which no amount of scrubbing or artful decorating could hide.

"Oh darling, it's very homey and cheerful." Raina stood in the centre of the room and turned slowly with a warm smile.

"Thank you." Nakita glanced at Nox to gauge his reaction to his new surroundings. It relieved her that his expression didn't show displeasure. His eyes lingered on the lemon-coloured walls where family photos were once proudly displayed. The hooks were still in the wall, while the paint behind where the pictures once hung was less faded. After Will was gone, she'd taken every one down; looking at them was too painful.

"I'm going to freshen the place up with a coat of paint," she offered. "This is the only bathroom. It's an awful squashed frog colour. I plan on renovating it one day."

"Well, make good use of Lennox while he's here. He knows how to do a thing or two," Pete said, good-naturedly slapping him on the shoulder. She smiled at the camaraderie between them.

"Let me show you Emmylou's room." Nakita took them back to the front door, turning right into a small hallway which led to two bedrooms. The small one on the left was for Emmylou, the larger one on the right was Nakita's.

"Poor little teapot was so wired all day about the big move, she exhausted herself and fell asleep on the way over."

Nakita smiled. She was looking forward to having Emmylou around, and from the sounds of it Pete was going to miss her. Her belly twisted with nerves as they stepped into what was to be Emmylou's bedroom, worried that they might think she went overboard or didn't decorate it right.

"Whoa. Emmylou's going to be in her element. You've gone to a lot of trouble," Nox said, his eyes making contact with hers. His eyes were so warm; they were both reassuring and somehow unnerving.

"I enjoyed it." She turned away to avoid eye contact, straightening a figurine of a fairy she'd sat on a small bookshelf amongst some other baubles. She had picked up a few bits and pieces from the local op shop, decorating the bedroom with frills, teddy bears and pretty things she hoped Emmylou would like.

"Yep, that will be worth being a fly on the wall for. I'm going to miss having this little teapot around the house. You could almost talk me into having another one, Rai."

Raina rolled her eyes at Pete. "They don't come out as four-year-olds, Pete. Or have you forgotten that bit?"

"Yeah, well, I'm going to miss her all the same. Though I think old Rodge will be glad to see the back of her."

The three of them chuckled.

"He's our cocky," Raina explained. "Emmylou put him through the wringer."

"To say the least," Pete laughed. "Okay, let's get this little whippet to bed."

Nakita pulled back the bedding that included a patchwork quilt that Miriam had made for her when she was little. Emmylou's eyes fluttered open slightly as Pete deposited her in the bed, and then she rolled over. They all stood silent for a moment, watching her sweet, sleeping form.

Pete clapped his hands together quietly. "Rai and I will go get the bags."

"I'll help, mate," Nox offered.

"No, you need to be taking it easy. You shouldn't overdo it, not just yet anyway."

They left Nox and Nakita standing there, both looking again at Emmylou. "She'll be out of her mind tomorrow. Is the cat ready for her?" Nox asked. She could tell he was trying to set her at ease with small talk. *Ugh, why must I always seem so socially awkward whenever I'm near him?*

"Yes, me and Mr Moops have had a little chat. Come. I'll show you your room." Nakita took him up to the mezzanine, which was more like a small loft. From his reaction, he seemed to like it. Nakita hesitated. "If there's not enough room for storage, I have more space in the garage/ I hardly use it."

"That's great thanks, I don't have too much. I'm pretty low maintenance."

"I didn't think you'd want Emmylou up here. I hope I made the right decision?"

"Yep, you did. It's perfect."

"In the morning, you'll see that it has a pretty view out the window."

Raina and Pete came back in with two large duffel bags.

"Would you guys like to stay for coffee?" Nakita asked, hoping to reduce the awkwardness. Something about Pete and Raina put her more at ease when she was in Nox's presence. They took the pressure off somehow.

"Oh sorry, we have to get going. Wyatt just called, all hells broken loose. Apparently Sy just blew up Ronan's world on Minecraft."

"Sounds serious," Nakita smiled.

"You'd think so, wouldn't you?" Pete shook his head. "Wouldn't have happened in my day. Would have gotten a clip over the ear."

Waving them off, Nakita and Nox wandered back inside, a peculiar quiet and unease settling over the house. "Well, I guess I'll leave you to get sorted. Let me know if you need anything. Oh," she dashed over to the linen press on the outside of the bathroom wall, "here's a towel if you'd like a shower. I really want you and Emmylou to feel at home."

He looked as though he wanted to say something, but just nodded, his jaw tight. She looked away, shifting on her feet. Was the house usually this quiet or was it only compounded because she was alone with Nox? Something about the thought of him sleeping just metres away was unsettling.

"Well, if you've got everything, I think I'll turn in for the night," she said, trying to sound casual.

"I'm good, thanks," he answered with an easy smile. "Night, Nakita."

"See you in the morning then," she tossed over her shoulder as she went to her bedroom. She lay in her bed, staring at the ceiling for a long time, listening to him moving around the house and the water running as he showered. She'd become so infatuated with the idea of him coming to live with her to complete the anti-bucket list that she'd never considered, until this moment, that it was quite possible she'd made a terrible mistake.

Bacon. Nox lay for a while, warm and comfy, listening to the sound of bacon sizzling and popping in a pan. He inhaled deeply, savouring the aroma. He hadn't woken disoriented as he thought he might, but it was unfamiliar. Only a matter of weeks ago, Nakita had been a stranger to him; now he was living in her house with his daughter. More than that, he was inextricably linked to her in ways he couldn't put into words. Moving in last night had him feeling like he was trapped in a weird dream, but he knew he was awake since he'd watched the alarm clock tick over every hour till three a.m. She'd been wound so tight last night he couldn't help but be a little on edge himself. He still wasn't sure he'd made the right decision. He wasn't worried about himself, but the last thing Emmylou needed was some strange upheaval, especially when the woman she was living with was clearly a little unhinged. Emmylou had near jumped out of her skin when he told her they were going to move in with 'Kitty.' To a four-year-old, the suddenness of it wasn't strange at all. They'd probably have a few kinks to iron out to begin with, which was only natural, considering the circumstance.

He would give it a few weeks, then they could re-evaluate.

Positioning himself on his side, he watched her working in the kitchen. She moved with precision, everything she did was deliberate and purposeful. He couldn't help but think this overflowed into other areas of her life. With the wintry chill of the morning closing in, he pulled on some warm clothes so he could take in his surroundings. He'd have to face her sooner or later. The old style beach house definitely had a cosy feel to it, but even from his brief tour last night, he could see it was badly in need of maintenance. Pausing at the bottom of the stairs, he watched her turn the bacon, her vibrant red hair piled high on top of her head in a messy bun. Only weeks before she'd been curvy in all the right places, now her grey tracksuit pants and flannelette shirt hung off her. As though she sensed him staring, she looked over her shoulder.

"Oh, hey." She turned back again. Any wonder it was a struggle for her to look him in the eye.

"I hope you like bacon?"

"Bacon and I are on good terms."

She smiled in that fleeting way of hers. "Did you sleep okay? I hope you were warm enough. The house can get kind of glacial in winter."

"I slept really well," he lied, watching as she busied herself setting out plates. "I hope you haven't gone to too much trouble; we're Weetbix any time of the day kind of people." She stiffened, her face stricken like the day she'd visited him in hospital. His insides tensed. "You okay?" What did I say?

"Ah yeah," she shook her head as though shaking out a memory. "I'm fine." She glanced around and he wasn't sure which of them felt more awkward. "If you're wondering where Emmylou is, she's in her bedroom playing with Moopsy. They finally met this morning."

"How long has she been awake?"

"About forty-five minutes, I'm surprised you slept through it. I don't think Moopsy knows what's hit him."

"Should I go get her for brekky?"

"Sure, I'll just finish with this."

He found Emmylou stuffing the cat into an old-fashioned dolly pram. The cat looked far from impressed, especially when she put a blanket over him and tucked him in. Whenever he tried to make an escape, she'd giggle, drag him back in and scold him in her sternest voice.

"Daddy! Look at my room Kitty made me. I have everything," her arms spread out as she spun around. It warmed his heart to see her surrounded by all the girly stuff he hadn't thought to give her since that feminine influence was missing in their lives. It hadn't really crossed his mind she'd be into girly stuff since she'd always made do with whatever was in front of her.

"No, Moopsy! Stay. Stay! Silly boy," she commanded, giggling as the cat tried to escape.

"Kitty—Nakita has made us breakfast, so we'd better go sit down."

"Yay." Emmylou was out the door and so was the cat, bolting in the opposite direction, into the sanctuary of Nakita's bedroom.

"You can thank me later, cat." Nox couldn't bring himself to say Moopsy. Returning to the dining table, he couldn't believe his eyes when he saw the plate of bacon, eggs, spaghetti, fried tomato and mushrooms, fresh juice and two steaming cups of coffee. He sat opposite to Nakita; his stomach tight, caught somewhere between anticipation for his breakfast and unsettled at the prospect of trying to make conversation over breakfast.

"Yummy." Emmylou skipped up and down, tongue wagging. She loved food and had never been a fussy eater; a good thing for him.

"Oh, no!" Nakita put a hand to her mouth. "I never thought—you probably shouldn't be eating bacon after heart surgery." She pushed back from the table and was already throwing open cupboard doors. "I have muesli and natural yoghurt?" She looked at him over her shoulder, her brows pulled together. "Or I could make you a fresh fruit salad?"

He put up his hands, alarmed. "Don't you dare. I haven't eaten decent food like this forever. You can't serve up such a feast and expect me to eat oats—that would be torture. The doctors said I could have everything in moderation, since I'm already fit and healthy. It's what I do eighty percent of the time that counts. Protein's good for me and bacon is protein, right?"

Her lips stretched into a slow smile. "You realise, you sound kind of desperate?"

"You have no idea," he half smiled. "Raina's been on my case since I left hospital. She's been forcing me to down these awful vegetable juices every morning. Get this: it's beetroot, kale, carrot and ginger. Mid-morning, its herbal tea followed by a handful of multivitamins the size of horse pills. Even Pete can't escape her radar since she wants him to shift a few pounds. That's the real reason he's glad to see the back of me."

"Well, you really do need to look after your health," she commented, her voice soft. They both watched as Emmylou shoved a whole piece of bacon into her tiny mouth with her fingers. "Emmylou, see your knife and fork, you need to cut your bacon or you could choke."

Nox watched as Nakita demonstrated how to cut the bacon with the knife and fork.

Emmylou picked up her knife and fork in the wrong hands, looking at them as though they were foreign objects.

"Looks like I've got my work cut out for me with Princess Fiona over here." He nodded at Emmylou with spaghetti all over her face as she took a huge gulp of juice with both hands, smearing spaghetti sauce all over the glass. Nakita pressed back a smile. "Eating with you kind of highlights some areas we are lacking. Table manners have been low on the list of priorities, but I think we need to take a look into it." At the Belle's place, it was all loud voices and elbows as everyone fought like seagulls not to miss out. This was definitely an unfamiliar experience.

"See your napkin, Emmylou? Yep, that's it. Wipe your face."

Emmylou held the napkin to her face and turned her head from side to side. Nakita watched her with a smile. Nox liked how she seemed to enjoy Emmylou like he did. She spoke to Emmylou different somehow, like she had more life in her voice.

"So what are you up to today?" he asked, after a long stretch of silence. Emmylou was concentrating hard on eating, and it seemed their light-hearted banter had come to a sudden end.

"For the next few days you won't see much of me. I'm going to be hammered—Finance Law." She grimaced.

"Sounds heavy."

"It's sucking the life out of me. It always has."

"Oh, is that right?" He questioned, surprised to hear her say so.

She straightened. "What do you mean by that?"

"Nothing, I guess, it's just that I thought people usually went to uni to do something they loved. Then again, I was a year ten dropout, so what would I know?"

"Some of us make hard choices to secure the future. We can't all follow our pipe dreams." She looked down at her plate as she kept winding the napkin tight around her forefinger.

"True." He'd obviously hit a nerve. "This is really good, by the way," he said, changing the subject and helping himself to more. She seemed to relax into her chair a little.

"I love cooking, but I haven't been able to keep much down lately." She sipped of her coffee.

Her quiet, emotional pain struck a chord with him. He never had brothers and sisters, so he couldn't imagine what it would be like to lose one so young; especially a twin. Not only that, but she seemed to have no other family at all. Maybe this was one of the practical ways he could help her. "How about I cut a deal with you?"

She looked him dead in the eyes; her face haunted. "That's something Will would say."

He stilled. The blood drained from his face. *Oh shit. I can't believe I said that; I sound like I'm channeling the spirit of her dead brother.* "I'm sorry, Nakita." He reached his hand toward hers, but didn't touch it. He was still trying to figure out the parameters.

"No, it's okay." She attempted to smile. "You've got my attention. What do you propose?"

"I'll eat anything and everything you cook, so long as you eat it too, and I get to wash up." He paused, taking a bite.

"Even veggie juices?"

He winced. "Yep, even veggie juice. So long as they don't have kale in them. Whatever that stuff is, personally, I don't think it's supposed to be consumed by humans. So, is it a deal?" he asked, around a mouthful of food, trying to keep casual.

She held the sides of her plate, looking down as though very interested in the mostly untouched food left on it. He could see she was trying desperately to have a normal conversation, to appear okay with what he just said. But she wasn't.

"Um, you know, I really better go. I have a lot on today." She stood up. "There's plenty of food. Make yourself at home and just text me if there's something that you need. Bye, Emmylou, have a great day, look after daddy." Her hands shook as she began clearing the table. He reached out and touched her wrist. She paused, looking at his hand on hers.

"Nakita, leave it to me, I'll sort it." He gave what he hoped was an encouraging look. She nodded silently and walked out; but not before he saw the tears falling from her eyes. He stood slowly and started shifting the dishes to the sink, wondering what he'd gotten himself into, knowing he was already in way too deep to get out.

CHAPTER 9

*N*akita was woken in the early hours of the morning by a tiny frame climbing into her bed and snuggling up to her. The past week had been a blur. Having a four-year-old living in the house, especially one as vivacious as Emmylou, gave an extra dimension to life and she couldn't help but love how the little girl approached everything with cheerfulness and awe. Even something as simple as feeding scraps to the chooks was wildly exciting, bringing a flurry of questions that Nakita's brain scrambled to find answers to. Diesel, their dog, had moved in too; so he and Moopsy had been working out their differences. Things were still a little awkward between Nox and herself, but they'd kind of fallen into a routine. It helped that she didn't see too much of him, since she'd been doing extra shifts at the Gull and had a lot of uni assessments due. Neither of them had mentioned the bucket list since he'd moved in; she wanted them to get settled first. But truth be told, she was stalling. What had seemed like the perfect idea at the time wasn't so easy to carry out in reality. She didn't know how to approach him to get started on the anti-bucket list when just being near him had her tongue-tied and self-conscious. Plus, there was nothing on her list that she had any desire to do—Will would have made it fun somehow.

Emmylou rolled over, allowing Nakita to admire her pretty, sleeping face. There wasn't much of Nox in her features, except for the shape of her eyes that were light brown with flecks of green, whereas his were a true light green. When she smiled, she looked more like her dad, yet she was cute and impish, while Nox's smile was disarming and did something in her mid-section that was unsettling. As she watched Emmylou's rhythmic breathing, she couldn't help but wonder what it would be like to be a mother. It's something she'd always secretly yearned for, but the cruel voice of reality would remind her, why invite more heartache? That's what she hated about life now, the crippling fear of loss; loss was inevitable and she couldn't love freely anymore, not now.

Hearing a movement, she lifted her head to see Nox's reflection in the mirror. He stood at the door watching them. Stepping in, he said in a relieved voice, "Sorry, I've been looking for her everywhere. She's been known to get up early at Pete and Raina's and go play outside or lay with the dogs. I didn't even think to check in here. Sorry to wake you."

Sitting up so as not to disturb Emmylou, Nakita pulled her bed sheet up, aware that she was only wearing a thin singlet top. She could only imagine what a wreck she looked, her slept-in red hair no doubt in its usual manic state.

"No, really, it's fine. You didn't wake me. She climbed in about forty minutes ago. It's been nice snuggling with her."

"I'm just grateful it wasn't me. Usually, she ends up sideways on the pillow. Last time I copped a huge scratch down the side of my face from her toenails."

Nakita smiled. "Actually, I was just admiring how pretty she is. She has your eyes and smile. Does she take after her mother at all?" As the words fell out of her mouth, Nakita regretted them. They hadn't talked about the whereabouts of Emmylou's mum, though she'd been eager to know.

"Emmylou's prettier than her mum ever was."

Was? So he's a widower?

"She passed away a few years back. It's a long story," he said, answering her unspoken question. He didn't appear bothered, rubbing his chin as he studied her.

"Emmylou seems to be adjusting well," she said, sensing she should change the subject. "She loves Moopsy and the chickens. I was thinking of getting some guinea pigs. I had guinea pigs when I was her age—Porky and Petunia. I loved them."

"Porky and Petunia, eh? I was a Looney Tunes fan."

"Me too, my favourite was Bugs Bunny. My family were avid Looney Tunes watchers."

Nox slowly eased down onto the edge of the bed next to Emmylou. The muscles in his biceps worked as he leaned forward, resting his chin on his hands. After a moment he said with a tentative smile, "I always liked Road Runner myself. You know Wile E. Coyote got Road Runner in the last episode, but he was too small to eat him."

"Road Runner was Dad's favourite. You know, it's really an allegory for obsession when you think about it. Coyote didn't even care about eating Road Runner, it was about the chase. He was the ultimate OCD character."

Nox turned and gave her a level look. "You know, I think you possibly just took the simplest cartoon of all time and killed it for me." She shoved him in the arm at his playful jibe and his face broke into a smile.

"Okay, I admit I can tend to over-analyse sometimes. I guess I'm too much like Coyote in some respects; I can be a little obsessive."

"Yeah, I think I saw a little of that when you cut those carrot sticks last night."

"Hey, carrots sticks should be cut uniformly."

"Well, Bugs never cared, did he?" He paused. "You know, this is a really strange conversation to have at—what time is it? Six in the morning?"

"True, I have no idea how we got here."

"Guinea pigs... Porky and Petunia." He laced his fingers together. She couldn't help but admire his profile and hands. Last night they had enthralled her as they deftly plucked the guitar.

"Hey, I'm going to take a wander around Dorley Point and maybe go for a walk to the lagoon when Emmylou wakes up. Want to come? The locals keep telling me how nice it is."

She smiled at his cheeky comment, since she was the one who kept telling him how stunning the lagoon was. Even though he'd surfed at Dorley Point Beach, he'd never taken the road to the nearby lagoon.

"Yeah, that'd be nice. Emmylou will love the park."

"I'm going to take a shower; by then she'll most likely be up."

"We can walk past the bakery and get coffee and croissants for breakfast," Nakita suggested.

"Now you're talking my language." Nox eased up from the bed.

Watching him stand, she couldn't help her eyes being drawn to his broad chest, where Will's heart was beating. It was crazy knowing that her brother's actual heart was right there. Weirder still was the fact that she wanted to reach out and touch his chest. But why? Because of Will's heart? She wasn't sure if that was it entirely.

She watched as he glanced down at his own chest, noticing the direction of her gaze. She looked away. Embarrassed.

"Nakita." The way he said her name, she felt compelled to look back. His green eyes held hers with plain sincerity. "Look, I know this whole situation is... well, I was thinking it has to be a first. But I just want you to know that even though I'll never be Will, I hope to be worthy, at least somehow." He stood for a moment as though he wanted to say more, then turned and walked out.

She pondered his words.

If nothing else, she was grateful that out of all the people who could have received Will's heart; it was him. She cuddled into Emmylou while he showered and wondered how she was to cate-gorise him in her life: a housemate, friend, brother? He had her brother's heart pumping in his chest, so that definitely put him in the category of totally forbidden.

Within the hour of Nox suggesting they go to the beach, they were out of the house with an already wide-awake and very bouncy Emmylou between them. The morning was brisk as they set off to the bakery and bought piping hot lattes and warm croissants fresh out of the oven. They wandered to the lagoon; the wintry morning sun suffusing everything in its pale glow. Each breath of frigid air reminded Nakita of winter's stark beauty. There was something about winter she'd always found revitalising. There was the familiar tug of hope and joy she usually felt this time of year—then came the pull back to reality. It grabbed hope and joy by the ankles and yanked them back down into the dark where they belonged.

They approached the camping area where sand dunes merged into an inlet that flowed into the picturesque lagoon. On the shore was an open, grassy, tree-lined knoll where people camped or picnicked. A few keen campers sat around early morning fires, cooking barbecue breakfasts and speaking in lulled tones while kids whizzed around on bikes with tangled hair and bleary eyes. Emmylou ran straight for the climbing frame as they made their way to the water's edge; both watching as a pelican skimmed the glistening water, landing gracefully close to the shore. Even during winter, the sights, the sounds, the smells—everything hummed with life and activity.

"This place really is quaint," Nox said, inhaling the wood smoke from the early morning fires. His voice held the reverence she felt inside. Something about death seemed to magnify every tiny facet of life. She pulled her army-green jacket tight around her, driving the grief inwards, but as she gazed at the smooth surface of the lagoon, she couldn't suppress the memories that flooded her mind.

"When we were little, we'd rug up and go for family walks in winter. Will and I would play while Mum and Dad sat right there by the lagoon and cuddled." She could see them clearly, the memory so sweet; but the way it was now, the sweeter the memory, the more it burned like a searing, white-hot poker. "It would get so cold that we'd run till the air set our lungs on fire. It hasn't changed all that much since I was little."

Nox was quiet, as though waiting for her to say more, but she couldn't.

"I've never felt a strong association for a place like that," he said, after a while, "we moved around a lot. Most of my memories of the places I grew up in are fairly sketchy. I fended for myself from fifteen onwards; probably even well before that come to think about it."

"I guess in some ways we've both had to fend for ourselves. After losing Mum, then Dad when we were seventeen, Will and I mostly took care of ourselves. Antony and Mim were our legal guardians, but we didn't have any other family." She willed herself to have the courage to ask him the question she'd been wanting to know for some time. "Can I ask you something?"

"Yeah, go ahead."

"Can you tell me how it was you came to be needing a heart transplant?"

He nodded as though he'd been waiting for her to ask him. "They think a virus I had when I was young gave me cardiomyopathy. It's where the heart muscle becomes enlarged, and after a while, it can't pump normally. Doctors think I had it for years and just didn't know until it started taking its toll. I made it worse by treating my body like an enemy for so long." He exhaled. "Nakita, now is probably a good time for me to be completely honest with you." He looked at her with those evergreen eyes and her heart missed a beat; but she wasn't sure if it was his eyes, or what he was about to say.

"I don't deserve this chance, another chance. Five years back, I was pretty messed up. If it wasn't for Emmylou, I don't know where I'd be. When I was fifteen, I left home. My stepdad was a violent alcoholic, he put me in hospital more times than I can count. I'm not trying to make an excuse for my behaviour, but I wasn't, I don't know..." he grasped for the right word. "I had nothing in my life to anchor me. I hated him. I hated my mum for letting herself be a victim, for choosing that life for both of us." He grimaced. "I always had this noble idea growing up of who I'd be and what my life would be like. But somehow, I got way off track." He got down on his haunches, picking up a smooth black stone from the shore, turning it over and over in his hand.

"It's the same old story. I gravitated to the kids who were heading nowhere, fast. They just seemed to be my fit. It all started out with the usual partying, drinking, smoking weed. But it never filled the gaping hole inside me. I got into the drug scene and spiralled down from there. It wasn't about the party anymore, it became about the fix. That became the most important thing, drugs were my friend. Or so I thought. I got to the point where I well and truly lost sight of living a reasonable life. I'd do anything for a hit. That's all I cared about." He shook his head, as if disturbed by the memories. "I didn't realise I was ravaging my body and accelerating the damage done to my heart. When I finally got off the drugs and was ready to make a new start, instead of getting better, I just got worse. I was weak, tired, and had all this funky stuff going on. I started seeing specialists, and it became pretty clear that I wouldn't make it to old bones unless I got a heart transplant. The medication I was on wasn't really working for me."

Nakita stood transfixed by his story. It didn't shock her; there was something about the way he carried himself that told he was a survivor.

"How did you end up getting off the drugs?"

There was a shriek. They both turned and watched helplessly as Emmylou fell from the climbing web. Nox ran over and picked her up, dusting her off. She sobbed in the circle of his powerful arms. After he carried her home, Nakita watched on as he tended to the grazes on Emmylou's tummy and chin with Betadine and kisses. There was something about seeing him, exuding strength and masculinity, yet treating his daughter so tenderly that had her yearning for something; something she couldn't put words to or understand.

Watching them also reminded her of how her dad had done the same for her when she was little. He'd put his hand over wherever she was hurting and whisper repeatedly, 'Take the pain and put it in my hand. Take the pain and put it in my hand.' Now she had no one to take her pain away. Everyone she loved dearly had been snuffed out, just like the flame of a candle. And now here she was again, groping in unfathomable darkness.

CHAPTER 10

*N*akita coaxed her aching legs up the porch stairs, the sorrowful call of an Eastern Koel from nearby bush land matching her mood. Standing a moment in the dark void of night, she wished she could be that bird and fly away; having just worked a shift at the Gull that had her hiding in the storeroom in tears. Everything inside of her seemed to implode when she saw Will's friends talking and laughing as they watched a game of football on the big screen. Miriam found her sitting in the storeroom in a hot mess of tears and handed her a serviette to blow her nose. She remembered a time she'd made such a fuss when Miriam had decided to go from cloth to disposable serviettes; things that had seemed so important were so trivial now.

Miriam pointed out in her no nonsense way, that the boys were laughing through their pain and trying their best to move on 'as they should.' Nakita knew Miriam was right, but she was helpless to rein in her irrational anger. In a tirade of emotion, she finally told Miriam there was a man living at her house with his four-year-old daughter who, by a twist of fate, had received her brother's heart. Although Miriam knew Will's organs had been donated, she had no idea about

Nox, having been away the past few weeks settling her older sister with Alzheimer's into a nursing home. As Nakita told Miriam the story, the older woman sat down utterly flabbergasted.

"You mean to tell me that the boy who received Will's heart is living with you right now?"

"Mim, he's not a boy."

"I'm sixty-nine, Nakita, he's a boy. Why did you keep this from me?"

Nakita could tell Miriam was indignant that she hadn't been told until now. She'd squeezed her shoulder. "Mim, you've had a lot on your plate lately and I didn't want to worry you, especially with you visiting family and everything going on with your sister. This thing with Nox, it's new. I wasn't sure it would last."

"Last? What do you possibly hope to achieve, having him live with you? Are you in some kind of relationship with him?"

"Of course not! That would be wrong. He has Will's heart! Mim!" she cried, distressed by the thought it would cross anyone's mind that she'd do something like that. She had to explain herself. "I don't know, it's like I still have a piece of Will close by. A real living piece of him." Miriam had taken her hand, and they'd wept together in the storeroom for a long time.

The house was dark as she came inside, except for the flashing of the television. Putting down her handbag, she walked to the lounge room. Some obscure movie was on mute. She stopped short of turning it off when she saw Nox asleep on the lounge. Emmylou was curled up in a ball, her cheek resting on his stomach. Nakita's eyes were drawn to the coffee table and the single smooth black stone lying in its centre, the same stone that he'd collected a few days ago at the lagoon. She reached down and picked it up, turning it over in her hands just as he'd done. Something in his story resonated with her. If she'd allowed herself, she could have gone down a similar path to him, but the control freak in her had her hitting the books harder, aiming higher. She found more security in structure and routine than in being reckless.

The stone warmed quickly in her hand; she held its smoothness to her lips as her eyes drew back again to the sleeping forms on the lounge. They were so peaceful—her heart ached—especially to think that Emmylou had almost lost him. She took the opportunity to take in his features while his green eyes weren't upon her; inevitably sending her stomach plummeting to her toes. Everything about him exhibited strength: his forehead, his brows, the shape of his square jaw, shadowed over night with stubble. She'd never seen him with his hair free of the knot at the back of his head until now. If he slicked it back, she imagined he'd look quite stylish.

Her eyes were drawn to his chest as it had been that morning. She still couldn't believe Will's heart was there within reach. She had the urge to put her head on his chest and listen. Shifting, he half-opened his eyes, snapping her back to reality. He looked a little confused for a moment, then a lazy smile spread across his face.

"Nakita." There was something about the way he said her name that she liked.

"Hey." She moved the stone from her lips, embarrassed to have been caught watching him.

"Is she still asleep?" He tried to look down at Emmylou.

"Yeah, gone by the looks of it. I'll take her to bed."

"Thanks. I was going to a while ago, but I got stuck. I couldn't get the right angle to get up with her on me." She leaned down to scoop Emmylou up into her arms. Touching him was unavoidable as she slid her hand under Emmylou's head, which rested on his abdomen. His eyes regarded her the whole time. *I wonder how he feels towards me? If he's as confused by all this as I am?*

After tucking Emmylou back into bed, she returned to the lounge room. He looked deep in thought, his forearms resting on his knees while his fingers raked his hair. She sat on the edge of the coffee table and let out a heavy breath.

"How was work?" he asked, watching her.

"Terrible," she plucked at the material of her work pants to avoid his eyes. "Will's mates were there."

"That would've been hard."

"I didn't handle it well. I was a real cow, actually."

He eased further back into the lounge. "You need to ease up on yourself. Grief is always unchartered territory. You navigate it your own way, in your own time. There's no right way."

"True, but I'm just not like that normally, you know? With Mum and Dad, it was bad enough, but at least I had Will," She rubbed her temples that throbbed from too much emotion.

"When I was struggling through stuff, I'd try to focus on the tiny grains of hope in my life and hold onto them, just like how an oyster holds onto that one tiny grain of sand and over time turns it into a pearl."

She looked up at him, struck by his words.

"Would you mind telling me the rest of your story?"

"Sure." He reached for the stone on the coffee table beside her. "You asked how I got off the drugs. I'd been into the heavier gear for about three years, mostly party drugs, and my life was a mess. I'd started getting into trouble with the law, DUI's and that sort of thing. I was twenty-four when I ran into Emmylou's mum at a party. I'd gone to school with her for a while when we were younger. I stayed away from her back then because she had a reputation; but by this time, I was pretty messed up and just didn't care about anything. It was one night—I still can't believe how one night can change the course of your entire life."

She could believe it. One night had shattered hers.

He shook his head as though still confounded and continued. "What I thought was a curse turned out to be the biggest blessing in my life. I was twenty-four and had nothing to show for it, except a record, a drug addiction and a pregnant wife who was also a hopeless addict. I learnt pretty quickly that her drug addiction was on a whole other level to mine. Even though I didn't want a baby, especially with Mel, I couldn't make peace with that tiny life being ditched because we couldn't get our shit together. There was no way I could sit by and just let an innocent life be destroyed by—if you'll excuse my French

—two fucked up parents. I thought if I married Mel, it might change her mind. I knew she wanted to get off the drugs. She always talked about being respectable. So we got married."

"Did you love her?" She wasn't sure why that was important for her to know, but somehow it was.

"No, but sometimes decisions get made for us by the choices we make, you know? I loved the idea of making it work. I always wanted to live a good life; you know, have a family and settle down. I guess I just never knew how. My thinking was clouded when we married. I never had functioning parents, so I always had this dream that my life was going to be different, but I was just recreating the nightmare. I'd grown up thinking I could save the three of us, but it turned out I was wrong. At first, for a month or so, Mel tried really hard. She wanted Emmylou. When Emmylou's older, I'll be able to tell her without a word of a lie that her mum loved her. But she wanted a fix more. The drugs take a hold and before you know it, you're their slave." He ran his fingers through his hair.

"When Emmylou was born—somehow she was perfect, even though she had the worst start. Things improved for a few months, Mel went to rehab. I began the process of turning my life around. I met Pete when I was in rehab with his younger brother Tyler. Pete and I hit it off. He knew I was interested in getting into the tattoo industry. Once I was clean, he gave me a loan so I could get set up."

For the first time since he started telling his story, Nox really looked at her, "You know, even though Pete hadn't known me long and had no guarantee I could or would ever pay him back, he took a gamble on me. Something about him having faith in me gave me faith in myself. If it weren't for him, I don't think I'd be here." He tossed the stone lightly, catching it as he spoke. "It wasn't easy, but I cleaned myself up and put the past behind me. That's when I noticed something really wrong with my heart. By then, Mel had hooked up with an old boyfriend at rehab. She took off with him and Emmylou and returned to her old habits."

"You must have been freaking out," Nakita said, unable to imagine the horror he would have felt.

"Yeah, Emmylou was my reason to live. I tracked them down and asked Mel if she'd give me sole custody. She went rabid at first, but then her boyfriend, Briggs, got her to cut a deal." The light of the muted television glowed as he re-lived those moments. She could feel his despair. "It's still inconceivable to me how a mother could sell her own flesh and blood for a few hits."

"Did she ever come back for her?"

"Yeah, she tried. I was pretty paranoid for a while. Briggs was a mean guy. I wouldn't have put anything past him. I pretty much slept with one eye open for a long time."

"What happened to Mel?" Nakita asked into the silence.

"Briggs was violent, not just physically, but verbally too. Mel was already broken, but he destroyed her on a whole other level. I tried to get her out of there, but in the end she overdosed. She left Emmylou a note, but I'm not sure if I'll ever give it to her. It's the ramblings of a junkie; it's not her. She had a past she never overcame. I just wish she'd made it too; you know? She could've had a good life." He stopped speaking, sounding heavy-hearted, and put the stone back down on the coffee table.

She sat there silently, feeling the weight of his sadness, trying to find the right words to say. Nox cleared his throat. "You might feel differently about me living here now that you know my past. I should've told you before we moved in. I totally understand if you want us to leave."

"Don't suggest such a thing." She leant forward, touching his forearm to add weight to her words. "Your story changes nothing for me, except that now I know you're an even more remarkable person." She drew her hand back as the intensity that burned in his eyes met hers.

"I know this sounds crazy, and I don't know if I should say it, but I really just feel like I'm living life now and I'm almost thirty."

"Don't ever feel guilty for being alive because of what I've lost. I'd never begrudge you that."

"I know."

She could see the sincerity in his eyes, but resisted looking into them for fear he'd see something in hers she was struggling to contain.

"You have no idea how many times I wished all this could have ended differently."

"If it had, you wouldn't be here. Emmylou wouldn't have a mother or a father."

"True, but maybe there would have been a miracle, and you'd still have Will. I would have a different heart; Emmylou could have met Moopsy, and we'd have had a tea party together."

She could read his unspoken suggestion. He was admitting his attraction to her and acknowledging he knew she'd felt something too. And she had. But it wasn't meant to be. God, or the universe had made that clear enough, that was certain. Her very soul seemed to weigh her down as she stood, her eyes fixed to the late night cowboy movie on the television. "One thing I've learnt in all this is—wishful thinking helps no one. It is what it is. Everyone I held dear is gone and I'm never going to wake up from this nightmare." She walked over and switched the TV off, drenching them both in the pitch black. "But I'm glad you got your miracle, Nox. That's my grain of sand to hold on to in all of this—you having Will's heart." She spoke hope into the dark, but her grief was like an oversized woollen coat that she was trapped inside of. "I'm off to bed, night."

"Nakita?" His voice broke through the stretching darkness.

"Yeah?" She paused, but didn't turn around.

"I don't know if now's a good time to tell you... the crematorium called today. Will's ashes are ready to be picked up."

CHAPTER 11

*N*akita wasn't sure if her limbs were still attached to her body as she stepped forward to receive the deep blue urn with silver embellishments that rested on a lone marble bench. Everything swam as she reached out, taking the urn very deliberately.

After a few moments she heard Nox's low voice. "Let me drive, it's no problem for me now."

She nodded, her attention still on the urn in her hands. The gentle but firm pressure of Nox's hand on her lower back guided her to the car; she was vaguely aware that he took the keys from her handbag and helped her in. They drove in silence, the heaviness of the atmosphere outside reflecting the mood inside. Dark clouds rolling in from the South were backlit by the sun that was losing its battle to break through.

The urn was cold and uncaring in her lap. Will, warm and sunny, so young and spirited—his whole life stretched gloriously before him —now reduced to a pile of ashes. *Ashes to ashes, dust to dust. Dust. Age twenty-four and his destiny was dust. What was the point? It would have been better to never have known him, than to know this pain.*

She looked down at the urn. "This is not Will." Her fingers twitched with the sudden urge to wind down the window and fling the urn out; to let the ashes fall to the ground. She held it tight, her knuckles white with exertion as desperate fingers of grief wrung at her throat from the inside out. She looked to the place where she knew a piece of Will still was; a warm, vital piece of Will that was keeping Nox alive.

Nox watched as Nakita placed the urn onto the fireplace mantle and without a moment's glance, disappeared into her bedroom. He didn't try to console her with words; there weren't any. Going to the crematorium with her to pick up Will's ashes had been one of the hardest things he'd done in his life. Something about the place disturbed him to the core. Even though its gardens were spacious and well manicured, a grim reminder of the finality of death hung in the air. Everyone seemed to walk in quiet reverence, as though they themselves were apparitions. Nox knew it should have been him laid out in the ground—not Nakita's healthy twin, now just a pile of ashes in an urn. From the moment they pulled into the crematorium, sickening guilt unfurled in the pit of his stomach. He knew he was the beneficiary of someone else's loss when he received the transplant, but now that someone was Nakita; now it was personal. Her torment was his torment. How could she even stand to look at him?

He wandered along the beach, deserted save for him; hoping to give her the space she needed. *What have I ever done to deserve a second chance?* He knew he should be grateful, but that jagged rock of guilt sat heavy in his stomach. For reasons he couldn't understand, he knelt in the cool, gold sand; he'd said a prayer or two in his time, but right now he didn't know what words to say. He watched as the ocean hammered the beach with foamy whitewash. It was as if the sea itself was a living, moving impression of the turmoil inside him right now. Inhaling deeply, the enormity and strangeness of life washed over him. All he could do was go with it; circumstances were beyond his control; he was at the mercy of this thing called life, just as the shore was at the mercy of the ocean swell—casting itself upon it again and again and again.

As the afternoon faded and the shadows of the grass on the dunes stretched longer, he knew it was time to face her. He couldn't shake the devastating image of her clinging to that urn. If any metaphysical part of Will existed in him, maybe he was just the person to help her navigate through her grief?

He found her sitting on the edge of her bed, a comb loose in her hand, eyes and nose red, her long hair dripping wet. She looked so vulnerable, he tensed against the door, longing to take her into his arms and hold her close. "Nakita, Emmylou's staying the night at Pete and Raina's. Let's go get something to eat." She lifted the comb to her hair, as though jolted back to reality.

"Thanks, but I don't want to be in public."

"I've got something different in mind. It's cold outside, so rug up. I'm taking you to my special thinking spot."

She looked at him, her velvet brown eyes red-rimmed. "I don't want to think right now."

"Then we won't think. C'mon, I'm not taking no for an answer. Dress as warm as you can and meet me at the door in ten minutes."

Soon after, they were bundled up in his van, stopping to pick up takeaway Indian and a bottle of red before heading to Fickleback Headland. It was one of many beaches that dotted the coast. He knew it was a gamble taking her near a beach, but his instincts told him it was a small step towards the healing process. Parking close to the cliff with the back of the van facing the roar of the ocean; from their vantage point they could see the rise and fall of the crashing waves. For a long time, Nox leant against the back of his car, watching Nakita's long hair whip wildly around her face. She stood at the cliff's edge with her arms wrapped around herself, looking mournfully into the ocean. It was like watching a moving scene in a painting. They'd been thrown together through crazy circumstances; in many ways they were still strangers, and yet oddly, the magnitude of what they shared gave them an inexplicable intimacy. Turning, she smiled over her shoulder. His stomach clenched. God, but she was beautiful.

"I haven't been to this lookout for years," her voice was carried by the salty wind. "Thanks for bringing me here, Nox. Somehow it's just what I needed." Climbing into the back of the Kombi, she observed the thin mattress beneath her knees. "Wow, you have the full set up. I'd always heard that guys with vans had mattresses in the back, but I thought it was just a stereotype. You've proven me wrong."

"Yeah well, us van guys never know when we're going to get lucky, so we're always prepared." When he saw the expression of distaste on her face, he couldn't help but chuckle as he eased in next to her. "I don't usually have the mattress in here, but with the move I needed somewhere to put it. It's usually packed with surf gear and tattoo paraphernalia."

"Tattoo paraphernalia?" She raised an eyebrow.

"Yeah, apparently living with you is having this weird effect on my vocabulary." Smiling, she shook her head as she set out the curry containers while he poured them both a glass of wine. For the first time since everything had happened, she seemed a little light hearted. He wanted to keep it that way.

He handed her a glass. "Here's to not thinking," he proposed and she touched her glass to his.

"To not thinking," she toasted. "Look at the sky and the waves. It's incredible," she breathed, looking out at the ocean. The sky was battered and bruised; a visible, thick, salty mist hung in the air while the wind blustered against the van. They ate in easy silence, enjoying the wildness of the elements and the ocean roaring and tumbling before them. Dusk set in and the evening darkened. In the eerie light, her eyes gleamed as she looked at him. "You know Nox, as much as it pains me to say this, I think it's time for us to get started on the anti-bucket list."

"Yeah, I was going to ask you about that. I was starting to think that you just made the whole thing up as a ploy to get me to move in with you." At his playful comment she nudged him with then toe of her ankle boot and he couldn't help but enjoy how easy it could be between them.

"I wanted to give you and Emmylou time to settle in first, plus, I've had a lot of uni work. I guess, the truth is, my only incentive to do the things on my list is so I make good on my promise. It would have been important to Will too."

"Your anti-bucket list is fairly typical bucket list material."

"I guess for most people, but it's the kind of stuff I dread. It was a whole lot harder finding things Will didn't want to do. He was pretty much up for anything. I suspect he put some things down just so he had something to bet. Will thought I needed saving from my boring, do-gooder existence." She crossed her arms and shook her head as if to release the thought of her brother.

Nox wanted to reassure her that she was far from boring. Unlike some women he found loud and grating, there was a tempo about Nakita that intrigued him in ways no other woman had. "It's a shame that a picnic in a Kombi van isn't on your list," he said. "You could have crossed that one off right now."

"True. Maybe I'll write it on just so I can put a line through it." She tried to keep her voice light but he could tell it was an effort. Her shoulders slumped; the grief had set back in. "I honestly don't know if I can face the rest of my life without him. I know it sounds dramatic, but he was my light—" she blurted, her voice faltering.

He was silent for a moment. For someone so young, she'd experienced so much grief.

"I've heard that when you turn a light off it seems to disappear, but in reality it's just been absorbed by everything around it because it's taken on a different form."

She wiped at the tears with the sleeve of her jumper and took a shaky breath, giving him an equally shaky, unexpected smile. "You know; you remind me a lot of Antony. He says things in this special way that makes the situation seem different somehow. You'll have to meet him. He's so wise."

"That's a first. No one's ever compared me to someone wise before."

"Nox, thanks for doing this. I can honestly think of nowhere else I'd rather be right now. I love the sound of the beach." They were silent as they listened to the rhythmic pounding of the waves and the wind buffeting the Kombi. She had her eyes closed, her lips curled ever so slightly at the edges. It wasn't that she was smiling, but her face was the most relaxed he'd seen since he'd met her. "It reminds me of my childhood when everything was good." She never talked about how her mum and dad had died. The walls and side tables in her house were devoid of any sign that she'd had any family at all.

"Can I ask you something?" Her voice was soft and hesitant.

"Sure."

"Do you feel any different? Even a tiny bit, I mean, having his heart?"

How am I supposed to answer that? Does she want me to feel different? Just tell her the truth.

"The truth is, I feel stronger and healthier every day. And I have a newfound awareness and gratitude for life that I never had before. But I still feel like me, if that's what you're asking?"

"Sorry, I don't know what I'm asking." She ducked her head, "I guess I've heard that sometimes people who have had transplants end up acquiring some of the traits of the person whose organ they received."

"Yeah, I've heard stories like that. Perhaps when you're ready, you can tell me more about Will, then I'll know if I'm having Will-like tendencies," he said, trying to bring back the earlier light-hearted-ness they'd shared. She gave a small laugh. He was surprised how much it pleased him to make her laugh and smile.

"When you start stuffing your dirty socks in the corners of the lounge and leaving crumbs in the butter, I may get suspicious."

"What about when I leave the toilet seat up?"

"All boys do that and I have noticed that you're improving."

Ominous looking clouds were forming above the backdrop of flushed sky while an orange glow peeped above the ocean's horizon, painting an ethereal hue. The moon was soon to rise in all its fullness.

"Can I ask you something else?"

He looked at her. "Nakita, you can ask me anything."

"It's just that, I thought if I could...well that is...I've been thinking: Would you mind if I listened to his—your heart?"

Her request wasn't unusual. He'd been wondering if she'd ever ask to listen to her brother's heartbeat. He didn't mind, especially if it brought her peace. His heart wasn't his own any more.

"Sure, come here," he motioned.

"Are you sure it won't hurt?"

"No, it only hurts when pressure is put on the middle of my chest or if I move suddenly." He took off his thick jacket, leaving his long sleeved T-shirt on and grabbed a few pillows, putting them behind him. He settled back. She looked so unsure, biting her lip as she often did. "Come on." He took her hand and pulled her towards him.

She curled into his left side, dragging the blanket up over them and very tentatively lay her head on the side of his chest. He wrapped his left arm around her, his hand on her shoulder, his chin resting on her head. Inhaling her fragrance of honey and woman, he decided he'd best stick to shallower breathing. By instinct, his fingers found their way into her hair and he couldn't resist the temptation of fiddling with the long strands. Her body gradually relaxed into his as she listened, her left hand resting on the right side of his chest.

As they both watched in silent awe, the moon, now an orange disc, suspended itself above the fury of the ocean, gradually paling as it moved higher into the evening sky. He had to remind himself that she was listening to her brother's heart and hoped she couldn't tell it was beating harder and faster than normal.

She felt too good in his arms.

CHAPTER 12

"*W*ater," Nakita rasped, her tongue and throat bone dry. She rolled onto her back and groaned, her head thumping abominably, her bladder ready to burst. Barely able to put a coherent thought together, she slid off her bed and staggered to the bathroom, sticking close to the hallway wall for support. *What on earth happened last night?*

Nox as in the kitchen, whistling while he turned sausages that sizzled frantically in the frypan. The smell simultaneously turned her stomach and set it clawing in hunger. She went to the bathroom and splashed her face. Hoping it would clear her mind a little. Coming back, still dazed, she leaned against the back of the lounge; Nox turned and looked at her.

"That good, huh?" he chuckled. "I've got your brekkie on the way. Nothing beats a hangover like a sausage and egg muffin with barbecue sauce."

She touched her throbbing head. "That's what this is; a hangover?"

He grinned. "Don't tell me you've forgotten about last night?"

Last night? Last night... What did I do?

What did they do?

"You should see your face." He laughed. "Don't stress, it wasn't whatever you're thinking. I have scruples." She sagged in relief. "You can't remember?"

She rubbed her temples, wracking her brain to get a handle of what they had done; she could only remember up to a certain point when they'd come home from the beach. They'd sat on the lounge room floor, by the old wood fire, and listened to her dad's old-school music on the crackling record player; for the first time since meeting him, she had been totally at ease and relaxed in his company—that she could remember—after that, everything was a blur.

Filling up a glass of water, he brought her two aspirin; she took them, still confused. "You drank me under the table last night, after we got home." He supplied.

"So hang on a minute, if I drank you under the table, how are you so bright and cheery?"

"Let's just say my body is more accustomed to the effects of alcohol than yours." He turned, but his smile gave him away. He was enjoying this *way* too much.

"So I can't remember the bit where I went to bed? I still have my clothes on."

"Well, I thought you could strike two things off your anti-bucket list in one hit." He went to the fridge and pointed. "'To drink someone under the table and sleep a whole night fully clothed.' The fact you've never done that before last night baffles me." He pulled out a glass, filled it with water and popped an orange tablet in it. "Here, drink this. Another good hangover cure."

She took it. She'd try anything at the minute. Taking a swig, she grimaced, her stomach clenching in protest. "I didn't really drink you under the table, did I?"

"Let's just say you gave it your best shot. I did get under the table, if you remember?"

"Mmm, it's sort of coming back to me." She managed a smile that felt more like a grimace. "I think I'll take a shower now. You really shouldn't hang out with me. I'm obviously a bad influence. And you shouldn't drink anyone under the table when you've just had a heart transplant." She tilted her head to the side as the night before started coming back to her in vague impressions. "Come to think of it; you didn't drink much at all, did you?" His eyes crinkled. "You kind of cheated by letting me think I'd won." After another sip of the vile, orange flavoured drink that sent a shudder through her, she decided she'd best shower. She felt ghastly.

"Hey, anytime you're up for a rematch, I'll be ready," he called to her back as she walked down the hall.

"No, I think I pretty much nailed it last night." She dismissed his suggestion with a wave of her hand. His throaty laughter followed her to her room, awakening another flash of memory of last night, how he'd made her laugh till tears rolled down her cheeks; she couldn't remember exactly what he'd said that was so funny, but she hadn't laughed that much in years.

As she stood in the shower, her mind drifted again to the night before: The wind; the crashing waves; the moon full and orange as if it was being birthed from the ocean; the musky male scent of him mingled with the salty air as she laid her head on his chest and listened to Will's heart. The experience had been real, but to think she was listening to her brother's heart beating in another man's body was unfathomable. For that person to be Nox, and to have her body pressed up against his, plunged her mind and flesh into a state of conflict. Somehow, she couldn't reconcile her brother's heart by her ear with Nox's strong, warm arms holding her, his fingers playing with her hair. The whole time she kept reminding herself that to have any kind of physical response to him was totally wrong, yet her body seemed to have a mind of its own. And worst of all, it wasn't just her flesh; the more she got to know him and move past her discomfort, the more she realised she enjoyed their conversations. She enjoyed having him around; his presence was easy and comforting, kind of like pulling on her old, pink dressing gown.

Wiping the small fogged up mirror, she caught her reflection and looked herself dead in the eyes. *Just finish that bucket list Nakita; that was the deal.*

Joining Nox and Emmylou again in the living room, she tried to ignore how her temples still throbbed even after the painkillers.

"So I was looking at the anti-bucket lists and if we're going to strike something off, I'm thinking, today is the day to do one of mine, since it's all fairly sedate," Nox suggested. She took a sip of coffee, thankful that he didn't bring up anything about last night in the Kombi.

"Sedate was agony for Will."

"Yeah, well, I reckon I may require intravenous caffeine to keep awake doing Will's list. I mean, look at this: 'Read an entire Jane Austen novel'."

Nakita straightened. "Are you suggesting Jane Austen is boring?"

"No, I'm sure she's not." His eyebrows drew together. "Who is she anyway? And why do I get the feeling from your expression, that I should know her?"

She looked at him in utter disbelief. "She is the most beloved female author of all time."

"Beloved, huh?"

"I don't have the energy for this," she said, holding her temples, "we'll get to Jane Austen soon enough. But I think with Emmylou home and the weather as it is, we should strike 'Disney Movie Marathon' off the list." She didn't mention the fact that she was extremely hung-over and not able to manage anything else. Besides, it really was a perfect day to stay rugged up and not feel guilty with the wind and rain lashing.

They set up in front of the television with blankets, pillows and a huge tub of popcorn. Emmylou nestled in between them, totally lost in Aladdin from the first scene. Nakita pretended she didn't notice Nox laughing at the Genie—he was into the story almost as much as Emmylou. Next, they watched The Little Mermaid, Nakita's personal favourite. When it finished, they ate chocolate brownies and ice-cream and Nakita could swear her clothes were already getting tighter. At one point, Emmylou remembered that Daddy had a mermaid on his arm that looked just like Nakita, but despite her nagging, Nox refused to show her the tattoo, and made a point of changing the topic; though intrigued, she let it slide, since he was obviously uncomfortable.

After brownies came Frozen, Nox groaned having already dozed throughout The Little Mermaid, but she bribed him, reminding him that it was a Disney *marathon*, and that two movies didn't qualify as a marathon. Emmylou made her way to the foot of the lounge bed, totally spellbound with the glittery songs. Nakita watched Nox from beneath her lashes, loving how much pleasure he was taking in Emmylou's enjoyment. Without Emmylou between them, she lay a little closer than she knew was appropriate, but something drew her to him. She kept trying to tell herself it was Will's heart. No part of her touched him, yet she was ultra-aware of every move he made and the musky scent that lingered around him. She looked at him from under her eyelashes and wondered what it would be like to be in a relationship with someone like him. The thought of it had her longing in ways she never longed before. He must have noticed as she switched off from the movie. Reaching down, he took her hand in both of his. She looked up at him and he gave her that sexy, tilted smile of his; his eyes crinkling at the corners. For the rest of the movie, he played absentmindedly with her fingers. As the credits rolled, she wondered how such a small act of friendship could throw her into such turmoil. Those two words she dreaded started resounding in her mind. Two words that had consumed her soul of late—*if only.*

Later when Emmylou was tucked up in bed, she washed up the day's dishes, Nox grabbed a tea towel, looking like he had something on his mind.

"You know I've been thinking. I feel sorry for chicks growing up with all that stuff. Did you see Emmylou at dinner combing her hair with a fork like that mermaid?"

"Ariel."

"Yeah, that one."

"You feel sorry for chicks, why?" She jibed at his use of the word. He swatted her on the butt with his tea towel, then took a plate and dried it. After last night, she could sense that something had subtly changed between them. There was an awareness of friendship and even affection that had replaced the awkwardness.

"Well, the way I see it, it's all just a fantasy, right? I don't want Emmylou to grow up with all this bullshit, thinking there's a Prince Charming around the corner destined for her, when the reality is, there probably isn't. I think I've ruined my daughter."

"A little dramatic, don't you think?" she laughed. "What's the difference? Boys are fed the whole superhero thing. Disney feeds girls' romantic fantasies, boys get their egos stroked."

"Yeah, but the difference is boys do grow into superheroes," he said, holding the tea towel around his neck like a cape.

She rolled her eyes.

"I just don't believe in all that soul mate, destined for one another crap. Apart from Raina and Pete, I've never seen it and I reckon they probably fluked it."

"Well, I have seen it," she said, unsure why she felt so prickled by his words. Growing up, she'd never questioned these notions. Her parents had always been so in love, "Antony and Miriam. Rosie and Donald from the nursing home. Mum and Dad..."

"C'mon, admit, it's few and far between. Most of the time, relationships end badly. Not worth the hassle if you ask me."

She knew he'd experienced the worst from his own dysfunctional relationship and that of his parents, but she wasn't about to let him tar all relationships with the same brush. "Well, no one asked you. True love is worth the hassle." She said, in what Will had always called her 'highfalutin voice', which was really just another way of saying she sounded like a snob. But it was really that she did want to believe it;

she wanted to defend the worth and the cause for True Love and Destiny. Which she still believed in, didn't she? She wasn't so sure herself anymore. True Love may be worth the hassle, but was it worth the pain and loss?

"I might sound cynical, and I suppose I am, but in the end it's the kids who are sacrificed."

"Maybe, but I've seen the kind of love that endures even the most dreadful circumstances. The 'in sickness and in health' kind of love. The kind of love that even death cannot part." Nakita heard herself speaking, strangely distant, her words made hollow by her own skepticism.

"Hmm." He sounded unconvinced, but didn't push it further. "What if you don't get your Prince Charming? I mean if you're a, a—"

"A virgin?" She raised an eyebrow at the direction of the conversation. *Where is he going with this?*

"But what if you wait and wait and he doesn't exist?"

"Well, I shall be thoroughly disappointed. I'm hoping to fall tragically in love. I want the magic carpet ride."

He looked to be deep in thought as he dried a plate. "Sorry, the last thing you need is a depressing conversation about your Prince Charming who may not exist."

"Oh, he is out there. I'm completely brainwashed by Disney, but for now I shall do my chores, dance around the house and sing." She did a dramatic spin and bubbles from the dish cloth flung all over the floor. He looked at her, baffled. "Cinderella," she cried, exasperated.

"I thought she was the one who lived in a shoe and had dwarves or something?"

"Wow. Poor Emmylou. I see I need to do a lot of work with her. You're getting all your fairytales all mooshed up."

"Look, I think I've done a good job with the whole Disney thing. Would you mind if I left Emmylou with you and go to the pub? I need to get back to monosyllables for the rest of the night."

She grunted. He grunted back. Reaching into the sink, he flicked bubbles on her nose. She wiped them off with a tea towel, scowling at his audacity.

"Only if you admit one thing."

He leaned in closer, his physical presence so potent it dazed her. "Yeah what's that?"

"Admit you enjoyed Frozen."

"Not on your life." He grabbed a marker and put a thick line through 'Disney Movie Marathon' on the bucket list. With a satisfied nod, he grabbed his jacket and walked out. But just before he closed the door, he stuck his head back in. "Okay, I'll admit; the only thing that saved that movie was the talking snowman. The snowman and holding your hand. That was my favourite part."

She threw the dishcloth at his roguish smile as he shut the door.

"Be sure to be back in by twelve, or your beloved Kombi may turn into a pumpkin." She laughed, watching him from the kitchen window, shaking his head. Catching her smiling reflection in the window, she stilled, watching as it faded. A stab of shame rang through her. She'd been so focused on Will's heart being inside of Nox that she never considered the initial attraction she'd felt for him would remain... and grow. Last night, even today, had been a respite to the nightmare she'd been living. She'd allow herself that, but the fantasy was over—it had to be.

CHAPTER 13

*N*ox was strumming his guitar on the couch a few days later when Nakita came home and closed the front door. Instead of coming in, she stood for a moment, holding the doorknob, facing the door as though she didn't want to turn around. His guts twisted. *Where has she been? Something must have happened.* After the movie marathon day, he could tell that the little ember that was ignited in her had died back out. She was still more comfortable with him than she had been, but also kind of distant and tense.

He eased his guitar down. "Are you okay?" he asked, bracing himself.

"Don't you dare say a word." She turned and faced him, her eyes narrowed in warning. She was bright orange. The barest hint of a smile twitched around her tight mouth.

"Oh," he paused, trying not to look relieved. "You auditioned for a role as an Oompa Loompa in the remake of Charlie and the Chocolate Factory?"

"Of course. Of all the classics, you would have to know *that* one, wouldn't you?" She flung her handbag on the table. Emmylou came out of her room at the sound of Nakita's voice and ran towards her, her steps faltered as she got closer.

"Kitty, why you owange?" Her nose wrinkled as it did whenever she asked questions. She asked a lot of questions.

"It's really bad, isn't it?" She turned to him, her expression asking for reassurance he couldn't give.

He opened the fridge and started pulling out some bits and pieces to make a sandwich. "No, I like it. Orange is becoming on you, compliments your hair."

"I asked her for a natural, sun-kissed glow. Look at what she's done to me. I'm ruined," she motioned dramatically. "How can I leave the house looking like this? I'm literally fluorescent orange. It's like someone's spilt a tin of wood stain all over me. This is exactly why fake tanning was on my anti-bucket list."

Nox couldn't hold back his smile.

"At least it's winter and I can cover most of it up," she sighed, sitting down heavily, as though resigned to her fate.

"You tanned your whole body?"

She screwed her upturned nose a little, a habit he noticed she'd picked up from Emmylou. "What? Do you think I'd just get my head and neck tanned? Seriously." She strode over to the kitchen counter and turned to look at him, her arms crossed. He never realised living with a woman could be this enjoyable. But then, maybe it was just her?

"Well, I don't know. It would have been more economical if you had, wouldn't it?" He shrugged. "I mean, it's winter. It's not like anyone sees your body."

"Well, I have to see myself naked, don't I? I have to like what I see."

Now there's a thought. He swallowed. "Yeah, I suppose you do. Have you had a fantasy about being an Oompa Loompa? Or does this have something to do with the pole dancing course you just enrolled in?"

Her mouth dropped open. Something he was finding increasingly enjoyable was how easily he could get her to bite.

"How do you know about the pole dancing?"

"A woman by the name of *Gigi*," he emphasised the flamboyant name, "called and left a message. A spot has opened up for you." He squashed the lid down on his sandwich and gave her his best 'please explain' expression, then took a huge bite of his sandwich to hide the smile threatening to escape him. She stood by the kitchen counter, tapping the bench, glaring. He knew she didn't approve of how he prepared his sandwiches; he should have found it annoying, but it amused him more than anything. In her mind, there was a right way to do just about everything; everything had a place, everything was for a purpose. He liked to think of himself as fairly organised, but from what he'd seen so far, Nakita lived her life by a sequence of structures. She never seemed to waste time or kick back and just relax.

Her body language changed, and she shrugged, pretending she didn't care. "It was on the bucket list."

He pointed to the list on the fridge. "Attend a pole dancing *class*. It doesn't say *course* Nakita. What happened to the lecture you gave me the other day about over-sexualising women?"

She blew air through her lips and straightened her back at having been caught bending her own convictions, then threw up her hands in surrender. "Okay, okay, you got me." She walked over to the fridge, pulled out a carton of milk and poured a glass. "I've changed my mind."

"You changed your mind?"

"I may have been too quick to judge the sport."

"So it's a sport now?"

"The women are super-fit and strong."

"Well, if it's classified as a sport now, you won't mind if me and a few mates come and spectate then?"

"You'll do no such thing!"

"And why not? I thought it wasn't sexual?"

"It's not—well, it doesn't have to be. It's just... well, there are some rather compromising positions."

"I don't know any man who would see pole dancing as non-sexual."

"Well, you may be disinclined to think so if you saw some of the participants," she said, with a snicker when she saw his grimace.

"There you go again, painting vivid images."

Emmylou began tugging her skirt. "Kitty, what's pole dancing?" Nakita looked from Emmylou to Nox, giving him a sugary smile. "Sweetheart, I think Daddy's best to explain that." With a cheeky wink she left him with Emmylou looking up at him expectantly. He figured it probably served him right.

CHAPTER 14

*N*ox jerked awake. Something had woken him. Rolling over, he looked at the alarm clock on the floor by his bed, 1:22am. He could hear the shower. *Surely she's not having another shower to get that stuff off?* He cocked his head and could hear sobbing, muffled by the running water. Something in his chest clenched as he climbed out of bed into the freezing cold to go to her. Fumbling in the dark, he found his shirt and track pants, then went down to the lounge room. He waited for the shower to turn off, wondering what to say when she came out. Finally, the bathroom door opened and steam poured out. About to turn off the light, she gave a start, seeing him for the first time.

"Oh, you're up?" Her voice trembled.

"I heard you in the shower."

"I'm sorry. I didn't want to wake you. I had a bad dream. I prefer to cry in the shower. It's weird, I know," she said, in a watery voice.

"Come here." He reached for her in the semi-darkness and pulled her into his arms. He held her close and stroked the back of her head while she sobbed; he tried not to think about how perfectly she moulded into his body.

"I should get to bed." She stiffened and pulled away.

"Nakita, if it helps, you can lay with me and listen," he said, tapping his chest.

"Really? Would you mind?" she asked, as though he were throwing her a lifeline.

"Come on." He took her hand and led her up the stairs to the mezzanine and they both climbed into his bed. As Nakita slid down next to him under the covers, resting her cheek on his chest, he was thankful he still had his track pants on and for the cold dampness of her hair that lay across his arm. He tried to concentrate on that, rather than the curves of her body—curves that were pressed up against him. *Okay Nox, it's one of those times in your life when you need to be the hero. She's a sister, right? Just like the sister you never had.* Pete's voice came back to him.

"So you had a bad dream?" He hoped she didn't notice the strain in his voice. She was silent for a long moment and then took a long, shaky breath.

"I dream about him all the time. The dreams are always bad; he's always fading away or dying. Sometimes I know that I'm dreaming and think, if I can just get a hold of him somehow, I could bring him back."

He put his hand over hers where it rested on the right side of his chest. Her voice giving way as fresh grief wracked her body. Holding her close, he rubbed his hand along her shoulders and stroked her hair. After a long time, the shudders subsided. She lifted her face and turned to look up at him. Even though it was dark, the silvery moon lit up the room enough that he could make out her features in the dark. Her eyes gleamed like ebony stones. "Thank you for being here." Her lips barely brushed on the underside of his jaw, then she nestled back down into him. Or did he imagine it? He forced his body —his mind—to submit. *Brother and sister. Platonic. This is a completely non-physical relationship.*

She ran her foot along his and then snatched it away. "Ooh, your feet are freezing."

"Yeah, well, I did stand in the cold waiting for you for a long time."

"Can you tell me something about yourself?"

He let out the breath he'd been holding. "What like?"

"I don't know, anything, a story about your childhood or something?"

"I don't like to think about it too much. It wasn't great."

"Funny, isn't it? That people who've had difficult upbringings are either destroyed by it or become stronger and more decent. You're the decent variety." *She wouldn't think you were so decent if she knew the thoughts you were having right now.* "I know." She half sat up, sounding brighter. "If you had to write your own anti-bucket list, what would you never want to do?" He didn't have to think about it, he knew right away, but felt stupid saying it out loud.

"What? Say it." She nudged him, as if she knew he was holding something back.

"Fishing," he muttered into her hair.

"Fishing?" she laughed, sounding intrigued. "Why in the world would you hate fishing? Is it the smell? Baiting the hook? Do you find it boring?"

"No, nothing like that." He wasn't sure how much further he wanted to delve into his past. Every time they shared with each other, it was another tie binding them closer. He knew he needed to keep his distance, but something in him just felt an irresistible tug towards her. He told her what he'd never told another soul. "Okay, so it's more to do with my old man. My real dad. He's a mad, keen fisherman. It's pretty much all he does, all day, every day. Drink and fish, drink and fish." He exhaled, he couldn't leave it at that. "He left us when I was about four."

"That would have hurt," she commented, as he stroked his hand down her long hair; he couldn't help what came naturally.

"Anyway, not long after he left, Mum hooked up with Ron who I told you about." He was glad that he could talk about it all now, say his name without the hatred and anger he used to feel. The black dog inside of him; that splinter in his mind was dead and buried. "They never married—she and Dad are probably still legally married to this day—but I always knew Ron as my stepdad. Like I told you, things were pretty bad, really bad. I ran away on and off from when I was about eight-years-old. Mum never did a single thing to change anything, just took it. He was so hateful, he must have been sick in the head, the things he used to do. His idea of reasonable punishments." He heard her sharp inhale and gave her a light squeeze to show her he was okay. "Mostly I just tried to stay out of his way, but as I got older and bigger, I stood up to him more. I'd get between him and Mum. When I was thirteen, he busted me up pretty bad. Mum said I asked for it because I got in the way. I was so angry, I took off. I had an idea where my real dad lived from a few things Mum had said over the years. I hadn't seen or heard from him since I was six; that was the last time I got a birthday card. I don't know what I was expecting at the time." He let out at a deep breath. The pain of his dad's rejection had always been a deeper wound than any physical pain inflicted upon him by his stepdad. Occasionally, it still got him like a punch low in the guts. "So, I hitched North. He was living in a caravan park. His obsession in life was fishing; there was no room for anything else."

"Didn't anyone try to persuade you to go home?"

"No, I was one of those kids that looked older than I was."

"Did you find him?"

He nodded. "He knew straight away who I was. He was fishing at the time. I'll never forget it. He barely turned his head and said, 'Hi son,' and kept fishing. It was as if I'd just come back from popping down to the shops." He could feel her body tense alongside his. "Remind me, why am I telling you my sad story?"

"I asked you to tell me something about yourself."

"Yeah, but I could have told you something funny, not a depressing story about my childhood."

"What happened then?"

"We ate fish. He was an alcoholic, but more of the quiet, reclusive kind. He told me to go home, basically that there was no place in his life for me."

She took his hand and squeezed it. "He wasn't mean about it. Just straight down the line. Kind of emotionless, but it still hurt pretty bad. I cried, I begged and pleaded, yelled at him, even tried to cut a deal with him. But he wouldn't have any of it, he didn't want me. He bought me a ticket, and I bussed it back home. Nothing changed. Mum didn't even realise I was gone. I guess that was a defining point for me. I knew then that I had to make my own way, but I screwed that up too." He stared at the ceiling. *All that wasted time.*

"But look at you now. You have Emmylou, your own business, and you're a good man. Some people never move on from their past. Do you know where your dad is now?"

"Nah, not really. Last I heard, he was still at the same place. I'm not bitter about it. I'm not going to waste any more of my time on him. It's his cross to carry."

"What about your mum?"

"She's doing the same thing she was years ago, still cleaning hotels."

"Do you ever see her?"

"Every now and again, but I reckon she thinks she can't change, that unhappiness and hardship are her lot in life. I just hate how she lets herself be a victim, that she never tries to get out of the hole she's in. Her and Ron aren't together anymore, he just up and left her one day. She pretty much lets the men in her life define her existence. Anyway, that's the long story of why I don't fish. Maybe I'm secretly afraid I'll take a liking to it," he chuckled.

She took his left hand and held it to the warm silkiness of her lips, kissing the sensitive skin on the palm of his hand. His belly tightened, his heart speeding up a few notches. His mind started going places. *Stop it, heart. Brother. Sister. The sister you never had...*

"Do you want to cross one more item off your anti-bucket list?"

"Well, that depends. If it's a puzzle or a crossword, I'll pass. But if your mind's heading down the track of strip poker or skinny dipping, I'm definitely in." She jabbed him in the ribs.

"I was thinking, since I'm already in bed with you... perhaps we could cross one off Will's list and I could sleep here with you the night without doing anything?"

His body tensed at the idea of her lying in his arms all night. He'd been with more than a few women in his time, and yet the idea of lying with Nakita and doing nothing was more appealing than all those women put together. "On one condition."

"Yeah?" she quizzed, rolling onto her side with her head resting on her palm.

"That you promise not to take advantage of me."

"That's such a cliché," she gave him a playful shove.

"No, I'm serious," he said, smiling into the darkness. "I've never slept with such a beautiful and cultured woman as yourself."

"Sure," she scoffed, "I can only imagine how many opportunities you get in your line of work."

"Well, that may be so, but just because opportunities arise doesn't mean I take them." He didn't want her to think he was some sort of womanising sleaze; common in his industry. "Look, it's not like I've been an angel by any means, but I do stay away from clients. And the truth is, with Emmylou, it's not like I have time for relationships. I'm trying to give Emmylou a different kind of upbringing to what I had. I don't want women coming and going from her life. Her being happy and secure is more important to me than any relationship."

"Nox, thanks for what you've done for me, for taking a risk and moving in when it probably went against your grain and didn't really make any sense."

"Yeah, it didn't make too much sense at the time, but you know what? It kinda makes sense now. I'm not one for fate or destiny, but I'm grateful our paths crossed."

She curled into him, breathing a sigh of contentment.

He had to know, he'd been itching to know all this time. "So you can tell me to shut up, but I have been wondering, how is it that someone gets to your age and hasn't had sex?"

"It's a long story. But I guess it was sort of a promise I made to myself when I was sixteen. After Mum and Dad were both gone, I wasn't really coping. I started drinking—a lot. There was no one around to stop me. One day, after I'd had way too much, I ended up in a situation with one of Will's friends that I had a crush on. He pretended to care, but really he was just using circumstances to get to me. I was too drunk and vulnerable to see it, but Will came home at just the right time and saved me from making a decision that I really was powerless to avoid and would have regretted. It's kind of ironic now... but after I sobered up, I realised I had to be my own protector from then on, Will couldn't always be there... so I swore off alcohol for a long time and decided then that my virginity was a part of myself I wanted to share with the right man. It just made sense, like its something sacred almost." She put her hands over her face. "I know it sounds old-fashioned. You probably think I'm naïve."

He rolled to his side, coaxing her hands off her face. "Actually, I admire a woman with strong values. You have so much courage and strength."

He let out a long breath. All this talk was too heavy, too intimate; he needed to lighten the atmosphere. He was getting too close. His hand made its way to her armpit undetected. "I can't believe I get to snuggle with an Oompa Loompa; all my boyhood fantasies have come true at once." Arching back, she shrieked at the unexpected attack. As she dissolved into fits of squealing laughter, he tried to think of a time in his life that he'd ever lain like this with a woman; if there was, he couldn't remember it. There was something about Nakita that made all the other women he'd been with utterly forgettable. As she settled back into in his arms to go to sleep, he gave himself a stern talking to about duty and honour. It was a homily that he continued as he held her close; savouring her womanly scent and the sensation of her curves pressed against the hard lines of his body. It was only when he felt the rhythmic rise and fall of her chest that he finally drifted off to sleep, relishing the feel of her in his arms. Living with Nakita was an exquisite form of torture.

Nakita was remotely aware that she lay in his embrace. She could hear the comforting sound of steady rain and feel the side of his face pressed into the curve of her neck. She snuggled in closer to narrow the gap between them. In turn, he tightened his strong arms around her, his lips brushing along the delicate skin of her neck. Blissful sleepiness turned into sudden alertness. Everything went still; they both held their breath. Nox's hand slid tentatively to her hip and came to rest there with a light squeeze, sending electric thrills into her belly. His fingertips, roughened from playing the guitar, became bolder, tracing lazy circles on her exposed flesh. Becoming less feather-light, they roamed more insistently along the contours of her body, stroking along the side of her thigh, sliding hesitantly just under the hem of her pyjama top to caress along her waist, his palm splaying flat on her abdomen. His jaw, scratchy with stubble, sent shivers coursing down her spine as he ran it up along the length of her neck, his breath hot in her ear. Instinctively, she reached up and squeezed his bicep, arching her neck back.

The theme song of the Lion King blared from his phone next to the bed, breaking the spell.

Nox hissed between his teeth and rolled over to answer it.

"Kara? Hi, oh shit... is it that late? Yeah, I'm okay. I slept in. Yeah alright, I'm on my way." He rolled onto his back. "I have to change the ringtone... Emmylou..." He didn't finish.

She peeked over at him. He lay there a moment, as if willing himself to get up. She lay there willing him to go—hoping he'd stay—pleading with her body to stop doing that zingy thing; it was thrumming, as though awakened for the first time. He heaved himself off the mattress, the sudden cold engulfing her hot, flushed skin. She rolled to her back, frustrated. *Pincushion*. She didn't know whether to thank her or throttle her.

He kept his back turned as he busied himself getting dressed. "Well, I guess I got that one scrubbed off the bucket list then." He commented, his voice husky. She figured he was feeling as awkward as she was. They were borderline making out—though they'd both kind of been half-asleep and not totally in control of their actions. Okay; whichever way she looked at it, they had just made out.

"As providence would have it, yes." She watched the corded muscles in his back flex as he pulled the shirt he'd been wearing off, a tattoo on his right shoulder blade she'd never seen before; a chiselled Atlas bracing himself, bearing the weight of the world on his shoulders, caught her eye. He turned, tugging a fresh shirt on, giving her a flash of his taut abdomen, causing her own to belly to tighten. "I don't know about you, but this is a definite first for me."

His grin was rakish as he pulled his hair back into that knot that she still found intriguing. She concentrated on pulling the quilt back over her.

"For me too, but I guess in a different way."

She presumed he meant because they never went the whole way. *What had she been thinking?* Her cheeks flamed a deeper shade of pink as she knew exactly what she had been thinking.

"Well, I guess I better change these elsewhere," he said, holding up a pair of jeans, "I have a client in ten minutes."

She nodded, pursing her lips together, hoping that their lapse in judgment wouldn't make things weird between them.

His gaze lingered over her a moment. "Just for the record, Nakita, even though nothing happened between us last night, what didn't happen was far better than nights I've spent with a lot more happening."

He never gave her a chance to respond as he strode out, leaving her determined to throttle Pincushion next time she saw her.

CHAPTER 15

*N*ox was glad to to get outside doing something useful with his hands. It had turned into a fine winter's day, so he'd mowed the backyard, pruned some overgrown bushes, and worked on a few things that needed repair; the chook pen being one of them. It being a Sunday, Nakita went to the nursing home with Antony for a couple of hours in the afternoon; while Emmylou spent the day playing on the tyre swing he'd hung up in a sprawling mulberry tree that Nakita talked of playing in as a child. When she wasn't on the swing, she was playing with Pinky and Flower, two Guinea pigs that Nakita had surprised Emmylou with a few days ago. He wasn't sure what he was going to do with them when he and Emmylou moved out; not that he was itching to move out. Dorley Point wasn't a bad place to live, by any means. It was a step back in time, everything was at a pace that much slower. Most mornings, he got up early and went for walks with Diesel around the headland; the dawning sun resting against the watery horizon so that everything blushed pink and gold. They'd stand on the shoreline and watch the flickering lights of the prawn trawlers and fishing boats as they returned from their nightly catch, seabirds circling overhead squawking. The simplicity of the moment drew him in, reawakening his yearning for a simple life; it was a tiny taste of something that always seemed just out of his grasp.

Going inside to get himself a quick bite and a much needed drink, it surprised him to hear a knock at the door. A tall, slim woman with silver-white hair greeted him with a smile. She looked to be in her late sixties—he knew by instinct it was Miriam. They hadn't met yet, but Nakita spoke so of her so often; he felt like he already knew her.

"Hello, Son. I'm Miriam, more or less a grandmother to Nakita. I thought I'd come by and meet her housemate."

Nox opened the door wide, returning her smile. She'd picked her timing well, waiting for Nakita to be occupied with Antony. He couldn't help but wonder how they'd feel towards him, knowing he had Will's heart, especially since Will was more or less a grandson.

"Would you like a cup of tea? I'd offer you coffee, but I don't know how to work the coffee machine."

"Tea would suit just fine."

Something about the way she carried herself, calling him son, had Nox warming to her immediately. He could see she was a no-nonsense, salt-of-the-earth kind of woman. After chatting with Emmylou and striking up an instant friendship, they sat on the back deck and had a pot of tea while Emmylou played with Diesel. A short time later, Miriam regarded him with intelligent blue eyes, seeming to want to get to the actual point of her visit.

"I've been around the traps, son, and I'm not stupid, Nakita's a beauty; she's clever, but she's not worldly wise by any means. She's dated boys who are safe that don't get under her skin, but she hasn't dated a man yet. You're pretty easy on the eye and just the kind of man that'll turn her head."

"No need to worry about that, Miriam. We're polar opposites and I'm not her type at all," he slipped in, hoping to set her mind at ease. He could take a warning when he heard one. "You see, there are a number of reasons why we'd never get together." She raised her eyebrows as if to encourage him to continue. "To start with, I have a long history of adopting the baggage of just about everyone who has come my way and making it my own. I've spent most of my life unpacking baggage. I mean this with no disrespect to Nakita, but I think you'll agree, considering the circumstance, Nakita and I would equal a lot of baggage. When, and if I have another relationship, I want it to be with someone who is uncomplicated."

Miriam put down her teacup and threw her head back in throaty laughter. "When you find that person, let me know and I'll marry them myself. There'll be a lineup," she gestured. Then composing herself added, "Son, there's no such thing as an uncomplicated person; everyone's got baggage." Her dark blue eyes sparkled as she smiled indulgently over her cup of tea.

In spite of himself, he couldn't help smiling back at the attractive older woman.

"I know, I know. But any relationship with Nakita would be just... I don't know." He shook his head. "There's baggage and then there's luggage. Not to mention I'm older, I've got Emmylou and I'm really just at a different stage of life. Anyway, the two of us would be strange because—well, you know..." he faded off, not wanting to bring up the fact that her brother's heart beating in his chest was keeping him alive.

Admittedly, something about just being near Nakita sent his body into overdrive, but that would pass sooner or later. He was a man and she was a gorgeous woman. Sleeping with her had been on Will's bucket list, and it wouldn't happen again. Waking up next to her, so close that he could see the smattering of freckles across her nose, her hair in a glorious tangled mess and the way she'd responded to his touch, had been pure torment.

"I love that girl like my own grandchild. I loved Will the same. Nakita has been through hell. I don't want to see her get hurt again."

"Miriam." He tried to reassure her as she looked at him with shrewd eyes. "She's safe with me; she sees me as a brother and I'd never do anything to hurt her. I owe her everything."

"And how do you see her?"

Damn, but the woman's straight to the point. She refilled her teacup and stirred in two heaped teaspoons of sugar. He paused, knowing he wasn't going to pull the wool over her eyes.

"I see her as Nakita."

"At the moment, when she looks at you, she sees another chance of having a part of her brother with her. You're not Will. One day, the reality will come crashing down and the cards will fall," she spoke as though she were some kind of prophetess.

"I've always been good at cards," he countered, hoping to disarm the direction of the conversation. Miriam smiled, and the conversation moved on. But he could tell they'd formed the beginnings of a mutual respect.

Once she left, he couldn't help but mull over her words. They were already getting too close. He wasn't sure if he liked the idea of Nakita laying any claim to his heart, even though it was really her brother's. He'd already had enough of his own fuckups in life. He didn't need more. After years of being out of control, he'd learnt the hard way—he chose his own destiny—and Nakita was not his destiny.

I hate you commerce. No, I loathe and detest you with my entire being. Nakita slammed her laptop shut and put her face in her hands, rolling her shoulders and work out the kinks. She brought to mind the memory that always got her through moments of self-doubt: That day bursting through the front door with her school report, excited because she knew it was good and that her parents would be so proud. Will trailed miserably behind, his report unopened in his bag. Report time was never easy for him.

"Mum! Dad! Come and have a look." Her dad hadn't been long home and was filthy from a hard day's work. Washing his hands ceremoniously before taking her report, he sat at the small kitchen table; while her mum peered over his shoulder, beaming while her dad read out the glowing report. Nakita remembered feeling like she'd burst with pride.

"You know, sweetheart, with a report like this, the world will be your oyster. You can go to uni and do whatever you set your mind to." Her father retold the same story he had told them repeatedly over the years. How when he was twenty-two and in his second year of accountancy, they'd discovered that her mum was pregnant with twins; he'd quit uni right away and got a job with his cousin in construction. He never went back to finish his degree, but always wondered how different their lives would have been if he had. To Nakita, he'd always seemed regretful each time he told that story. She decided she'd have a different future and make him proud. She remembered the words she spoke as though it were yesterday.

"Dad, I've been thinking, I know what I want to be when I grow up. I want to be an accountant just like you dreamed of being."

"That would make your mother and I very proud, Nickle," he said, calling her by the pet name only he used. He'd spun her around like when she was little. From that moment on, she promised herself that she'd become an accountant no matter what. Not long after, cancer had weaseled its way into their lives. They diagnosed her mother with ovarian cancer, and life as Nakita knew it changed forever. While her mum wasted away physically and eventually lost her battle, her dad became a hologram of his former self. Nakita assumed her mother's responsibilities and her dad stopped calling her Nickle. She'd had to grow up overnight. When her mum passed away, they lost their dad too. Though it was some years later that it became a physical reality. Losing him made it clearer in her mind that she *needed* to become an accountant; so she could fulfil his dream. Once she made that decision, everything else became crystal clear including the reality that she would have to be the one who held everything together for her and Will. She was the one who took care of all their practical needs—but looking back, now she could appreciate that it was Will who kept her sane. Moments of him getting her to lighten up, that seemed so inconsequential at the time had become precious memories that played in her mind's eye.

She stood abruptly to push the sweet and painful memories from her mind. *Tea, that's what I need, another cup of tea.* She turned the kettle on, settling for chai. Her eyes came to rest on the white paper chemist bag, still folded down with sticky tape. She thought back to yesterday; Nox said he was out of medication and went to the chemist late in the afternoon, but left in a rush this morning. *I best take it to him.* She needed a distraction and seeing him was a bonus; he'd been so busy lately with work and seemed to spend a lot of afternoons at Pete and Raina's; working on what he called 'a few projects.' Whenever she quizzed him about his so-called projects, he was evasive and uncomfortable.

Things had been weird between them ever since she'd woken up in his arms. Not in a bad way, just in an awkward kind of way. She'd convinced herself that she'd made half of it up. Plus, Nox had let it slip that Miriam had visited. For the life of her, Nakita couldn't get anything much more out of him than that they'd had 'a nice cup of tea and a chat.'

She grabbed the paper bag, went over to the stereo and turned it off. As she turned to leave, she saw Nox's hoodie bunched up on the lounge. Picking it up, she held it to her nose, inhaling deeply, savouring his cologne and that scent that was uniquely his. It made her tummy hurt with some peculiar longing. Opening her eyes, she realised what she was doing and flung it back on the lounge, far from her. *Try to explain that one when Nox catches you sniffing his clothes.*

She noticed his sketchpad jutting out from under a lounge cushion. Picking it up, she ran her hand over the leather cover. Often she'd catch him sketching, but his body language always showed he didn't want her to see.

It's just a bunch of drawings. What would it matter? I've seen tons of his sketches at Ink Guild. She bit her bottom lip, overcome with temptation. *He left it on the lounge. He mustn't care too much who sees it. I'll just take a quick peek.*

Opening it, she eased down on the edge of the lounge, turning each page slowly, struck by the complexity of the drawings. They were intense and utterly absorbing. A few times when the subject of his art came up, he'd been fairly vague in answering her questions. He was increasingly sought after as a talented tattooist, but he seemed to lack a wider belief in his artistic abilities. But here was evidence that he was far more than a tattooist—he was a true artist. There was something unique and cutting edge about his work. Maybe he just needed a little push in the right direction? Often an aspiring artist just needed the right contact, and Nakita knew just the person.

～

Kara wasn't at the front desk. Nakita peeked inside the door to Nox's studio, which stood wide open. She couldn't see anyone, so she wandered into the large storeroom out the back. Pushing the door open, she found Nox kneeling down, mixing paint in front of a large canvas. He was so engrossed he didn't notice her. She wandered in to see what he was working on, excited to see him in action on one of his paintings.

"Nox, I have something important—" she said, coming around the side of the painting, glimpsing briefly a naked woman lying in a field of flowers. He jumped up, turning the canvas from her view, knocking over his pallet as he did. "Nakita—"

"What? You do nude portraits too? Can I see?" She maneuvered to push past him, her belly stabbing at the thought of him painting a woman naked; it just seemed so tacky. If he were a proper artist, then maybe it would be different.

"Nakita, you can't just barge in." His broad chest blocked her view.

"Is it one of your clients?" she tried asking in a casual tone, but her voice came out sounding more like a jealous lover. His face was flushed as he glanced up at her from trying to salvage the spilt paint.

That he looked so guilty was all the more grating. It was like she was suddenly discovering a side of him that she didn't know about, that she didn't want to know about.

"Nakita, what I do in my own time is my business."

He's right. Who he paints, what he does, has nothing to do with you. Her voice of reason rang out; but she couldn't help feeling offended at him saying so.

"I'll go," she turned.

"No, you're here now. Let's go out there though." He ushered her into his studio. *He clearly doesn't want me to see the painting.* She watched as he busied himself organising boxes. He wasn't himself.

"So, I found something when I was cleaning today." The memory of smelling his hoodie sprang to mind as the white lie rolled off her lips.

"Oh yeah, what's that?"

Now that she stood in front of him, she no longer felt so confident about what she'd done. "Your sketchbook." She held her breath, waiting for his response. He paused what he was doing, giving her his full attention. She took in his raised eyebrow and slightly flared nostrils.

"Look, I know I shouldn't have sticky-beaked, but I've seen your artworks here and I couldn't resist." She spoke faster. "Nox, they're really good. I mean really, really amazing," she emphasised, unable to wipe what felt like a stupid grin off her face.

"And?" his voice was flat, his eyebrows drawn together. She could see by his response he wasn't happy with her for looking at his sketchpad.

She balked a little at the thought of telling him what she'd done. "I really didn't think you'd mind."

"Well, I do. I really mind," he said, the muscle in his jaw flexing like he wanted to say more. Waves of heat flushed through her body as she realised she may have made a big mistake.

"Then you may not like what I did..." she trailed off.

"What did you do?" His eyes looked a deeper sea-green than their usual, leaf-green, soothing oasis.

"I have a friend, an art dealer in Melbourne. She's really clever," she moistened her suddenly dry lips, "I took some photos and emailed her for you."

"Please, tell me you didn't." His hands went to the back of his neck as he looked towards the ceiling.

She could hear herself speaking double-speed again as she stepped towards him, her hands out in supplication. "Nox, she's really trustworthy, I swear. I wouldn't have sent them to her if I didn't trust her implicitly. I'm certain she can help you, that she'll get you the break you need—"

"Oh, and now you're the one to tell me what I need, are you?" His eyes flashed. She'd never seen him angry before; even when Emmylou was at her worst, he was always so patient, so calm and laid back.

"Nox, I was only trying to help." She said, shocked by his response. *What is his problem?*

"Did it ever occur to you I don't want or need your help? That I'm not looking for a break." He rubbed his forehead as though he couldn't quite believe what she'd done. "Is this how it's going to be? Do you feel a sense of ownership over me now that I have Will's heart?" He didn't wait for a response. "Just go. I need to get to work. I didn't sign up for this." He pushed the door open.

"Yeah, I'm sure you've got much better things to do, like painting nudes." She mumbled, a plume of satisfaction rising inside her as she saw the look of shame in his eyes. With her shoulders thrust back and neck straight, she walked out; but not before turning to have the last word. "And for the record, I never signed up for this either!" She burst forth, staring straight at his chest then slamming the door.

CHAPTER 16

*N*akita wrestled with the sheets, kicking in frustration. No matter how she lay, she couldn't get comfortable. It didn't help that she was wide awake or that it was late and Nox hadn't come home. Any wonder? She'd done the wrong thing. In hindsight, it was so glaringly obvious; it pained her. Not only had she massively breached his privacy and trust, but she'd acted more like a psychotic, jealous lover than a housemate or friend.

At what point had she become so completely irrational? Deep down, the truth, if she could admit it to herself, was that she did feel like she owned a little piece of him—a really important piece of him, actually. But he didn't owe her anything, so why was she acting like he did?

The crunch of wheels on the gravel driveway signaled his return; his Kombi headlights momentarily filling her bedroom window. She slid out of bed and peeked through the blinds, feeling a little like a stalker as she watched him get out of the car and pull a sleeping Emmylou from the seat. He planted a kiss on Emmylou's forehead before carrying her towards the house. Something inside her moved at his tenderness towards his daughter. *Why did you have to go stuff this up so badly?* Releasing the blind as he looked towards the house, she dived back into her bed and lay there holding her breath. His boots clomped lightly on the wooden floor as he walked down the hallway towards hers and Emmylou's bedrooms. After a moment, he came out of Emmylou's room, towards hers; his shadow hovered at her doorway. Her belly tightened. Was he going to knock? What would he say? She heard his heavy exhale before his footsteps faded back down the hall.

After how she'd carried on today, he'd leave. There was no question. She knew enough about him now to know he wasn't one for drama; she knew he only came to stay in the first place because he felt like he owed her, now she was acting like he did. As he moved quietly around the house, she tried to picture going back to a life without him and Emmylou in it, hating herself that it was all her fault. They'd only been there a short time, and yet they were so much a part of the fabric of her life now.

I can't take this. She slid out of bed and pulled on her old, pink dressing gown. Somehow she had to change his mind.

The house was dark as she crept up the creaky hallway to see him standing by the open back door. He turned his head, startling her.

"Nakita?" She hesitated, not sure what to say or do. His voice gave nothing away.

"Come sit out here for a bit," he said, nodding towards the backyard. This didn't bode well. She followed him, taking a blanket from the lounge; it was so late and cold outside. His wanting to talk now could only mean one thing—he was leaving.

She approached him in the middle of the backyard. He was leaning back on his hands, looking up at the stars. The shyness and uncertainty that overtook her that first day she saw him grabbed hold of her all over again; but this time it was different. Now she knew him and living together, they were coming to share a connection that went beyond Will's heart. She lowered herself on the carpet of grass beside him.

"Here, do you want to put this over you?" She held out the blanket.

His focus was on the night sky. "Just look at those stars." Nakita tipped her head back for the first time.

"Wow," she breathed. "They seem extra bright tonight."

"No moon." For a heartbeat she thought back to the time they'd lain together while they watched the moon rise over the horizon of the ocean and wondered if he ever thought about it too.

"It's such a clear night."

"Quiet too," he said. A neighbour's dog erupted into barking nearby. They both looked at each other and couldn't help but smile at the timing. Nox lay back with his head in his hands and continued staring up at the stars. She followed suit and lay next to him, glad of her thick dressing gown, which mostly protected her from the night dew on the grass. Willing herself to say what was on her mind, she turned toward him.

"Nox, I'm so embarrassed about how I carried on today. I'm really sorry. There's no excuse, I don't even know what I was thinking. I betrayed your trust, big time; and invaded your privacy and worse, I was plain mean. I'd like to say that this was totally out of character, but truth be told, I always drove Will crazy, interfering in his business."

He turned to her. She could feel him looking at her profile. "I'm not Will, Nakita."

"I know," she huffed, fiddling with the ends of her dressing gown cord; unsettled by his words and his eyes on her, as though he could see straight through her. "I get it." She turned her focus back to the sky. "So, are you leaving?" she asked, her body tense with expectation at his answer.

He breathed out heavy. "To tell you the truth, what you did today really pissed me off. I planned on telling you tonight that we were leaving. But then I came out here to see Diesel and looked up at the stars and thought about my dad, wondering if he was standing outside right now looking up at the same stars. Walking out was his first instinct. But I don't want to be like that. I don't want walking out to be my first instinct."

Now, it was her turn to look at him as he stared into the sparkling abyss. Finding his hand underneath the blanket, she squeezed it. "Thank you. I know we're still sort of just getting to know each other, but somehow Emmylou, and well... both of you, are starting to feel like family."

He pulled her in closer so her head was on his shoulder. For a moment, she could pretend that everything was right with the world as they lay silent. There was something dizzying about being this close. Or maybe it was the stars winking above, dazzling her senses so her body wasn't entirely her own.

"Can you tell me something about him?" He didn't need to say his name; she knew who he was talking of. A bubble of grief rose within her, but with it a memory came that she spoke into the night.

"We used to sneak out here at night when we were little. We'd wait till Mum and Dad were asleep and then come and play on the tyre swing in the mulberry tree. They had no idea." Hot tears found the corners of her eyes. "Will just had this way about him. I'd never have told him, but nothing made me happier than pleasing him. He was the only person who could get me to do pretty much anything, eventually." Nox wrapped his arm around her and rested his palm on her forehead, brushing her hair back. Her body relaxed into his and she felt the sudden need to keep talking, to tell him more about Will. "You know, one night we got fully dressed, packed our torches and went on a mission on our bikes around Dorley Point? We were so prepared, we even made peanut butter sandwiches. Will's idea." She smiled at the memory. "We had so much fun. We went everywhere: the lagoon, the park, the beach. We played spotlight in the sand dunes and came home just before sunrise. Mum couldn't wake us for school the next day. We pretended we were sick."

She wondered how a memory could simultaneously bring so much pain but somehow joy at the same time. *This must be what bittersweet is.*

"Did you always make bets with each other?"

"Yeah, Will was always betting me to do things I didn't want to. I wanted to be the good girl and do the right thing, but I guess there was a side to me that only he knew how to bring out. The thing was, whenever something went wrong, Will would always take the rap for both of us." She didn't want to think about the last fall he took for her. "The next weekend we did it again, but Will wanted to up the ante. Our bus stop was right in front of this old woman's house. Every morning she'd yell at us if we so much as touched a blade of grass; we truly thought she was a witch," she chuckled. "Anyway, I swear it was Will's idea—we stole every garden gnome we could find."

"You didn't."

She nodded. "All night we ferried them on our bikes and set them up out the front of her house, on the path facing the front door. There was an army of gnomes, they were popular around here at the time. Anyway, the next day we heard she'd had a turn and ended up in hospital from the shock. She thought someone was out to get her, I think. Everyone knew about it. There was a lot of speculation about who did it. Will of course was a suspect, not me. I was a nervous wreck for months; I was sure we'd get busted."

"Did you?"

"No, we never told a soul. We swore on it. You're the first person to know. I guess it doesn't matter now." She whispered the last words, aware that Will's heart lay so close to hers.

"Sounds like you have lots of wonderful memories."

"Yeah, but I try not to think about him because it hurts. But tonight it feels okay, somehow." A shiver coursed through her as his fingers tugged gently on the lengths of her hair.

"What were your mum and dad like?"

"Mum was just like Will. She had the blonde hair, olive skin and the same baby blue eyes. She was beautiful. She was always so laid back; she just made you feel peace when you were around her, somehow. She loved nothing more than getting out in the garden, and drove Dad totally crazy, always starting new projects and never finishing them. He complained that she was useless with money, but said it in a way that you knew he wouldn't have changed a single thing about her. I guess I'm more like Dad. He worked in construction, but it was his dream to be an accountant. Dad was so good with numbers; that was one way that Will was more like him than me. Funnily enough, I'm the one that promised to do accountancy, yet I struggled the most with maths. It comes... came naturally to Will."

"So that's why you're doing accountancy, because you promised?"

"Partly," she said, choosing not to elaborate. It didn't have to make sense to anyone else, just her. "There is a lot of career security in accountancy, plus it pays well. Mum didn't really work, except for some casual shifts now and then at the bakery. We lived pretty frugally. When we were twelve, they diagnosed her with ovarian cancer, so Dad worked less and less to look after her, then he lost his job altogether. After she passed away, he struggled to cope, and sank into deep depression. He must have been in such a dark place to leave us behind like that... We have no other family; dad was an only child, his parents died in a car accident when we were babies. Mum's family disowned her when she was much younger; she was from money and her parents never approved of dad; he was never good enough for her in their eyes."

"Harsh. Do you have any contact with them now?"

"No, and I don't want to. It's like they don't even really exist in my mind. Losing mum was so painful, but we all got to say our good-byes, there's a beauty in that. But with dad... I don't blame dad, I never blamed him for leaving us. He just couldn't live without her. He always did his best for us. I just wish I could tell him somehow." She trailed off, trying to reframe her sad memory to the happy picture that she held of him in her mind; his smiling dark eyes and large work-roughened hands. "After dad passed I promised him, and myself, to look out for Will, even though he was the same age, he just needed looking after." Nox's strong arms squeezed her tight, his warm breath in her hair. He lifted the long strands of her copper hair into the darkness.

"So is this your dad's doing?"

"No. Dad had jet-black hair. It's the doing of my great grand-mother Agnes, a Scottish woman."

"Agnes, eh?"

"Yeah, awful name, but she was apparently a great beauty in her day, well, before she had nine children. Dad always said I had a temper like hers. Whenever we were having a fight, Will would call me Agnes or Aggie. I'd totally lose it." She sighed and snuggled in closer while he continued to stroke her hair. She savoured the feeling of lying close to him, so warm and contented by his presence that she could ignore the cool fingers of night air on her nose and cheeks, and the slight dampness of dew seeping through her gown.

"I miss him so bad. I just wish I could turn back the clock; you know? I got so caught up in everything I was doing, everything I was working towards. So many times he asked me to do stuff with him. Most of the time I blew him off because I thought I was doing something more important. I was just too busy living this structured life that I wouldn't deviate from. I'll never get that time back, not ever. Antony always says 'Lost time is never found again.'"

"You quote Antony a lot, you know?"

"I probably do..."

"Emmylou is quite taken with him. She said he read her face."

She nodded in the dark with a smile. "I took her there the other day, and they hit it off straight away. Antony's been blind for nearly twenty-five years. You know, he sees people through his fingertips?"

"How does that work?"

She half-sat up in a moment of lightheartedness. "Want me to show you?" She patted the ground. "Antony always taught me to see through my fingertips, and I've watched him do this my whole life." Nox sat cross-legged in front of her. Her eyes had adjusted to the darkness, allowing her to make out the contours of his firm jawline. Her stomach squeezed tight. "So I'm going to close my eyes and see you with my fingertips, then you can close your eyes and see me. Ready?" she asked, not really sure she was ready herself.

Feeling a little giddy at the thought of touching his face, she closed her eyes. Even still, she could see the image of him staring at her; his chin slightly upturned, as though intrigued by what she was about to do. Taking a deep breath, she tried to empty her mind of any visual image, then reaching out hesitantly into the darkness her hands came to rest on his shoulders for a heartbeat or two, before sliding across the hard planes beneath his shirt. As she skimmed her palms up his neck to the back of his head, she marvelled at how much heat was coming off his body considering the coolness of the evening. She had to lean forward slightly, allowing her hands to roam through his hair, feeling its texture, then pulling her fingers through the lengths. On a whim, she leaned forward and dragged his hair back into the place that he wore it in a knot every day, then let it fall back to where it hung below his ears. A shudder ran through him and she smiled into the darkness. "Ticklish?" she asked, emboldened.

Next, her fingertips traced along his cheekbones and temples to where she lay her palm flat along his forehead. His thick brows tickled her hand as her palms glided along their smoothness. From his eyebrows, her fingertips felt down his nose. His long eyelashes brushed her thumbs as she gently found the contours of a pair of eyes that, on one hand, brought reprieve to her soul and yet had the ability to unravel her. Her palms found his cheeks and made their way down to the spiky stubble of a three-day growth. There was something about such a simple, manly thing; that brought with it its own type of awe. She ran her hands back and forth to feel the bristles along his jaw. Resting one palm there, she slowly outlined his lips with her index finger. An impulse urged her to lean forward and taste his lips; her belly squeezed as she wondered if he could somehow sense her thoughts. Playfully, he nipped at her fingers. She opened her eyes.

"Looks like I found your sensitive spot." She said, tying to look and remain unaffected. "Yep, you look just how my fingertips pictured you."

He sat still, smiling wordlessly back at her, and she knew they'd just shared an intimate moment. But had she crossed a line? Her eyes slid down over the hard angles of his chest. Placing her hands deliberately in her lap, she was afraid that she wouldn't be able to restrain them from roaming over a lot more than just his face. "Okay, now it's your turn." She realised she'd been holding her breath, but now her breathing quickened in anticipation of his hands on her.

He nodded, closed his eyes, and then reached out. She studied him in the darkness. As his warm hands came to rest on her shoulders, her body seemed to liquefy. Touching him was one thing, but being touched was a whole other. He squeezed her shoulders lightly, before sliding his hands up her neck and into her hair, cradling her head with both hands before tangling his fingers through her hair and rubbing it between his fingers, making it crackle. She lost all thought as his hands roamed over her face without the slowness and hesitancy that she had used. She couldn't help but close her eyes against the pleasure of it. His roughened fingertips, alternately traced, outlined, caressed and moved over her features: back through her hair, up and down her neck and throat, her ears, her eyes. The only place they didn't traverse was her lips. She was vaguely aware that she was nuzzling her face into the palm of his hand like a feline, but she couldn't resist. She had no idea how much time had passed when he stilled his exploring, one palm splayed across her left cheek, his other hand gently cupping her chin. Something in the atmosphere made her open her eyes and found herself pinned by his penetrating gaze. Her heart beat fast, seeming to keep in time with her breath. The air was thick with desire. His eyes held the same intensity she saw when they were focused on tattooing her, but this time there was something more.

Stop this, Nakita. It's gone too far.

His eyes moved to her lips. She reached for his forearms to pull him away, but she couldn't command her flesh, so she just held them. His muscles were taut under her fingertips while his thumb traced her lips seductively, as if touching something profoundly desirable.

140

He stilled his thumb in the cleft of her bottom lip. She couldn't take her eyes off his face.

Will.

She pushed his arms away.

"You cheated. You were supposed to have your eyes closed." Her voice wavered.

He pulled his hands away, lacing his fingers together in his lap. "Yeah, I suppose when I touch something exquisite with my hands I can't help but want to see it with my eyes."

"Well, now you know how Antony sees people. He'll probably want to see you when he meets you in person," she said, reaching for the blanket.

"Now I'll be prepared. But somehow I think it might be an altogether different experience."

"Maybe."

His teeth flashed in the darkness. She stood, pulling her gown close around her.

"Where are you going?"

"I'm off to bed. I've got loads of uni work tomorrow." He was still looking at her. "Goodnight Lennox."

"Night, Nakita."

With each step she felt the distance between them grow as she left him sitting in the dark. She slid between her sheets; they were positively icy against her hot skin. She lay for a long time, tormented physically and also for that deeper connection that she'd never shared before.

Think of Will, Nakita. What you are thinking about disrespects the sacrifice he made. Just finish the bucket list.

A long time after she heard him go to bed, she crept into the lounge room and stood in front of the urn. Reaching one hand to the urn, with the other over her heart, she uttered a silent vow.

CHAPTER 17

The aroma of a roast lamb in the oven greeted Nox at the door. His stomach rumbled in anticipation; it had been a long day's work, and he'd had no time to eat. He couldn't remember a time in his life when he'd eaten so well; if he wasn't careful, he'd be toting a paunch like Pete soon. Nakita sat at the table doing craft with Emmylou. Something about the smile she cast over her shoulder did him in. She was eating again and looked too much like she did the first day they'd met. He just stood watching. Often when he came home from work, Nakita would be doing things with Emmylou that he imagined a mother would do. It wasn't unusual to find them baking, doing craft or gardening; Emmylou was blossoming in ways he'd never thought possible by this one change in her life.

He couldn't think clearly when Nakita was around. Every day he was finding it harder to control the feelings he was trying to deny. Her sense of propriety belied the raw sensuality he knew lingered just beneath the surface, and the smattering of freckles across her nose that she hated—he loved. Even the things he found irritating, like her relentless desire for structure, he admired. It was becoming increasingly difficult not to stare when she absentmindedly twisted and piled her red mane on the top of her head in a tangle that she didn't secure; inevitably, it would loosen and fall down to where it belonged, skimming the small of her back. He didn't know what was going on with himself; he was like a kid mesmerised by a piece of candy he couldn't have. He'd made a habit of cracking his knuckles so he didn't just grab her, kiss her and drag her to the ground where she stood.

Since that night when they'd explored each other's faces, the walls were well and truly flung back up. They were on strict brother-sister-housemate, or whatever they were, terms. What was he thinking? They had nothing in common. He was just a tattooist with a kid, a dark past and no place to call home. Not exactly a catch for someone like Nakita. Maybe that was what got him? She was so out of reach.

Either way, he had to put his raging lust or whatever the hell it was to death. He felt uncomfortable with her lately, which unsettled him even more. Women rarely got under his skin, but she was burrowing right in.

He'd been spending more than a few days doing some avoiding of his own with odd jobs at Miriam and Antony's. They reminded him of what it might have been like to have grandparents. Nakita had been right; Antony had wanted to 'see' him with his fingers. It had been quite a humbling experience standing in front of the stately, older gentleman, his sightless watery eyes upon him; his papery fingers travelling over his face as they chatted easily.

He cleared his throat, "Hey, guys."

"Hi Daddy," Emmylou said, preoccupied with her craft.

"How was your day, Chipmunk?"

"Daddy, I've been making the garden, and I found worms." She scrambled down from her chair and tottered off in a tatty pink tutu and new sparkly silver gumboots.

"Poor worms," Nakita murmured, focused on the craft in front of her. "They've been dragged around the house all day. She had eight to start with, but when she screwed the lid on their new home—well, let's just say, now she has nine." She turned to look at him, "Hey, how are Mim and Antony?"

"They're good. Antony told me to tell you 'The Posse,'" he made quotation marks with his fingers, "missed you on Sunday,".

"Did you remind him about my assessment that was due?"

"Yeah, he knew. Apparently Doris was very disappointed."

"Oh dear. God love her." She smiled and shook her head at the mention of the old woman at the nursing home. Each Sunday afternoon, Nakita would go with Antony to the nursing home. First was a few rounds of bingo, then Antony would play old tunes on the piano, before Nakita read to the residents as they enjoyed afternoon tea. He didn't know any other twenty-four-year-olds who did things like that. She just didn't add up; she was a small-town girl with big town dreams. He trained his eyes to the little foam craft shapes on the table, trying not to think about how his fingertips had memorised her face only nights before.

She stood from the table. "Hey, I have a gift for you."

Nox went straight to the fridge and pulled out a beer. From the look on her face, her pink cheeks, and the way she was trying to bite away the smile on her bottom lip, he was going to need it. She bent over the couch to get whatever it was. His only bonus was getting a good look at her arse, which was looking far too delectable. When she turned, he quickly averted his eyes. She didn't need to know.

"Okay, what is it? I can see by the pleasure on your face that I'm not going to like it." He took the package, set his beer on the bench and tore it open: Crocs, fluorescent yellow Crocs. "You've got to be kidding me." He held them out, looking at her. They were the ugliest things he'd ever seen.

She jumped up and down on the spot in anticipation, clapping her hands. "I saw them on special today and remembered the list. They're perfect."

"Yeah, perfectly hideous. I'm not wearing these."

"Oh yes you are, tomorrow all day at work and afterwards. I have a little plan."

"No way, not to work, I have a reputation. Couldn't you find anything less... fluorescent?"

"Hey, you said yourself we need to focus on the bucket list more. We're going to kill two birds with one stone with this little errand."

"Why do I get the feeling I'm not going to like this 'errand'?" He set the shoes down on the bench and picked up his beer, giving her a look of skepticism before taking a swig.

"Oh, you're going to love it," she assured him, her brown eyes dancing.

And for that reason alone, he knew he'd do anything she asked.

Nakita jumped into the car with an explosion of laughter.

"That's it, these are coming off. I've had enough." Nox lobbed the Crocs into the back of the van as she dissolved into more peals of laughter, holding her aching belly. He threw the car into reverse. "Did I tell you that when I was getting fuel this morning, a biker elbowed his mate in the ribs and pointed at my shoes and they both laughed? And you know the homeless guy with about five teeth? He saw me opening the shop and asked me if 'my missus had gone colour blind.' I told him he could have them. You know what he said? 'A bloke has to have some standards,' and walked off laughing." Nakita slapped her leg; beside herself with laughter.

After a few minutes, she calmed down enough to remind him. "Lennox, the day's not over; you've got one more thing to do." He looked at her, his nostrils flaring in unwilling compliance. "We are off to the library to find you a hot date. And yes, you will be donning the Crocs."

"Donning?"

"Yes, donning."

"You sound like a bloody grandma."

"Nox, don't swear. It's an unpleasant habit."

"Nakita, I said bloody; it doesn't count as swearing."

"Well, it did when Emmylou couldn't tie her 'bloody shoelaces' and you sent her to the naughty chair."

"Point taken," he sighed, "where's this library?"

"You don't know where the library is? You're kidding me?"

"No, I don't know where the bloody library is because I don't bloody well hang out in libraries, let alone pick up bloody chicks from them."

"Chicks? How Neanderthal of you. Just remember 'picking up' doesn't include clubbing them over the head."

They pulled up outside the library. Nox took the Crocs from where he'd lobbed them in the back of the van. His expression was pained as he scuffed his feet into them.

He really doesn't want to do this. Should I let him off the hook? She thought to herself in a soft moment. *No. This is an anti-bucket list. The whole point is doing those things you'd never want to do. The stuff you found challenging, confronting and downright mortifying.*

"Wow, this library has a lot of books," he said with a low whistle as they walked in.

"Hey maybe that could be your pickup line?" she scoffed, then grabbed his forearm. "Okay. Stop, close your eyes, inhale." She took a deep breath and slowly exhaled. Opening her eyes, she saw his were still shut.

"Okay," he whispered, "why are we doing this?"

"We're inhaling the aroma of books." He opened his eyes and smiled at her, as though surprised by her answer. "Sorry, but I really love the library. It's like its own universe."

"I can see that. You know you suit this place?"

"I'll take that as a compliment," she said, certain that suiting a library couldn't possibly ever be a compliment.

"Okay let's do this." He clapped his hands together. "See that young lady over there?" He pointed to a woman standing by the photocopier. He cracked his knuckles and gave her a cheeky look, knowing she disapproved of his knuckle cracking. It never ceased to make her skin crawl. "Watch a master in action."

Everything about him exuded manliness as he strode up to the young woman who looked about her own age. As he began talking to her, she responded eagerly, her black bob nodding under the bright lights of the library, eyes wide and expressive. She was clearly smitten. Nakita couldn't blame her; he really was something. Her face changed as a tall man stalked over and had words with Nox. Before she knew what was happening, Nox had made his way back over to her hiding position with a stricken face.

"What happened?"

"Oh man, that was awkward. No way can she be seventeen. She looks about your age; that was her dad," he said, running a hand through his hair, blowing out air through his full lips.

Nakita covered her half-shocked smile. "Her father? Oh no, what did he say?"

"Exactly what I would have said if someone that looked like me tried to pick up my seventeen-year-old daughter in a library." He rubbed his hand over his face. "Okay, let's go."

"Nu-ah," she wagged her finger at him, "you haven't picked up yet."

"Hang on, what are you expecting? For me to take a chick home to bed or something? Because you know, I'm not that easy."

"I expect a giving or receiving of phone numbers. That's all."

"I could be having a beer with the lads," he groaned, scanning the library. "Okay, let's do this. See the chubby brunette at one o'clock reading? She's next. This'll be a piece of cake."

He went over, looking more than slightly ridiculous in his Crocs. Leaning casually on a bookshelf in front of her, he said something, his smile friendly. The girl gave him one glance and hunched further over her book, ignoring him completely. He spoke to her again. This time she turned her body away from him, her face concentrating hard on her book. She would not budge. Nox looked at Nakita and pulled an amusing face. He stood there a moment longer and then came back over.

"Did you see that? I had her eating out of my hand."

"Um. I'm pretty sure you didn't."

He sighed. "Nakita, we could be here all evening. This place is not a good pickup joint. How about we have a rematch at the club?"

"No way, that one's on my list, yours is specific to the library."

"So you're telling me you'd rather pick someone up at the library than the club?"

"Ah, yeah." It was a no-brainer. The thought of clubbing, let alone picking up at a club, was terrifying. "Well? Run along." She motioned with her hand.

Nakita watched on as Nox did a few laps of the library, looking for his next target. Spotting a tall blonde wandering through the front door struggling to carry a massive pile of books, he made a beeline to her, stooping to pick up a book as one slipped from her pile. He was so damn gorgeous, he was probably part of the reason she dropped the books to begin with.

They ended up chatting and laughing as she put the books in the return chute, with his help of course. It seemed to be going really well —too well. The blonde fiddled with her hair and looked up at Nox with flirtatious eyes; he seemed to be enjoy his interaction with her a little too much. An unreasonable part inside of Nakita, stabbed with envy. He must have asked her for her number because they both seemed to be trying to locate their phones.

Oh my goodness, she's going to give her number to him! Who even does that? Who randomly meets a stranger and gives out their number? It wasn't something she'd ever had the confidence to do.

From their body language, neither of them had their phone. Haha! Bad luck for Nox. It didn't surprise Nakita, Nox frequently left his phone at home when he wasn't working. He motioned for her to wait and went over to the front counter with a small piece of paper. Something in Nakita's belly squeezed; with the irrational desire to be the girl giving him her number to him.

She had a very satisfied look on her face as she checked him out. But once her eyes dropped to his feet, her smile vanished. She turned and left without a word. Nakita couldn't believe her eyes—she'd done a runner! Nox turned, pen in hand. He stood there for a minute, a bewildered expression on his face; he looked over at Nakita and shrugged his shoulders. He had no idea. "What? Where'd she go?"

"She did a runner!" she barely managed. "She took one look at your Crocs and bolted. I think I'm going to pee myself." She crossed her legs, dissolving into more peals of laughter, tears rolling down her cheeks.

"So, clarification... The rule is I have to pick a woman up from the library, right?"

She nodded, trying, but failing to pull herself together. He stepped forward, grabbed her around the waist and heaved her over his shoulder.

"Nox!" she shrieked. "Put me down! You'll hurt yourself. What are you doing?"

"I'm picking up a woman at the library."

And with that, he strode out with her dangling helplessly over his shoulder, squealing for him to put her down.

CHAPTER 18

"Hey darlin', what a nice surprise. Come on in," Raina greeted Nakita in her warm way. "Great timing, we're just about to stoke up the wood oven for the first time and make some pizzas."

"Oh, the one Pete and Nox were building?"

"Yep, they finished it today. It looks great. Nox is out in the back shed working on something else now and I have no idea where Emmylou is." Raina shook her head and smiled in her way.

Nakita felt less awkward about just turning up on their doorstep, since Raina didn't seem to find it unusual at all. "He mentioned this morning he was coming over. I've spent the entire day with my head in the books and I couldn't stand it anymore, so I thought I'd see what's happening."

"Seems a crime to be studying on such a beautiful day." Raina led her through their home modest home that was decorated with an assortment of antique odds and ends. "But, I'm sure, it'll be worth it in the end," she added with a smile, picking up bits and pieces left around as they went. "These kids, I tell you." She shook her head, exasperated. "I run them around to their sporting commitments all day Saturday and as soon as they're in the door, they just drop everything where they stand. I'm my own worst enemy picking up after them, and Pete's no better; you'd swear I have five kids."

Nakita laughed, enjoying how easily conversation flowed with Raina. She'd spent a growing amount of time with the Belles over the past weeks since they were like family to Nox and Emmylou. They were always easy company, though at times, watching them together made Nakita nostalgic for what she'd lost.

"How have you adjusted having Nox and Emmylou? I hope Nox has been pulling his weight?"

"Oh, he's great around the house."

"Yeah, he's pretty good like that, and Emmylou?"

"I adore her."

"I'm so glad it's working out. Emmylou is more settled than I've ever seen her, and Nox seems happy too, which is nice to see. He deserves to be happy." Raina looked as though she wanted to say more, but seemed to think better of it.

"Hey, let me show you what I've been working on." She led the way to the massive open shed outside where Pete worked on his vintage classics. It was late in the afternoon, and the sun was only moments away till it would hide its face behind the craggy mountains in the distance.

"Aye, love," Pete greeted her as he stuck his head up from beneath the bonnet of an old car, Nakita had no hopes of identifying. "Ready to give that pizza oven a workout?"

"Sounds perfect." She couldn't help her smile widening whenever she was around Pete. He had a special way about him. In a short time, they'd made her feel she was very much a welcome part of the Belle family.

"Let me just finish up here and we'll stoke her up. I swear it'll be the best pizza you'll ever eat. Did you get the anchovies, love?" He turned to Raina.

"For the last time, yes. You've asked me about ten times already."

"Just have to be certain. We can't be eating our wood fire pizza without anchovies now, can we?" He looked to Nakita for support while Raina rolled her eyes and led her to a part of the shed which seemed to be her own corner.

"So I spent the day working on this beauty." Raina rubbed at a smudge on the wood of an exquisite teal, antique dressing table with elegant, twisted gold handles. "I was going to sell it online, but now I've got to thinking, I might keep it. I've fallen in love. That's the problem with these restorations, they become hard to let go of."

"Wow. I love how you've distressed it in all the right places. I can see why you want to keep it."

"Thanks." Raina smiled. "I just work with what's already there, bringing out their natural beauty, with a bit of sanding here, a lick of paint and polish there."

"Where did you learn to do this?"

"Just picked it up along the way. It makes it easy if you're passionate about it. I love restoring old stuff. This is nothing compared to what Nox can do. His work is amazing." Raina stressed the word 'amazing,' shaking her head as if in disbelief. Nakita couldn't help the tug of envy that Nox trusted Raina enough to show her his work, which was clearly a lot more involved than what she'd stumbled upon in his art book.

As if his ears were burning, Nox stepped out of a shipping container that ran parallel to Pete's shed. As he turned, Nakita took note of his grimy jeans, black singlet and the welding helmet he had flipped back. It was the first time she'd seen him in a singlet. Since it was still mostly cold, he always had his tattoos covered. Her eyes ran over his sculptured arms and shoulders that were both inked in elaborate designs she wanted to study. There was something about them that stirred her.

"Lennox." She inclined her head.

"Nakita." He tipped his helmet, revealing that lazy grin. She peeked over his shoulder, hoping he'd invite her in. Raina's comment piqued her interest further. She was already more than a little intrigued since Nox would regularly disappear to the Belles for long stretches of time, saying he had work to do. It was like he had a secret part of himself he wasn't sharing, which she so badly wanted to understand.

"What are you working on?"

"Not much, just tinkering." He turned back, shutting the door before her eyes could adjust to the darkness of the container.

"How was your day?" he asked, hauling a crate full of heavy tools to Pete's shed.

"Exceedingly dull and tiresome." She watched the muscles in his back and shoulders strain under the weight of what he was carrying. "But it's improving somewhat."

He flashed a grin over his shoulder. "You know, it's a pity you aren't doing a degree in purple prose, because I think you'd do 'exceedingly' well at it." He heaved the crate up onto the workbench.

"Will always said I spoke too much like Anne of Green Gables. I think it's the red hair to tell you the truth." She pulled a face as she slid up onto the workbench next to where he was working.

"She one of Jane Austen's friends?" He winked as he put the tools away. She rolled her eyes and tried to ignore the effect that the simple wink had on her.

"So what are you creating in there?" She eyed the tools, her curiosity getting the better of her once again. *Whatever he's doing is obviously far more than drawing or painting.*

"Like I said, just tinkering."

"I don't believe you." She raised her brows at the crate. "They are not tinkering tools."

"Quite the busybody, aren't we?" He flicked her nose.

"You did *not* just flick my nose and I am *not* a busybody." He leaned towards her so she could see the tiny flecks of gold in his light green irises.

"You are a proven busybody and your nose has this way of turning up, begging to be flicked."

She bit her lip, knowing he was referring to when her nosiness had gotten the better of her. "I'm just curious, is all. You spend an awful lot of time over here. Actually, part of the reason I dropped by was to tell you my art dealer friend, Michelle, emailed me back. She wants you to contact her," she said, still feeling a little guilty as she handed him a slip of paper with Michelle's email address and phone number on it. He took the slip of paper and gave her a look she couldn't interpret before folding it up and stuffing it into his pocket. Embarrassed, she wanted to change the subject. There was a magazine folded in half, sitting on the windowsill, she took it down looking for a distraction.

"Hey, look a crossword. Someone's already started it. All we need is a pencil." With a cheeky look, she slipped the well-worn carpenter pencil from the belt slung low around his hips. "Fancy that. Let's finish it while you pack that stuff up. It's on our list, anyway. It'll be fun."

Nox sighed. What was it about this girl that drove him crazy, but also got so far under his skin that he wound up doing things he had zero interest in?

"Okay, 'ability to mutate'? Let's see 'morph'? Ten across, no it doesn't fit, neither does 'modify' hmm..." Nakita soon had them both hard at work on the crossword. Truth was, he was more taken with pretending to be busy, while in reality he studied her face as she held the battered pencil to her lips, her forehead furrowed in concentration. Her cheeks were back to their honeyed glow when he first met her, reminding him of the silkiness of her skin. It took all his self-control not to burrow his hands in her long hair and kiss her senseless. Pete's words flitted through his mind.

Like the little sister you never had.

"Have you tried mutability?" His voice came out hoarse. Her eyes narrowed as she counted the letters on her fingers before jotting it in. Then putting the crossword in her lap, she tilted her head, regarding him.

He knew that look; there was something on her mind, but he turned back to his drill, knowing that she would say whatever it was she wanted to say without a lot of encouragement.

"You know; I think you're a lot smarter than you or anyone else gives you credit for."

"People don't think I'm smart?" He looked at her aghast, but she knew he was just fooling around.

She pursed her lips "You know that's not what I mean. I don't know; you just seem to know a lot of stuff."

"It wasn't that hard."

"But you've done better with this crossword than me and I do them all the time."

"What makes you think I don't know 'stuff'?" She looked away, flustered. He loved it when she blushed.

"It's not that I don't think you're intelligent. I guess I'm just increasingly surprised by how intelligent you actually are."

"Is it the tatts?"

"It shouldn't be..." She squirmed.

He shook his head in mock disappointment. "Judging me by my dust-cover, Nakita?"

She eyed the tattoos on his arms. "Can you tell me about them?"

"What, my tattoos?"

She nodded. "Which was your first?"

"V for Vendetta," he said, pointing to the Guy Fawkes mask on the inside of his right forearm. "I got it when I was sixteen. My mates and I were into the whole punk scene. 'V' was anarchist and at the time social anarchy and revolution appealed to me."

She smiled. "I can just picture you, all grungy, getting around on a skateboard, breaking girl's hearts."

He grinned. "I had a Mohawk for a while."

"No way? Do you have any photos?" Her smile was wide. Damn, he loved her smile.

"Nope. I only have a couple of photos from when I was real little."

"I would have given you a wide berth if we'd ever crossed paths."

"I would have done the same with you. I stayed away from girls who were the marrying kind." Their eyes met for a glimmer of a moment. *Idiot. Why did you say that?*

Averting her eyes, she reached for his fingertips; leaning forward to study the matrix of cogs, gears and screws that began at his elbow and ran up to his shoulder; her fingers cool and light against his warm skin as they danced over the lines and contours. His bicep twitched slightly as she traced over the tattoo of a woman with emerald green hair, her face partly obscured by an old-school leather gas mask, the goggles around her neck reflecting the image of a burning Ferris wheel. On her head was a jaunty looking top hat.

"I like this one. And the antique clock. Steam punk influences a lot of your designs."

"Yeah. There's just something about it: the past combined with future possibilities. It's not defined by what it once was, it's influenced by what it once was, but a transformation has taken place."

"Which is your favourite?"

"I don't really have one. They've all meant different things to me at different times. Some of them I don't feel the same affinity for anymore, like the 'V,' but I guess they remind me of who I was and they are part of who I'm becoming. The atlas on my shoulder blade was at a time when I felt like I was carrying the weight of the world. Atlas was condemned to hold up the sky for all eternity; I guess sometimes I felt like I was condemned."

"Do you still feel like that?" she asked, tipping her head to the side, looking at him in that intent way of hers.

He shrugged. "I don't know, sometimes I guess."

"I hate that you have ever felt like that," she murmured, focusing her attention on his tattoos, her long hair falling forward into her lap, "What does that inscription down your side mean?"

He lifted his shirt to reveal *Veni, Vidi, Vici* engraved on his side in old English script.

"That was my second tattoo. It means *'I came, I saw, I*

conquered'. I was young and arrogant. A few years back I got this," he pointed at the inscription that ran just below both his collar bones, "'*Vincit qui se vincit*'. It means '*He conquers who conquers himself*,' I guess it made more sense to me."

"I wonder what your next will be? It's like each one tells a part of your life." She reached out and took his left arm. "What about this warrior?" She pointed to the Japanese-inspired Samurai on his arm. In profile, his hair was in a knot, similar to how Nox wore his own. Windswept, with sword drawn, the warrior's features were pensive with autumn leaves falling around him.

He shrugged. "I drew him one time, it just kind of captured how I was feeling."

She nodded, her brow knitting together as her index finger outlined an autumn leaf near the warrior's sleeve. Her fingertips came to the mermaid, her touch playing havoc with his system as they danced across the sensitive skin on the inside of his arm. He sucked in his breath.

"Why did you get her? She's somehow out of place with all the others."

"A couple of years ago, I hadn't long been back into surfing. A wave took me out. My board hit me in the head and it must have knocked me out for a few seconds, I let go, but then I had this vision of a mermaid that looked just like her, telling me to hold on. Something in my subconscious must have kicked in."

Nakita nodded, running her fingertip along the long red hair of the mermaid that drifted upwards around her face as though underwater. She traced along the turquoise tail that curled around his arm. "She's beautiful." Even though the light in the darkened shed was reduced to a few fading rays that streamed through the dusky haze, he didn't doubt she could see the eerie resemblance to her;

"You look just like her."

She returned his gaze but pulled her hands away as though she knew they were on precarious ground. He wanted to take her right there and then on the workbench.

You're getting too close, his inner voice warned him. Ignoring it, he leaned towards her and spoke low. "Just for the record, Nakita, I've been known to do a crossword or two when I'm at an extreme level of boredom, but when it comes down to it, I'm really at my best with Sudoku." He flicked her nose again before walking away.

She called after him, "That's it, I'm pulling out my most tedious puzzle this week."

"I can't wait," he threw back.

And damn him, but he couldn't.

A couple of hours later, they sat by the fire with a glass of red wine after having eaten pizza that was crisp and smoky, and just as Pete had promised—the best of her life—though she still wasn't so sure about the anchovies. Poking a stick into the glowing coals, she listened, captivated by the richness and humour of their stories. Hanging out like this with no real agenda was kind of new. Ordinarily, everything had to have a purpose or some function to fulfill, aimlessness was not really her forte, but for the first time since she could remember, she felt truly relaxed.

Nakita found herself alone with Nox by the crackling fire while Pete and Raina got their younger ones sorted, Emmylou having already fallen asleep. He stood up after a few moments of serene silence. "Come here, I want to share something with you." He motioned to where the neighbour's property lay cold and misty before them. Moving away from the heat of the fire, she shivered and followed him into the darkness. At a point, when it got further and darker away from the fire, he held out his hand for her to take. Holding his hand, they stopped in front of the dilapidated fence, separating the two properties. He reached into his jacket pocket and pulled out something long that she couldn't make out in the dark.

"I bought this for you today. It's on your bucket list, and I reckon tonight is as good as any to smoke your first cigar. I'll light it for you."

She watched, mesmerised, as he struck a match, the flame momentarily lighting up his handsome face. He puffed until the tip glowed red. Thick, pungent smoke swirled in a white cloud around them, stinging her nostrils. He passed it to her with a nod of encouragement.

"Okay, here goes nothing." She put it to her lips, then paused. "Wait. What do I do?"

"Okay, so it's not like a cigarette. Hold it like this." He took the cigar and placed it in her fingers correctly. "Don't inhale. Just puff on it and let the flavour permeate your mouth."

"Permeate. Okay. I can do this." She concentrated, taking a gentle puff. When she felt like she could handle the flavour, she had a few more puffs. Squinting, she blew out a thick column of smoke into the night air, smiling at Nox, who stood watching her with an odd expression on his face. "I'm not doing it right, am I?"

"You look every bit the aficionado. You sure this is your first time?"

"Of course. Good girls don't smoke. But I have to admit, it's kinda fun as a once off."

"This cigar marks a special moment for you."

"Oh, what's that?"

"Apart from this," he made a sweeping motion to the stars and her, "I have something else for you. I bought it last week." He pulled an envelope out of his jeans pocket. Holding the cigar between her teeth, she opened it. He struck a match so she could read it.

"A skydiving voucher," she choked, pulling the cigar out of her mouth. "You can't be serious?"

"It's on the list."

"Whew," she let out a determined breath. Her first reaction was to reject it; but she steeled herself, knowing deep down she had to go through with it at some point; she was committed to completing that list, no matter what. "Okay. I guess it had to come sooner or later, though the thought absolutely petrifies me."

"I won't deny the first time's a bit hairy, but it's a real buzz."

"I need to build up to that. I'm not quite ready yet."

"There's no pressure. Just hold on to it for now. You'll know when the time's right."

"Ugh. It's not fair. Your list is easy. Mine is awful."

"Hey, mine was *not* easy. Respect levels from my clients are at an all-time low. I don't know if I'll ever make a comeback. Although I've got to say one thing those Crocs were pretty comfy."

"Oh, now he admits it." She laughed into the cold night air. They were quiet for a few minutes, and Nakita's thoughts turned to Will as she looked at the zenith of stars hanging in the night sky. "You know, Will loved skydiving. Every country he went to—he sky-dived. He always said you've never really experienced a place until you've eaten with the locals and seen the landscape while falling from fourteen thousand feet."

"Sounds like he lived every day to the fullest."

"Yep, every moment. Mim always said he wrung the possibilities out of every day. What are the words to that John Lennon song? Something like, 'Life is what happens when you're busy making other plans.' I think that's what Will was trying to tell me, but I just didn't get it." She was quiet for a moment, needing to say something that had been on her mind; something she'd been working up the courage to say. And that moment that was about to happen in the shed made her even more determined. "Nox, I need you to make a deal with me."

"Yeah? What's that? Should I be worried?"

She felt suddenly very shy about what she was about to ask. Say it. "We need to make a deal," she took a deep breath, "that nothing will ever happen between us."

She heard his intake of breath at her strange request and held her own as she waited for his response. In the stark moonlight, she found herself spellbound by his eyes.

"If that's what you want."

"That's what I want." she said, her voice distant to her own ears.

"Okay. It's a deal."

"Put your hand over your heart and swear it."

He put his hand over his heart and looked into her eyes. "I swear on my heart that nothing will happen between us." *Can eyes leave a mark on your soul?* His eyes captured and held hers so it felt more like he was declaring his love to her, when in fact he was pledging to stay away.

Dazed, she shook her head and opened her mouth to repeat the vow.

"Smells like someone's holding out on me. Who's got the Corona and what's the occasion?"

They both turned towards Pete's penetrating voice. The spell was broken.

"I do. Here." Nakita responded more brightly than she felt as she passed the smouldering cigar to Pete. "Apparently I'm going skydiving."

Pete took the cigar and puffed away as though it were second nature. "When you go, you'll meet Rob. He's a good friend of mine; owns the place. He's one of my best customers, he'll look after you." Raina nodded in encouragement, her straight, white teeth reflecting in the dark, "It's not my cup of tea, but it's worth trying. Only way to find out if you like it or not is by giving it a go."

"Have you done it, Pete?"

"Hell no. I prefer solid ground." He patted Raina on the thigh. "Rai keeps my feet firmly planted, don't you, Rai?"

Till well past midnight, the four of them chatted around the fire. Nakita was curled up, content to watch the slowly dying embers, relieved to have had that conversation with Nox. It made her feel safer somehow. Yet, a tiny splinter of doubt sat uncomfortably in the region somewhere between her belly and mind. It bothered her that Nox had sworn so easily—but she hadn't verbalised her own vows. What troubled her more, was that she was searching for a way out of a vow she hadn't even made, but knew she must keep.

CHAPTER 19

*N*ox looked down at the fresh-cut flowers in his hand; unable to deny to himself any longer; he had a thing for her—a little infatuation. Emmylou was still at preschool and he was supposed to have been on the other side of the city picking up supplies, but halfway there his supplier had cancelled, giving a woeful excuse as to why he could no longer meet with him. It was frustrating. Nevertheless, since he'd rearranged his appointments to free up the day to make the trip, he was hoping to catch her since they hadn't crossed paths much over the last week. She'd been at uni a lot and apart from working, he was using all his spare time on his artwork. Now, here he stood; the bunch of flowers looking out of place by his tattooed forearm. He was in deep water.

What are you doing, Nox? Shit.

She was taking over his mind every sleeping and waking hour, all the while he had to pretend she didn't affect him. He had to stop replaying every scene; stop contemplating those lips. He'd bought the flowers from the markets on a whim, the deep purple irises contrasting with the red roses, reminding him of the contrasts within her personality. Just when he thought he had her pegged, she'd surprise him all over again. He paused for a moment, contemplating whether he should chuck them in the bin. No, she deserved them. She did so many things for him and Emmylou every day; he was just showing his appreciation.

Yeah, bullshit, that's all you're doing.

The house was quiet, which wasn't unusual considering she was most likely studying. She wasn't expecting him back till evening, but why were the kitchen curtains drawn? Maybe she had a headache? He opened the door, sucked in his breath and pulled up straight. Wearing only an emerald green satin bra and underwear set with lacy black trimming, her flaming red hair spilled loosely in waves down her back. She tapped away on her laptop, humming along to whatever she was listening to as she sat at the kitchen table facing the backyard, totally oblivious to his presence. He stood stock-still, rooted to the spot, with no idea what to do. Part of him thought he should get the hell out of there before he was detected. The other part was utterly hypnotised by the image in front of him; her curves, gorgeous in all the right places.

Something in the atmosphere must have changed. Perhaps it was a cold draught when he opened the door, or maybe the heat emanating from his body, but she turned and stood bolt upright—suspenders, stockings, red stilettos. His eyes travelled down and back up again over the curves and valleys of her body. He was only brought back to reality when she reefed her earphones out and attempted to cover herself with her hands. He wasn't sure who felt more like a deer in the headlights.

"What are you doing here?" she demanded, her lips painted a deep scarlet like the roses in his hand.

"I was going to ask you the same thing," he croaked.

His eyes roamed over her as though needing to be quenched. Hers were wide open in dismay.

"Go!" She squeaked.

He looked down at the flowers in his hand; everything seemed to be in slow motion. "These are for you." He walked over and put them down on the kitchen bench before turning and leaving without another word.

$$\sim$$

He came home fairly late that night, waiting till he knew Emmylou would be asleep, not knowing what he would walk into. Most likely Nakita was going to be pissed that he'd seen her in her lingerie. After leaving, he'd driven straight to the gym in a daze and worked out long and hard, trying to block images of her out of his mind. He couldn't for the life of him figure out why she was dressed like that. He'd already seen glimpses of the other side of her. On one hand, she was totally neurotic and proper; overthinking everything and maintaining an outward wall of composure; yet just below the surface lingered a volatile, barely contained part that seemed to want to break out; a part of her that could do a list of things that were the last things she'd ever want to do; a part of her that would...

Stop thinking about her.

After an intense workout, he went to Pete's for a beer. Pete seemed to have a radar for when something was amiss. As they leaned over the guts of a '69 Mustang Pete said, "Alright mate, something's up. Come on, out with it."

In the end, he couldn't help himself. He told Pete. Pete had spluttered on his beer. "Hey, maybe she turns tricks to put herself through uni?" When he saw Nox's face, he was more serious and suggested she was trying to seduce him. Nox made it clear how shocked she was, and just so Pete didn't get any other ideas about her, he let him know she was a virgin. That shut him up. After that, he made no more suggestions and went quiet, except to slap him on the back. "C'mon buddy, let's go down the rifle range and shoot something."

Deciding it was best to act as if all was normal, Nox went to the fridge and pulled out his dinner. Next thing he knew, she was standing there in sweat pants tucked into fluffy socks and an ugly, oversized brown woollen jumper that looked like it may have been a moth-eaten hand-me-down from her dad. It was as if she'd gone out of her way to appear her frumpiest. But he knew what lay beneath.

She stood there looking at the floor, her arms folded across her chest.

"Hey." She rubbed a spot on the floor with her pointed toe.

"Hey." He continued to unwrap his dinner, waiting for her to speak.

"Emmylou's asleep."

He glanced up. She let out a deep breath. "This is so embarrassing." Her hands were encased in her jumper as she rubbed her cheeks. "Okay. I've just got to say it. What you saw earlier was me trying to write."

"Yeah, I gathered that. You always do your uni assignments dressed like that?"

She gave him a look with delicious brown eyes that said, 'take me seriously,' but she still couldn't maintain eye contact.

"I'm writing a novel. It's a murder mystery... well, a romantic murder mystery." He nodded, as if that explained everything. The microwave pinged. He didn't move. "Oh, I sound so stupid. I'm so embarrassed." She turned her face from him.

"How about we sit down?" He suggested.

She walked over to the lounge and sat across from him, her face burrowed in the sleeves of her jumper. "Right. I'm just going to say it," she took a deep breath, "I have this novel I was writing a couple of years ago, but I just stopped. I got too busy, and it didn't seem like a good use of my time. But the other day, after seeing you, Pete and Raina all doing what you love, I kind of felt jealous. It got me thinking I need to rediscover what I'm really passionate about," she paused. "I guess that doesn't explain the other bit... what I was wearing..." He watched as she bit the corner of her bottom lip and tried hard not to let his face betray his amusement. "The thing is, I totally suck at writing the love scenes, probably because... well, you know. So sometimes I get dressed into something, um... appropriate, and it helps, I think?" She put her face back into her hands and after a few moments peeked up at him, bright red. "Say something," she moaned.

Oh crap, what do I say? He knew what he wanted to say and do. But he didn't know what she wanted him to say or do.

Women.

"I don't know what to say. Really, I guess, ah, it makes sense?" But the image he had permanently tattooed on his brain had nothing to do with writing. She gave him a look of dissatisfaction. "I could help you work on the love scenes if that would help?" She arched an eyebrow at him. "I mean, strictly from a writing point of view, of course. But if the sexy lingerie thing is working for you, just stick with that," he offered with a grin. She threw a cushion at his head. Making light of it seemed to be working. "Or you could just write, and I'll proofread over your shoulder?" This time she stood up and attacked him with a cushion. He had her down on the floor in seconds, tickling her till tears rolled down her face and she begged for mercy. Her hair fell from its messy bun and splayed out in a fan behind her. She looked up, her eyes sparkling, her cheeks flushed pink from laughing.

He'd made a vow to her. He needed physical space—fast. He moved to the safety of the lounge.

There was a moment's silence as she sat up, adjusting herself. "Thanks for the flowers, by the way. They're lovely."

"I reckon those flowers wilted today in the presence of your beauty."

"Well, count yourself lucky. No other man has seen that much of me."

"Believe me, Nakita, I've been counting myself lucky all afternoon. I have a replay button in my mind, you see." He tapped the side of his head. She launched herself at him again, attacking him where he sat. This time he pulled her onto his lap and let her wrestle with him, knowing all the while they were on dangerous ground.

"Do you think I'm crazy?" she asked, breathless, her hands coming to rest on his shoulders.

"A total lunatic," he answered, trying to regulate his own breathing.

Oh man, she's straddled over me and her lips are so close. A change in the atmosphere sparked and the air between them ignited. Her body was luscious, pressed against his, and it was only natural for him to rest his hands on the curve of her hips. He stopped breathing as he watched her eyes travel over his face and pause momentarily at his lips. Her mouth opened slightly; her breath catching, eyes widening. She suddenly shifted off him, snatching her hair band off the floor and tying her glorious hair back. Some primal part of him couldn't help feeling satisfied, knowing that he had that effect on her. He needed a shift of focus.

"All jokes aside. I reckon it's great that you're sinking your teeth into something you're passionate about. I mean, you're so into books and writing, why not pursue something more along those lines? I know it cliché, but life is short, why not do something you love?" He picked up his guitar and began strumming it. "You know, I was looking at the paper at lunch the other day and I'm sure I saw a job going at the library you love so much."

"Nox, I've been working towards getting this degree for years, I will not pack it in now on a fleeting fancy." She stood up, dusting her tracksuit pants with more vigour than necessary. "You just don't understand. Anyway, who are you to talk? It's not like you're really doing anything with your passion. You spend all your spare time working on something you keep hidden under lock and key in a shipping container. You won't even show anyone, what's with that?"

"Fair point, but I'm not spending my time doing something I hate. You talk about financial security, but is that really what it comes down to? Or are you holding yourself to a promise made when you were a little girl?"

CHAPTER 20

The rain, consistent all day, chose right then to emancipate itself from the steel-grey clouds that were closing in as she drove home from Uni.

"Seriously, what next?" Nakita mumbled, straining to see through rain-battered windows, her windscreen wipers working overtime. Finally beat, she pulled over to wait it out, slapping the steering wheel, frustrated at wasting the best part of a day when her uni work was piling up.

It had been a totally crap day on so many levels. First, was the ridiculous lack of parking at uni that meant she had to walk in the pouring rain, having stupidly left her umbrella at home on the front porch. Second, she'd gone in early, having made an appointment to speak with a lecturer to discuss a paper that was due the next day. After a wild goose chase to locate him, she found he wasn't even there. Next, she had the humiliation of filling up a tray of food at the cafeteria, only to realise she'd left her purse at home. Red-faced, cold, wet and with a rumbling belly, she'd left the tray of food and headed to the library to study. The library was packed, humid and noisy, so she'd basically achieved nothing all day.

The final straw came when she made the long trek back to her car through more rain, only to find that her battery was flat. Eventually, after finding a guy who could jumpstart the car for her, the kind deed turned into a hopeful, but very unwelcome pick up opportunity. But the worst part that she couldn't block out of her mind, was seeing Will's old girlfriend from school, Shelley, at the bus shelter snuggling up on some guy's lap. Even though she'd been Will's ex, his death had devastated her. Clearly, she'd well and truly moved on. Turning the air conditioner to demist the window, a pang of guilt overcame her... The past months; the things she'd done with Nox; the fun she'd been having. *How am I any different? Am I moving on already? Am I starting to forget Will?* She'd laughed so much the day Nox wore the Crocs, she'd become so preoccupied with him to the point of even forgetting that it was Will's heart beating in his chest...

Will.

People always said that over time the mental image of loved ones faded. She only wished she could forget Will's face and yet it was perfectly branded into her memory—almost every time she closed her eyes he was there. Almost. There was another face that came increasingly unbidden to her mind. Somehow that face was in competition with Will's now. One face brought her gut-wrenching grief; the other was like a soothing balm on an open wound. She sighed as the rain relented enough so she could see through the windscreen. All she wanted was a long soak in a hot bubble bath and a warm meal. The rest of the night she'd have to dig deep to work on her paper.

Knowing Nox was home as she opened the door, she tried to ignore the quickening thrum of her pulse, her thoughts turning to last night and how he'd looked at her, how she'd nearly succumbed to tasting his lips.

Emmylou was at the table absorbed in her craft, singing, 'Let it go' in her chipmunk voice.

Nakita paused for a moment, watching her. She had some kind of powdery substance all over her, and an operatic expression on her face. No matter how she was feeling, Emmylou never ceased to bring her delight and entertainment.

"Hey, Sweetheart," Nakita said, feeling better just having seen her. She put her handbag down. "What are you doing, Gorgeous?"

"I'm making potions. I'm Elsa."

"Potions? Sounds interesting. Where's Daddy?"

Emmylou didn't answer, clearly too enthralled with her potion making. Nakita could hear the shower running. *Well, that answers that.* Turning to go to her room, something caught her eye, then every organ in her body convulsed at the same time.

Emmylou had one hand in a mixing bowl that was filled with a light grey powder. She'd poured pink and gold glitter into the bowl; but it was the blue and silver urn with its lid carelessly discarded and the ashes spilled all around the table, and on Emmylou's face and clothes that paralysed Nakita. Emmylou reached for the water, humming to herself as she did. She was just about to pour it into the mixing bowl, when Nakita shrieked.

Nox stood with his hands against the tiles of the shower, relishing the scorching water on his sore muscles; he only wished there was more water pressure coming from the shower head. Now that he was better, he'd be able to focus on getting a few jobs done around the house. His eyes snapped open as a blood-curdling scream snapped him from his thoughts. Crashing out of the shower, he grabbed a towel and found himself standing, dripping wet in the living room with what turned out to be a hand towel barely covering his crotch. He tried to assess what appeared to be an ordinary situation. When he'd left Emmylou to shower, she was alone. Now Nakita was home, and everything in the room looked completely normal—except for Nakita. She stood with her hands on either side of her face, her mouth gaping in horror. Emmylou arm was poised in mid-air; her eyes wide on Nakita.

That's when he saw the problem.

The open urn.

The ashes. Everywhere.

"Oh, fuck."

There was nothing else to be said.

Nakita's eyes swept over him, and came to rest on his chest, to the place where her brother's heart beat furiously. When her eyes met his, he couldn't fathom what was in them. Not really sure of what to say or do and forgetting his near-naked state, he stepped towards her with one hand out. "Nakita... I..."

Pale-faced and gulping back sobs, she shook her head and turned. Snatching her bag from the kitchen bench, she left. He stood still for a moment, not knowing what to do. Should he go after her? She probably needed space. Plus, he was butt-naked. He looked at Emmylou, eyes still large in shock.

No, he needed to deal with Emmylou first. She had no idea what she'd done. If the situation wasn't so grim, he'd see the funny side of it. But this was anything but funny.

"Okay, Emmylou... everything's okay." He approached her with his hands stretched, feeling as though he was reasoning with a terrorist. "I just need you to do something for me. Just don't move, okay? Be still like a statue and don't touch a single thing."

"Like on Frozen, Daddy?"

"Yes! Just like on Frozen... Oh, and whatever you do, don't lick your lips!" He kept instructing her as he raced into the bathroom to turn off the shower and grab his clothes. No point putting on clean clothes for the job ahead.

Still standing in the same spot that he'd left her in, Emmylou was trying very hard to stay in position, but it looked like it was taking all her focus.

"Why did Kitty scream, Daddy?" she asked, as he came back in to clean up the mess.

"Well, I guess you could say that the dust in the, the," he wracked his brain trying to think of a word that she could relate to other than urn.

"Lamp, daddy."

"Yes, the lamp... it's... special to her." Realisation dawned on him that to Emmylou's eyes, the urn probably looked something like the genie lamp from Aladdin. She was undoubtedly expecting a talking genie to pop out. It was a wonder she hadn't gotten into it sooner. Come to think of it, he had seen her eyeing it off on a number of occasions.

Scrunching up her nose, which still had ash on its tip, she squinted, inspecting the ashes mixed with glitter all over her hands and chubby forearms. "Are they magic, Daddy?"

What to say?

"Well yes, kind of," he said, eyeing the kitchen chair under the mantelpiece; evidence of her heist.

He had no idea how to clean up the ashes respectfully. It didn't seem right wiping them up with a dishcloth or rinsing them down the sink, so he dusted the ashes off as best he could and took her to the bath, filling it with so many bubbles they reached to her chin. She giggled riotously as he scrubbed her till her skin was rosy all over; totally oblivious to the drama she'd unwittingly just caused.

"C'mon, time to get wrapped up like a sushi roll," he said, wrapping her in the biggest, fluffiest towel he could find, kissing her on the nose and depositing her on the floor of her room. It was their night time ritual. She would laugh, scream and try to wiggle free, then take her high time getting into her pyjamas, stalling bedtime any way she could. Usually he'd help her dress. But tonight she was on her own.

He went to the kitchen and carefully dust-panned the ashes into a pile, pouring them into the glass bowl on the table, still dusted with pink and silver glitter. It was surreal to think these ashes were the very reason that he wasn't a pile of ashes himself. He had no idea how Emmylou's 'potion making' could get so out of hand in a matter of minutes. There was nothing he could do about the glitter, so he poured it all back into the urn and put the lid back on, returning it to its prominent place on the mantelpiece. He didn't know whether he should cross himself or say a prayer; so he just stood there looking at the thing. Not that he had much experience with urns, but it seemed strange that it could be opened so easily. He was tipping that it must have been the kind someone would choose if they wanted to scatter the ashes. Nakita had mentioned nothing about it to him.

He made sure everything was spotless, vacuuming and mopping the floors, not wanting to take any chances. All the while his thoughts were consumed with Nakita. He wanted to be the one to give her the comfort she needed. He couldn't help but wonder what was going to happen now.

Just as Miriam had predicted, the walls she'd so carefully constructed around herself had come crashing down, and he was no longer confident of the place he held in her life.

CHAPTER 21

"*N*akita, pause it. I need a bathroom break. You have to come with me. I'm terrified." Annie unswaddled herself from her blanket cocoon and snatched the remote from Nakita to pause the horror movie. Nakita stumbled after her to the small bathroom that opened off the kitchenette of the granny flat. She'd been staying with Annie, who lived out the back of her mum and stepdad's house. It had been a few days since 'the incident' and she'd pretty much set a routine of drinking herself into a state of oblivion, then watching movies till the early hours of the morning. Sleeping until midday, she'd start the process all over again.

She still couldn't bear to think about what she'd walked in on. The most important person in her world, reduced to a pile of ashes spilled around the table while Nox stood there with nothing but a hand-towel to cover his nakedness; a look of complete dismay on his handsome face. His scar, an angry red line running lengthwise down his chest, a reminder of what lay beneath. It was right then that her brain reduced to a switchboard in overload. She could only walk out. She couldn't let Nox and Emmylou see her completely unhinged. In a state of shock, she'd driven to Annie's house, collapsing into the arms of Annie's mum when she opened the door. Eventually, Annie and her mum got to the bottom of her breakdown and decided it was best she stay for a few days.

Three o'clock in the afternoon seemed like a reasonable enough hour to start drinking. There were more than a few folks at The Gull who started earlier than that. Okay, so it was kind of dysfunctional, but she was well and truly over appearing composed. Being dysfunctional had its short-term benefits, such as not having to face responsibility, not having to get dressed or do one's hair. The fog from being inebriated in the middle of the day until late in the evening gave her the sheer relief of not having to think or feel. With each drink she consumed, she welcomed the numbness that overtook her body; she could understand for the first time how people became addicted to substances.

Life could be so raw, so unforgiving.

While Annie was at work, Nakita was left to her own devices until evening. She tried watching the movies she'd always loved. It wasn't unusual for her and Annie to wile away a day watching old classics like Doris Day movies or BBC period dramas; but right now, they made her feel worse; being either too romantic, when she didn't want to think about romance, or too comedic when she had no laughter in her. Annie's fifteen-year-old brother, Clay, suggested horror, and so in the end, she found her escape in horror movies. In the evenings Annie joined her, albeit very vocal in her disapproval. She lay in bed with the quilt over her face, holding onto Nakita's arm while Nakita sat transfixed. Under normal circumstances she'd never watch horror, she'd have been petrified, but now she was numb.

"Annie, I've been thinking," she said, leaning back on the bathroom doorframe for support, trying to keep her eyes focused when the room seemed to tilt.

"I'm sure this is going to be eloquent," Annie remarked, relieving herself. Nakita ignored her sarcasm.

"Okay, here it is: Life is like a horror movie."

"Life is like a horror movie?"

"Yes, that's it. It really is a horror movie. We're all getting picked off. One way or another, it's going to happen. We don't know how or when, but somehow we're all going to get taken out."

"Where's all this talk coming from?" Annie's eyebrows tugged together in a look that reminded Nakita of a kewpie doll. "Oh bugger, you haven't replaced the toilet roll. Can you pass me one from under the sink?"

Swaying towards the sink, Nakita fumbled to open the doors. "You know, I don't think you should watch horror movies, it's clearly not good for your mental health. How about tomorrow we watch 'Seven Brides for Seven Brothers' or 'Calamity Jane?' They're always good for a laugh, huh?"

"Anyway, I think Nox's dad has the right idea," She plucked unsuccessfully with clumsy fingers to detach the end of the roll. "Did I tell you he's a hermit?"

"Only about five hundred times. Pass it here." Annie motioned for the toilet roll. "What's Nox's hermit dad got to do with anything, anyway?"

"He like—just fishes!" She flung her arms out, not entirely in control of her limbs. "He keeps to himself and that's smart, because everyone we love is going to die and that totally sucks! Just like in a horror movie. One minute you're taking a shower and you're happy singing away to yourself, then the next thing you're being strangled with a shower curtain and you're dead, and there's blood… everywhere."

Annie took Nakita's toothbrush, put toothpaste on it and handed it to her. "Brush."

Doing as she was told, she scrubbed vigorously; talking around a mouthful of toothpaste. "I mean, why would you even bother loving someone or having a family? They're all just going to die." She spat into the basin and rinsed her mouth, her throat constricting. Annie cuddled her from behind, resting her face on her back.

"You would make a dreadful fishmonger, Kit. Now, stop all this talk. I'm freaked out as it is. Let's talk about something positive." She led her back to her queen bed. "Ugh, there's popcorn in the bed. That was my only rule; no popcorn eating in the bed. I already have to listen to you snore and breathe in your fumes all night. It's enough to give *me* a hangover. Now move over."

"Stop whining. I need to snuggle." She wiggled in closer. "You feel nice, but not as good as Nox."

"You slept with Nox?"

Nakita yawned. "No, I slept next to Nox."

"Yeah, that's what I meant."

"Well, it was on our bucket list. We had to."

"How many times did you sleep *next* to him?"

"One night for the whole night and then two other times I just cuddled into him and listened to his heart—well, not his heart..."

"And how many times was it written on the bucket list?"

"Once."

"Did anything happen?"

"No, well, not really... well, stuff kind of happened... but nothing, really."

"Stuff?"

"Yeah, you know, inappropriate touching..."

"Kit, have you considered that Nox may have feelings for you?"

"He doesn't," she said emphatically. "I'm like his little sister now."

"Kit, trust me, if he thought of you as a sister he wouldn't be touching you at all. And what about you?"

"What about me?" She yawned again.

"What do you feel towards him?"

"He's like a brother."

"Okay... and so are you attracted to your *brother*?"

Nakita rolled onto her back, her hands on her face. "If I am, I'm gross."

"So are you gross?"

"I can't be. He has Will's heart. It would be incestuous or unethical, or something. Not to mention just plain weird; you have to admit it."

"It's just an organ—a pump. It fulfills a physiological function, that's all."

"Do you really think so?"

"I do."

"Well, I don't." Nakita pronounced lifting her chin. Annie sighed. They lay there silent for a moment. "I love you, Annie." She added.

"I love you too."

"Annie?" She said after a moment.

"Yeah?"

"Please don't ever leave me, even if I become a hopeless drunk, kill all my brain cells and can't string a sentence together. You're all the family I've got now. You and Miriam and Antony. Well, there is Emmylou, she's like family... and well, I guess Nox... since he does have Will's heart and all."

Annie rolled over. "Oh seriously, Kit, face the other way, your breath stinks. What have you been eating?"

"Clay and I ate garlic and chilli beef jerky, while we watched Silence of the Lambs."

"I don't know what's more disturbing, you eating beef jerky while watching Silence of the Lambs or you watching it with Clay in my bed." Nakita started to drift off. "Kit?"

"Hmm..."

"I wouldn't be a good friend if I didn't tell you the truth. I know you're so confused, but I think you have been for a long time, even before Will died."

"What do you mean?"

"I mean, maybe this terrible thing that happened will set you back on a path to finding out who you truly are and what you truly want out of life?"

"What I truly want, Annie, is for the people I love to stop dying."

"Nakita, I know. Will would want—"

"Annie, just stop." Nakita sat up, suddenly wide-awake and angry that Annie was pushing her, forcing her to think when she just wanted to forget. "Will wants nothing. He's dead, remember? He's more than dead. He's just a pile of ashes spread around my kitchen. Oh, hang on a minute—no wait—that's right, his heart's inside my housemate's body. And who knows where his liver and kidneys are, not to mention his eye corneas!"

Annie sat up, drawing her knees to her chest. Even in her inebriated state, realising she'd made her friend cry, she lurched onto her. "I'm sorry. I'm such a bitch." Her lash of anger dissolved to regret and tears that she hadn't shed in days. "I don't know how I'm supposed to do this... to live with this. I want to forget him, but I can't, and then I feel so guilty if I'm not thinking of him every second... when I laugh, when life starts to feel like it could be normal."

They sobbed in each other's arms for a long time. As she finally fell asleep, she welcomed the momentary respite of enveloping darkness.

～

"You arranged what?" Nakita demanded, as she and Annie pulled into the hospital car park a few days later.

"We are here to cuddle the babies in the NICU," Annie said, unruffled by her tone.

"What's the NICU?"

"The Neonatal Intensive Care Unit. We are going to cuddle the premmie babies. Remember Irene, my Filipino friend? She coordinates the program."

"Cuddling sick and dying babies? I can't think of anything I'd less rather do. I'm not going." She crossed her arms and pressed back into her seat. Annie had been doing her best to get her out of the house the last few days. Nakita had assumed they were going to a café, not the hospital of all places. "No, I've already got plans with Clay to watch the classics. We're starting with Poltergeist and I positively can't wait."

Annie rolled her eyes. "For your information, My Fair Lady is a classic. Colin Firth, plunging into a pond fully clothed, is a swoonworthy classic. Don't put fake blood and a little girl sitting in front of a fuzzy television on the same level as classic." Annie paused, taking Nakita by the elbow. "Nakita, you need to find a better way to deal with this grief."

"Oh, and you think more grief is going to help, do you?" She was angry again. "I'm doing exactly what Will always wanted—I'm letting loose and not controlling life."

"No, Nakita. You're out of control. You're not dealing with life. Look, it was okay for a few days, but now it's just out of hand. You passed out last night for goodness sake. That's not you."

Nakita folded arms tight, unwilling to process her friend's words.

"I was thinking the other night, if Will was to come back and say one thing to you, what would he say?"

"Annie. Don't," she warned. The last thing she wanted to think of right now was what Will would say if they had a last moment together.

Annie was quiet, then climbed out of the car. "Let's go."

Nakita followed a few moments later, slamming the car door behind her. "Annie, you seriously suck." She strode past her towards the hospital doors, her shoulders rigid. *God, how I despise this place.* As they stood in the waiting room of the ward, she tried to comprehend how Annie had managed to get her there. That Annie had arranged for her to come and cuddle babies who were fighting for survival when she could barely deal with Will's death, was beyond her. "Annie, this is insane," she hissed under her breath.

Irene introduced them to Karen, the head nurse who appeared as stern as she was sturdy. After instructing them about hand washing, which Annie already did to a level that bordered on OCD, she took them over to the tiniest baby Nakita had ever seen. The newborn had tubes and wires coming off her everywhere. A nurse was tending to her carefully. Nakita looked at her crib and saw her name was Shae.

"This little treasure is a fighter; she's been with us for a little over three weeks. She's battled every odd against her. At the moment, our biggest battle is getting her to gain weight. She's a NAS baby."

"NAS?" Nakita asked.

"Neonatal Abstinence Syndrome; her mother is a user." Karen showed them how to handle Shae without disrupting the tubes and other apparatus. Nakita couldn't help thinking of Emmylou being born to a drug addicted mother. Something deep inside hitched in her throat. Life was so delicate. The nurse offered for Annie to hold Shae. Annie took her with great delight, cooing and crooning nonsense words.

"I can't believe we're allowed to do this." Nakita said in disbelief. The nurse who was looking after Shae nodded.

"It's a privilege, isn't it? The idea is that volunteers come in and cuddle the little ones and give them human contact. There's been a lot of research to suggest that premmies who have more physical contact, not just their basic needs met, recover more quickly. Human touch releases chemicals in the newborn's brain, so our volunteers come in and cuddle them because, for various reasons, their mums and dads can't be here all the time. Of course, the parents have to give permission first."

"Nakita." Karen waved her over. "I have a little man for you to hold over here. His name is Adam. This little fella is a trooper. He's fought hard and just turned the corner this week." She leaned over the crib. "Hey there, little buddy." Nakita peeked inside and saw not one, but two babies. All at once the air was sucked from her lungs. She braced herself on the edge of the crib, her hands tingling as the room swayed. Karen's voice faded.

Gradually, the room returned to normal, but she felt far from normal. "He's a twin. His little sister, Ava, is having surgery on her bowels tomorrow. She's not doing so well. He could probably go home, but we're keeping him here for her. Together they'll put up a fight."

The hair on Nakita's arms stood on end. She couldn't take her eyes off the babies, snuggled together. They each had a beanie on their tiny heads. Ava was much smaller than Adam, even though he was still so, so tiny. Her skin was yellower, and she just didn't look as well, in general. Adam still had the look of a premmie, but his skin had a better tone to it, his face a little more filled out. They lay on their backs, their tiny fingers entwined. Nakita's breath was heavy to her own ears, as though she'd just run a race. She wanted to get out of there; but it would be wrong on so many levels. If these two little ones had not long been born into the world and were fighting for their survival, who was she to run away from them because she couldn't cope?

"I was a twin," she blurted.

"Oh, you were?" Karen stopped fiddling with medical equipment and gave Nakita her full attention.

She nodded. "I had a brother. His name was Will."

"Oh, I'm sorry for your loss, love. When did he pass?"

"Earlier this year. He was killed." As she uttered the words, disbelief crept over her to hear them spoken out loud; by herself. Karen put a firm, warm hand on her arm; her face full of empathy.

"Then you are just the person to hug this little man and give him advice on how to look after his little sister. You understand the connection between twins." Nakita nodded, barely holding it together. Karen reached into the cot and pulled him out, smiling and chatting to him the whole time. "You sit over there, darling, and I'll pass him to you." She nodded to a single blue lounge-chair facing the window; a cosy spot in filtered sunlight. Nakita sat down as instructed, her breath coming out in tiny gasps, not unlike Ava's in the crib.

"Open your shirt a little, sweetheart. The skin on skin contact will keep him warm and help him feel the connection even more." Karen put Adam into her arms and positioned the side of his face and body into her chest, then huddled a nest of flannel blankets around him. "I think you'll find that just holding him brings strength to you and to him. Cuddling him will heal you like nothing else. There's something special about holding such a tiny, defenseless baby in your arms and knowing that their little bodies are fighting every inch of the way to be here. It's the human spirit." Letting out her pent-up breath, Nakita allowed the lines of her body to relax along Adam's. Karen gave her a satisfied smile. "Sing out if you need anything, love."

Nakita looked down at Adam's face in her arms and couldn't hold it in any longer. Tears rolled down her cheeks and neck, onto her chest where Adam lay, curled into her. She let them flow. The tears weren't the hopeless kind; they were the healing kind. With sudden clarity, she knew, with this little boy in her arms, and his sister fighting for her life, that it was time she stopped fighting the healing. It was time to be brave and let the healing come, even though it hurt so badly.

Stroking the downy softness of Adam's cheek, she put her finger in the little divot of his tiny chin, smiling through tears at the faces he pulled. When he opened his barely focused eyes and looked up at her, she chuckled. He was utterly adorable, a tiny beacon of hope.

She started talking, hesitantly at first, but then it overflowed. While he lay there, content in her arms, she didn't even know exactly what she said, but she told him about the beauty in the world and all the things he was going to see, about how annoying sisters could be and how to be a good brother. Then she started telling him stories about Will. She marvelled at his minuscule hand wrapped tightly around her finger, and in that moment she knew that she'd been given a precious gift from just holding Adam—the courage to embrace the pain and to live on in the hope of each new day. She said a silent prayer for him and Ava, thanking God for her own life and the opportunity to have Will as her brother, even if it had been for a short time. There never could be enough time with loved ones—only forever would do.

After a while, Adam drifted back to sleep. She didn't know how long she stayed, truly contented, deep inside for the first time since Will had died. Realisation came, that all those years she spent thinking she had been the responsible one, looking after Will—how wrong she'd been—all along he'd been the one looking out for her, guiding her back to her truth. He was a mirror, reflecting part of her true essence that she'd lost somewhere along the line.

Karen eventually came back and said it was time for Adam to rejoin his sister for a cuddle. She handed him back reluctantly, with many kisses to his brow and a whisper of thanks in his ear. Karen settled him on his side as Ava was on hers. In their sleep they nestled back together again, their bodies intertwined as one, giving strength to each other. She stood and watched them for a long time. Annie joined her and took her hand, lacing their fingers together. Nakita looked at her through a teary smile and mouthed the words, 'Thank you.'

It was time for her to move forward and start dealing with her loss instead of holding onto it tight with two fists and compressing the pain down deep.

It was also time for her to face Nox.

CHAPTER 22

"Kitty!" Emmylou clomped up the stairs and threw herself at Nakita, arms around her neck, almost in a stranglehold. "I'm sowwy I played with your special dust."

"That's okay sweetheart, Kitty just needed to have a little time out." A rush of love hit Nakita; she rained kisses all over her upturned face. Emmylou took both sides of Nakita's face in her hands and looked into her eyes. It was her childlike way of imparting something to Nakita she couldn't put into words. In that moment, she wished with all her heart that she could somehow lay claim to Emmylou as her own.

She could sense Nox before she saw him. He stood in the doorway watching them. Resisting the urge to throw herself into his arms, she held Emmylou even tighter. He was incredibly handsome in an army-green T-shirt that moulded to his chest, revealing his tattoos, which she had to admit, she now found incredibly sexy. The last time she saw him, she was shaken as much by his physique as anything else—his broad chest with the red line down the middle, tattoos snaking up around his shoulders and one side of his neck with another across his taut abdomen. He was all man.

She turned back to Emmylou. "There's a surprise for you on your bed."

"Yay!" Emmylou skipped off. This left Nox and Nakita alone, staring at each other. Her belly clenched. A muscle twitched in his jaw and she had the strongest desire to reach out and take his face in her hands like Emmylou had done to her.

"Nox, I'm so sorry for walking out on you. I just lost it there for a few days... well, more than a few really."

His calming green eyes met hers. "You don't need to apologise for anything, Nakita. Your reaction was perfectly understandable." She watched his throat work as he swallowed. "Remember at the beginning we agreed that as soon as you got uncomfortable that we would move out? I think it's time Emmylou and I started making plans—"

She stepped forward. "No. Please don't. That is, unless you want to. It's just that Emmylou and well... *you* have come to mean a lot to me, you're like my family in a way." She wrung her hands, distressed at the very thought of them leaving. "If you will, I want you to stay. I just needed time to sort through everything. The truth is, it had nothing to do with what happened with Will's ashes. It just triggered something that was already below the surface. It's been building for some time, but I guess I was distracted."

"Okay, then, we'll stay, but only if you accept that I pay our way from now. My pride rests on me paying our way. Deal?"

"Deal." She moved closer and slipped her hand into his. It wasn't so much of a handshake as a clasp. He pulled her into his warm embrace so that her head rested against his chest.

"I missed you." His voice was barely audible, his cheek against her forehead.

"I missed you too," she murmured. His heart beat firmly by her ear. Standing in his embrace felt so right; his musky scent had become familiar somehow. His hand stroked her hair down the length of her back. She shivered.

"What you said about being like family. I feel that too," he said tentatively. She pulled away slightly to look up into his face, touched by his words. He looked like he wanted to say more. The muscle in his jaw tensed like he was conflicted. Maybe he wanted to leave? She knew it was selfish, but she needed them to stay. His strong hands took the sides of her face gently as he leant forward and kissed her forehead, tenderly, as though she were something precious.

Emmylou came noisily clip-clopping up the hallway in the plastic, light-up, high-heels that Nakita had bought her. She entered the room in a flouncy dress, a lopsided tiara and plastic necklace; struggling to pull on her long, satin gloves. Nakita couldn't help but smile at Nox.

By a strange twist of fate, they'd both been given a second chance at family and the last thing she was going to do was mess it up.

Taking her time helping Emmylou get ready for bed after dinner, Nakita read a few of her favourite Pamela Allen stories. As she tucked Emmylou in and listened to her say her prayers, Emmylou looked up at her with luminous eyes.

"Kitty. I missed you when you went away. I cwied to daddy evewy night."

"Oh, sweetheart. I'm so sorry. I just had a little problem I had to work out."

"Is the pwoblem better now?" she asked, in her innocent way.

"Let's just say it's getting better. Now roll over and I'll tickle your back." Emmylou did as she was told and Nakita watched her little body relax as she stroked her, a rush of love and tenderness surging through her.

"Kitty?" her voice was muffled and sleepy.

"Yeah?"

"Will you be my mummy?"

Nakita's heart squeezed. What was she to say? "Oh honey, your daddy has to choose your mummy. Think of me as your big sister or aunty, and daddy is like... my big brother." Emmylou nodded as though she understood, yawned, then drifted off straight away. Nakita turned to see Nox leaning in the doorway. She could tell by the brooding expression on his face that he'd heard their conversation. He walked over and bent down to kiss Emmylou on her forehead.

"I'm only just starting to realise how much she's missing out on not having a mother. She really missed you." He looked down at Emmylou sleeping, his hands on his hips.

"I missed her too." She tucked the blankets around her chin and kissed her forehead. "When I was away, I had a revelation. It took an encounter with... someone special." She wanted to keep her precious encounter with little Adam to herself.

Nox shifted, and she could feel his eyes level on her face. "Anyway, it made me realise that I haven't been letting the healing process take place, but I think I'm ready now. I wonder if you'd help me do something? Are you free tomorrow?"

"Yeah. I can be free," he said, his eyes on Emmylou.

"Thanks. There's something important I want to do and I need you to be there."

Nox woke from a frustrating sleep. All night, he dreamed about a woman he couldn't have. The dream was on repeat. A change had definitely taken place in her; she seemed to be centred somehow. He was more at ease knowing she was back home, but with that came the familiar tug of yearning. He'd been so worried about her state of mind when she'd walked out. As much as he'd wanted to comfort her, some part of the grieving process could only be sorted through alone.

He wondered who she'd had a 'special encounter' with. It made him sick to the guts. Damned if he was going to keep moping around after someone who had him in some kind of brother zone. If that was the only future she saw, then he guessed he either had to take it or get out of her life altogether. Somewhere along the line he forgot he'd made his own commitment to himself that she was off-limits. He needed more mental resolve or something else to distract him.

He looked out of his loft window. She was already out in the early morning sun, feeding scraps to the chooks, her hair in a loose ponytail, hanging down her back. She wore her old dressing gown that did nothing to hide her shapely calves. She smiled down at Emmylou climbing out of the chook pen with a freshly laid egg in her small hands, a huge lopsided grin on her face as though she'd just discovered treasure. Turning, the sun lit up her red hair like the burnished coals of a fire. Tearing his eyes off her, Nox flipped onto his back.

This is going to be a lot harder than I thought.

He headed down for breakfast and some time later Nakita walked out in a simple blue dress that reminded him of the fifties. When he saw the dress, he knew they were up to something special. He ate his Weetbix silently, watching as she took the urn from the mantelpiece and turned to look at him.

"So you know how I asked if you could join me for something special today?" He nodded, his mouth full. "Well, I decided that today is the day to scatter Will's ashes."

Inhaling sharply, his breakfast went into his windpipe and he erupted into a full-blown coughing fit, causing tears to roll down his face. They'd never talked about the cleanup process of the ashes, and never in a million years did he consider that the ashes were going to be scattered. Apart from ashes, only he knew that the urn was full of pink and silver glitter. It was going to look more like the sprinkling of ashes of someone who was a regular at the Mardi gras.

A few hours later he was standing at what had been Will's favourite beach. For early spring, the weather was spectacular with perfectly sized waves rolling in, leaving him determined to get out on his board as soon as he could manage it. But right now wasn't the time for daydreaming about surfing. Standing with the small gathering of people that she'd invited to the informal ceremony, he was sick to the guts that she would be upset with him for returning the ashes back into the urn after they'd been played with and dust-panned off the floor.

What was the protocol in these situations, anyway? She seemed so at peace and had a quiet joy about the whole damn thing that he just had to keep his trap shut and hope for the best. Maybe she wouldn't notice?

As the warmth of the spring sun gazed down on them and the waves chanted their rhythmic beat on the shoreline, they stood in a loose huddle by the rocks, barefoot with the sand between their toes. They paid their respects as breakers rolled in and sucked back out, gurgling and slurping at their feet. Nakita invited everyone to say a few words or to share a story if they wanted to. There wasn't a dry eye as Miriam, a quietly spoken, teary Antony and finally Toby, shared special tributes. The term bitter-sweet had a whole new significance to Nox now. The awe mingled with dismay that he still felt at being the beneficiary of Will's heart, gripped him once again.

With her long hair swirling loosely in the salty breeze, set on fire by the sun, Nakita took a deep breath, her brown eyes glistening with tears as she spoke a tribute from her heart.

"If you think of just about anything beautiful, there's always light. Light is warm, it's comforting. It captivates the soul. Light extinguishes the darkness. It gives life. It's the first thing we see when we're born, the last thing we see when we die. Light is magnificent, breathtaking. That was who Will was to me. He was my light in a world that sometimes grew too dark. He drew people in with his light. When his light went out, it took my breath away. In the words of W. H. Auden, 'He was my North, my South, my East and West.'" She closed her eyes for a moment, the tears streaming freely down her face. "These past months, I've been struggling to let go of my brother. Will may not be here in the flesh, but his light lives on inside each one of us, in the memories we have of him. Just as I feel the sun rays on my skin, I feel his presence. I have to choose to see him; to feel him in each moment. And it has to be enough. It is enough." She lifted the lid on the urn and released his ashes into the gentle breeze. "Goodbye Will, thank you for always giving us your light."

There was a pause, followed by a collective gasp of delight as the sun caught the glitter, and the glitter and ashes caught in the breeze, shimmering off into the elements that would continue their ceaseless rhythm. Nakita turned and looked at Nox, a radiant smile lighting her gorgeous face. With a stab, he realised an inconvenient truth: At some point, he'd fallen hopelessly in love with her.

CHAPTER 23

*E*xhausted from the emotion of the past weeks, Nakita awoke from a peaceful sleep when she felt her toes being tickled. She knew it wasn't Emmylou, since she'd stayed the night at the Belle's. Opening her eyes, Nox was at the end of her bed. *Ugh. How did he always look so good in the morning without trying?* Wearing a simple fitted white T-shirt and black jeans, his hair tied back, he stood there smiling down at her.

"You slept through your alarm," he said. She rubbed her face with a groan, pulled her doona up higher and rolled over, determined to go back to sleep.

"Go away, I've changed my mind," she said crankily, knowing deep down there was no way she would truly let herself off the hook. Today she was going to face one of her greatest fears—skydiving. After scattering Will's ashes, she decided that doing something he loved was the ultimate way of celebrating his life.

"I'm heading out for a bit. Eat a light breakfast. We'll aim to leave in forty minutes."

"And where are you going?" she asked as he headed out her bedroom door.

"You'll see."

After showering, she forced herself to eat some toast and Vegemite, opting to not have her usual cup of tea since her belly already felt queasy at the mere thought of what she was about to do. Quivering with nervous energy, she went outside to check the sky, hoping that the meteorologist had got it wrong and that it was going to be a horribly overcast day instead of the sunny day that had been forecast.

Damn. It's going to be a stunning day. Oh my gosh, I am really going to do this. I can't believe it.

Minutes later, she watched as he rolled in on a sleek motorbike in black jeans and a leather jacket, every bit the sexy tattooist she met that first day at Ink Guild.

"Whose is that?"

"She's mine,"

"She's yours?"

"She sure is." He patted his bike.

"Why did I not know you had this, umm her?"

"I had her stored away in Pete's garage. I don't get to ride all that much these days with Emmylou and all."

"Well, that's wise considering they are a death trap. You'd be better off not to ride it at all. Are we going now?"

"Yep." He walked over holding out a helmet to her.

"You're not expecting me to ride on that?"

"Yes, Nakita, this is our form of transport today."

"Look, I know motorbikes are on the list." She spoke fast; hands out, refusing the helmet, "but honestly, they scare me to death. Skydiving seems crazier, but statistically, I'm more likely to die on that thing—her—than I am skydiving. This is not about fear, it's about common sense. I've heard of too many people who have either died or sustained permanent injuries on these things."

"Wonderful speech, Nakita and yet..." He pushed the helmet into her hands, his secret dimple flashing at her. "It's on the list. Deal's a deal." She scowled at him. "Go get a warmer jacket."

Resigned, she squared her shoulders and stomped up the stairs. "Don't even get me started about the poetry recital that I'll be escorting you to."

Moments later, she was seated behind him, clinging in sheer terror as he drove down the lane, through the short main street of Dorley Point and up the steep, narrow road that laced around the mountain. Thankfully it was early, and there was less traffic on the road as they passed through town to the back roads that led to the vineyards. Forcing her body to relax, to her surprise, she found herself enjoying the thrill of the meandering, stunning drive through the spectacular countryside. Still, she kept her arms wrapped tight around his waist, moulding herself to the broadness of his back; never in her wildest dreams had she expected to find motorbike riding peaceful and even kind of exhilarating.

When they pulled up outside the skydiving hangar, her legs began their involuntary shuddering all over again. Nothing about skydiving appealed to her, except that it was something Will had loved.

"Okay, we're up. Let's do this." James, her skydiving instructor, motioned to her after taking her through the drill a few times; it was as if someone had knocked the air out of her. She walked on leaden feet to the Cessna. Her legs faltered. *I can't do this.*

"Nakita?" She turned. Nox stood by an old plane used for practice. He smiled and saluted her; the simple action reminding her of something Will would have done. She saluted back with a shaky grin. Then, unable to resist, she ran over to him and hugged him tight. On a whim, she kissed him on the left side of his chest, over his heart. "That was for Will—this one's for you," she kissed the underside of his jaw; lingering a moment as he held her close in his embrace. She pulled away. "Thank you, Nox. I couldn't have gone through half of that list without you. Actually, I couldn't have survived these last months without you, and that's the truth." He held her chin between his thumb and forefinger and looked into her eyes as though he were imparting strength to her.

"You got this, Nakita. Be fearless."

Everything after that was dreamlike: going up in the plane to reckless heights; the brilliant, endless blue of the sky, puffs and wisps of clouds with sun rays bursting through; the feeling that she was being beckoned upwards into the heavens, suspended in time. There came with it a tingling awe—Will had done this. All the while she was struck by a combination of deep, abiding sorrow and delirious joy in who he was; that she'd been lucky enough to have twenty-four years of her life with him. She stood at the edge of the plane's open door, with the wind and the roar of the engine howling in her ears.

"This one's for you, Will," she said, under her breath, ready to take a leap of faith. The next moment, with James propelling her from behind, she released an almighty shriek and was suspended in thin air, falling from the clear blue.

She let go.

Several hours later and her legs still shuddered sporadically. She and Nox spread out on a picnic blanket under a twisted, oak tree gnarled by the passage of time. Nox had suggested they have lunch in the wineries since they were in the area. Having come across a charming vineyard tucked away from the usual tourist traffic, they decided to settle in for the afternoon with a bottle of wine, a plate of fancy cheeses and antipasti.

"To overcoming fears," Nox proposed. Nakita couldn't wipe the smile from her face as she touched her glass to his, still unable to believe what she'd just done. "Do you think you'll ever do it again?" Nox asked, stretching out his long legs.

"Never," she said, widening her eyes. "I'm glad I did it. There's something thrilling about facing your fears, and it has brought me closure, but I never want to do it—like, ever again."

"Will would have been so proud of you, Nakita. I'm proud of you. I've never known anyone like you." He looked off into the distance. "Hey, I have something for you." He jumped up and walked over to the small leather rucksack attached to the back of his motorbike then sat back down holding out a gift, wrapped in purple tissue paper with a floppy yellow ribbon.

"What's this for?" she asked, touched that he'd bought her a gift and taken the time to wrap it.

"It's just something I found the other day in a second-hand bookstore and I thought of you."

Smiling, she untied the ribbon and found a small, hard-cover poetry book. She ran her fingers over the aged cover and opened it carefully. The yellowing pages had several names handwritten in the front cover, only to be crossed out by the following owner. She flicked through. "Oh wow, listen to this:

> *You who demolish me, you whom I love,*
> *be near me.*
> *Remain near me when evening,*
> *drunk on the blood of the skies,*
> *becomes night,*
> *in its one hand a perfumed balm,*
> *in the other a sword sheathed in the diamond of stars.*
> *Be near me when night laments or sings,*
> *or when it begins to dance,*
> *its steel-blue anklets ringing with grief.*
> *Be here when longings, long submerged*
> *in the heart's waters, resurface*
> *and when everyone begins to look:*
> *Where is the assassin?*
> *In whose sleeve is hidden the redeeming knife?*
> *And when wine, as it is poured,*
> *is the sobbing of children*
> *whom nothing will console—*
> *when nothing holds,*
> *when nothing is:*

at that dark hour when night mourns,
be near me,
my destroyer, my lover,
be near me."

"Whoa, that's incredible, who wrote that?"

"Let's see... Faiz Ahmed Faiz. This has been translated from Urdu, it's called *Be Near Me*. Such powerful imagery." She held the open book to her nose and inhaled deeply. "Thank you. I love it, Nox."

"It's nothing much and I know it's old, but I figured you kind of like the older ones, since they have that funky smell." He fiddled with a blade of grass.

"I do. And I love how this book has its own history. You know, when I find books that have names in the front like this, I daydream about what the past owners were like, what kind of life they'd lived, that sort of thing."

"Pass it here." He motioned for the book. "Okay, let's see, 'Ingrid Marsh'." He squinted, making out one of the printed names inside the cover.

She settled back on the rug, looking up through the knotted boughs of the old oak. "Oh, she was definitely a seamstress. Tall, angular, mousey hair, a pleasant face with slightly bucked teeth. She lost her husband in World War Two. There was a short, bandy-legged man who lived around the corner whose clothes she mended. He would do odd jobs around her house and helped her remember how to laugh. Oh, how he made her laugh, till her cheeks ached. He was in love with her, but was too shy to tell her. One day, he plucked up the courage to tell her. He bought her a bunch of daisies and declared his love. He was a good man. She could imagine life with him would make her happy again, but just as she was about to say yes, the memory of her husband's hands drifted to her. She hung her head and said, 'I'm sorry, I can't. I have an immense pile of clothes to tend. I really just don't have the time.' He left that day and she never saw him again." No longer lost in her daydream, she turned to look at Nox. He was staring at her, his mouth open. He turned to the inside front cover again. "I can't quite make this name out. Ah, Lennox... Conrad."

She laughed and rolled onto her back again, closing her eyes.

"Hmm. Definitely, sounds like a tattooist name: tall, broad, light green eyes, wears his hair in this knot at the back of his head. He's a man with a past who doesn't realise just how noble he is. He has the sweetest little girl that he dotes on and this amazing artistic ability that he's quite secretive about. Nothing ever seems to get to him. He keeps his cards close to his chest and has this irritating habit of cracking his knuckles."

"What do you see in his future?"

"That's easy. Arthritis from too much knuckle-cracking, a comb-over tied into a knot and a gorgeous teenage daughter who has him wrapped around her little finger. But it won't matter because his sexy green eyes will always set his ageing client's hearts aflutter."

He launched an olive at her, hitting her in the forehead.

"You did not just throw a Kalamata olive at me." She picked up the offending olive, throwing it back at him; he caught it mid-air with infuriating accuracy and popped it into his mouth with a smile. "That bit about you being noble, I take it back."

"Nope, what's said is said and now I know you think my eyes are sexy."

"I did not say that."

"Deny it all you like, Nakita," he teased.

The wine and the sun made her too relaxed to care. "Isn't this just a perfect spring day? Just look at the colour."

"Nice change of subject. But yes, I agree, there's so much light green around, it's—well, just plain sexy."

She pursed her lips and tried to give him her best version of the stink-eye that she'd learnt from Emmylou, but ended up laughing in the process. They lay there for a long while, content by the warmth of the sun, the light breeze on her skin and the sounds of bees humming, busy doing their thing, in a nearby hive.

After a long pause, she sat up. "Nox, there's something I want to tell you. Over the last few days, I've had an epiphany and I've made a decision—a totally crazy decision, I've been too scared to say it out loud because I know that if I do, I'll have to follow through and I'm kind of... well, petrified." She took a deep breath, "So you know that special person I told you about that I had an encounter with?"

"Yeah, who was that again?"

"Never mind. That's not the point. The point is, he made me realise so much about everything. Life is so short and I realised I was holding myself to a promise that I don't think even Dad would hold me to. He would have wanted me to have peace... in myself." She took a deep breath. "I've decided to pull out of my degree. I know I'm so close to finishing, but I think I just need to be radical. Who knows, maybe I'll do a whole other degree at uni? Something to do with writing. Maybe even get a new job? I don't know, but for the first time in my life, I'm throwing caution to the wind. I'm going to pursue my dreams from now on Nox."

"Nakita, I want to show you something on the way home," Nox said a little later as they mounted his motorbike to go home. She'd never admit it, but she was secretly thrilled to be getting back on the motorbike. It felt good to be doing things and making decisions that were utterly reckless; it made her feel so alive; her body, not to mention her mind, tingled with new possibilities, new adventures to be had.

"We're visiting Pete and Raina?" she quizzed, more than a little intrigued when some time later in the evening, they pulled up outside the Belle's home. "It doesn't look like they're home." He didn't respond, but took her hand in his and led her behind him, through the dark to a shipping container. Her heart sped up as she realised he was finally going to show her what he'd been working on all this time. He pulled open the heavy door that welcomed them with a rusty creak, then drew her into the inky darkness alongside him.

"There's a light somewhere... around about. Here." Bright light rudely engulfed the pitch-black, pinching Nakita's eyes. "Here it is. My other workshop. But I guess you already knew that." He stood, legs apart, running his fingers through his hair. Nakita turned around, her eyes still adjusting, trying to take it all in.

Made almost entirely of scrap metal, bolts, screws, springs and moving cogs, countless industrial styled sculptures of all shapes and sizes lined the shelves in the container. Representations of both earthly and otherworldly creatures, living organisms fused with inanimate life forms. A few pieces she recognised from his sketches, some from the drawings she'd taken photos of.

"I can't believe you've kept this to yourself."

"I have another container with larger sculptures along the same theme."

"Nox. I'm speechless. This is far more than tinkering." She gasped, picking up a ladybird that fit neatly in the palm of her hand. For its size, it was heavier than she expected.

"It opens." He slid the wings out so that the ladybird looked to be in flight. Inside were cogs and gears that turned, making the wings move back and forth. "I had my own 'epiphany' today when I watched you sky-dive. You see, I've been watching this amazing girl face all her fears these past few months." Pausing, she turned to him, touched by his words. "Anyway, I realised that it's high time I started facing some of my own. I guess showing you my art is a step towards revealing a part of me that runs kind of deep. In a way, these works are a metaphor for my life; you know, taking junk and making something new out of it? I've been given this second chance and even though I enjoy what I do—this," he gestured, "keeps me awake at night. This is what truly excites me. I guess at some point I've got to take a risk with it, especially since I'm running out of shelf space and somehow I doubt Pete will let me put another shipping container on his property." He ran his finger along the dust on a shelf.

"Nox, I'm so proud of you." Overcome with excitement, she hugged him. "I love these; each design is so unique, so complex and so... thought provoking. I mean, the detail is just incredible," she said, touching an amusing looking angler fish that had been made into a light fitting. The bulb hung forward in front of its face. "This is remarkable."

"You think so?"

"Yes!" she exclaimed, alight with enthusiasm. "What do you mean? You're brilliant. Why do you still doubt yourself?"

"I don't know. I've done nothing with my life for so long and I suppose I've listened to so many voices over the years telling me I'd amount to nothing; you get to believe it after a while."

"You are already someone, someone pretty amazing, even without all this talent."

His green eyes held hers for one, two, three heartbeats. The space where they stood suddenly felt too small, too intimate. His presence occupying all her senses.

"Thanks. That means a lot."

"It's just the truth, Nox." She broke eye contact and moved past him out of the danger zone to distract herself with another shelf of extraordinary creations.

"I have something else for you," he said, after a while. She turned to see him take something from his jeans pocket. "I was going to give it to you earlier, but then I realised it was a copout and I needed to bring you here." He held out a long chain from his closed hand. A heart-shaped steam punk pendant dangled from the end. The mechanically inspired cogs and gears overlaying it, gave it an industrial feel, and yet there was a delicacy too. A red stone that appeared to be a ruby was cleverly placed off centre so that the light shone through, giving it a hint of romance. She reached out almost hesitantly and touched it. "Nox, it's exquisite," she breathed, unable to lift her gaze from the pendant. "But I don't understand... what is it for?"

"It's for you. I've been working on it for some time. You'd be surprised how long all the detailing takes."

"I know, but why?" She wasn't even sure what she expected him to say.

"I don't know. It just came to me." He looked so vulnerable, even boyish, as he stood there. "If you don't like it. It's okay, I understand. The style isn't for everyone." He closed his fingers abruptly over the pendant and it disappeared in his fist.

"No, no," she moved towards him and took his fist in both her hands, opening it gently, "I love it. I want it. I just don't understand why."

His eyes were steady on her.

"There's not always a why, Nakita."

"Can you help me put it on?" she asked, still absorbed by the heart in his hand.

He nodded. "Come here."

She turned, lifting her hair over her shoulder to give him access to her neck. Heat emanated from his body as his arms went around her to lower the chain, his fingers against the nape of her neck as he joined the clasps, sending electrical tingles down her spine. "You have all these tiny ringlets," he murmured, his breath warm on her neck. She had to keep herself from swaying towards him as he took one of the curls between his fingers, tugging it gently. She closed her eyes at the pleasure of his touch. "They're like these tiny corkscrews."

He's too close.

"I've always hated those," she said, forcing her voice to sound light and normal, though she was physically paralysed. "I wish my hair would make up its mind if it wants to be curly or straight." As soon as he withdrew his touch, she felt its loss. He remained behind her, silent and unmoving. Drawing her hair back over her shoulder, she covered her exposed neck; turning, she stepped away from the heat of his body, her focus on the pendant.

"I can make the chain shorter if you like?"

"No. It hangs close by my heart. It'll remind me of Will," she lied.

Something she couldn't comprehend flickered in his eyes as he nodded, his eyes moving to the door. "C'mon, let's go." His face gave nothing away as he moved to the light and switched it off, drenching them both in the pitch black once again.

CHAPTER 24

$\mathcal{H}$e was in no mood for the club. He was supposed to be 'escorting' Nakita because it was her turn to pick up. It wasn't all that fair, since for a smoking-hot redhead, picking up wasn't exactly a challenge. Besides that, it'd been a long, hot day, and he'd spent the whole of it ripping up the rotting timber decking on the back of the house. He was already sore from his first ever yoga class, with Nakita, the day before; the yoga instructor had him in positions he was sure he hadn't been in since the womb. If he was quick enough, he could check Nakita out doing the 'downward dog', but got whiplash for his efforts. All he really wanted was to have a quiet night in with her, watch a movie, even do one of those boring as hell puzzles she liked to do—anything but the club.

Heading downstairs, he pulled out a cold beer, heavy-hearted, even though he knew he should be happy for her. It seemed that her 'encounter' with this 'someone special' had brought her to a point of closure. Pulling out of her accountancy degree was a huge deal, and he knew she hadn't come to the decision lightly. He hadn't seen that one coming, but that was the way it was with Nakita—you never knew what was coming next. They had gone back to the list with a vengeance, and he could see that she wasn't going to ease up until they struck every item through. She'd come to some point of closure, even some old photos of Will and her parents had been returned back to their rightful places on the walls.

The past few weeks flashed through his mind. The evening cooking class he failed after scalding his hand and ballsing up the main. He had no doubt Nakita had a certain level of sadistic, competitive pleasure in his failure, since she was constantly biting back a smile. In spite of his humiliation, because it brought her pleasure, he didn't mind in the least. After that, she'd dragged him along to a poetry recital, which even she finally conceded was boring, except for when they were both trying to contain fits of laughter. They'd been forced to excuse themselves after Nakita, trying to contain her laughter, had ended up snorting.

Following this was a visit to a Jane Austen book club to study 'Pride and Prejudice', which was also as boring as hell—well, for him at least. The group had scrutinised, dissected, and over-analysed the book, all of them way too opinionated. He couldn't understand why they had to go make a club about a book, anyway. A good book was a good book; once you read the thing you moved on. He didn't care about Mr. Wickham's motives for running off with Lydia Bennett—they were pretty clear as far as he could tell. That had been the only thing he'd bothered voicing, but wished he hadn't. When he spoke up, eight pairs of female eyes turned to him and he was asked to justify his opinion. Nakita listened, apparently enthralled with everyone's thoughts, head slightly tilted, her eyes glowing like dark topaz. The only good thing about it was the lead up before the book club. She'd pretty much figured out that he was never going to read it by himself so each night for a week, after Emmylou was tucked up in bed, she'd lain on the lounge room floor and read him a few chapters of Pride and Prejudice. He'd end up stretched out on the floor too, not at all interested in the story it would have bored him to the point of tears if not for the sensual cadence of her voice. When he wasn't engrossed watching her, he was visualising every which way he'd make love to her, given the chance.

He tried to shake his mind clear of the images as he realised he was getting lost in yet another Nakita fantasy. Loving her was an inconvenience, one he'd get over sooner or later. Overcoming unrequited love would probably be on par to coming off any illicit substance. He behaved and acted like a friend or a big brother, but under every act and gesture of friendship, was his stupid, barely suppressed, searing love.

Ugh! I'm even thinking in poetry.

He stood before the fridge, beer in hand, and studied the two 'anti-bucket' lists, side by side. A list had appeared by the other two, attached to the fridge with every available fridge magnet. Nakita must have helped Emmylou write her own bucket list, except hers appeared to be a bucket list of all the things she wanted to do. She'd drawn a little picture beside each one: Dance in the rain, a tea party in the cubby, my own pony, Olaf tattoo, ice skating, Disneyland, fishing with Daddy. He stopped reading at that point, cringing. Even though she didn't share Nakita's DNA, they both shared the same pig-headedness and Emmylou could become a bloody little hellion when she didn't get her way. He stuck the list back on with a sigh and wondered what was taking Annie and Nakita so long to get ready. They'd been in her room for more than an hour, primping and preening; it made him glad to be a bloke.

As though they could hear his thoughts, they both stepped into the kitchen. His beer almost turned sour in his mouth when he saw the red dress Nakita was wearing. It fit her hourglass figure perfectly, skimming just below her shapely thighs. Everything about her was red hot, reminding him of a 1940s pin-up. She and Annie stood arm-in-arm, both in ridiculously high stilettos.

"So whatchya think?" Annie asked. He was certain by her smug expression that she knew exactly what he thought.

"You're fine, Annie." She had something blue on. "But you can't wear that, Nakita."

Annie's face broke into a grin. "Perfect. Let's go." Nakita looked at Annie, panicked.

"I knew I shouldn't have let you talk me into buying this. Redheads shouldn't wear red."

"Fiddlesticks, Kit, you're gorgeous." Annie's eyes bored holes into Nox, daring him to say anything else. "Besides, if you're going to pick up tonight, you'll probably feel more comfortable trying a new persona."

"Hey, let's set the record straight. I'm just getting a phone number. That is all."

He pictured her asking for a guy's number in that dress. "I think she should just be herself," he said, taking a swig of beer. *Since when did I become the voice of reason?*

"Well, I think you should stay out of it." Annie narrowed her eyes at him. If anyone felt more like a sister out of the two of them it was Annie. She was ultra-annoying. Though they did have moments when they put the sarcasm aside and could have a serious conversation.

"Well, I'm not going with her like that."

Annie rolled her eyes at Nox and pulled Nakita's arm. "Fine. Don't come. You'll be a hindrance, anyway."

"Ouch."

"Annie, don't be mean. He's just being brotherly. Come on, Nox, please? I won't have fun without you, and besides, you have to witness me pick up for it to be legit."

"Yeah, well, it'll be the fastest pick up in history," he said under his breath.

Nakita wiggled out the door on her heels, giving him a view of how her dress cut low at the back, and hugged her high, round arse.

"Thanks for looking out for us and being so 'big brotherly', Nox." Annie said, following the direction of his eyes, her voice dripping with sarcasm as she stood beside him with a knowing look.

He averted his eyes. *Annie knows. It's probably obvious to everyone but Nakita. Re-distribute. Re-Categorise. Sister.*

Tonight was going to be like ripping off a Band-Aid. Fast and hopefully painless.

~

It was as bad as he thought, if not worse. Every eye was on Nakita, who was totally oblivious to the attention, since she was so freaked out about having to pick someone up. He remembered why he hated clubs as they stood in line to get in. He hated everything about the atmosphere, the music, the pretence, the smell of stale beer and sweat, which no amount of perfume or cologne could cover. It brought back memories he'd rather forget.

He clenched his fists tighter, reasoning with the impulses that ran through his body as he watched other men ogle Nakita.

Annie dragged a protesting Nakita to the dance floor. *Argh. What are you doing here, Nox?* Sighing, he wandered over to the bar for a drink, wondering how he ended up in love with someone so completely wrong.

"Nox, hey, how you doing, mate?" Of all people, his lawyer, and now mate, was standing at the bar next to him.

"Proctor, hey, man." They shook hands, and Proctor's sheer size struck Nox all over again. Not only did he stand a full head taller, he was all round burlier. With head shaved to the skin, his hooked nose slightly crooked, he looked more like the Russian mafia than a lawyer. Maybe that was because he saw him in the chair getting new tattoos more than he saw him in his office. Although, when he'd seen him in lawyer mode, he was every bit the part. They'd been mates ever since he used his services to get custody of Emmylou.

"How's life treating you?" Nox asked, relieved to have someone to talk to.

"Yeah, well, mate. I hate this place though. Reminds me of why I love being almost forty. I just finished dinner with a few workmates and my daughter texted me to pick her and her girlfriends up to take them to the next venue since I was in the area, but now they seem preoccupied." He nodded towards a bunch of young girls dancing in a group in the corner. "Thought against my better judgement that I may as well have a drink myself, instead of sitting in the car waiting." He clinked his glass against Nox's, wincing as he took a mouthful of whisky.

"I'm with you, mate. This place messes with my equilibrium." Nox felt like he needed to explain why he was there. "I'm just settling a bet with a friend, then I'm out of here." He nodded towards Nakita and Annie. Proctor looked over and his lips blew out into a whistle that Nox couldn't hear over the music.

Easy. Friend or not, he was not letting Proctor have any ideas about Nakita.

"Who's the buxom beauty in the blue dress?"

"What? Annie?"

"Yeah. Is she a friend of yours?"

"Ah yeah, but more so the one in red. Well, she's my housemate, actually." He hoped Proctor couldn't hear the tightness in his voice. Proctor gave him a knowing smile, a gleam in his eyes.

"Stay away from redheads, mate. The redhead's temper is no myth; believe me, my mother was one." Nox wondered if the same was true for Proctor. The guy could be pretty cutthroat in the courtroom, but in reality he was as mellow as they came.

"They're coming over. I'll introduce you to Annie, but she's only twenty-five and probably more suited as a friend of your daughters than for you." Nox jibed.

"Bullshit." Proctor adjusted the collar around his thick neck, "I'm in my prime, mate."

"So age isn't an issue, but hair colour is?" Nox chuckled. Annie and Nakita both arrived breathless and pink-cheeked.

"Whew, this is so much fun. Why don't we do this more often?" Annie exclaimed, Nox could see why a man like Proctor would be interested in Annie. She definitely had something going on. But compared to Nakita, every other woman paled to insignificance. After the preliminary introductions, he could see that Annie had

Proctor's full attention. Sharp as a tack and adept at holding up her end of a conversation, she had Proctor throwing back his head in hearty laughter. When it came up that Proctor was there to pick up his daughter, Annie didn't bat an eyelid; and as the conversation eventually came to a close, Proctor asked if he could see her again. Nox was surprised at just how straightforward Annie was. She was never one to pull punches.

"Look, I'm a straight shooter and I won't muck you around," Annie said. "I'm done wasting time doing the whole indiscriminate dating thing. I'm ready for something more serious. If a man wants me, he will have to work hard for it." Nox watched as Proctor's intelligent eyes honed in on Annie as though no one else were present.

"Annie, I respect you being up front more than you could understand. I'm not a time-waster and I'm not looking for someone who isn't looking for something serious." Annie blinked twice. Proctor had her attention. "Name the time and place tomorrow and I'll pick you up."

"Sure, give me your phone and I'll put in my number."

Proctor shook his head. "Don't bother with that. Tell me your number and I'll remember it."

Nox stood there, bemused. He knew the guy had the gift of the gab, but it was like watching a maestro in action. He was sure if Proctor had asked him on a date, he'd end up eating out of his hand too. But he knew Proctor well enough to know that he said what he meant and meant what he said. In that way, he was a lot like Annie.

"I'll call. Number's on file now." Proctor tapped his temple and smiled. Annie grinned at him, dragging Nakita behind her.

"Call me tomorrow. If you don't, then don't bother at all. Simple as that," she tossed over her shoulder.

"Stay away from redheads, eh? Looks like Annie's broken your balls already," Nox laughed.

"She can have 'em." Proctor raised his glass, then threw back the rest of his drink. His daughter and a bunch of her friends came over to drag him onto the dance floor. He waved them off with a smile.

"Hey, I've been meaning to ask, mate, how's the ticker? You're looking much better than when I saw you last." Nox wasn't surprised at the question since the last time he'd seen Proctor was five months ago when he hadn't been in the best of shape.

"I just had a heart transplant a little while back," he said, glad Nakita wasn't in earshot.

"You're kidding?" Proctor's face broke into a huge grin and he clapped him on the back. "No shit. That's great, man. You must feel like you've won the lottery."

"Yeah, pretty much."

Always. Well, almost always.

"Looks like I'm going to have to make tracks. Sounds like we need to have a quiet whisky and a catch up soon."

"Sounds good."

Proctor paused. "Hey, before I go, tell me something, have you had any weird changes in tastes or habits lately?"

"Nope, not so far."

"The strangest thing, one of my clients had a wife who had a heart transplant; he reckoned her personality changed. Apparently she became a big beer drinker and started eating seafood. Thing was, she'd always hated seafood. He couldn't stand her sudden obsession with country music either. They ended up divorcing. And get this, she later discovered her donor was a country music fan who loved seafood and drank schooners."

Nox nodded. He'd heard a few stories like these before. "Well, fortunately, I've had nothing like that going on, but if I get any sudden desire to shave my legs or cravings for vodka cruisers, I'll let you know," he joked, hoping to put an end to the conversation. Proctor had no idea what a minefield it was.

"That story always stuck with me. Fact is stranger than fiction." Proctor chuckled.

Nox tipped his glass. "I'll drink to that." Proctor threw his back. Nox watched as he walked away; his little anecdote drove nails further into his coffin of senseless hopes and dreams, confirming exactly what he already knew—this whole Nakita thing could never happen. People would always bring up reminders.

Nakita made her way over to him. "Okay, Nox, I'm going to do it right now," she said in his ear over the music.

"Who's the lucky guy?" She pointed discreetly to a guy that looked about her age. He had the squeaky-clean uni boy look about him, Nox imagined she'd go for.

"We met a few weeks back at uni." She fiddled with her hair, squirming as he watched her.

"Hang on a minute, that's cheating." *A few weeks back? It has to be the guy she had her 'special encounter' with...*

Let her go.

"You know what? Go get him. He sounds perfect." He forced a smile.

"Wish me luck." She took a step and faltered, turning back around. "Can I bring Annie?"

He shook his head. "You know the answer."

"Am I okay?" Her eyes pleaded with Annie's, as she yanked the hem of her dress in an attempt to pull it down. It was a lost cause.

"Still perfect."

"Oh... I'm so nervous. What if he refuses to give me his number?" She straightened, tucking in her chin. "No. I can do this. For Will."

Nox shook his head in disbelief. *Women.* He watched her walk away to ask for another guy's number. Just as he expected, she picked the uni guy up in two seconds flat. He watched the exchange, how the kid's face lit up like a Christmas tree, then regained a type of manly composure. Metro-uni-geek was her fit. He was suddenly aware of Annie squeezing him on the shoulder.

"Buck up, Nox. It's just a number." He looked away, hating that she knew. He was about to deny it, but saw Nakita leading her pickup over to them.

"Trent, this is my best friend, Annie, and this is Nox." Nox shook Trent's hand harder than he normally would, pinning him with his eyes. Trent's eyes widened slightly. "Nox and his daughter Emmylou live with me. He's pretty much my adopted big brother," Nakita explained, completely oblivious to what was transpiring.

His intestines twinged at her words. *Big brother.* He figured deep down that's all he really was to her, some kind of proxy, stand in brother. As Trent took in this additional information, Nox was sure it was obvious Nox wasn't feeling as big brotherly towards Nakita as he should. He glanced around the club, feigning disinterest.

Enough is enough. This fixation stops right here.

CHAPTER 25

"*B*e with you in a minute," Nox called from the back room.
Nakita was hoping to catch him for lunch since she'd
hardly seen him the past few weeks. He'd become withdrawn and
distant, either working or taking Emmylou over to Pete and Raina's.
The coolness of the shop was a relief to the scorching sun outside.
There'd been a heat wave the past few days and even in tattered
denim shorts, a singlet and flip-flops, it was still impossible to keep
cool. It was good to get out of the house. She'd spent the best part of
the day working on job applications and was particularly excited
about the position at the local library that Nox had mentioned.
Telling Miriam she wouldn't be at The Gull much longer had been
hard, and yet Mim seemed to know it was coming. As she slowly told
the people who mattered the most about her decision to finish with
her accountancy degree, not only were they supportive, they seemed
to be relieved for her.

She stood for a moment, hearing his low voice, then the sound of
a female giggle from the back room. Her stomach clenched tightly.
*Have I walked in on something? Maybe he's painting someone back
there?* She waited a moment longer, not knowing whether she should

turn and leave. He would never know it was her. He said something else she couldn't make out and stuck his head out through the doorway, grinning back to whoever was in there. When he saw her, his face changed and the smile that had once been for her, disappeared. The dull anxiety in her belly twisted and arched up like a cobra.

"Oh hey, Nakita." His face and voice were devoid of any enthusiasm in seeing her. Another snake twisted up.

"Sorry to... ah barge in, I made you sushi. I thought we could have lunch together if you're free?" She held up the cooler bag, feeling suddenly very foolish to have just turned up like last time.

"Oh thanks, but I just had lunch with Bree. I can eat it later though, which would work out well, since I'm here late tonight."

Bree? Nakita went through her mind, trying to remember a Bree, but came up with nothing. "Actually, I was going to text you to see if you could mind Emmylou tonight? I've got a client coming who can only do nights." He walked towards her and she could see something was off; he was cagey. Her stomach sank.

"Um, I already have plans to go out with Trent..." She watched as he ran his fingers through his hair, a habit that still never escaped her notice.

"Oh yeah, Trent, it's okay, I'll sort her out with some colouring-in or something." He wasn't making eye contact; it was as if they were strangers, less than strangers.

A voice piped up from the doorway. "I can look after Emmylou. I'll pick her up this afternoon and she can play with Jacy." Nakita turned and instantly recognised Bree as a mum from preschool. Emmylou had pointed her out from the car one day. She was quite taken with Jacy, who looked to be a miniature version of her mother.

"Bree, this is Nakita, my housemate." Nox kept his eyes on Bree. *Housemate?* Nakita and Bree smiled politely at each other. Bree looked to be in her early thirties with a perfectly shiny, bleached bob and bright blue eyes. Petite in every way, she didn't have an ounce of fat on her. "Nakita's been hearing about Jacy all week," Nox said, sharing a smile with Bree that didn't include her.

"I don't know if that will work," Nakita said, responding to Bree's offer. She could feel Nox's eyes on her as she continued. "Emmylou has gymnastics at five."

"No worries. I can take her, Jacy's been nagging me to try gym ever since she found out Emmylou does it. I've been meaning to check it out, anyway. If it's okay with you?" Bree looked between her and Nox as though she wasn't sure who she needed to get permission from.

"That'd be great, thanks, Bree." Nox's eyes passed over Nakita back to Bree. With a jab of alarm, she saw his hooded eyes keenly fixed on Bree's pretty features as he gave her one of his disarming grins.

"It's fine with me," Nakita lied. She loved watching Emmylou. "Except she won't have her gym clothes with her."

"That's easy fixed, she can borrow something of Jacy's." Nakita just nodded with a smile that must have looked as pasted on as it felt. "Okay, well, I better head off," Bree said, turning to Nox. Their mutual physical attraction was obvious.

"Are you sure? I never had time to draw up that tattoo you were thinking about."

"Yeah, I stayed longer than I meant to. I need to get to the hardware store to get something to fix a broken tap in my kitchen." She looked towards Nakita. "Hazards of being a single parent."

Seriously? Could you put yourself out there any more? Nakita tried to ignore the pang of dismay in her gut.

"I can take a look at that tomorrow if you like?" Nox offered, his eyes darting to Nakita before fixing his full attention back on Bree.

"That'd be great, actually," Bree smiled.

As she walked towards the door, Nakita couldn't help but envy her trim figure in cargo capris and black singlet. She wondered if Nox went for the well-groomed, petite, blonde type. Her stomach sank. Idiot Nakita. What man wouldn't go for that?

"Hey, thanks for lunch, it was really good." He grinned stupidly.

Nakita shifted from one leg to the other with her cooler bag of sushi, trying to appear the casual observer when she felt anything but. She wondered what Bree had made that was so damn special.

Bree turned and smiled. "No worries and thanks for showing me your artworks. They were great." He waved the compliment off. "Nice to meet you," she added, her eyes sweeping Nakita from head to toe, making her wish she wasn't dressed so shabbily. She usually took a little more pride in her appearance, but it was so hot she hadn't been overly bothered today. Even her hair was in the remnants of a fish braid that she'd slept in.

"Yeah, you too," she attempted to inject some enthusiasm into her voice, "Oh, by the way, if you could take Emmylou to the bathroom before gym that would be great, otherwise she might have an accident."

"Sure, no worries. See yas."

Nox stood and waved her goodbye from the door, looking larger than life. Somehow he seemed taller, broader and more tanned than before. He turned and looked at her, his expression wary.

"She seems nice." The truth was, Bree was nice and probably a perfect match for him. But an unreasonable part of her wished she'd go away. She just wasn't ready to invite another person into the little nucleus that she, Nox and Emmylou shared, no matter how nice they were.

"Yeah, she's really down to earth. Matter of fact, she's just taken over the hair salon in the plaza." He continued straightening furniture in the room.

Perfect. They'll be meeting up every lunch break. "Can I put this sushi in the fridge? I don't think it will hold up in this heat, even in a cooler bag."

"Yeah, sure, pass it here." She gave it to him, trying to make eye contact, but he deliberately averted his eyes from hers.

"So she's getting a tattoo?" Nakita asked.

"Who?"

"Bree."

"Um, yeah. She already has a few... so she tells me." If she hadn't arrived when she did, maybe something would have gone on. Maybe it already had. She wondered which artworks he'd shown her. Maybe a painting on one of the canvases out the back? Maybe she had even modelled for him?

"Are you okay? You don't seem yourself." There was that quaver in her voice again. Looking up from an invoice, he made eye contact for all of two seconds. Exhaling heavily, he lowered the paper.

"Yeah, I just have a lot of stuff to do." His eyes travelled over her briefly, then turned back to the desk. Was he comparing her to prettier, olive-skinned Bree? She'd come to terms with being a pale-skinned, red-head over the years, but right now she felt a lot like she did when she was thirteen, standing in front of her mirror willing away curves, colourless skin and thick red hair. All she wanted was to be stick thin, blonde and have fine, straight hair.

"Sorry, Nakita. I've got to get back to work." He was totally blowing her off. "Hey, thanks again for the sushi." He opened the door, dismissing her. "Have a nice time tonight. Where are you two off to?"

"I don't know, it's a surprise." She couldn't disguise the flatness in her voice.

He nodded and smiled, but it didn't reach his eyes. "Nice. I guess I'll see you later."

"Okay. Bye." She made her way to her car with leaden feet, knowing that it was only a matter of time before he left. In many ways, he was already gone.

"Hey, you look beautiful." Trent handed her a bouquet of pink gerberas. They'd had a few dates together over the past weeks and every time she saw him, he looked sharp and smelled good. He took a lot of pride in his appearance, which was a change to the guys she knew. Will and his mates had spent most of their time getting around shirtless and barefoot in boardies, and Nox looked good with no effort. It was the first time in years that she could picture herself being in a relationship with someone. Trent was intelligent, quick-witted and had her laughing easily. He knew where he was headed in life, which was nice since she had no direction of her own lately. If she was to write her most desired qualities down, which she was sure she had done at different times over the years, Trent ticked all the boxes.

"Thanks. I wasn't sure what to wear since I don't know where we are going." She was dressed in a simple sundress with a cardigan and sandals.

"Well, actually, you're perfect for where we're going. Except you'll be needing this." He produced a blindfold. She'd always hated being blindfolded, but didn't want to make a thing of it. He put the blindfold on her and she had to force herself to sound bright and cheerful. As they drove on, she sensed the direction they were heading, knowing each and every twist and turn in the road. Trent was taking her to the very beach where Will was killed and she was, almost...

Her heart went from an irregular wild beat, to a full-blown sledgehammer against her ribcage. They stopped. Trent opened the car door; she barely heard the pounding surf over the blood thrumming in her ears. Her body was rigid. He took the blindfold off. She kept her eyes steady, forcing herself to smile up into his beaming, clean-shaven face. He has no idea, Nakita. Misreading her eye contact, he leaned in for a kiss. Their first kiss. She pulled away and took a shaky breath. He pressed his forehead against hers.

"Sorry. I couldn't resist. My plan was to save that for later on the picnic rug when we were looking out into the ocean with some wine." Squeezing her fingertips after touching his lips to hers again, he turned to open the boot of his car, pulling out a picnic rug and a basket overflowing with food. He took her hand and drew her down to the beach. She kept her eyes fixed to the sand, knowing she was only metres from the place she was dragged by a rapist and her brother's murderer.

He spread the blanket and lay out a perfect array of food that would normally have been mouth watering, but she wasn't hungry. *Nakita, he's gone to so much effort.* She willed herself to imagine she was at another beach and pushed her anxiety down deep while she listened to stories of his childhood; laughing a little too easily while she drank her champagne quickly, hoping to relax. For a short time, it worked and she could almost forget where she was; but as the late afternoon drew on and only a few stragglers were left in the dimming light, memories of that night started to flash in her mind. Memories she'd blocked out until now.

Reaching over, Trent brushed her hair off her cheek. "Where did you just go? Sorry I sometimes talk too much."

Oh no, what had he been saying? She scrambled to respond. "No, no, I was just admiring the waves." He smiled and shuffled in closer, his fingertips stroking her arm; she resisted the urge to yank her arm from his touch. The shivers that ran through her spine were for all the wrong reasons. He leaned in for another kiss and she returned it with a passion she wasn't feeling. As she did, Trent eased her gently backward onto the blanket.

Rough hands forced her down. She could feel the sharp tip of a blade digging into the soft skin on her side. A voice gruff by her ear, "Now Princess, you can do it my way, or the hard way."

Princess. Princess. Princess.

An eerie orange glow from the automatic lights lit the side of Trent's face.

His face.

The ghostly outline of his face loomed over hers. As he moved in to kiss her again; she gulped in thick air, pushing hard against his chest, his face, anything. She thrashed to get from beneath him. He pulled away.

"Nakita! What's wrong?" She wrapped her arms around herself, unable to quell the shuddering of her body. "Did I do something wrong?".

"No. I just—I don't feel well all of a sudden. It must be the wine."
She put her hand to her forehead.

"You're shaking like crazy."

"I just need to go home. I'm sorry."

They were silent the whole drive home; she couldn't bring herself
to say anything to make it better. When she shut the front door, she
slid to the floor in a mess of hot tears.

Alone. Again.

Nox hadn't come home at all last night. She couldn't shake the
mental image of perfect Bree lying in his arms. Slipping into her
lemon sundress, she went to put food out for Moopsy and Diesel.
Coming back inside, she was taken aback to see him in low-slung grey
jeans and a white T-shirt, plucking her now burning muffins out of
the toaster. Turning, his gaze rested on her.

"Is he...?" he asked in a low voice, nodding towards her bedroom.

"Is who what?" She couldn't disguise the irritation in her voice.

He exhaled. "Trent, I mean. Did he stay the night? I'll just go and
come back later when he's gone."

"What? No. What do you take me for?" She screwed up her nose,
appalled.

"Well hey, I don't know. You were the one who talked about
having an 'encounter with someone special.'"

"But that wasn't him."

"How was I to know who it was?" he said, his hands out.

"Who *it* was, was a newborn infant, struggling for his life in the
neonatal intensive care unit," she said with her hands on her hips.

His dark eyebrows drew together. "A newborn? So Trent's not
here," he said more by a statement than a question. Infuriated, she
shouldered past him to get the milk out of the fridge. "Then why are
you looking like that?"

"Like what?" She looked down at herself. Okay, so her hair was a tangled mess, and she wasn't wearing her bra, which she was sure he couldn't notice, but she wasn't *that* bad.

"Never mind." He turned and looked out the kitchen window.

"Who are you to talk, anyway?"

"What?" He turned.

"Oh, forget it," she frowned, putting two new muffins in the toaster.

"Was your date okay? You seem kind of tense."

"I don't want to talk about it." She could feel his eyes on her.

"Are you okay?"

"I don't want to talk about it," she barely managed, the lump in her throat rearing its ugly head again. A car pulled into the drive and Nox looked out the window.

"Nakita, I hope you don't mind. Emmylou asked Bree and Jacy to come around for a tea party. It all just kind of happened," he said, as if the matter had been completely outside of his control.

"A tea party?"

"Yeah." A car door slammed. "You might want to get dressed... ahh," he averted his eyes.

"Of course, Lennox. It would have been helpful if you told me about five minutes ago. I wouldn't want to appear shabby in front of our special guest now, would I?" She spun on her heel and made it to her room just before the front door burst open.

"Where's Kitty?" she heard Emmylou ask, out of breath.

"She's in her room, she'll be out in a minute." Even from her place by her bedroom door, she could hear the strain in his voice.

"Kitty? Who is Kitty? Your cat?" Came Bree's, overly cheerful, voice.

"No, silly," Emmylou giggled.

"She means Nakita."

"Oh, I was wondering who she was talking about whenever she spoke about Kitty." Bree laughed.

"She's my mummy," Emmylou declared. Nakita leant against the door, her heart squeezing at Emmylou's words.

222

"No, she's not." Nox's voice came flat. Nakita stiffened. Even though his words were true, there was something in his tone that cut her to the core. Throwing on some old tights and a loose grey singlet, she thrust her unruly hair back into a ponytail. *I need fresh air. I've got to get out of here.* Heading to the front door to leave, their laughter drew her out the back as if against her will. She stood in the doorway, their chemistry knocking the breath out of her as she watched on. Emmylou was showing Jacy around the chook pen while Nox was grinning down at Bree, her blonde head thrown back in laughter.

Here she was, an intruder again, but this time in her own home. She didn't fit into their happy family portrait.

"Kitty!" Emmylou raced up the back stairs and body slammed her. Nakita knelt down, cuddling her tightly. Emmylou took both sides of her face as she did when she wanted her full attention.

"Hey, I missed you sweetheart," Nakita said, unable to help but smile.

"Guess what? I went to Jacey's, and we ate pizza, but I wet my pants at gymnastics so now I won't get my reward."

"Oh, did you go to the bathroom before gym?" Nakita looked up at Bree, noticing for the first time that she and Nox were watching them. Emmylou shook her head, her eyes large. Bree stepped forward.

"Sorry, Nakita, I feel terrible. I completely forgot."

"Bree, you don't need to apologise, she's not Emmylou's mother," Nox interjected. Nakita stood slowly, her eyes meeting his at the weight of his comment. He stepped forward. "Nakita, I didn't mean..."

She didn't need to hear the rest. She walked out.

But with each step away from him, came the dawning realisation that she'd very stupidly fallen in love with the man who had her brother's heart.

CHAPTER 26

*A*n hour later, Nox waved goodbye to Bree. He knew she sensed there was more between him and Nakita than just the ordinary housemate situation, but she said nothing and he wasn't about to go into it. As he wandered around the headland to find her, he thought about Bree. She was single, attractive, only a few years older than him, had a daughter the same age as Emmylou and from what he'd seen, was low maintenance. She'd given him all the signals she was interested. He needed to give it a go. Yesterday, when she'd come by the shop, he'd shown her through, then they ate a homemade lunch, the conversation was easy between them as it had been on other occasions. He had to admit, he couldn't help but compare everything she said and did with Nakita, but that would pass; infatuations always did, and so would love.

He hadn't wanted a relationship, but obviously, on some subconscious level, he needed one or else he wouldn't be pining for a woman he couldn't have. Not only that, when he swore off relationships, he hadn't really considered that Emmylou would be so affected by not having a mother figure. Hearing her say Nakita was her mummy was the last straw. Emmylou had always been so adaptable, but living with Nakita must have made her realise something was missing. Nakita had well and truly fulfilled this role, yet she wasn't Emmylou's mum or his partner; it was becoming a big drama he had to put a stop to, before Emmylou got hurt.

He'd been avoiding her as much as possible, keeping her at arm's length, trying to move on. He thought he was doing well until she turned up in denim shorts with her hair hanging down in some kind of messed up plait. The most primal part of him wanted to take hold of her and kiss her till she gave in.

Last night he'd had an uncomfortable night on the Belle's couch, deciding to give her and the boyfriend some privacy, even though it'd near killed him. He convinced himself the reason he'd thrashed around all night was because the lounge was uncomfortable, not because he was sick with jealousy. That morning he'd gone to Bree's to fix her broken tap, and before he knew it, he was swept up in the girl's plans for a tea party with the dog and the cat out the back. When he'd come home, seeing Nakita standing there in a pale yellow dress, sleepy and rumpled, all he could think of was Trent in her bed. The desire to smash him was overwhelming.

Thunderclouds loomed as an apocalyptic backdrop to Nakita, who cut a melancholic figure, sitting unmoving on the swing. There was a calm eeriness to the air that he could taste. As Nox drew close, he took in a deep breath. Bree's easy smile flashed in his mind. It was time to cut ties with Nakita.

She stiffened as she saw his approach. Having been there for some time, turning her scrambled thoughts and stupid reaction over and over. How could she have been so blind to her own emotions? It was so obvious. One thing she was now sure of, she was wholly and unequivocally in love with him. And she adored Emmylou. How had she not have seen this before? She couldn't pinpoint when it happened, nor could she remember a time when she wasn't aware of his presence in relation to hers. It was as though their trajectories were destined to collide; but their paths could only ever exist in parallel.

"Nakita."

"Lennox." She could barely look at him for fear he'd see the longing in her eyes.

"Where's Emmylou?"

"I dropped her to Miriam's for a play." He took a deep breath. "Look, I'm sorry about what I said before, about you not being Emmylou's mother—"

"No, you're right. It's true. It shouldn't have upset me. Bree must think I'm crazy."

"Nakita, I can never repay you back for how you've cared for Emmylou." She didn't respond. He pulled on the swing to get her attention. She glanced up briefly and nodded, but sadness threatened to spill over.

"Where were you last night?"

"We stayed at the Belle's."

"Oh." Her mind raced to keep up with this new information. So he didn't stay with Bree? She could feel him watching her. A cool gust lifted her hair. He moved to squat on his haunches beside her, looking out into the lagoon.

"Nakita, I know I have Will's heart, but I can't keep this up for much longer. As much as we have this brother-sister-friend connection and I've enjoyed living with you, I have to get on with my life, with Emmylou's life. We've almost finished the anti-bucket list." She looked at him, knowing what was coming. "There's no easy way to say this... I've found a place. It's amazing how it's all worked out, actually. Emmylou and I will move out within the next fortnight." She took a deep breath, studying his profile.

"I understand, Nox. Really, I do. It's time for us both to move on with our lives." Her words came out more certain than she felt.

Thunder rolled in the distance and the first fat droplet of rain fell to the hot earth.

He turned to look at her. "So we can still be whatever we are to each other and finish those lists?"

"Yeah." She nodded, smiling despite the tears that threatened to escape. They were silent, watching a lone figure with his dog, rowing his dinghy to a row of mismatched houses on the other side of the lagoon.

"So you didn't have a good date?" He moved to sit on the swing alongside her.

"That," she snorted, dragging her toes in the dirt, glad for a distraction from her thoughts of him and Emmylou leaving. "It's just... well, I kind of freaked out."

"Freaked out?"

"Trent was trying to surprise me. He took me to the beach blindfolded. It was the beach where everything, you know... happened. He didn't know. He started kissing me and I don't know, I just lost it I guess." Her face flushed at how juvenile she sounded.

"I'm not surprised you freaked out. Going back there would've been confronting."

"With Will dying, I thought what happened to me was insignificant. Who was I to complain? I was only 'almost raped.' Will lost his life. I realise now I haven't dealt with it, but I don't really know how I'm supposed to. How does someone deal with being 'almost raped'? Some days I wish he'd finished the job and that Will never found me, then at least he'd still be here. Sometimes I wonder if my dress had only been a little longer, or I didn't wear those stupid heels. If I could have reacted quicker, or I'd got to that party on time, maybe none of it would've happened." He took her hand. "Nox, what if I can never let a man touch me again? What if I always just freak out? I always dreamed of marrying and having babies."

"The magic carpet?"

"Yeah, I guess, the magic carpet." She shook her head, feeling every bit the tragic romantic. "Maybe you were right. Maybe I've built a sandcastle in my head."

"Maybe Trent just isn't right for you?"

"Maybe," she said doubtfully, "but he should be. If he's not right, who is?" Her insides burnt with 'if only's' once again. If only Nox was right—but he wasn't. He couldn't be.

He let go of her hand and stood in front of her. "Someone else."

He held out his other hand, and she took it. He pulled her to her feet. This time she felt a droplet of rain on her scalp. The static in the air was palpable, the thunderclouds about to burst open. He touched underneath her chin and tipped her face. She lifted her dark eyes to meet his light ones. Overwhelming desire twisted her insides, intoxicating her senses.

It's too late.

A raindrop fell on her cheekbone like a single tear from heaven. She watched him take it in with a smile.

Slowly, he brushed it away with his thumb. Their eyes met. His head tipped slightly towards her. Her mind said no; her hands moved to reach for him. A mighty clap of thunder cracked. She jumped back.

He let go of her chin as the heavens opened up all at once, drenching them where they stood. Tapping her on the arm, he shouted above the roar of summer rain. "Last one back's a dirty rotten egg."

And with that she dashed after him, exhilarated and thankful that even though he could be nothing else, he was still her friend.

It had to be enough.

CHAPTER 27

$\mathcal{N}$ox sat in his studio listening to music; relieved his mates were gone. Every now and then they'd get together on a Friday night and have drinks and a jam session at Ink Guild. It'd been a good night, but the truth was, he just wanted to be by himself. Even though he hadn't drunk much, he'd still probably be over the limit, so was content to sit there and wait it out instead of catching a taxi. He didn't want to go home to an empty house. Nakita was out for dinner with friends while Emmylou was having her first sleep over with Miriam and Antony. Tomorrow, he and Emmylou may be moving out of Dorley Point, but Miriam and Antony's relationship as grandparents was well and truly cemented.

Last night, he and Nakita had tacos, Emmylou's favourite. It was their farewell meal and even though they'd tried to keep it light-hearted, it just wasn't. No matter how many times or in how many ways they explained the move to Emmylou, she was devastated. It felt wrong somehow, almost how he imagined an amicable divorce to be. But deep down it had to be right. A sleepover was a good distraction.

Even though things appeared to be normal, there was a peculiar unspoken tension, a little like his guitar now, just slightly out of tune. He had started seeing Bree more regularly, and Nakita had made amends with Trent. What was doing his head in, was his and Nakita's continued close proximity, centred around that damn 'anti-bucket list.' She'd enrolled them in private tango lessons, which was on Will's list. Nox had been adamant that he'd only do it if it wasn't a group thing. Determined to play the brother role, he congratulated himself on his feigned lack of interest; it helped that they argued the whole time over who was doing the steps incorrectly. Nakita never let him take the lead. Their teacher, Madame Lannetta, in her early sixties, would shake her head and 'tsk tsk' in her foreign accent, saying they had to 'feel' the connection and let the music 'move' them, but they just wanted to learn the steps and get out of there.

He strummed his guitar lightly, humming along with his own nonsense lyrics. There was a knock. Nox looked at his watch. Strange, it was pouring outside. One of the fellas must have left something behind. He put his guitar down and looked through the blinds. *Nakita.* He unlocked the door, and she walked in without explanation, shaking rain off her umbrella before coming in.

"Lennox."

"Nakita." He followed her lead, greeting her formally as she did when there was something on her mind; she was complicated like that. He locked the door again and turned towards her. "I thought you were having dinner with friends?" His eyes took in her high-waisted black skirt and midnight blue silk blouse with high heels. She was beautiful. This struck him every day.

"We just finished dinner and I'm on my way home. I saw your car here, so I thought I'd drop by. I still can't believe you guys are leaving tomorrow."

"Yeah, after work." He didn't point out that driving past Ink Guild was hardly on her way home. A tiny flame of hope kindled. Was it possible she had feelings for him? So many times, he swore she'd felt it too. Like the other day at the swing; electricity coursed between them. At least, he felt it.

"I'll help you once I'm done with my job interview at the library."

"It won't take long; we don't have much. Pete's picking up the bike."

"You can just leave it there and work on it whenever you want. You know I don't use the garage, anyway."

"Thanks, but Pete's got everything I need at his house." She sat heavily with a loud sigh. "Hey, don't worry, we'll still see you. We've got a few things left on that bucket list. I need to get to the old folks' home to do a reading if I remember correctly?"

"Well, that's partly why I came by." She stood again, biting her lip and inspecting his artworks as though she were wandering around an art gallery.

Okay, something is definitely up. "Out with it, Nakita."

She turned, "Okay, well I'm just going to say it."

"That's usually the best way." He walked into his studio and picked up his guitar, figuring the more casual he appeared, the more likely she was to say what was on her mind. She followed him in.

"So after dinner we had a game of cards and, well, it reminded me there are only two items left on my bucket list." His abdomen tightened. Suddenly he knew where this was heading. He sat on a stool and started strumming. She produced a deck of cards. "I thought we could kill two birds with one stone again."

He had to give it to her. As much as she was uptight and straight, when she made up her mind about something, she was ballsy. *God, I love that about her.*

"Look, I know this may seem weird, but I figure since you've already done nude portraits, and it doesn't mean anything... your kind of with Bree, I'm with Trent." She rolled her eyes as if to punctuate what she said, as if it were old news.

Yeah, he was with Bree, sort of, to try to get *her* out of his system. Her words put cold distance between them, but could barely douse the flame raging inside him.

"So what are you thinking?" He was coiled tight, too tight. "We play strip poker, then I do your nude portrait since we're already halfway there?"

She nodded, biting her lip again and casting her eyes to the floor. He leant his guitar against the wall, then stood and clapped his hands together once as though it were decided.

"Okay, let's do it." Her eyes widened. Part of her must have been expecting him to say no again.

"Okay. When?" Her eyes flicked to the front door.

"How about right here, right now?"

"Fine." She let out a decisive breath. He strode over to the coffee table in the corner where he worked out his designs and cleared it of folders. He motioned with his head for her to join him. She stood, her handbag in front of her. There was a heartbeat in time where she looked like she'd back out, but when he saw her tuck her chin down, he knew it was on.

She sat primly on the edge of the chair. "Okay, so what are the rules?"

"Just a sec." He walked over to the kitchenette, pulled out two glasses and took some cubes out of the ice tray. Placing them on the table, he got the bottle of whisky he and his mates had been drinking. Their eyes fixated on the amber liquid as it glugged from the bottle. "Dutch courage." Reaching for their glasses, they chinked them together without a word, eyes focused on each other. The liquid blazed a trail, searing his already hot insides. Unexpectedly, Nakita downed her whisky in one hit; he couldn't help but smile as she held the table and shuddered, blowing air through her lips. The girl had way too much spunk for her own good.

He poured another glass.

"Okay. So we each get five cards. Aim of the game is to get the highest points. If I get a higher hand, you lose an article of clothing and vice versa."

"So either way, one or both of us get naked?"

"Ah, yeah," he cleared his throat, trying to focus on shuffling the deck, which felt clumsy in his hands. "You familiar with pairs, straights, flushes, full houses and all that?"

"Roughly," she tugged on her hair, twisting it around her finger.

"Okay, since there's only two of us, we'll play the quick version, so no raising or folding and one exchange only from the deck." He dealt them five cards each. A rush of adrenalin surged through his veins as he picked up his hand, unable to believe the situation he found himself in. He looked at his cards; they were terrible.

"You want to exchange?" he asked, surrendering two of his, only to get a worse hand.

"Nope."

"Okay, show us what you got." Her hand shook as she lay her cards on the table.

"Two Jacks." He laid his hand out.

"Yes!" she hissed, fist pumping the air.

"Beginner's luck." Nox tried to sound nonchalant.

She raised an eyebrow with a look of expectance. "Maybe. We'll see."

He reached down and pulled off his black flip-flops, dangling them in the air with a cheeky smile. "Unfortunate occasion to be wearing no socks, I'd say," she jibed.

"Maybe." He smiled at how quickly her competitive nature kicked in.

This time she dealt.

A pair of Queens. This was looking more promising. She exchanged two cards, her eyes lighting up.

"You go first," she directed. He laid his hand on the table.

"Yes!" She slapped a flush down on the table. "Got you again. Beginner's luck, my foot."

He conceded with a nod and stood up. His hand went straight to the button of his Levis as he made out to undo them. She looked up at him; the shock registering on her face.

"Haha, just kidding. But they'll be next to go if you beat me again." He grabbed the back of his shirt and pulled it forward over his head, self-conscious of the clearly visible scar. Her gaze swept his bare chest. She swallowed and looked away.

He dealt the cards again, trying to keep focused on the game. He looked at his cards and rubbed his chin. He had to win soon or he was going to be the only one sitting there, butt-naked. That was not going to work. She lay her cards down. She had two nines and two fives.

He lay his down: *Three of a kind. Phew.*

"I thought I'd give you a little breather," she teased, sliding off her sleek high heels.

Collecting the cards, Nakita reshuffled and dealt, humming along to the tune in the background. The arches of her delicate brows went into a deep furrow as she looked at her hand for some time before exchanging two cards and smiling to herself. He exchanged one. "Ready?" she asked, clearly confident. She lay down two aces, trying not to smile. He laid down a straight flush. Her back stiffened, sighing she started to undo her earrings.

"Hang on a minute, what are you doing?"

She looked at him, confused. "Taking out my earrings."

"Hate to break it to you, but earrings don't count."

"Of course they do, they're part of my ensemble."

He shook his head. "Nice try, but they don't count as clothing or I could take off my watch and you've got all your rings." After looking like she might argue the point, she stood in her huffy way, but then paused suddenly as if to weigh up what she should take off first. Reaching behind, her eyes on him the whole time, she undid the zip of her skirt; stepping out of it, she laid it neatly on a chair behind her before quickly sitting back down. He had to concentrate to clear his mind after seeing the flash of black underwear contrasting her creamy white thighs. Pushing the hair out of his eyes, he took a gulp of whisky, knowing the next round was going to be a game changer. She followed his lead, wincing slightly as she gritted her teeth.

"Okay, let's do this," he said, with more swag that he felt. He looked at his cards, nothing special. He could see it was only moments till he was stripping down to his jocks.

"Okay, let's put them down at the same time." Nakita suggested.

They looked into each other's eyes. "One, two, three," they counted. They lay their cards on the table.

She had a queen of diamonds, a nine of spades and a five. He let out a breath; he had a queen of hearts, a nine of clubs and a seven. His seven trumped her five.

Their eyes met and with silent resolution she stood; her hand went to her blouse to undo the first button, the second, the third. Her blouse parted. His mouth went dry.

He closed his eyes. "Nakita. Stop." He didn't have the strength to play the game any longer. The game of pretending she didn't mean more to him. It had to stop. She paused, confused. He ran his hands through his hair and stood up, walking over to the counter and resting his hands on it. He couldn't look at her. "We can't do this."

"Is it Bree?"

He turned and looked at her. Her blouse was already buttoned.

"This has nothing to do with Bree." Suddenly everything was crystal clear. "Wait there. I need to show you something." He disappeared into the back storeroom, his mind screaming at him, his heart determined. When he came back, she'd already put her skirt back on and stood there watching him, her expression somewhere between unease and confusion.

"What's this about, Nox?" She nodded at the canvas in his hands. He didn't answer.

Here goes nothing. He pulled the sheet off the canvas. She gasped; her fingers at her lips in shock. She stood for a moment taking it in, then came closer, not taking her eyes off the painting. She reached out and ran her fingers over it.

It was her, lying in a grassy field, naked except for her unbound hair flowing around her and wildflowers that barely covered her nakedness. He'd captured the wistful expression of her velvet brown eyes.

Her eyes met his. "This is the painting you were working on that day, isn't it?"

"Yeah." He found it easier to look at the painting than at her. "I guess you inspired me."

"So if you've done this already, why won't you paint me now?"

He could hear the tremor in her voice. He rubbed his temple, not knowing where to start. "Nakita, you said it would mean nothing to you." He looked her in the eyes. *Don't play the game, Nox.* He took a deep breath. "The thing is, it means something to me. It's always meant something to me." She looked into his face intently, her head tipped to the side as though she was grasping to take in his words. "I'm tired of pretending, Nakita. Pretending to be some stand-in brother. Pretending to be everything you want me to be, except what I am, what I want to be." He stepped in closer, his body craving to be closer to hers. "I'm tired of pretending that I care about you, when the fact is—I'm in love with you." She inhaled sharply and took a step back. *You've gone too far to back out now man, may as well go the whole hog.* "I can't pinpoint a moment in time since I first saw you that I didn't love you." He stated it as plainly as he felt it; he was baring his soul to her.

Dismay registered in her face; she crossed her arms over her stomach as though he'd punched her. Averting her eyes from his, she lifted her chin. "You can't."

"Why? Because I have his heart? Is that it?" She didn't answer, her chin set, her eyes veiled by her eyelids. "Well, I do, Nakita. I love you. And I really don't think Will has any say in it." He couldn't help his frustration bubbling to the surface.

Is that all this is ever going to be about? Will's heart? Surely she feels something too?

"I have to go." She went to the coffee table and grabbed her earrings, tossing them in her bag. She looked at her watch.

"So that's it? You're just going to keep avoiding this?"

"Avoiding what, Nox?" she cried, "Don't you see? I can't love you!"

"You can't love me? Or you don't want to love me?" He looked at her levelly.

"Is there any difference?" She didn't wait for his response. "We swore to each other, Nox. I swore an oath to Will that this would never happen."

"Is that what this is about? A deal?" he demanded, frustrated, so incredibly frustrated. "Look around, he's not here, Nakita." She kept her head down, balancing herself on the nearby counter and pulled on her high heels before walking over to the front door, her back stiff. He dropped his head back and rubbed his hands over his face in disbelief, groaning. "You're always talking about finding your one true love. Doesn't following your heart mean more to you than a hastily spoken promise?" He strode over to her and took both her hands, thankful that she allowed him this even though he saw her apprehension. "Well, I made another promise a long time ago. I swore to myself if I was ever one of those lucky bastards who found love, I'd take hold of it with both hands and not let go." His mask was off. She lifted her eyes to his, her lips gently pursed. He didn't bother trying to conceal his love and desire for her as he looked down at her, into her eyes. For the briefest moment her eyes softened, and she returned his look. *She desired him too.* His body was tight with need as his gaze landed on her full, soft lips as they parted. He wanted to kiss those lips a thousand different ways for the rest of his life.

Her eyes widened. She pulled her hands free and stepped away. "Don't you see? Whether you like it or not, you have his heart. You deserve to be loved unreservedly, I'd always be holding something back."

"No, Nakita, that's only what you've convinced yourself to believe." He stepped into her space again, resting his right hand against the door next to her so she stood encircled by him. Her back was to the door as he touched the knuckles of his left hand to the smoothness of her cheek. He leaned in closer; resting the weight of his hand on her hip, he bent to murmur close by her ear. "I know you felt it too, that first time we met." Her eyes closed; she swayed at his breath by her ear. "I know you feel it now. You've felt it all along. Admit it."

Everything seemed to pulse between them.

"I can't do this, Nox," she said unmoving, as though she were immobilised by her own need. She was fighting it; it was so obvious to him now. She craved him too. This sudden knowledge sent his body into overdrive; but he didn't want to scare her off. He was mere inches from her. He gently nuzzled the stubble of his jaw inside the curve of her neck. She tipped her head to the side, helpless. Both of his hands moved to her neck; he pressed his open mouth to her throat, just enough to sample her bared flesh, to feel the electric sensation of his lips and tongue against her salty skin. She moaned softly, her hands moving to his bare chest. She paused there for a moment, then stiffened, shoving hard against him. "I have to go. This wasn't supposed to happen."

Her hands trembled as they worked to smooth her hair and her clothes. "Maybe, but that's just like life, isn't it? It happens. You can't control everything." Nox steeled himself against his own desire. He ran a hand through his own hair, taking a shaky breath.

"You don't need to remind me," she said, her voice full of barely suppressed emotion.

She was afraid. He had to let her go—for now. He turned the key to unlock the door, but held it closed momentarily.

"I'm not playing the game anymore, Nakita."

She paused, her eyes were dark, polished stones; glowing with undisclosed desires. She walked out with an almost imperceptible nod of acceptance.

CHAPTER 28

To say she hadn't slept would be an understatement. No matter how hard she tried, she couldn't hide the bags under her eyes. He never came home. She knew, because she'd slept in his bed, she just wanted to be close to him even though it was wrong. Him loving her was a dream; one she couldn't entertain.

Her job interview was at the library today. First she had to pick Emmylou up from Mim and Antony's before dropping her to Ink Guild. There was no way she'd be able to avoid Nox. Pulling on a white blouse and black pencil skirt that skimmed just below her knees, she teamed it up with some tasteful black heels and twisted her hair low at the nape. Swiping on a hint of mascara, she said a silent prayer that no one on the panel would recognise her from when she was goofing around with him in the library.

As she pulled in alongside Ink Guild, she became increasingly nervous at the shift that had taken place between them, a shift that was outside her control. Emmylou raced up the stairs into the shop while Nakita lagged, partly because her skirt was restrictive, but mostly because she wasn't ready to see Nox.

"We're in here, Kit," Annie sang out. Nakita stepped into the room to see Proctor face down, getting a cover-up tattoo across his shoulder blades. He was broad and heavily muscled across his freckled back. Annie and Proctor were totally smitten; somehow they just made sense. Even though he was much older than her, she'd always been an old soul deep down.

Nox was straddling a stool, focused on his work as she walked in. She couldn't help but admire his brow, furrowed in concentration. He really suited this place. She leaned against the doorframe for support since her body wasn't cooperating in his presence. They were moving out this afternoon. Her stomach sank at the thought of them not being a part of her everyday life anymore.

"Kit, you look good—" Annie paused "but tired. Were you too nervous to sleep?"

"Hey, Kit," came Proctor's muffled voice.

"Hi, Proctor."

Nox glanced up at her, his eyes stamping hers with the memory of last night. Her belly squeezed. Emmylou sat beside Annie, fiddling with her hair while Annie swung her legs, looking pretty and chirpy.

"So the plan is, I'm going to take Emmylou for the tallest ice cream in the world and then we're going to the blood bank and she's going to watch me give blood, aren't you Emmylou?" Nox paused what he was doing momentarily and looked at Annie, his eyebrows drawn.

"You're taking my daughter to watch you give blood?"

"Yes, I am; it's educational, and she needs to realise the importance of donating."

"She's four."

"Yes, but before you know it, she will be twenty-four and, due to my guidance, will already be a regular blood donor." She turned to Emmylou and said in her, 'I'm-now-talking-to-a-four-year-old,' voice, "you see I'm a very important person to the blood bank, Emmylou. I'm an AB which only three percent of Australians are, so when the other ABs out there are in a trouble they need me." Nakita doubted that Emmylou had a clue what Annie was talking about, but she nodded expressively as if she understood every word.

Nox shook his head and went back to the tattoo. He was used to Annie's unconventional ways; even though they really liked each other, they bantered on as if they didn't.

"What's your blood type, Nox?" Annie asked.

"Just plain, old regular O," he said, wiping the tattoo.

"Okay, guys, I really need to go now. Bye, Emmylou. Have fun and remember to use your best manners with Aunt Annie." Nox stopped what he was doing and looked Nakita over. Her body flushed as his gaze ran over her deliberately.

I'm not playing the game anymore, Nakita.

"You sure you're going for an interview at the library?"

"Yeah, why? Is this too much?" She looked at Annie, panicked.

"Kit, don't listen to him, you're perfect."

Proctor looked over his shoulder at her. "You look great. I'd hire you in a flash."

"Are you going for the sexy librarian look? If you get the job, I might even get myself a library card," Nox teased.

Stress dumped into her system. "I don't want to look sexy. I want to look smart and sophisticated."

"Well, you nailed that too," he said, his eyes regarding her in that heart-clenching way. His demeanour towards her had definitely changed. She shook her head, dismissing him.

"I've got to go. I don't have time for this."

Nox gave her a rakish grin, his eyes still warm upon her. "Good luck, Nakita."

"We'll say a prayer for you, won't we, Emmy?" piped up Annie, crossing her fingers.

Nakita was heading out the door just as she heard Emmylou say, "Daddy, what's sexy mean?"

"I guess it means I want to kiss her," Nox answered. Laughter followed her out the door. Nakita was only glad that she was already on her way, as she didn't want them to see how she'd gone to jelly in her high heels.

He wasn't playing her game any longer. He was playing his own, and she didn't know the rules.

~

Rivulets of sweat made pathways down her back as she drove home from the interview. Fortunately, her hair had kept it together, but now, it was partly fallen with damp tendrils curling wildly at the base of her neck. She had both windows down; the wind blasting her. Her aircon was broken, but she didn't care. Her interview had gone well, and she was in a state of relief knowing there was the possibility of a life for her beyond accountancy. Pulling up at home, she noted Nox's van loaded, ready for the move. Her moment of hopefulness came to a standstill and was replaced with dread. *They're leaving*. She knew it was coming, but even still it didn't seem real.

Emmylou was in the wading pool in the backyard, shooting Diesel with a water gun. As the little girl giggled infectiously, Nakita couldn't help but smile even though her own heart was heavy. She walked towards where she could hear music coming from the garage, then faltered mid step. But this time it wasn't Emmylou who had her attention. Nox was squatting before his dirt bike in the garage, wearing only a pair of grey jeans, reminding her of last night. He looked up at his daughter, grinning at her antics while Nakita stood transfixed, until his gaze slid over to her, a smoky gleam coming to his eyes. Lightheaded, she concentrated on every step she took towards him, trying to appear unaffected. The scar on his chest no longer looked red and angry; it had faded to a thin pink line.

"Nakita," he said, taking in her dishevelled state with a salute and a tip of his head.

"Lennox."

"How was it?" he asked, rubbing a cloth on some motorbike part. She squared her shoulders and tried to bite back her confident smile.

"I think it went really well."

"I expected nothing less." He walked into the garage and she followed him, resting her back against the wooden bench covered with tools.

"But there are other candidates, so I can't be sure."

"When do you hear?"

She stared dumbly at the muscles flexing in his arms as he concentrated on wiping grease off his hands with a rag. He smiled and leaned in towards her. She stiffened, her breath caught. He was going to kiss her, and she was helpless to stop him. He came in closer, his eyes following the trickle of sweat that meandered down her neck to the base of her throat, giving her visions of the last night: his declaration of love, not just with words but with his lips, hot from whisky, his jaw scratchy from the shadow of a beard. Those damp, open-mouthed kisses on her neck, coaxing her till her body was liquid with desire. As she relived the moment, her breathing quickened; knowing how much he wanted her was as intoxicating as it was unsettling.

He pulled away slowly. "Looks like you need to cool down," he teased, waving a tool in his hand that she now understood he'd been reaching for. He turned back to his motorbike. She was glad his back was turned as she silently let out her pent-up breath; her heart thrumming at his gall. *So this is how he played the game? Well, I can play the game too.* An idea formulated in her mind.

"I'm going inside to change." She announced then went over to Emmylou and gave her a cuddle, whispering some instructions in her ear. After she had everything ready, she gave Emmylou the signal.

"Daddy, Daddy! Come here, there's a big black spider in the pool."

Nox strode over to inspect the pool, and Nakita let the full force of the hose blast him from her hiding spot. She got him good, except he ran towards her, instead of retreating as she expected he would. Realising he was going to seek revenge, she dropped the hose and tried to run, but her heels dug into the grass, impeding her escape.

Roaring, he grabbed her around the waist, lifting her off her feet.

She shrieked as she saw he was carrying her to the wading pool. She held onto him so tight; he went down with her. With an almighty splash, they both ended up half submerged in the water. She lay there unable to do anything but belly laugh. He looked down into her face, smiling, and she realised his arms were still wrapped around her. Her laughter ceased as she caught the look in his eyes. She was breathless, paralysed. His thumb and forefinger came to her chin, the intensity of his gaze tracking from her eyes to her lips as though he couldn't decide between them. Closing the final inches between them, his mouth pressed against hers. Her lips parted by instinct to meet his. There was the exquisite sensation of his open mouth meeting hers; the first taste of his soft, firm lips.

It was a fleeting moment; a heartbeat in time.

The dog leapt into the pool barking while Emmylou squawked, "Daddy the water's coming out!" Nox pulled back with a groan and they both turned to see a fountain of water spraying up from the side of the pool; perhaps from her high heel or the dog sitting, panting expectantly, his eyes and tongue lolling.

"Diesel. Out," Nox commanded. Diesel jumped out, his tail between his legs. "Nooo," Nox shielded Nakita with his body, his forehead pressed against hers as the waterlogged dog shook himself. Nox rolled off Nakita, his back and arms covered in flicks of dirty water. "You sure know how to wreck a moment, Diesel," he groaned.

"Good boy, Diesel, perfectly timed. We got him, didn't we?" Nakita laughed as though she'd planned the whole thing.

"Right, that's it!" Nox dove onto her again. She came back up, still laughing and sputtering.

"What's all this then?" Pete demanded, in his playful, gruff way as he turned the corner.

His arrival to the scene gave Nakita the perfect opportunity to withdraw herself from the situation. Because, no matter how she looked at it, as brief as it had been, Nox had kissed her and she had kissed him back.

CHAPTER 29

*T*he next day it was Miriam and Antony's fiftieth wedding anniversary, and Nakita went to Annie's to get ready so they could arrive together. She'd organised a formal celebration at Sophia Grace's—a vintage restaurant overlooking the Marina. Nakita had been friends with the current manager since primary school. Shepard, or 'Shep' as he was widely known, had given her an amazing deal that she couldn't pass up. Miriam and Antony would love the antiquated atmosphere of a bygone era. The catering was all part of the deal, as was the jazz band that Nakita knew would put Antony in his element.

Nakita's biggest challenge was getting out the invitations. Not knowing names and addresses of Mim and Antony's closest friends and family; in the end, she'd temporarily liberated their well-worn address book. Luckily for her, they were still old school in their ways.

The next challenge was to make sure they were dressed. Fortunately, Antony had the perfect suit for the occasion, which she had dry-cleaned without either of them knowing. Then all she had to do was work out Miriam, which wasn't too hard since she was tall and slim. It wasn't too hard tricking her to get her measurements and even finding a dress online that she liked was easy. With Nakita pretending to browse through a website of various dresses for fun, she got an idea of what Miriam liked. She went by early in the morning and took around the beautiful gown and shoes she'd bought online and set out Antony's suit, letting Miriam know that she had booked her a hair appointment. This was when Miriam discovered Nakita had booked them to go somewhere special for the evening; little did they know that it was going to be a monumental occasion. Nakita had a stroke of genius and asked Pete to pick up Antony and Miriam in one of his vintage cars to take them there.

Nakita checked her hair and makeup one last time in the oval mirror, admiring her sleek black satin dress that fit like a dream. It split up one side to mid-thigh, showing just the right amount of cleavage in front, and scooped low at the back with a sheer insert. She'd fallen in love with it instantly as she browsed a boutique for an outfit for the occasion. Tonight she opted to keep her hair smooth and sleek, as much as the straightener would allow, putting the focus on making her eyes look smoky, leaving her lips with just a hint of colour.

"Nakita," Annie called in her sing-song voice. "There's a surprise out here for you."

A surprise? She was the one doing the surprising as far as she knew. At the front door, standing beside a black vintage Cadillac, was Proctor, looking handsome in an expensive dove-grey suit and tie. But it was Nox who drew Nakita's attention. Looking a little more casual than Proctor, it was like he'd stepped out of some Italian cologne advertisement with his longish hair slicked back and usual three-day growth shaved clean. He wasn't wearing a jacket since it was warm; instead, he wore black suspenders with his white sleeves rolled up. He was totally swoon worthy.

Proctor had a huge bouquet of flowers in his hand. Annie skipped into his arms, planting kisses all over his face. They looked a good pair, her dark purple dress setting off her eyes and complimenting his suit. Nakita and Nox watched them, smiling indulgently. Nakita walked over to Nox, unable to avoid him any longer; the entire time his gaze burning upon her.

"Lennox." Her mind was on the kiss in the kiddie pool yesterday. She'd replayed the whole guilty scene over and over again, all last night, all day today. She couldn't help but wonder if he was thinking about it too.

I can't believe this man loves me.

"Nakita." He tipped his head, a spark in his eyes.

"You look good," she said, nodding towards his outfit, overwhelmed by his presence and the spicy, wooded scent of his cologne.

"This old thing?" he joked, looking down at himself. "It's not my usual style, but I figure Miriam and Antony are worth suiting up for."

She watched him with a smile, knowing she had to keep her guard up.

"You also look... good." His eyes lingered on her, telling her everything she already knew.

"Looks like Pete got me." She changed the subject, nodding to the car. There'd been no talk of her arriving in one of his vintage cars.

"Yep," he grinned. "Looks like he did. He's on his way to get Miriam and Antony now, so we better make tracks and get there before they do." He motioned her into the front passenger seat, holding the door open and guiding her in. The heat of his hand through the fine netting on her back gave her a shiver she couldn't contain. As she slid into the smooth leather interior, she caught his sexy smile and had to work hard at constructing walls fast. He was too skilled at pulling them down.

∿

Miriam was regal in a soft gold gown that sparkled at the bodice and dropped sheer and flowing to the ground while Antony wore all the finery and fripperies of a dashing, aristocratic gentleman. Nakita described the venue in detail to Antony as the three of them walked arm in arm. Friends and family came and greeted them. Antony, overcome, pulled out a hanky to mop his tear-rimmed eyes. Miriam scolded Nakita for being sneaky and having the audacity to steal their address book. She told Nakita how she'd blamed Antony for being vague and misplacing it, even though he'd heartily denied it. Miriam quipped she'd been so cranky about the matter that they'd almost divorced before they made it to their anniversary.

There was a great vibe in the room, and from Nakita's perspective, everyone appeared to be having a wonderful time. The finger food and wine flowed freely while everyone was taken with the jazz band and smooth female singer who performed Miriam and Antony's wedding song. Nakita wept, as a blind Antony lead a radiant and blushing Miriam around the dance floor with finesse.

"Shep. You're here!" Nakita exclaimed, launching into his arms.

"I had to check in with my favourite girlfriend and make sure everything was in order."

Nakita laughed and rolled her eyes. "Wow, you are suave tonight."

"And you, are positively divine." He held her at arm's length. "Tell me, who's the guy with the dreamy eyes and tatts standing by the fireplace giving me death stares?" She glanced over to see Nox, drink in hand, scowling at them.

"Oh, that's my former housemate, Nox. He just moved out yesterday."

"You sure that's all he is? By the looks of it, he wants to pulverise me." Shep took her hand and pulled her to the dance floor. "Come on. Let's give him something to be really jealous about." He swept her up in a dance that was as over the top and as flamboyant as his personality. At one point she looked over at Nox and saw the muscles flicking in his jaw, eyes narrowed under dark brows. By the end of their dance she was laughing riotously, dismayed by how many people watched.

After heart warming speeches and toasts all round, dessert, and more dancing; the last people left were Nakita's favourites. And, for the first time since Will had died, she didn't wish in vain that he was there. She simply enjoyed those present; those whom she loved.

~

Nox kept silent as he drove everyone home while Annie prattled on about everything and nothing in her usual overeager way. They dropped Proctor off first since there was no way he'd be staying the night at Annie's; her mum and stepdad being devoted Christians. Proctor seemed happy enough with their arrangement; he knew it was the full deal or no deal and he was in hook, line and sinker. He spent most of the time grinning like a Cheshire cat. Nox envied the bastard; it had all been so straightforward for him.

He sat there with Nakita in awkward silence as Proctor and Annie kissed goodbye, yet again. He was pissed off, but he didn't know why. Well, he did really. This whole unrequited love thing was not for the fainthearted; it totally sucked. Especially when the person you loved danced the way she did with a suave, Italian stallion, who'd set most female's pulses racing. His heart near imploded watching her in his arms, all pink, flushed and laughing. He wanted her to look at him with the same sparkling, dancing brown eyes. Instead, her eyes avoided his all night. He realised for the first time in his life that something as simple as eye contact was enough to keep a person breathing.

Annie got back in the car babbling and singing Proctor's praises. He couldn't help himself any longer.

"Annie, it never ceases to amaze me with all that kissing, that you can still manage to speak; it's a wonder your lips aren't worn off." He knew he was being juvenile, but she was driving him crazy.

As he expected, she arched up. "You know what?"

"No, but you're going to tell us, anyway."

"You're being a total ass, Nox." She sat forward in the middle seat as if he couldn't already hear her. "Look, I've kept my mouth shut for way too long—"

"You reckon?"

"You know, you two are pathetic. Sorry, Nakita, I love you, but it's true. Look at you, ignoring each other and pretending there's nothing going on. Aren't you exhausted from it? In fact, pull over, I'm walking. I'm exhausted. Not from dancing the night away or kissing the one I love every chance I get. No, I'm exhausted from you two. If you can't get it together, just move on and give the rest of us a break from your stupid games. Pull over Nox; right here."

"Argh! Okay, just quit hitting me over the head with your handbag."

"It's a clutch purse!"

"Okay, stop! I'll pull over."

She jumped out. "Bye, Nakita. Call me tomorrow. Best party ever." She gave Nox a look before slamming the door shut, leaving them in silence.

"Well, she went psycho," he said, rubbing the back of his head.

"Yep, but I guess at least now you know the difference between a clutch purse and a handbag."

Nox shook his head, pulling back onto the road. In a moment of inspiration, he fiddled with the radio, wondering why he hadn't thought of putting it on before. He found a station that played old classics that fit the vintage of the car and the theme of the night.

"I never got to introduce you to Shepard, the guy I was dancing with."

"Oh yeah," he said as if he didn't care, even though they both knew he did.

"We went out for a bit when I was fifteen. For a while actually, until he came out."

"Came out? What? You mean—" he faltered.

"Yeah, I was about the only person who didn't see it coming. For a long time, it was a running joke at school for the guys to keep clear of me in case I turned them gay." She shook her head with a smile. "It seemed such a big deal at the time."

Nox kept silent, relief soothing the tension in his tightly corded body. How did he fail to see that one? As he drove past the river, on a whim, he pulled the car over.

"What are you doing?"

"Looking at the moon reflecting on the water," he said, more casually than he felt. He turned off the engine. He had no idea what he was doing, but he felt the need to clear the air between them. He hated to admit it, but Annie was right. "Let's get out for a few minutes," he said, turning to look at Nakita.

She had her eyes fixed straight ahead; but after a moment's consideration, squared her shoulders before climbing out.

Even though it was late, it was a balmy evening with the scent of recently blossomed, wild jasmine drifting on the air. Nox leaned against the bonnet of the car, at a loss for words as she wandered to the river's edge, bathed in the moonlight.

"It's a gorgeous night." She gazed up at the moon.

"Hey, tonight was great, Miriam and Antony were chuffed. I saw both of them shed a few tears."

"They tore up the dance floor, didn't they? Their love after all these years—"

He watched her profile as she smiled to herself at the memory. "I wanted to dance with you all night." He needed to know where he stood; where *they* stood. She turned and looked at him.

"Well, you could have asked."

"Your dance card was pretty full." He didn't need to point out that she'd avoided him all night. "Will you dance with me now?"

"What, here?"

"Yeah. Here, now."

"The grass is more than ankle deep."

"So dance with me on the road?"

"We'll get run over."

"Nakita, it's the quietest road ever, and it's the early hours of the morning. I'm sure we'll see and hear if anyone's coming." She stared at the river. From the outside she appeared serene, but he could sense her inner turmoil. She was torn.

"Come on."

She considered his outstretched hand, but didn't take it.

"Please?" Her eyes lifted to his. "Throw me a lifeline, Nakita." He tried one more time, his eyes pleading with hers.

She bit her lip and stepped towards him, putting her hand in his, her eyes luminous marbles in the light of the moon. He led her over to the car and turned up the music. He had no idea if he was going to trample her toes like when they had lessons together, but tonight he'd watched closely as Antony guided Miriam around the dance floor with grace and style; they had that connection that Madame Lannetta was talking about.

Turning, he pulled her into his arms, letting out a pent-up breath. He was sure she must feel the heat coming off his body just from being near her; but she was careful to avoid eye contact as he took her right hand in his left while her left hand barely touched his shoulder. Her face was a whisker close to his, but still not touching. She kept it deliberately turned to the side. Electricity coursed between them as he positioned his hand on the small of her back. He took a breath and without words, guided her with his weight and the movement of his body. For the very first time, she allowed him to lead. He put the steps out of his mind, realising he knew them, and they danced by instinct. Her sensual body was close as he pushed, pulled and turned her around the moonlit road while some old timer crooned a song that didn't really match the beat of the dance. Finally, as the dance came to a natural end, he led her in a move that had her snapping her face towards his in breathless surprise. He pulled her luscious curves along the hard lines of his body, then dipped her backwards so that her bent knee was parallel to his waist. Deliberately, she extended her pointed toe towards the sky like he'd seen in movies. He looked down into her eyes, breathless, while she gazed up at him, before leisurely tipping her head back, baring her throat; her mouth stretching into a slow smile of satisfaction. He couldn't help himself any longer. Tracing his nose and his lips from the base of her throat, up her neck and along the underside of her cheek to her ear, he marvelled at her honeyed scent and the silky smoothness of her skin. He groaned as his mouth and tongue working together with a mind of their own, exploring her neck, her throat, her ear; his lips whispered how exquisite she was by the thrum of her pulse as he pulled her in against the tautness of his body. He could feel as she gave in to him— and she was his. She looked up at him, her eyes gleaming, feverish. He drew his face up so he was looking down into hers. Hers smouldered; her lips parting as he touched his to hers, hesitantly at first, tasting her lips, her mouth, and her breath in hot, open-mouthed kisses. When she arched towards him with a sigh and met his lips with tastes of her own, he took hers completely, kissing her deep and long, pulling her upright and cupping the side of her face. Their kisses became more urgent as his mouth searched hers, ravenous for more. Her full lips were sweet and sensual as she kissed him back unashamedly, her hand reaching behind his head, weaving into his hair and pulling him closer still. Everything in him wanted to ravish her there and then—to be one. He pulled back to control himself, but the way she looked up at him with her eyes half shut and her lips swollen from his kisses, he went back for more. Unrestrained, he kissed her with increasing fervour.

The game was lost.

Nakita tore herself away, her breathing ragged as she heard her phone ringtone.

"Oh my gosh, that's going to be Mim's niece, Julie," she exclaimed, disentangling herself from him. "She's down for the party. We organised that she'd stay at my house tonight. I completely forgot." She raced over to the car, grabbing her phone and answering it just in time. She looked over at Nox standing in the dim headlights of the car, his hands laced at the back of his neck, his eyes on her. She was still reeling from the dance, those kisses and his lips that had branded her in a way no tattoo ever could.

"Julie? I'm sorry. I... was held up. I'll be right there... yep, okay, bye." She held her fingertips to her lips. "We have to go. I completely forgot. She's waiting out the front."

"Saved by the bell, eh?" He grinned in his lazy, cheeky way, coming closer and placing his hand on her shoulder, his fingers hot on her neck where her pulse still pounded. "Then we better go. Just one last taste," he murmured, leaning forward, his green eyes almost translucent in the moonlight as Etta James started crooning 'At Last' on the radio. His head dipped to hers once again.

She welcomed him. Never in her life had she been kissed the way that he kissed her right now. She didn't know if she'd ever get enough of his mouth, his breath. It was almost primal, a meeting of two souls that hungered to consume each other. One hand remained at the base of her throat where her pulse beat wildly, while the other went to her waist and slid down past her hip, squeezing there lightly; his hands on the curve of her butt, lifting her onto the bonnet of the car. Their kisses became more urgent, their breathing heavier as his mouth found her throat, leaving a trail of hot kisses to her ear where he paused to nibble gently, his breath sending electric spasms down her spine, causing everything inside her to bloom. His right hand roamed down her thigh, finding the split of her dress, skimming tentatively under the folds. She moaned again as his work-roughened hands found her upper thighs, pulling her closer against him. By instinct she wrapped her legs around him, her fingers working at the front of his shirt.

He chuckled into her ear, his hands restraining her. "Let's not start what can't be finished." He pressed his forehead against hers, his breathing heavy. "Come on, we better go," he nodded towards the car. "Best not leave Julie waiting."

She pressed her lips together, still seared by his kisses, her body in overdrive as she gazed up at him, the fire of desire surging through her. He took her by the waist and somehow as he guided her back-wards, his lips moving on hers the whole time, they made their way to the front seat of the car. In the end, with a reluctant groan, he disentangled himself from her.

Moments later, as they pulled up on the driveway, they could see Julie waiting patiently in the dim porch light. In the darkness of the car, Nakita reached out and took his large hand in hers. Nuzzling her cheek against the palm of his hand, she pressed her lips inside.

"You know what you asked me the other night? I felt it too. All along I've felt it. Right from the start." She let go of his hand and climbed out of the car, but turned at the last moment. "I love you." She mouthed the words that had been the echo of her heart before she even knew.

CHAPTER 30

The very next day, Pete and Raina's neighbours, Dolph and Martina, were throwing a barn dance as a farewell to friends and family as they were selling up and moving on. The weathered old barn, the only original piece of construction on the property, already looked the part without even trying. Complete with bales of hay, saddles, bridles, rusted pitch forks hanging on the wall and a long wooden table with bench seats, they'd simply strung up a few fairy lights and hung some dried flowers here and there. An old tractor in the corner completed the picture, as did the stray chooks, flapping and squawking in the rafters, terrorised by kids trying to catch them. All of this just added to the atmosphere, as did the delectable aroma of a spit roast wafting through the open doors. For the occasion, they'd thrown together a band to play some country and folk music to liven up the old place. With a few of Nox's connections mixed in, Martina as lead vocals and on the fiddle, Pete on the banjo and playing the spoons, and Nox on guitar and backup vocals, they put together an amazing sound.

Every time Nakita looked at Nox, his eyes were on her, sexy and intent. They held a look of promise in them when he smiled that knowing smile; it was hers alone. She couldn't help the clumsy smile she returned to him, or the way her heart felt like a rose that had bloomed in her chest. She knew she was love struck. And putting aside all feelings of guilt, she allowed herself to be overcome; to be love-struck by him. As if by some unspoken agreement, they'd kept their distance since last night. Nakita had been caught up with Miriam's informal family gathering since many had come a long way for their anniversary. Against her better judgment, she took to drinking punch, which one of Pete's mates always seemed to be only too happy to provide, topping her up from his hip flask. It didn't take long before the whole room was spinning as she danced with the young, the old and everyone in between. It seemed that every time she looked Nox's way, his eyes were glued on her as he played and sang. For the first time, she allowed herself to feel the exhilaration of being wanted by him and allowing herself to want him. She spun from one dance partner to another in euphoria.

"If you're planning on making it to the end of the night, you need to slow down, girl," Raina laughed, bringing her a cup of water.

"Oh, it's boiling hot in here." She held the stitch in her side that she'd been trying to ignore. "This is my first barn dance and I can't believe how much fun it is. I never knew Pete could play the banjo! And I had no idea how well Nox could sing. I love his voice."

"Mmm? Is that all you're loving?" Raina's eyes and voice teased. There was no point trying to keep it a secret from Raina.

"Well," Nakita said, feeling a little sheepish. "As of last night, we may be something... but we haven't had a chance to speak since then, so I don't really know what's happening." Raina gave Nakita a huge squeeze.

"I knew it. I've been watching you two making eyes all night. I've never seen Nox as happy as he is today. He's been walking around like a lovesick puppy since he met you, but today he was more like a mooning teenager. Oh Nakita, if there's anyone I know that deserves to be happy, it's Nox. He's like the brother I never had, and I couldn't be happier. I had my misgivings to start with about the whole moving in together thing because I didn't want to see either of you get hurt, but I can see now that you belong together."

"You really think so?" she asked, needing assurance from someone else. She still had so many doubts, but she was trying not to think about them. "We're so different. Do you really think I could make him happy?"

"You'll make him plenty happy, Nakita, I've already seen it. And yes, you are both different, I agree, but you're just the right amount of different that it could work."

Nakita couldn't wipe the smile off her face at Raina's words as she helped herself to another punch.

"Want some punch?" she asked to change the topic, not wanting anyone to overhear. "It's so good. The mint is so refreshing."

Raina bit her lip. "Actually, I don't think I'll be drinking your kind of punch for a while." Her face broke into a wide grin.

"You're not?" Nakita exclaimed, as she got the gist of Raina's meaning and threw her arms around her. "I'm so happy for you. But I thought you were done with babies?"

Raina nodded smiling, "Apparently they weren't done with me. Anyway, Pete and I couldn't be more delighted, though it was a huge shock and it did take a little to get us used to the idea. I thought I was way past it. We wanted to tell you guys sooner, but first we wanted to be sure. Wyatt was thoroughly disgusted to know we still do that sort of thing; but secretly I think he actually likes the idea of having a baby brother or sister."

"I'm so excited for you," Nakita squealed.

"Heard about our good news, huh?" Pete wrapped his arms around Raina and nuzzled into her neck.

"Yes! Congrats, Pete, looks like you got your wish."

"Yeah, well, I can't keep this one off me."

"Pete." Raina shoved him in the arm. He grabbed her, planting a solid kiss on her lips before heading back to his banjo to get ready for the next song.

"So can I have this dance?" Nox asked in low tones, his warm breath by her ear. A shiver worked its way down her neck, making her lower spine tingle.

"Shouldn't you be playing with the band?"

He took her hands and ran his thumbs over her knuckles. "They'll make do. Let's get out of here."

"I thought you wanted to dance with me?"

"Not here, I want you all to myself."

He drew her away from the din of the party, his arm slung low around her hips. Stopping by his van on the way, he took out a blanket. They wandered past all the parked cars in the paddock, making their way to the tiny shelter that stood by the curve of the river in front of the jetty. Someone had thought to string up red Chinese lanterns that swung languidly from a weeping willow in the balmy evening breeze.

"Look at this—it's enchanting."

"You're enchanting." He spun her towards him, catching her up in a playful dance, crooning the silly words of a country song that floated from the barn in the distance. She giggled at his outburst and he suddenly stopped, his face serious. She stilled as he reached out and ran his knuckles along her cheek. Lacing his fingers in hers, he held her captive by the magnetic pull of his eyes.

"You've made me the happiest man, Nakita. I want you—all of you." Holding her chin between his forefinger and thumb, he tipped her head back, his mouth against hers in a slow, aching kiss.

She'd been waiting for this moment since last night after finally submitting to her feelings. Leaning in closer, she savoured this entirely new sensation of her body pressed against his. Her fingers wound in the knot of his hair, pulling it free as she kissed him back without reserve. Together their lips became more insistent, more demanding. She dared, for the first time, to allow her hands to wander over the hard surfaces of his body, down his shoulder blades, his muscled back. She slid her hands under his shirt, lost in the plea-sure of the feel of the smooth skin of his hips. All the while, his lips worked on the curve of her neck. Without a thought, she proceeded to unbutton his shirt. This time he didn't stop her. Her hands roamed and pressed against the tautness of his abdomen, gliding up to the planes of his chest where she felt his heart beating fast against her hand. Groaning at her touch, his hands were doing their own explo-ration; awakening her flesh.

Right then, she knew what she wanted more than anything. She stopped his hands and stepped back; he looked at her, confused, his eyebrows drawn together. Reaching behind herself, she unzipped her dress and let it fall to the jetty. His face changed from a look of concern to comprehension, then unmasked need and desire. He took her hand, leading her to a shadowy section of the riverbank. He lay the blanket on the ground amongst the reeds that swayed with each gentle gust of warm, flower-scented breeze. Taking her in his arms, he kissed her with fervour and reverence; then pulling her down where he sat on the blanket so she straddled him, he continued his explo-ration, uninhibited, until neither of them could bear it any longer. In one effortless movement, she found herself beneath him. He gazed down at her, branding her with love and desire matched by her own. As his hands, his mouths, his body embraced her, she gave herself to him; holding nothing back.

She lay in his arms, gazing up at the moon, unable to remember a time in her life when she felt so alive, so content. He nuzzled into her hair.

"I can't help wondering if this is all just a dream I'm going to wake up from," she murmured.

"Me too."

She shifted with a sudden idea. "You know, there is one way for us to test if this is real or a dream."

"What do you suggest?" He nipped playfully on her collarbone. She turned and kissed him on the tip of his nose and pulled free of his arms, reluctant to let go.

"You have fifteen seconds to be in that water." She nodded towards the river.

"What?"

"Or you can stay there and miss out on this glorious moment." Overcome with delirious joy, she skipped to the end of the small jetty. With the moon reflecting liquid silver on the still water of the river, the last thing she registered as she cast an inviting glance over her shoulder were his eyes, wide open in disbelief. *Good, I shocked him.* Diving headlong into the embrace of the river, air bubbles rippled over her skin and she knew now—she wasn't dreaming. As she came up, he was diving in after her, his powerful arms wrapping around her waist, pulling her towards him. He took her face in his hands, his mouth meeting hers once again. The water was slightly cooler than the warmth of the outside air; and she was in a fever. She kissed him back with a passion, far too long withheld. His lips found the base of her throat, her neck, her ears as she wrapped her legs around him and he pulled her closer still, the feel of her body against his; finally close as they needed to be. Everything about him filled her with a dizzying elation.

He pulled away, disentangling himself so she was standing on the riverbed; his breath ragged like hers. He took her hands and gazed at her as though she were infinitely precious. "It's like I've been in love with you forever. The idea of someone like you, someone I never thought existed..." He pressed his forehead against hers. "Nakita, I don't have the magic carpet ride you want and I don't have much. All I have to offer you is me—all of me. Share this life with me. Marry me, Nakita?"

She swayed at his words. "Did you just ask me to marry you?"

"Yes. I know it's sudden, and I don't have a ring; but I know you, and I want all of you, just as you are. Nothing is going to change for me. I want you to be my wife."

Now that she'd tasted him, there was no going back.

"I want to be your wife." She spoke the words from her heart; they rang true from the depths of her being.

He pulled back from her. "So is that a yes?" he asked, as though he couldn't believe his ears.

"Yes!"

"Swear on it." He gripped her tighter, his voice husky in emotion and disbelief.

She put her hand over his heart and took his hand and put it over hers and looked into his eyes.

"I swear on it." She threw herself onto him again and kissed him with glee, submerging them both in the river.

CHAPTER 31

"*W*on't be a sec," Nox called out, hearing the doorbell of Ink Guild chime.

"Nox, it's just me." Annie's voice came from the door.

"Annie, hey, come in," he said, wiping down the leather upholstery of the tattoo lounge. He wasn't sure if Nakita had told Annie about them yet, so he decided it was best to keep his mouth shut. That was a best friend's prerogative, not his. Annie would probably have a hernia in excitement.

Something in her demeanour was unsettling. He'd never seen her looking so drawn. Maybe she was having issues with Proctor?

"Annie, what's up? Is everything okay?" When she didn't respond, he knew something was definitely up.

"Are you okay? Come, sit down." He led her to a chair in the corner.

"Nox, I think you are going to be the one who needs to sit down."

"What? Why? What's happened?" The valve in his heart released hot blood.

"Is Nakita okay?"

"Yeah, she's fine. That is, I haven't seen her. Nothing like that."

"Oh, thank God, you nearly gave me a heart attack." He watched as her eyes drew to his chest—she had a queer look on her face.

"Nox, I need to tell you something."

"So tell me." He sat on a stool, giving her his full attention. She stood in front of him and he became increasingly nervous as he watched her pace around the room. "Annie, tell me. What the hell is going on?"

"Remember the other day when Kit went for her interview and Proctor and I were here?"

"Of course."

"I was talking about donating blood and you said your blood type was 'O'?"

"Yeah?" his eyes narrowed, unsure where she was headed.

"Nox, I won a bet against Will once. He ended up giving blood. I went with him because he was terrified of needles. Nox, I know for a fact that Will was Type B."

She didn't have to state the obvious; he knew the implications immediately. If Will had Type B blood, he couldn't possibly have Will's heart—it was incompatible. He felt as the blood drained from his face.

"Let me finish." Her forehead was creased with two intense frown lines as she continued. "When I was working at the hospital the other day, I told my friend who takes care of record keeping about your situation and I asked her to check the records. I thought if maybe there was some kind of mistake and you had someone else's heart, then maybe it would help. I mean, we never knew one hundred percent if it was Will's heart to begin with; though chances were that it was because of the timing... Nakita has been so emotionally stilted by you having Will's heart. Nox, I wished I hadn't done it. I thought there might have been some confusion I could clear up."

"Annie, it's fine." His cheeks puffed out as he blew out a breath, rubbing his forehead. "So I don't have Will's heart? Wow. I guess I suppose I should be relieved. It might make things easier for us now."

"Make what easier?" she asked, her face set in stone.

He grinned widely. It was his turn to be the Cheshire cat. "Well, I was going to leave it to Nakita, but I guess I can't now." He stood to tell her the news that had him whistling all day, knowing he was the luckiest bastard alive. "We finally got our act together, not that you can take full credit, though I know you probably will... I guess what you said the other night may have had something to do with it." He looked into Annie's blank stare, still reeling a bit from the bombshell she'd just dropped. "Nakita and I are together now. I was going to leave it for her to tell you but I don't think she'd mind considering..." He took a deep breath, "I've asked her to marry me and she said yes." He waited for Annie's reaction, but it didn't come. She shut her eyes like he'd just landed a blow to her stomach.

"Marry? Already?" She looked as dumbfounded as he felt. He shrugged, feeling a little defensive at her reaction. The last thing he needed was Annie to be against them now.

"Yeah, well, we want to be together and that's never going to change."

She put her hand to her temple as if she was about to be sick. "Oh no, this is not good."

He frowned. "Why? I thought you of all people would be happy about it."

"No. Nox, it's not that. There's something else."

"What?" he demanded, a stab of alarm shot through his gut.

Collapsing into a chair, she placed her face in her hands.

"Nox. There's no simple way to say this... You have the heart of the man who tried to rape Nakita—the man who killed Will."

The air sucked out of the room.

"What?" His heart was a violent pump at her words. "Is this some kind of fucking joke, Annie? Because it's not even remotely funny."

She shook her head in denial. "Nox, I wished I left well enough alone. I wasn't going to tell you, but Proctor said I'd never be able to look either of you in the eye again."

"Annie, how is it even possible? I mean, what are the chances of that even happening?"

"Remote; you would think," she lifted her face. "At the time, everyone was so focused on Will's death and... Nakita... we knew that Gregory Reynolds had died within days of Will, but none of us cared what happened to him."

"No, this can't be happening." He paced the room in denial, then turned to her. "Annie, there must be some mistake."

Her eyes held his as she shook her head again. "Not this time, Nox. Reynolds was brain dead... he wasn't recorded on the donor registry, but when his father heard what he'd done, he gave permission for his organs to be donated; hoping to make amends, I suppose. I saw the records with my own eyes. You have his heart."

He stood still, his head upturned with his hands on his face as the truth sank in. Of all the cruel jokes, this had to be the worst. He had the heart of a rapist and murderer beating in his chest. He staggered forward to a chair, stone cold and lightheaded. He was going to be sick. He lurched to the sink, retching until there was only bile left. He barely registered Annie's hands on his shoulder, trying to comfort him as he washed his mouth and face with cold water.

"I'm so sorry, Nox. Are you okay?"

He didn't answer. He'd never be okay, not now.

"Listen; I've been thinking, we don't have to tell her. It can be our secret. I promise I will never, ever say a word of it again," her voice stretched tight.

He turned and looked at her. "Do you really think I'd lie to Nakita? I love her more than my own life. She has to know the truth."

"Don't be crazy. It's all a big mistake," she begged. Her eyes levelled with his, "You know what it will mean if you tell her. She doesn't need to know. It's not going to help her. You're still you, Nox; it doesn't change a thing; it's just a stupid pump, for crying out loud. It's all in her head, it always has been."

"Annie. I want to spend the rest of my days looking into Nakita's eyes. Do you really think I can do that knowing this?" He grabbed his wallet and keys. "She has to know." He went to the door and stopped.

He looked down at his chest. It was as if he'd just found out that an imposter, a parasite, had infiltrated him.

And it had.

"All this time I thought I had the heart of someone free-spirited, someone loved and noble... I have the heart of a rapist—a murderer. I have the heart of the man who took everything from the woman I love. The woman I gave my heart and soul to. She has to know." His resolve was bittersweet.

"Nox, don't do it, she'll never marry you." Annie pulled at his forearm. He turned, yanking free from her grip, a wave of grief and rage consumed him, roaring, he punched his fist into the wall, leaving a hole in the plaster. Pain lanced from his hand to his forearm, but he ignored it and strode out of the room.

Nakita had to know.

Nox stood for a moment, watching her working in the garden in her denim shorts, ankle boots and a loose T-shirt by the light of the dwindling afternoon sun. Her cheeks were pink from exertion; her hair hung in two long braids. When she saw him, her face broke into a huge grin. Throwing down her hand-trowel, she hurled herself at him exuberantly, wrapping her legs around his waist, her lips catching his. He'd only had two days of this. Two days of pure joy, and now *this*. He allowed himself one last kiss; one last, throbbing, aching, uncontaminated kiss—knowing it'd be his last.

He wrapped her up in his arms and kissed her slow and long, hoping in that one kiss, he could impart the depth of his love.

Kissing her was the reality that told him that this wasn't a nightmare

He was contaminated—polluted.

Arms still wrapped around his neck, she pulled away, gazing and smiling down into his face; adoration plain on her face. Even so, he wouldn't contemplate not telling her.

"If you keep kissing me like that, the neighbours will talk." She murmured.

He eased her down to the ground; his heart thrashing against the wall of his chest.

"Wait—why are you back so early? Where's Emmylou? Are you okay?"

He took her dirtied hands in his, his movements slow; while turmoil raged inside of him. As she saw apprehension in his face, fear registered in hers.

She grabbed his forearm. "Nox? What's wrong? Where's Emmylou?"

"She's fine, Nakita."

"Then what's wrong? You don't look right. My God, you're bleeding. What have you done to your hand?" He looked down at it. He may have broken something, but he barely registered the pain. It was nothing compared to the searing agony in his chest.

"Nakita. There's something I have to tell you."

"Okay," she said, but he could see that she was bracing herself. "Do we need to sit down?"

"Yeah, that would be good."

She held his hand, and they walked over to a garden bench, looking into his face the entire time.

He stood in front of her and let out a long breath.

"Nakita. First, I want you to know that every part of me loves every part of you. You and Emmylou are my world—my reason for living."

She stood. "Nox, you're scaring me. What's happened? Don't you want to marry me anymore? Because we can postpone. I understand if it was too quick." Her voice trembled.

"Nakita, with all my heart..." he stopped, closing his eyes, searching for better words. "With all my soul and mind, I want nothing more than to grow old with you." Her smile was tremulous as she sat back down. "Annie came by today—"

"Did you tell—" He reached out to brush his knuckles gently to her jaw, but refrained, who was he to touch her?

"Just. Listen. Okay?" He kept his voice low and gentle. "Annie came by today because something I said the other day got her doing some research at the hospital." *Just say it.* "Nakita, my blood type is 'O.' Will's wasn't."

"So?"

"So, a heart transplant can only work if you have compatible blood types. Mine and Will's blood types were incompatible."

She blinked. "So I don't get it. How was yours made compatible?"

"It wasn't." She looked at him, confused. He let out another breath to deliver the first blow. "Nakita, I don't have Will's heart."

She stood again. "Are you sure? How can you be certain?"

"Annie saw the hospital records." He watched the shock in her face as she took this news in.

"I'm astonished... I don't know if I feel relieved or not. Why didn't Annie tell me?" She sat back down heavily, her mouth opened in shock. "It seems so strange, all those times I listened to what I thought was his heart." She turned and took a deep breath, seeing the look on his face. "Nox, it's okay. I'll deal with it. It will probably take me some time to get used to. It's probably a good thing, I guess. It's just such a shock and kind of unsettling. Who has Will's heart then?"

"We don't know." He tried to swallow around the hard lump in his throat.

"That's not all," he looked at the ground, unable to look in her eyes for the pain he was about to cause her. For the complete and utter shame that he felt. "Annie found out something else."

Her downcast eyes lifted to his face.

Say. It. Just say it.

"They gave me the heart of Gregory Reynolds, the man who killed Will."

It was done. The words tasted worse than the acrid bile in his mouth earlier.

"Nox, this isn't funny," she stood bolt upright, her face stricken.

"Nakita, I wouldn't joke about this."

"That's ridiculous, there has to be some mistake. Why would you have that monster's heart? It has to be Will's heart, or... or someone else's."

"Annie saw the records. Think about it, Nakita, Reynolds died from a brain haemorrhage two days after Will passed away. My transplant was the date Reynolds died. I don't know how we never realised... it can't have been Will's, we all just assumed. I was hoping Annie had made a mistake..." Each word he spoke nailed his hopes and dreams into a coffin that would never again see the light of day. He could only watch on as the colour drained from her. He wanted to touch her, to comfort her.

"Oh my God—" Her hands went to her face as her whole body swayed in dismay. He reached out to steady her, but she snatched her arm away, as though his touch revolted her. "Don't touch me... Please... I—"

"Nakita, I know this is an enormous shock to you. It was for me too; it will take us a little time to get used to." He stepped forward, palms out. She put her hand up and turned her face from him, her voice barely a whisper.

"Please... I can't. Please, don't touch me."

Leaning in, he spoke fast in supplication, his voice barely holding out. "Nakita, you're my everything. I love you. I want you as my wife, by my side, forever. We can work through this. We can work through anything." She didn't move. Her eyes were clamped shut, so he continued. "Nakita. I'm not him. I've never been either of them. We have to fight for this. Fight for us."

"Fight for what?" she was panting now, her arms wrapped around her stomach as though winded. "It's not possible. You have his heart." He wanted to embrace her, to protect her, to make it all go away. "I despise him."

"Nakita, I'm not him." His frustration turned to desperation as he realised she'd already shut down on him. "Remember that time in the kitchen you said to me true love was worth the hassle? Remember. This is worth it."

"It doesn't matter." Her eyes were closed as tears streamed, unchecked, down her cheeks. "I can't do it, Nox, you have to understand... some things... are just too much. This is just too much..."

"Don't do this. Don't throw us away. Just take some time. I'll give you some space."

"He took everything. Now he's taken you." She was walking in circles, fists clenched by her side as though she were in the midst of a panic attack. "To think... I laid my head on your chest and listened to *his* heart. I gave myself to you, to him," she shuddered in disgust. "He got me. In the end, he got me."

He reached out to touch her on the shoulder, but thought better of it.

"No, he didn't. I'm not him. I have his heart, but you have mine. From that very first time we met—it was yours."

She spun around in sudden fury, stabbing a finger to his chest where his heart lay underneath. "This heart is black with filth." Her face was twisted with rage and revulsion, when only moments before it had shone with admiration and devotion. "See this heart?" She jabbed him again. "It's dead to me—I want to tear it out of you."

"You just did." His voice broke as he turned and left.

His heart was a cold, steel blade in his chest.

CHAPTER 32

$\mathcal{N}$akita found herself back to where she'd been before Nox and Emmylou had entered her life, back to trying to forget. If someone were to scratch her starchy, librarian exterior, they would see that just below the surface she was red raw. She knew that she well and truly wore the caricature librarian look now, complete with sensible clothes and shoes, severe hair and the scowl of a young woman who'd already sucked too many bitter lemons in life. At the very least, she knew she should be grateful that she had the job she'd always secretly wanted, but somehow everything felt like it was for nothing.

The cover of the book in her hand caught her attention. It was some Fabio-like creature in all his glory, dressed in a pirate's outfit with a smouldering look on his face and a raven haired beauty draped across his lap, her cleavage heaving out of her dress and lips parted.

"Still My Beating Heart," he muttered, "you've got to be kidding me." Her voice came loud in the silence of her cubicle. She slammed the book face down on the counter then looked up, hoping no one heard. Everyone continued in their usual state of oblivion—except for two people. A young guy was down an aisle slightly hidden from view from most people in the library. He had his arms around a pretty girl, burrowing his face into her neck while she had her head tipped back, giggling. Nakita watched knowingly as things between them progressed into a full-blown, make-out session. Something stabbed inside her, jolting her to action.

That's it. I'll put an end to this. She strode up to them.

"Excuse me." She used her sharpest tone. They pulled away, both looking sheepish. "In case it escaped your notice, this is a library where people come to borrow books." She enjoyed the sound of her voice, dripping with condescension. "To read, to work, to learn." The girl looked at the floor, her face bright red. "I suggest if you want to make-out, that you go elsewhere. This is not the place."

"Yeah. No problem. We were just leaving anyway," the guy snarled. He put his arm around his girlfriend, drawing her close. "Freaking librarians, they're all the same. Just a bunch of uptight bitches; pissed off at the world." He didn't bother lowering his voice.

Heat flooded Nakita at his words as she saw a flashback of the time she and Nox had fooled around in the library, acting like teenagers themselves. Shaking her head, she straightened her shoulders and went back to the glass enclosed room that was like her own emotional bubble. Her phone was vibrating on the bench. She ran over to it, a small part of her hopeful that it would be him. Even though she was certain if it had been, she wouldn't have answered it. It had been six weeks since he'd walked out, since the day she had treated him like the monster that had killed her brother. She would never forget the look of shock and hurt on his face. She grabbed the phone. *Annie.* Her shoulders sagged.

"Hey." She kept her voice even, though nothing inside of her felt even. Nothing felt good or okay anymore.

"Nakita, are you ready for this? I found him. Marie contacted the family and asked if they'd like to meet you and they said they would. His name's Tristan—Tristan Blake—he's seventeen. Kit? Kit? Are you there?"

~

"Suzie?" she asked the plump, middle-aged woman sitting on the bench seat.

"Hello, love." Suzie stood and grasped her hands, dark blue eyes shining. Something about her presence instantly set Nakita at ease.

"Thanks for agreeing to meet with me." Nakita squeezed her hands in return.

"Oh love, please, think nothing of it. We're so happy to meet with you. You've given us the greatest gift. Tristan," she called. Nakita followed the mother's line of sight to land on a shaggy-haired, shirt-less teenager. He wore black jeans in spite of the intense blanket of afternoon heat, made more merciless by the glare of concrete. In typical teen style, he kept skating, barely giving his mum a cursory glance.

"That boy, I tell you," Suzie said in an exasperated voice, but Nakita could see the pride and love that gleamed in her eyes.

"He's fine." Nakita reassured her. "I don't want him to feel weird or pressured. I'm sure he isn't feeling entirely comfortable. It's such an unusual situation."

"That's lovely of you, darling. He's really such a good boy. When he's not at school, he's always keeping active by skating, riding his BMX or surfing. He's got a great bunch of mates; they really look out for each other."

"Oh, that's great to hear. He's looking well."

"He is, isn't he?" she said, talking to Nakita, but watching her son as he did a slide on a rail; the ease with which he pulled it off, a fair indicator of how much he must practice.

"He recovered so quickly, the doctors were amazed." She turned to Nakita, tears in her eyes, "I'm so glad you contacted us because I've been wanting to thank you for letting my boy have a chance to live. He's all I've got in the world. His father left us when I was pregnant." She sniffed. "Without getting into the details, Tristan is my everything. I nearly lost him, but thanks to you and your dear brother, I didn't."

Nakita felt a surge of warmth towards the single mum and her son—her world. She knew how it felt to have your world ripped away. She reached out and pressed her hand to Suzie's shoulder. Suzie reached up, patted her hand and gave Nakita a tremulous smile.

"I can never pay you back or tell you what this gift means for us. I know this comes at a great cost to you and I have no words to say except thank you for your selfless act."

"It means a lot for you to say so. And you know, it makes me happy, knowing that Tristan is living his life." Thunder reverberated across the sky. Suzie looked up and pulled a face.

"I think there's going to be a downpour. I'll call him over so you can meet him. Tristan!" she called again, in a no-nonsense voice.

Nakita watched as he paused, taking in Nakita standing with his mum. He flicked his deck up, grabbing it by the end, and walked over. "Tristan, where's your shirt?" his mum scolded, sounding embarrassed. Nakita knew it was more to do with the exposure of his scar than him being shirtless.

"Oh yeah, sorry, it was hot," the teen mumbled and pulled on the shirt that hung from the back of his pants, but not before Nakita noted the pink scar that ran from the top of his angular chest, to the bottom. He put out his hand.

"Hey," he said, simply. She took his outstretched hand in hers and smiled.

"Hi, Tristan, I'm Nakita. I'm really pleased to meet you."

He gave her a brief, shy smile, then his eyes slid to his mother, and she nodded slightly to reassure him. He looked back to Nakita and took a breath.

"I just want to thank you... ah, for your sacrifice, and for giving me a chance to live. I want you to know that I'm going to try my hardest to make the best out of the rest of my life." She watched him blush as he stumbled on his words. Even though they sounded rehearsed, she knew by his demeanour they were heartfelt. Tears sprang to her eyes.

"Thanks, Tristan." She dabbed at the tears. "I know Will would be proud that you have his heart and he'd ask nothing more than for you to live your life to the absolute fullest—that's how he lived his."

Suzie passed her a tissue as she held one to her own eyes and they both laughed. Tristan looked between the two, shifting on his feet as though unsure why they were crying and laughing at the same time.

"Do you reckon one time when you're feeling up to it, you could tell me a bit about him? I'd kinda like to know what he was like," His question warmed Nakita's heart. It was as though he were giving her the ultimate gift.

"I'd love nothing more. Would you find it weird if I gave you a hug?"

He shook his head and smiled "No. I'm okay with it. I guess in a weird way, your kind of like a sister now."

She laughed, leaning in to give the tall, skinny teenager a tight squeeze. "I guess in a way I am. You know, I can almost hear Will groaning. He always thought I was way too bossy."

"Well, you couldn't be any worse than mum."

Suzie rolled her eyes in feigned exasperation. "Now I told Tristan that there was the possibility that you may want to listen to his heart-beat and he's fine with that too."

"Thanks, guys, that's really kind of you. But you know, I think I'm okay for now. His heart belongs to you. It's a good thing." She smiled at them, glad that she was truly okay with it. Even kind of elated somehow. Though she'd lost Will, something beautiful had come out of it. One time, unbeknownst to her, he'd made the choice to donate his organs, never dreaming it would become a reality. Will being someone who lived from moment to moment—the very fact he had the forethought to be an organ donor meant it was important to him. And here was Tristan's life now, stretched out before him. Her brother was gone, yes, but now a young man lived, and not just him; but others who had received Will's other vital organs.

Nakita could tell Tristan was itching to get back on his board. "Hey, go for it. Don't mind me."

"You sure?" He asked, spinning the wheel of his skateboard.

"Yeah, we've got plenty of time to catch up."

"See you again soon, I'm sure Mum will be all over it." He threw his board down on the ground and skated off with a grin.

"He's something special," Nakita said. Suzie nodded in agreement.

"Are you doing okay yourself, love?" she asked after a moment. Nakita paused at the unexpected question. Somehow, meeting Tristan had moved her beyond mere acceptance, bringing her to a point nearer to true closure.

"Yeah. I am," she nodded. "This has actually helped me so much." There was peace knowing that even though Will's heart was in Tristan's chest, the true essence of him was in her heart.

Saying their goodbyes, they promised to keep in contact. As she walked back to the car, she smiled to herself at Tristan's words, promising to make good on his life. It stirred a memory, a memory of someone else who'd made a similar promise in the early morning hours in her bedroom...

The sweetness of the moment was gone. A sudden stupor overcame her, causing her steps to falter as she let her mind wander to a place she hadn't been permitting it to go.

She went home and even though it was still early in the day and she knew it was stupid, she lay in his bed, her head resting on the very same pillow that his had rested on. She hadn't been into the mezzanine since he left, but for some reason today, she wanted to be near him. She swore she could still smell traces of his cologne. She thought about Tristan and tried to imagine having done the bucket list with him as Will's stand-in, but she couldn't. Nox had been the perfect stand-in, not because he had Will's heart, but because he was Nox.

Nox. Emmylou.

Everything inside ached when she thought of them. Finding out that Nox had that monster's heart had utterly blindsided her. Grief, excruciating grief, had reared its ugly head again, but this time she was grieving for more. It was Will again, but now it was Nox and Emmylou as well.

Losing Nox was painful in ways that losing Will wasn't. Grief wasn't a blanket emotion, even though every encounter she had with it was agonizing; each face to face meeting revealed its own facets, it's own depths and rough edges that left her groping in the darkness, gasping, desperate to take another breath or to never want to breathe again. Nox was no different to Tristan; he deserved a chance at life. If he hadn't received Reynold's heart that night, chances were, he wouldn't be alive now.

Is that what you really want, Nakita—Nox dead? The very part of him he freely gave to you is the same part keeping him alive.

Rolling onto her side, more tears slipped out the corners of her eyes. She slid her hand under the pillow. Feeling something hard, she pulled out a deck of cards. She'd forgotten that she left them there after coming home the first night he'd told her he loved her. That night she lay in his bed, hoping he'd come back, knowing he wouldn't. Holding them to her chest, the knot of anxiety in her stomach sending spasms of grief convulsing upwards. Her life so far had been a cruel game of cards; dealing her one bad hand after another.

CHAPTER 33

*O*ne foot in front of the other, just focus on breathing. In. Out. Her hair was pulled back way too tight. Her head ached badly, but she invited the pain. It was a welcome distraction. *Breathe in. Hold. Breathe out. Just grab the groceries you need and get out of there.*

As she walked towards the main entrance, she sucked in a sharp breath. Out the front of the shopping centre, smoking a rollie and wearing tattered, ill-fitting jeans and a grimy singlet, was the homeless man that often hung around Ink Guild. But it was his fluorescent yellow Crocs that captured her attention. Her steps faltered. She stood rooted to the spot, panic clutching her throat. *It's just like Will all over again. I will never escape him.* Reminders of Nox were everywhere and even when they weren't, she still couldn't forget. Narrowing her eyes at the shoes, she stepped towards him. For reasons she couldn't comprehend, she had to have them.

"Excuse me?" *How does my voice sound so normal?*

"Why hullo there, pretty, young lady," the man answered from a mouth that had seen better days. She held her breath to avoid inhaling the stream of rank smoke that enveloped her. "Would you like a rollie, love?" He held out his pouch of tobacco with grubby nicotine stained fingers.

"No. I want to buy your shoes."

He paused mid-drag, smoke spilling out of his mouth. "What these?" He lifted his cracked heel, looking at his shoes, his expression dubious.

"Yeah, those." She glanced over her shoulder, hoping no one heard her strange request.

"How much?" She was relieved he didn't ask why, because she wouldn't be able to answer this herself. "How does ten dollars sound?"

"Ten? No can do lovey. A man needs a pair of shoes and these are the comfiest pair I've ever owned."

"How about twenty then?" He rubbed the back of his stringy hair and shook his head.

"No deal. These are pre-loved, lovey. Shoes like these are hard for a man of my means to part with."

"Look, I have to have those shoes. I'll give you fifty dollars. That's all I've got." He tipped his head to the side, contemplating her offer, then stuck out his hand.

"Deal." She shook his hand quickly and reached into her purse to fish out the fifty dollars. Handing it to him, she watched as he took his time putting it away in a worn wallet. Reaching down, he took off his shoes. Her agitation increased with every second.

"You won't get a better pair of shoes than these. Young bloke passed them onto me. I reckon I'm doing you a favour here." He passed her the shoes with a look of reluctance and she quickly stuffed them into her handbag.

"Thanks," she mumbled.

He tipped two fingers to his head with a nod as though he were wearing a top hat. Once inside the privacy of her car, she hurled her handbag onto the passenger seat. The Crocs fell out. Seeing them again, she burst into tears.

Nakita pounded on the front door. Finally, it opened.

"Antony," her voice broke. She collapsed into his large frame. He wrapped her in his arms and stroked her head with his oversized hand.

"What's all this now, love?"

"What have I done, Antony?" She buried her face into his shirt. "I trampled underfoot the best thing...that ever...happened to me, then I threw it away. Why Antony? Wasn't losing Mum and Dad and Will enough?"

He continued to pat her as she sobbed. Drawing comfort from him, she pulled her face away. He took a folded handkerchief from his pocket releasing the familiar tea tree smell she remembered from when she was little.

"Dry your tears and come out back, Nikko. You came at the right time. I just put the kettle on. I'll make a pot of our favourite tea."

She took a deep shuddering breath and went with him into the small kitchen, her body instantly relaxing in its familiarity. They didn't speak as Antony navigated his way around readying the teapot. Nakita prepared a tray with two china teacups and a small jug of milk. As Antony poured the hot water from the kettle with shaking, arthritic hands, Nakita didn't take over. Even though it wasn't easy for him and occasionally there'd be a spill, she knew that Antony was more than capable of the task and took great pride in his independence. The sharp aroma of Earl Grey tea caused her to wrinkle her nose; it tasted like dishwashing liquid. She never had the heart to tell him that she really didn't like it, even after all these years. It went against her grain to dislike anything that Antony loved. She carried out the tray to the small white table-setting in the sun, his preferred spot to drink tea in his flower scented garden.

"Now we'll just be careful with these love. Miriam will have my neck if we put so much as a chink in this china. I don't know what on earth has gotten into her, but after fifty years of never using it, she's decided that we'll only use the good chinaware from now on; God love that woman, stubborn as a mule." The last words were ones that she'd heard Antony speak affectionately a thousand times over the years. They sat in a long comfortable silence, sipping their tea. It was the rhythm of Antony.

"You know, Nikko, when I was your age, well actually a few years younger than you, I fell in love with a young lady—Shirley, her name was."

"No, really? Antony, I thought it was always just you and Mim." His face had the look that only those who'd really lived a lifetime could muster. His sightless eyes twinkled.

"That's the eternal folly of youth, my love; they think us old folk are one dimensional, long past being interesting. But it's only when they stop and listen that they hear how we have lived, loved and lost enough to weave many a good tale. The clever thing about the stories of the grey haired is that they always have a little pearl to take home.

"Lord, but she was a beauty. I fell headlong in love first time I ever saw her." He took a slow sip of his tea while she waited eagerly to hear his story. "Shirley was the new girl in town and when she and I met we hit it off. We became inseparable. There was no Facebooks and all the what-not that young folk carry on with nowadays. It was just me and Shirley, the trees, the rivers and wide open fields," he smiled, wistful.

"Now you remember I came from a God-fearing family. My father was the local minister and he was a good man. A big man, he was stronger than an ox. He had a lot of respect in the town we lived in and for miles around. My mother, rest her soul, was a tiny but formidable woman. Oh she had a heart of gold, but when she got something in her head, she could become a real shrew. Even though father was a powerful man, my mother knew how to turn his head when she wanted.

"When mum saw me knocking around with Shirley she knew trouble was brewing. Mothers have a special gift of sniffing out trouble where their sons are concerned. All it took was one word from mum and my father forbade me to see Shirley anymore." His eyes were moist with the reminiscence of youthful passion. "Oh and didn't I kick up a stink. I was young and foolish. I'd had a taste of one of Shirley's kisses and I was done for. Well, I just had to go see Shirley one last time. She convinced me to run off with her. I was all of seventeen and she was fifteen. Now I don't know how, but my dad got wind of our plan...I still blame Clem," he chuckled, with a glint in his eyes.

"Little sisters are notorious for getting into their big brother's business. She denied it all along; I guess I'll never know now. Anyway, my father found us some miles down the way to Borranggini and when he caught up, he took his horse whip to me. I couldn't stand or sit for weeks. He took Shirley home to her father and I never saw her again." He went quiet for a moment.

"What happened then, Antony?" she prompted, completely intrigued by this new revelation.

"I vowed I'd never speak to my father again, that I'd never forgive him. The way I saw it, he was ruining my life, stopping me from being with the girl of my dreams. I stuck true to my word; didn't speak to him for almost two months. He tried so hard to break through, but I had purposed in my heart to hate him forever...fool boy I was..." He shook his head, his aged eyes sad.

"Well life has a funny way of teaching you a lesson, doesn't it? My father ended up in a farming accident. He was helping out one of our neighbours when their young son climbed into a hole they were excavating. Dad jumped in and saved him, losing his life in the process." Tears fell from his sightless eyes. He pulled out another handkerchief and wiped his eyes and blew his nose. Nakita's heart broke for him, the passionate young boy that he was and the old man that he'd become, still missing his dad, still regretting a choice made in the rashness of youth. She reached out and took his weathered hand in hers.

"Well, you can only imagine, Nikko, the guilt and sorrow I had for being a foolish, stubborn lad. I learnt my lesson, forgave him straight away of course. The hardest person to forgive was myself. Not long after, I found out Shirley had a baby." Nakita stiffened and Antony patted her hand. "Not mine, love. She'd gotten herself pregnant in the previous town and was too scared to tell her father. She ended up running off with some other fool of a young man." He took another trembling sip of his tea. "A lot happens in a lifetime, both good and bad. The only regret I have is not letting go of the things that I should have and not holding on to the things that were most important. You see, sweetheart, sometimes we go around making mountains out of molehills and molehills out of mountains—then we can't see the true view of things, the things that really matter. We get so busy giving the best of ourselves to molehills that don't amount to anything and we minimise that glorious mountain that stands before us."

"But I've had so many terrible things to endure with Mum dying from cancer and Dad taking his life." She'd never uttered those words before, but she forced herself to face them. "Then there was Will, now Nox. How can I let go of that?"

"Darling, there is no mountain without a valley. The thing is, to get to that mountain peak you have to throw off the things that are weighing you down. Some valleys are deeper and darker than others, but if you are one of those special ones who make their way out of the valley and take the journey to the summit, the view is more breathtaking that you can ever imagine."

Hearing him speak this way when he'd been blind most of his adult life, gave Nakita goose bumps.

"How, Antony? Tell me how. I don't want to be like this."

"The same way anyone throws off the things that hinder them, love. Look at nature, it happens all the time—metamorphosis, transformation. Something has to be left behind, but a miracle takes place and something wondrous emerges. Resurrection, rebirth takes place. We all come to a point in our lives, time and again when we have to give ourselves over to being reborn, reawakened."

She was silent for a long time, letting his words sink in.

"I'm scared. Everyone I love is taken from me." He reached out large hands, gnarled with age and found hers.

"Darling, we are tiny ships sailing upon this earth, our rudders may control our direction, but as soon as you think you can control the waves you ride, the raging storms, the howling wind—you're mistaken." He patted her hand. "Tell me, what did you love most about Will, Nikko?"

She thought for a moment. "So many things...but I guess most of all, how he met life head on—without reserve."

"Then, my beautiful, that is the lesson you need to take from him. Meet life head on, unreservedly. Live and love unreservedly." She sat in stunned silence at the weight of truth in his words. The stark realisation that she'd probably made the most regrettable decision in her life was a stunning blow, and what left her terrified, was that it might be too late.

"Darling, I've been meaning to tell you something, but you haven't been by for a while."

"I'm so sorry Antony. I guess I just kind of shut down the last month or so."

"I understand, love. I was meaning to let you know that Lennox visited with us... 'the Posse.'" Her stomach clenched at the mention of his name. "He visited a few times actually and read us all a story."

"That was the last thing on Will's bucket list," she breathed, unable to believe that he'd completed the very last thing on the list after all that had transpired, the terrible things she'd said to him, how she'd reacted, how she'd just wiped both he and Emmylou out of her life.

"What was the story Antony?"

Antony reached out to take her hand again, his eyes searching but unable to see. "It was Frankenstein, love."

285

*P*ulling up alongside Ink Guild, her heart sank. It was closed again, but unlike the first time when there had been a closed sign in the door, now it was boarded up. He was gone.

Why would he close up shop? Maybe he's left town altogether? She slapped the steering wheel. *So stupid Nakita. Frankenstein, I made him feel like Frankenstein, like a rejected, patched together, sub-human—not the remarkable person he is.* She stopped for a moment to gather herself and to work out what to do next. *The Belles. They'll know where he is.* She was hesitant to face Raina since she hadn't responded to any of her calls and messages. *What if he refuses to speak to me? What if he's turned to Bree for comfort and they're together now? It would serve you right.*

When she pulled into the Belle's long driveway her stomach clenched in a vice-like grip when she saw Nox's van. She turned the engine off and headed to the front door. The house was unusually quiet as she knocked a few times. Finally, just as she was about to turn and leave, she heard light footsteps come down the hall. The door swung open and Raina stood there, her belly now visibly swollen. Seeing Nakita, she stiffened.

"Nakita." A deep line appeared between Raina's brows. "What are you doing here?" She didn't seem angry, though she had every right to be. If anything, it seemed more like she was guarded.

Nakita moistened her lips.

"Hi Raina, you look well." She gave her a shaky smile. "I'm sorry that I've come by unannounced. I'm looking for Nox." Raina looked over her shoulder, her expression strange. She shut the door quietly behind her and motioned Nakita to the side of the house.

"He's not here, Nakita. What is it that you want? Can I help you with something?" She spoke in low tones, again not unfriendly, but cautious somehow.

"I don't think this is something you can help me with, Raina. I need to talk to Nox. I stopped by at the shop and I noticed it was closed." The subtle scent of the flowering shrubs in Raina's garden wafted across, reminding her of the words Antony had just spoken in his own flower filled garden. She had to follow through on this.

"Well, he's not here." She noticed Raina wasn't looking at her.

Is she lying? What is she hiding?

"Do you know where he is?" Raina's eyes slid to hers, and Nakita saw for the first time the dark shadows around them. "Is Emmylou here? Can I see her?" She peered around Raina's shoulder to the backyard.

"Nakita, I think things are better left alone," Raina said, leaning forward to pull off a gardenia flower that was wilted and dying. "Things are... different now."

"Raina, look, I wanted to say this to Nox first, but I owe you guys some kind of explanation too. I know you must feel like I've discarded our friendship." She felt herself tugging on the strands of her hair. "But the whole thing with Nox's heart gave me a huge shock and I just couldn't cope with the idea of it, but I realise now that I have been so stupid. I know that I was wrong. I was so, so wrong and I want to ask for his forgiveness... and yours and Pete's, and well, the truth is I want him back." Raina's eyes widened the more she spoke.

"Nakita, it's impossible. Just leave it alone." She shook her head, the line between her brows deepening to a deep slash. The panic inside of Nakita began to rise.

"Raina, I'm sorry. I know that I hurt all of you, and especially Emmylou and Nox. I can't fix what damage I've done—"

"No, the damage is done," Raina echoed. Nakita stepped back, surprised by her words. Raina blinked and shook her head. "I'm sorry. I know I can't blame you. It's not your fault."

"That's the thing, you can blame me. I understand, I do. What I did was despicable, but I want to try to make it right."

Raina put her hand up as if to stop her. "Nakita, that may be the case, but what's done is done, and like I said, it's too late for you and Nox now." Her words were a stab in Nakita's abdomen.

"Why? What do you mean?" A sudden thought occurred to her. "Is he with Bree?" her voice cracked as she put a hand to her head. She didn't want to hear the answer.

"Kitty!" Emmylou came bounding out of nowhere and tackled Nakita.

"Emmylou!" Nakita squatted and squeezed Emmylou tight, holding the exuberant little girl close. Emmylou pulled back and rested her forehead against Nakita's with her eyes closed.

"You came back, Kitty. I knew you would."

"Of course, sweetheart. I missed you terribly."

"I said my pwayers, evewy night, just like you showed me. Daddy said that God couldn't answer some pwayers, but I knew he would answer me coz I wanted you to come back soooo bad. And he's not going to let my daddy die coz I pway for him every night."

Nakita froze.

"Emmylou, I think I can hear Wyatt calling you. Go see what he wants," Raina cut in with a choked voice.

"Okay!" Emmylou lunged at Nakita on tiptoes, giving her a quick hug before skipping off as best she could in her sparkly gumboots, "I'll be back in a jiffy," she tossed over her shoulder.

Fingers of dread seized Nakita. She stood, trying to keep level, her eyes on Raina.

"What's going on Raina, tell me?"

Raina put her face in her hands. "He wouldn't let me tell you," she choked.

"Tell me what?" She put her hand on Raina's shoulder, steeling herself. "What, Raina?"

Raina lifted her tear-stained face to Nakita.

"He's very sick, Nakita. After he came back here, he just seemed to give up, worse than before he had the new heart. He's still on all his anti-rejection meds, but they're not working anymore. The doctors can't figure out what's going on. It seems as though his body is rejecting his heart. They're running out of options." Her voice gave way.

No. This is not happening. The sensation of blood draining from Nakita's face and limbs took hold of her. Everything began to fade. "I did this. It's my fault." Her throat was gripped in a tight vice as it dawned on her. "He rejected his heart because of me. Because I rejected him."

"No. Nakita, it's not your fault. Really, don't listen to what I said before. He couldn't cope with the thought of that vile man's heart in his chest. Nothing could change his mind. It's as though he's given up."

"No matter how you put it, Raina, it's all my fault. I rejected him because of his heart. He gave his heart to me and I rejected it, so he rejected it." She spun on her heel.

"Where are you going?" Raina grabbed her by the back of her blouse.

She turned. "What do you mean? I'm going to Nox."

"No. You can't. He made me swear—"

"Why isn't anybody at the hospital with him?"

"He didn't want Emmylou's memories to be of him sick. He was adamant." Raina's voice dissolved into a sob. "You can't go—"

"Raina, I love him."

Raina took hold of both her shoulders. "Nakita, don't do this to yourself. You've been through enough." Nakita pushed her hands away, hit by a wall of anguish.

"I won't let him go!"

Raina looked into her eyes and Nakita saw their acceptance. She pulled her in close for a quick hug before propelling her away.

"Then go, now!"

Cruel fingers still had a throat hold on Nakita as she walked into the hospital and asked once again for Lennox Conrad's room number. Everything that meant anything to her was lying in a hospital bed, ill, quite possibly dying. Thankfully, the nursing staff were engrossed in conversation and didn't notice as she slipped down the corridor. After passing a number of rooms with mostly elderly male patients, she came to the last room where the door stood open. She peeked in, her heart leaping to her throat.

He lay deathly still, machines beeping around him. Her body swayed with the need to be closer.

There was a vase of flowers from Raina's garden and colourful pictures of stick figures drawn by Emmylou stuck all over the walls. She recognised a picture of herself; a figure with bright red hair that stuck up into the sky. Her heart sank as she thought of the hurt she'd caused. On trembling legs, she walked to the side of his bed, unable to tell if he was asleep or looking out the open window at the dimming sky.

As she came closer, she could see how ill he was. It wasn't just the colour of his skin, but how he wheezed as though struggling for each breath.

"What are you doing here?" He didn't turn his head.

"How did you know...?" Tears streamed mutely down her face.

"I can smell honey. You always smell like honey."

Eyes once a green, seductive haven turned to look at her. For the briefest moment, they were dark and feverish, as though he'd had very little sleep for a long time. "Did you come to make sure the job was done? Don't worry; it won't be long now. I can feel death's got a hold of me." He gasped for breath as he had a coughing fit. She rushed to the other side of the bed and held out a glass of water, but he pushed it away, not looking at her.

"Go," he rasped, "I don't need this now, I'm done. You got your wish." She shook her head, silently denying his words as the tears kept coming.

"This is not my wish. Please, Nox, I need you to listen to me."

"I don't have the energy."

"Why is this happening?" she whispered, broken inside.

"You want to know why?" His voice was dull, emotionless. "Because I don't fit into one of those neat little boxes that you want your life packaged into. I have a filthy black heart taking up real estate where my old heart used to live."

"Don't you dare say that." Desperate, she grasped his hand, but he was unresponsive.

"Nakita, you're giving me whiplash. You have since I met you. Just go."

"Nox. I didn't know you were here. I swear. No one told me. I literally just found out." She placed the palm of his hand against her cheek. In the past, his hand would touch her cheek with adoration, now it was indifferent.

"Please, I'm begging you, just leave. You'll forget me in time, so will Emmylou. She's young; she has a wonderful family now. I just want to go." He pulled his hand away.

"Please, Nox, just look at me and let me say what I've come to say, then I'll go." His eyes remained fixed straight ahead. "Please?" The anguish was almost too much to bear. She loved this man. *I have to make him see that I love him, that he still loves me.*

"Fine." He turned, staring straight through her, his eyes dull like his voice. "But once you're done, I want you out of here. I'm tired. I can't do this anymore."

She took his unwilling hand with both of hers, not bothering to wipe away the tears that ran down her neck. "I've been such a stupid, blind fool. I threw away the best thing in my life because I didn't know how to let go. Deep down, I think I was looking for a reason to give you and Emmylou up, because I just couldn't bear the thought of losing anyone again." His face remained unyielding as he looked down at the bedsheets, his chest labouring. "Nox, I can't live without you. I'm suffocating." She touched her hand to his face and the stubble on his chin. He didn't pull away, but his eyes remained averted from hers. "Since we first met, I tried to fight it, to stay away from you, to not let myself love you, but I couldn't. I can't. I'm helplessly, hopelessly in love with you and I want all of you. And I want Emmylou to be mine too." Through her blinding tears, she saw him swallow. "Lennox, I want you to marry me. We made a deal. Deals are binding. I want you to marry me as soon as we can. Right here in the hospital. Please marry me, like we said we would."

"Nakita, do you realise how crazy you sound? It's too late for me now, can't you see?" He pushed her hands away. "Go live your life. You've got years stretching before you. You'll find love again and forget me easily enough. You suck at letting go. Let me go." His voice came out hard.

"No," she buried her face, wet with tears, into the palm of his hand.

"I'm buzzing the nurse." He reached for the buzzer. She put her hand on his.

"Please, just let me do one thing and I'll go." She whispered, broken. He was not going to relent. She had to make him see somehow that he meant everything to her.

His mouth was a grim line of stony consent. She reached around to the back of his hospital gown and untied the straps at the neck.

"What are you doing?" he asked, jaw tight. She shushed him and pulled the gown down his arms. She couldn't pull it off completely since he had a drip, so she settled for pulling it down far enough to expose his chest. "Nakita?"

She lowered her face to kiss his chest where his heart lay underneath. She kissed it again and again as though it were something precious, something sacred and pure.

Because it was.

Now that it was in his chest, it was. Her tears mingled with her kisses. Looking up into his face, her red hair strewn all over his chest, she said the words she wanted to say more than anything. "I love all of you, Nox. I love this heart because it beats in your chest and it's keeping you alive, it belongs to you and for that reason I will cherish it till the day I die. No matter what happens, you will marry me."

"Nakita, my heart is black as ink," his voice cracked.

"No more than mine, and I happen to know that you're a master artist when it comes to ink." Leaning forward, she nuzzled her cheek into his. "You will marry me, Lennox Bradley Conrad. We swore on it."

"No, I won't do that to you. You have your whole life..."

"Lennox, you and Emmylou are my life. Nothing would bring me greater joy than to be your wife and Emmylou's mother." He put his hands on her shoulders and pulled her face away from his.

"Has anyone ever told you you're stubborn as hell?"

Her heart leapt as she recognised a light in his eyes. His hand came up to her head and stroked the hair back from her brow, tracing down the side of her face, resting next to her mouth. She burrowed her face into his hand.

"You have."

"Woman, when it comes to you, I'm powerless."

"Good." She looked into his eyes and smiled sadly. "I'm so sorry for how I treated you. I've been so stupid, so blind and selfish. How I wish I'd done things differently."

"Shh," he said, sliding his thumb over her lips. Another tear rolled out of the corner of his eye. "There's no time for regrets, Nakita."

"Then we'll get married right here, because either way, I am going to be your wife. Deal?"

She put out her hand.

"Deal." He took her hand in his and she smiled through bitter-sweet tears.

"Now come here. It doesn't count until you seal it." Nox wound his hand in her hair and pulled her face into his, kissing her gently. But it wasn't long before their tender, salty kisses changed to deeper kisses of longing and desperation.

Two days later they were married, much to the surprise and delight of the hospital staff, who decorated Nox's room with paper wreaths hanging from the ceiling, garlands of scented flowers and faux candles. For the small ceremony around a hospital bed, those present were Pete, Raina, and their kids. Proctor, Toby, and a weeping Miriam who watched as Emmylou bounced into the room dressed as a fairy princess, waving a wand and doing twirls as the other children blew bubbles.

Next was Annie, who did her own little Emmylou inspired pirouette, which ended in a curtsy. Finally, Antony followed, proud and dignified, in a navy suit with Nakita on his arm. She wore a simple white dress that had been her mother's on her wedding day. Around her neck she wore a gold locket that held three people close to her heart: her father, her mother and Will.

Nakita looked for Nox's handsome face amongst the great many people in the room as the hospital staff took snaps through the doorway on their phones. Once she found his face next to that of the hospital chaplain, she didn't take her eyes off him. Even though she knew she might not have much time with him, tears of joy slid down her cheeks as she saw his handsome face split into a boyish grin. As she stood beside him, still in a weakened state in his hospital bed, she took his hand in hers and they made a promise before their loved ones, each other, and God.

CHAPTER 35

*N*akita swayed in grief at the finality of the sound of his coffin being lowered into the ground. She was wearing the same dress that she wore to Will's funeral. She and Miriam leant on each other for support. Miriam wept as Nakita dissolved into fresh tears. Emmylou clung to Nakita's leg, her face crumpled in tears that she wiped onto Nakita's black dress.

"Miriam, why does everyone we love have to die?" Nakita barely choked out. Miriam shook her head, tears rolling down her tissue paper cheeks.

"He was a beautiful man. He loved you so much."

"I can't imagine life without him." Nakita's voice broke and Miriam held her tight, tears streaming down her own face.

"Remember, this is not the end, darling. I know when my time comes, I believe I will be in a place where our bodies won't be weary with age or disease. We will be joined together again."

"I want to believe that, Mim, but it hurts so bad." Bending, she took a handful of soil from the graveside; closing her eyes, she reminded herself of her promise to let go. As his darling face came to her, she knew that she had to live on with the memories that she had of him, memories kept dear to her heart. As the earth sprinkled from her hand, reminiscent of the sand of an hourglass, she whispered her farewell.

"Goodbye, sweet Antony." Nakita felt a gentle squeeze at her waist and rested her head on Nox's chest, kissing his heart in thanks as she did whenever she had the opportunity.

"I have a lot to thank that man for." Nox said, enfolding her in the warmth of his firm embrace.

Nox looked around at his wedding guests, close friends that had become family. They talked, laughed, and danced under the light of the moon; the stars, an array of twinkling fairy lights and glowing vintage bulbs that lit up trees and grassy fields. Annie had helped with the decorating and to say she'd gone overboard was an understatement. The simplicity of the country themed wedding by day seemed a bit lost in the twinkling lights that had it looking more like a country fair by night. But he didn't mind. What mattered was who was standing in his arms and that he was still alive.

While the sun bowed low, bathing them in its burnished, golden glow, they made their vows once again under a sprawling jacaranda in full bloom. Nox had to remind himself to breathe when he saw Nakita walking towards him, this time on Toby's arm. She carried a simple array of wildflowers in her hands and wore a fitted, calf-length, vintage lace dress, her hair pulled back in a low, loosely curled ponytail tied with a lemon ribbon. Her tan ankle boots, with frilly white socks, suited the simple country style. Their guests were watching on from rows of hay bales covered in hessian and cream crochet doilies with garlands of wildflowers adorning the sides. His wife couldn't have been more perfect.

Nox kissed her finely arched brow, then taking her hand, he played with her fingertips, admiring the antique styled, pink diamond on her finger he'd designed—a symbol of their promise to each other. She smiled as he lifted her hand to his lips and kissed her knuckles.

"I can't believe Pete's neighbours let us use their place for a wedding when they are so close to finalising the sale," Nakita said, standing in the circle of his arms. "Look at this. It's a fantasy."

"I haven't told you this, but your art friend Michelle from Melbourne flew up this way and looked at my work."

"Really? Oh my goodness, why didn't you tell me till now? That's so exciting, what did she say?" she gushed, grabbing his forearm in her exuberance.

"She loved my work. She's organised to have some samples shipped to Melbourne. She also gave me an advance on a few of my projects, and we signed a commission contract. She said it's only the beginning of much more to come."

"Oh, Nox, I'm so proud of you. I knew you'd do it. I'm not surprised at all." She hugged him, knocking him backwards, then leaned into him for another long kiss. He savoured the moment and then eased her back off him with a smile.

"So I guess I owe you thanks for prompting me to share my art," he said, looking a little sheepish.

"Mmm. You do, don't you?"

"That's not all" he said, holding her at arm's length so he could watch her face.

"Oh? What else?"

"The advance was more than enough to put a deposit on this place and there's more coming."

"What?" Her expression held the bewilderment that he himself was still feeling.

"You are standing on your own property, Mrs Conrad. This place is ours." He watched as her almond-shaped eyes widened; her mouth open in disbelief. Wrapping his arm around her waist, he pulled her in. "I was thinking we could move in here and fill this place with too many pets and babies." Nakita shook her head in amazement.

"Nox, this can't be real; you, me, Emmylou, our family, this place?" She wrapped her arms around him. "This is all too much to process. You know, you were right when you said that if I held onto the grain of sand that one day it would turn into a pearl. I am doubly blessed—I got two—you and Emmylou." She turned into him, pressing up close and took hold of his lapels, "I am not letting you go. Not ever."

"There's one more thing."

"Seriously? What else could there possibly be?"

"I took a gamble and did something." He pulled away, first undoing his tie, then unbuttoning his collared shirt. "I hope to God I've done the right thing."

"Nox... what?" He opened his shirt, revealing a steampunk inspired tattoo of a padlock on his chest. He watched her eyes gleam as they took in the design. She reached out and traced its lines, her simple touch sending his body into overdrive, reminding him that tonight she was all his. They hadn't made love since that night by the river. It had taken him a few months to get back to good health, and then Antony had passed unexpectedly. They'd both agreed to wait until they could renew their vows without the overarching sadness.

"It's a match to your key. I want you to know, Nakita, that you completely stole my heart. See the date?" It was dated the first time they met.

"Nox, it's perfect. I love it."

He pulled her back into the warmth of his chest. "You know what you said before, about not letting me go?"

"Yeah?"

"Can I get that in writing?" he breathed into her ear. She shivered in his arms.

"You've already got it in writing and I sealed it with a kiss."

"So seal it again." He dipped his head to hers and knew he could never grow tired of kissing her. She kissed him back with relish, then pulled away breathless. Her eyes held a dreamlike gleam that seized his heart and took it captive. After a few breathless moments, she pulled away.

"Come, let's dance. I made sure this dress split up the side so we could finish the night with the tango."

He took her fingertips in his and kissed her fingers just below the knuckles, giving her a wicked grin. "Oh, we won't be finishing the night with a tango. I have other things in mind." She arched into him, entwining her fingers in his hair and kissed him seductively. After some moments alone with his wife, he led her to the dance floor and, with her head pressed close to his beating heart, they danced under an expanse of shimmering stars. They were in no rush.

EPILOGUE

*ne Year Later*

"Nakita, can you tell me why we're doing this? This time we're supposed to be doing a bucket list of things we want to do and fishing is definitely top of my list of things I don't want to do," Nox said, sitting on the jetty of the property that he'd dreamed of being his home since he first saw it. Somehow he'd ended up with a fishing rod in hand, wondering once again how Nakita got him doing precisely the things he didn't want to do.

"I know. But it was on Emmylou's list of something she wanted to do. It was her turn, remember?" Nakita said, from the other side of the jetty as she baited her hook.

He sighed in acceptance. He wasn't going to win this one. "I really doubt we're going to catch anything."

"Fiddlesticks, I see fish jumping all the time."

"Me too, Daddy; I'm going to catch a fish."

Nox let himself relax in the moment. If you were going to fish, it was definitely the day for it. Apart from the endless, vivid-blue sky, there was a fresh breeze that made the reeds by the river rustle. The atmosphere all around seemed to be teeming with new life and activity. To Nakita's and Emmylou's constant delight, hundreds if not thousands of fluffy, white puffs floated through the air, giving everything a magical feel.

"Nox, quick, I have something."

"Nakita, you literally just cast in," Nox groaned, jumping up to help her as she pulled on the rod as though she'd just captured a medium-sized wobbegong.

"I know, but I've got something," she said, from underneath her straw hat, her cheeks flushed pink with excitement.

"Are you sure? The line looks kind of slack to me."

"No, I can feel it." He took the rod off her and started reeling it in.

"Yeah, you got something, but I'm pretty sure it's not a fish." She stood next to him, hands clasped, her eyes sparkling. How could she possibly be this lit up over fishing? No doubt, if she or Emmylou were to catch a fish of edible size, which was not likely, they'd probably feel sorry for it and demand he throw it back. "Yep, like I said, not a fish," he said as he reeled it in. "Hang on, what's this? Some kind of plastic attached?" He grabbed the end of the line and tried to take off the white plastic stick about the length of his finger, but it was well and truly stuck. "What the?"

"What is it, Daddy?" Emmylou piped in. It had a window with two blue lines. He looked at Nakita, standing there beaming, her hands clasped together at her lips. Then it dawned on him.

"Nakita? Is this what I think it is?" Tears glistened in her eyes as she nodded, smiling happy tears. He swept her up in his arms and kissed her heartily, knocking her sun hat off.

"What is it, Daddy?" Emmylou tugged his pants.

"You're going to be a big sister, Chipmunk, and I'm going to be a daddy again." Emmylou's eyes were almost as round as her mouth. Nox held Nakita tight. "Nakita, I can't believe I'm saying this, but I think you just redeemed fishing for me."

"Well, you said you wanted to fill this place with babies, so I figured we should get started." He stood behind her, spreading his hands over her stomach in awe of what their love had created.

"Aren't you glad you got that tattoo now?" he asked, tickling her hip. She reached her hand up to his neck as he nuzzled his face into her hair.

"With all my heart. It led me to you and Emmylou; my forever family."

He swept her up in his arms, spinning her around in the bright blueness of a perfect day. Her smile was sunshine itself. He gave thanks and decided right there and then he believed in happily ever afters.

The End

LAURINDA LAWRENCE

Thank you so much for reading, *Black Ink Heart,* I truly hope this story stays with you for a very long time. Would you please take a moment and leave a review? Great reviews and word of mouth are the lifeblood of authors. You can find Laurinda Lawrence on Amazon as well as Goodreads.

BONUS CONTENT

Nox and Nakita's love story is very dear to my heart and I would love to give you a copy of the actual *'anti-bucket list'* coasters that drew them together. Simple type the following into your web browser

bih.rm.laurindalawrence.com/bucket-list-coasters
Also available at **laurindalawrence.com**

The Law of Entanglement

He pretends she doesn't exist,

but now he needs her help to guard a secret.

Only she's hiding secrets too...

Secrets draw them together,

will lies tear them apart?

ACKNOWLEDGMENTS

I had no idea when I penned my first draft of *Black Ink Heart* in seven weeks that it would become such a huge undertaking. Nothing I have ever done has required so much commitment, dedication, and meticulous attention to detail.

To my three gorgeous kids, and devoted husband—thank you for empowering me and giving me space to write at all manner of times and in the oddest locations. Doing life with you is my absolute greatest joy.

To Mum and Dad—you always knew I had stories in me and you never stopped believing. I can never thank you enough for the life you've given me and your generous love.

To Annie Seaton, I am always blown away by your work ethic, positivity, tech-savvy creativity, and your graciousness. There is nothing like the encouragement of an amazing, real-life author believing in one's story.

A huge thank you to Wendy Parson—you were an absolute godsend at the perfect time when I was discouraged and ready to give up. You believed in this story and gave me the confidence to tell it with the authenticity it deserved.

To Elizabeth Troyer, my dear friend, and sounding board. Thank you for your valuable input, the surveys and 'marketing' groundwork you've done, and especially the laughter. Your excitement about my story has been a joy. You truly are one of a kind. Words cannot say what your friendship means to me.

Finally, to the One and Only who gave me the breath of life, and fills my soul with delight—thank you for taking me back to the place of fulfilling a dream that I had long let go of. Your praise will ever be on my lips.

LAURINDA LAWRENCE

Laurinda grew up on an oyster farm on the Central Coast where she enjoyed playing in the mangroves with her three big brothers on her creekside property.

A firm believer in happily-ever-afters, she fell in love with the power of story in grade five, when her mum bought her Gone with the Wind from a second-hand-bookstore on the Hawkesbury River.

Marrying her high-school sweetheart, Laurinda began her own love story, making her home in Newcastle with her husband, three teenagers and walking teddy bears, Banjo and Delilah.

When she's not working as a school chaplain, writing, and enjoying her family, Laurinda loves nothing more than sitting around a camp-fire with good music, a glass of wine and great company.

Laurinda believes we all have a powerful story to tell and that all in all: Love is a beautiful mess.

To discover what inspires Laurinda Lawrence and her writing, as well as free bonus content, just visit laurindalawrence.com